I0822453

THE ELEMENTAL TRILOGY

HORROR HISTORIA brings together the most influential monsters and original gothic stories in one blood-curdling collection.

Collect each volume and complete the ultimate nightmare pantheon.

Horror Historia Black
Nightmares and boogeymen of the phantasmagoria.

Horror Historia Brown
Werewolves, hellhounds, and other supernatural beasts.

Horror Historia Green
Carnivorous and lethal vegetation.

Horror Historia Indigo
Practitioners of sorcery and witchcraft.

Horror Historia Pink
Murderers, ghouls, and other monsters of the flesh.

Horror Historia Red
Bloodsuckers and vampire variants.

Horror Historia Violet
Magical beings of folklore and mythology.

Horror Historia White
Ghosts, phantoms, and visitants.

Horror Historia Yellow
Mummies and nightmares of the Nile.

The Elemental Trilogy

The Boats of the "Glen Carrig"
The House on the Borderland
The Ghost Pirates

William Hope Hodgson

Horror Historia: The Elemental Trilogy

written by William Hope Hodgson
edited by C.S.R. Calloway

Published by CSRC Storytelling
Los Angeles, California

ISBNs:
Hardcover: 978-1-955382-26-7
Paperback: 978-1-955382-29-8
Ebook: 978-1-955382-31-1

Cover illustration by Massai
Cover designed by Mena Bo

INTRODUCTION TO THE VOLUME

The boundaries which divide Life from Death are at best shadowy and vague. Who shall say where the one ends, and where the other begins?

— EDGAR ALLAN POE,
"THE PREMATURE BURIAL"

In the original Author's Preface to *The Ghost Pirates*, author William Hope Hodgson suggests his novels *The Boats of the "Glen Carrig"*, *The House on the Borderland*, and *The Ghost Pirates* are a trilogy of sorts. In his words, they share "an elemental kinship." In today's terms, the three books would be considered to form a thematic series—a collection of related works such as books, films, or television episodes that share concepts, motifs, or stylistic elements rather than characters or narrative continuity. While each work within the series stands alone as a complete story, collectively they explore a particular set of themes developed across the series. They may include recurring settings, overarching ideas, or similar narrative styles, altogether creating a cohesive artistic framework.

The Ghost Pirates was the only Hodgson novel I had initially considered when considering entries for the HORROR HISTORIA collection, looking to have a wonderful full-length ghost novel to include in the collection.[1] It's so short, however, that I was concerned it would appear a bit slender compared to the heavyweight horrors it would join, which include *Dracula*, *Frankenstein*, and *The Phantom of the Opera*. It was while revisiting Hodgson's preface, having been utterly transported by his captivating narrative, that I decided to combine the books in his implicit trilogy, marking a historic first in the world of publishing.

Thematic series are a prevalent format in television with anthology shows like *The Twilight Zone* and *Black Mirror* presenting unique stories every episode, and modern shows like *Fargo*, Mike Flanagan's *The Haunting* series, plus an entire Ryan Murphy cavalcade that includes *American Crime Story*, *American Horror Story*, *Feud*, and *Monster*, adopting a fresh storyline with every season. On the big

[1] For more of the most heart-fluttering ghost stories, thirty-one are collected in ***HORROR HISTORIA WHITE***.

screen, Sergio Leone's *Dollars Trilogy* (*A Fistful of Dollars, For a Few Dollars More*, and *The Good, the Bad and the Ugly*, released annually from 1964 to 1966) shares the same lead actor and Wild West setting, though the films aren't ever explicitly linked.[2] In literature, such thematic continuity is less common. The most notable example is Jules Verne's *Voyages Extraordinaires*, fantastical adventures with occasional cameos and cross-references, while each book largely stands alone.[3]

Hodgson's works, while individually distinctive in ways that show the wide range of his imagination, share an underlying thematic unity. They delve into eerie and supernatural occurrences, each exploring the uncanny and unexplained within unique and foreboding landscapes. *The Boats of the "Glen Carrig,"* published in 1907, straddles the realms of horror, fantasy, and adventure, chronicling the odyssey of the shipwrecked survivors of the *Glen Carrig* as they encounter monstrous entities and supernatural forces on a hazardous island.

Following in 1908, *The House on the Borderland* stands as a cornerstone of weird fiction and horror literature. Hodgson delves deeper into the realms of the supernatural, embracing the bizarre and the unknown, introducing readers to a visionary exploration of what would eventually become known as cosmic horror, serving as a precursor to the genre's future luminaries like Algernon Blackwood and M.R. James. This novel paints an evocative canvas of the unearthly—unearthly landscapes and unearthly phenomena, creating another disturbing narrative journey.

Continuing his foray into the esoteric and the macabre, *The Ghost Pirates*, published in 1909, has retained its significance as a landmark entry in supernatural fiction and maritime horror. Hodgson weaves a ghostly tale at sea, maintaining his most effective traits with presented terrors that are unsettling, unearthly, and—most terrifyingly—unexplained, making his titular ghosts a significant addition to the **HORROR HISTORIA** pantheon of monsters.[4]

Hodgson, despite his tragically short life and therefore equally short career, remains a master of the bizarre, the weird, and the uncanny—a paradigm of horror at its most relentless and all-encompassing. Individually, each book in this

---

[2] Despite being tagged "The Man with No Name" by savvy marketers, Clint Eastwood assumes the roles of "Joe," "Manco," and "Blondie" in each respective film.

[3] The series comprises 62 novels written by Verne and published between 1863 and 1905. Some of the most notable works include *Journey to the Center of the Earth* (1864), *From the Earth to the Moon* (1865), *Twenty Thousand Leagues Under the Sea* (1870), *Around the World in Eighty Days* (1872), and *The Mysterious Island* (1874).

[4] I want to highlight that the cover, illustrated by the talented Massai who has crafted artwork for all the standalone novels in the anthology, depicts a more straightforward version of "ghost pirates" per my aesthetic request. The phantoms in Hodgson's tale are less obvious and, consequently, far more frightening and tricky to express visually.

trilogy immerses readers in previously uncharted realms of the supernatural. Together, these works form a series that not only explores the farthest corners of imagination, but the dark corners of the human psyche as well, solidifying Hodgson's legacy as a literary maestro of the macabre.[5]

C.S.R. CALLOWAY

/

[5] A few of Hodgson's classic short stories can be found in the collections ***HORROR HISTORIA BLACK*** and ***HORROR HISTORIA BLUE***.

NOTES ON THE COLLECTION

Gothic grotesqueries, penny dreadfuls, pulp magazines, and other darkly inventive publications have produced a dread allure across the world, infiltrating culture and influencing language, becoming the source for multiple adaptations across all forms of media. HORROR HISTORIA brings together the most influential monsters and original gothic stories in distinctive blood-curdling collections, existing not as an exhaustive tome or panoptic omnibus, but as one hell of a starter kit for the archetypes, conventions, and motifs necessary to build the ultimate nightmare pantheon.

To make HORROR HISTORIA texts more accessible to the contemporary reader, minor changes have been made to spelling, punctuation, capitalization, italicization, hyphenation, and spacing. British spellings ("colour" instead of "color") have been altered throughout. Obvious typographical errors in the original texts have been corrected. Many of these stories contain depictions common during their day among writers from systemically majoritized backgrounds and cultures, though any outright slurs have been altered or removed. Neither the publisher nor the editor endorses any characterizations, depictions, or language that would be considered ableist, racist, xenophobic, or otherwise offensive.

Each book in the HORROR HISTORIA collection is dedicated to **Gerardo Maravilla.**

/

Contents

THE BOATS OF THE "GLEN CARRIG"

The thing, whatever it was, had come more forward over the rail; but now, before the light, it recoiled with a queer, horrible litheness. It slid back, and down, and so out of sight. I have only a confused notion of a wet glistening Something, and two vile eyes.

THE BOATS OF THE "GLEN CARRIG"

1907

Being an account of their Adventures in the Strange places of the Earth, after the foundering of the good ship *Glen Carrig* through striking upon a hidden rock in the unknown seas to the Southward. As told by John Winterstraw, Gent., to his son James Winterstraw, in the year 1757, and by him committed very properly and legibly to manuscript.

People may say thou art no longer young
  And yet, to me, thy youth was yesterday,
    A yesterday that seems
    Still mingled with my dreams.
 Ah! how the years have o'er thee flung
    Their soft mantilla, grey.
And e'en to them thou art not over old;
  How could'st thou be! Thy hair
    Hast scarcely lost its deep old glorious dark:
    Thy face is scarcely lined. No mark
 Destroys its calm serenity. Like gold
  Of evening light, when winds scarce stir,
  The soul-light of thy face is pure as prayer.

Madre Mia

I.
The Land of Lonesomeness

Now we had been five days in the boats, and in all this time made no discovering of land. Then upon the morning of the sixth day came there a cry from the bo'sun, who had the command of the lifeboat, that there was something which might be land afar upon our larboard bow; but it was very low lying, and none could tell whether it was land or but a morning cloud. Yet, because there was the beginning of hope within our hearts, we pulled wearily towards it, and thus, in about an hour, discovered it to be indeed the coast of some flat country.

Then, it might be a little after the hour of midday, we had come so close to it that we could distinguish with ease what manner of land lay beyond the shore, and thus we found it to be of an abominable flatness, desolate beyond all that I could have imagined. Here and there it appeared to be covered with clumps of queer vegetation; though whether they were small trees or great bushes, I had no means of telling; but this I know, that they were like unto nothing whichever I had set eyes upon before.

So much as this I gathered as we pulled slowly along the coast, seeking an opening whereby we could pass inward to the land; but a weary time passed or ere we came upon that which we sought. Yet, in the end, we found it—a slimy-banked creek, which proved to be the estuary of a great river, though we spoke of it always as a creek. Into this we entered, and proceeded at no great pace upwards along its winding course; and as we made forward, we scanned the low banks upon each side, perchance there might be some spot where we could make to land; but we found none—the banks being composed of a vile mud which gave us no encouragement to venture rashly upon them.

Now, having taken the boat something over a mile up the great creek, we came upon the first of that vegetation which I had chanced to notice from the sea, and here, being within some score yards of it, we were the better able to study it. Thus I found that it was indeed composed largely of a sort of tree, very low and stunted, and having what might be described as an unwholesome look about it. The branches of this tree, I perceived to be the cause of my inability to recognize it from a bush, until I had come close upon it; for they grew thin and smooth through all their length, and hung towards the earth; being weighted thereto by a single, large cabbage-like plant which seemed to sprout from the extreme tip of each.

Presently, having passed beyond this clump of the vegetation, and the banks of the river remaining very low, I stood me upon a thwart, by which means I was enabled to scan the surrounding country. This I discovered, so far as my sight could penetrate, to be pierced in all directions with innumerable creeks and pools, some of these latter being very great of extent; and, as I have before made mention, everywhere the country was low set—as it might be a great plain of mud; so that it gave me a sense of dreariness to look out upon it. It may be, all unconsciously, that my spirit was put in awe by the extreme silence of all the country around; for in all that waste I could see no living thing, neither bird nor vegetable, save it be the stunted trees, which, indeed, grew in clumps here and there over all the land, so much as I could see.

This silence, when I grew fully aware of it was the more uncanny; for my memory told me that never before had I come upon a country which contained so much quietness. Nothing moved across my vision—not even a lone bird soared up against the dull sky; and, for my hearing, not so much as the cry of a sea bird came to me—no! nor the croak of a frog, nor the plash of a fish. It was as though we had come upon the Country of Silence, which some have called the Land of Lonesomeness.

Now three hours had passed whilst we ceased not to labor at the oars, and we could no more see the sea; yet no place fit for our feet had come to view, for everywhere the mud, grey and black, surrounded us—encompassing us veritably by a slimy wilderness. And so we were fain to pull on, in the hope that we might come ultimately to firm ground.

Then, a little before sundown, we halted upon our oars, and made a scant meal from a portion of our remaining provisions; and as we ate, I could see the sun sinking away over the wastes, and I had some slight diversion in watching the grotesque shadows which it cast from the trees into the water upon our larboard side; for we had come to a pause opposite a clump of the vegetation. It was at this time, as I remember, that it was borne in upon me afresh how very silent was the land; and that this was not due to my imagination, I remarked that the men both in our own and in the bo'sun's boat, seemed uneasy because of it; for none spoke save in undertones, as though they had fear of breaking it.

And it was at this time, when I was awed by so much solitude, that there came the first telling of life in all that wilderness. I heard it first in the far distance, away inland—a curious, low, sobbing note it was, and the rise and the fall of it was like to the sobbing of a lonesome wind through a great forest. Yet was there no wind. Then, in a moment, it had died, and the silence of the land was awesome by reason of the contrast. And I looked about me at the men, both in the boat in which I was and that which the bo'sun commanded; and not one was there but held himself in a posture of listening. In this wise a minute of quietness passed, and then one of the men gave out a laugh, born of the nervousness which had taken him.

The bo'sun muttered to him to hush, and, in the same moment, there came again the plaint of that wild sobbing. And abruptly it sounded away on our right, and immediately was caught up, as it were, and echoed back from some place beyond us afar up the creek. At that, I got me upon a thwart, intending to take another look over the country about us; but the banks of the creek had become higher; moreover the vegetation acted as a screen, even had my stature and elevation enabled me to overlook the banks.

And so, after a little while, the crying died away, and there was another silence. Then, as we sat each one harking for what might next befall, George, the youngest 'prentices boy, who had his seat beside me, plucked me by the sleeve, inquiring in a troubled voice whether I had any knowledge of that which the crying might portend; but I shook my head, telling him that I had no knowing beyond his own; though, for his comfort, I said that it might be the wind. Yet, at that, he shook his head; for indeed, it was plain that it could not be by such agency, for there was a stark calm.

Now, I had scarce made an end of my remark, when again the sad crying was upon us. It appeared to come from far up the creek, and from far down the creek, and from inland and the land between us and the sea. It filled the evening air with its doleful wailing, and I remarked that there was in it a curious sobbing, most human in its despairful crying. And so awesome was the thing that no man of us spoke; for it seemed that we harked to the weeping of lost souls. And then, as we waited fearfully, the sun sank below the edge of the world, and the dusk was upon us.

And now a more extraordinary thing happened; for, as the night fell with swift gloom, the strange wailing and crying was hushed, and another sound stole out upon the land—a far, sullen growling. At the first, like the crying, it came from far inland; but was caught up speedily on all sides of us, and presently the dark was full of it. And it increased in volume, and strange trumpetings fled across it. Then, though with slowness, it fell away to a low, continuous growling, and in it there was that which I can only describe as an insistent, hungry snarl. Aye! no other word of which I have knowledge so well describes it as that—a note of *hunger*, most awesome to the ear. And this, more than all the rest of those incredible voicings, brought terror into my heart.

Now as I sat listening, George gripped me suddenly by the arm, declaring in a shrill whisper that something had come among the clump of trees upon the left-hand bank. Of the truth of this, I had immediately a proof; for I caught the sound of a continuous rustling among them, and then a nearer note of growling, as though a wild beast purred at my elbow. Immediately upon this, I caught the bo'sun's voice, calling in a low tone to Josh, the eldest 'prentices, who had the charge of our boat, to come alongside of him; for he would have the boats together. Then got we out the oars and laid the boats together in the midst of the creek; and so we watched through the night, being full of fear, so that we kept our speech low; that is, so low as would carry our thoughts one to the other through the noise of the growling.

And so the hours passed, and naught happened more than I have told, save that once, a little after midnight, the trees opposite to us seemed to be stirred again, as though some creature, or creatures, lurked among them; and there came, a little after that, a sound as of something stirring the water up against the bank; but it ceased in a while and the silence fell once more.

Thus, after a weariful time, away Eastwards the sky began to tell of the coming of the day; and, as the light grew and strengthened, so did that insatiable growling pass hence with the dark and the shadows. And so at last came the day, and once more there was borne to us the sad wailing that had preceded the night. For a certain while it lasted, rising and falling most mournfully over the vastness of the surrounding wastes, until the sun was risen some degrees above the horizon; after which it began to fail, dying away in lingering echoes, most solemn to our ears. And so it passed, and there came again the silence that had been with us in all the daylight hours.

Now, it being day, the bo'sun bade us make such sparse breakfast as our provender allowed; after which, having first scanned the banks to discern if any fearful thing were visible, we took again to our oars, and proceeded on our upward journey; for we hoped presently to come upon a country where life had not become extinct, and where we could put foot to honest earth. Yet, as I have made mention earlier, the vegetation, where it grew, did flourish most luxuriantly; so that I am scarce correct when I speak of life as being extinct in that land. For, indeed, now I think of it, I can remember that the very mud from which it sprang seemed veritably to have a fat, sluggish life of its own, so rich and viscid was it.

Presently it was midday; yet was there but little change in the nature of the surrounding wastes; though it may be that the vegetation was something thicker, and more continuous along the banks. But the banks were still of the same thick, clinging mud; so that nowhere could we effect a landing; though, had we, the rest of the country beyond the banks seemed no better.

And all the while, as we pulled, we glanced continuously from bank to bank; and those who worked not at the oars were fain to rest a hand by their sheath-knives; for the happenings of the past night were continually in our minds, and we were in great fear; so that we had turned back to the sea but that we had come so nigh to the end of our provisions.

II.
The Ship in the Creek

Then, it was nigh on to evening, we came upon a creek opening into the greater one through the bank upon our left. We had been like to pass it —as, indeed, we had passed many throughout the day—but that the bo'sun, whose boat had the lead, cried out that there was some craft lying-up, a little beyond the first bend. And, indeed, so it seemed; for one of the masts of her —all jagged, where it had carried away—stuck up plain to our view.

Now, having grown sick with so much lonesomeness, and being in fear of the approaching night, we gave out something near to a cheer, which, however, the bo'sun silenced, having no knowledge of those who might occupy the stranger. And so, in silence, the bo'sun turned his craft toward the creek, whereat we followed, taking heed to keep quietness, and working the oars warily. So, in a little, we came to the shoulder of the bend, and had plain sight of the vessel some little way beyond us. From the distance she had no appearance of being inhabited; so that after some small hesitation, we pulled towards her, though still being at pains to keep silence.

The strange vessel lay against that bank of the creek which was upon our right, and over above her was a thick clump of the stunted trees. For the rest, she appeared to be firmly imbedded in the heavy mud, and there was a certain look of age about her which carried to me a doleful suggestion that we should find naught aboard of her fit for an honest stomach.

We had come to a distance of maybe some ten fathoms from her starboard bow—for she lay with her head down towards the mouth of the little creek—when the bo'sun bade his men to back water, the which Josh did regarding our own boat. Then, being ready to fly if we had been in danger, the bo'sun hailed the stranger; but got no reply, save that some echo of his shout seemed to come back at us. And so he sung out again to her, chance there might be some below decks who had not caught his first hail; but, for the second time, no answer came to us, save the low echo—naught, but that the silent trees took on a little quivering, as though his voice had shaken them.

At that, being confident now within our minds, we laid alongside, and, in a minute had shinned up the oars and so gained her decks. Here, save that the glass of the skylight of the main cabin had been broken, and some portion of the framework shattered, there was no extraordinary litter; so that it appeared to us as though she had been no great while abandoned.

So soon as the bo'sun had made his way up from the boat, he turned aft toward the scuttle, the rest of us following. We found the leaf of the scuttle pulled forward to within an inch of closing, and so much effort did it require of us to push it back, that we had immediate evidence of a considerable time since any had gone down that way.

However, it was no great while before we were below, and here we found the main cabin to be empty, save for the bare furnishings. From it there opened off two staterooms at the forrard end, and the captain's cabin in the after part, and in all of these we found matters of clothing and sundries such as proved that the vessel had been deserted apparently in haste. In further proof of this we found, in a drawer in the captain's room, a considerable quantity of loose gold, the which it was not to be supposed would have been left by the free will of the owner.

Of the staterooms, the one upon the starboard side gave evidence that it had been occupied by a woman—no doubt a passenger. The other, in which there were two bunks, had been shared, so far as we could have any certainty, by a couple of young men; and this we gathered by observation of various garments which were scattered carelessly about.

Yet it must not be supposed that we spent any great time in the cabins; for we were pressed for food, and made haste—under the directing of the bo'sun—to discover if the hulk held victuals whereby we might be kept alive.

To this end, we removed the hatch which led down to the lazarette, and, lighting two lamps which we had with us in the boats, went down to make a search. And so, in a little while, we came upon two casks which the bo'sun broke open with a hatchet. These casks were sound and tight, and in them was ship's biscuit, very good and fit for food. At this, as may be imagined, we felt eased in our minds, knowing that there was no immediate fear of starvation. Following this, we found a barrel of molasses; a cask of rum; some cases of dried fruit—these were moldy and scarce fit to be eaten; a cask of salt beef, another of pork; a small barrel of vinegar; a case of brandy; two barrels of flour—one of which proved to be damp-struck; and a bunch of tallow dips.

In a little while we had all these things up in the big cabin, so that we might come at them the better to make choice of that which was fit for our stomachs, and that which was otherwise. Meantime, whilst the bo'sun overhauled these matters, Josh called a couple of the men, and went on deck to bring up the gear from the boats, for it had been decided that we should pass the night aboard the hulk.

When this was accomplished, Josh took a walk forward to the fo'cas'le; but found nothing beyond two seamen's chests; a sea-bag, and some odd gear. There were, indeed, no more than ten bunks in the place; for she was but a small brig, and had no call for a great crowd. Yet Josh was more than a little puzzled to know what had come to the odd chests; for it was not to be supposed that there had been no more than two—and a sea-bag—among ten men. But to this, at that time, he had no answer, and so, being sharp for supper, made a return to the deck, and thence to the main cabin.

Now while he had been gone, the bo'sun had set the men to clearing out the main cabin; after which, he had served out two biscuits apiece all round, and a tot of rum. To Josh, when he appeared, he gave the same, and, in a little, we called a sort of council; being sufficiently stayed by the food to talk.

Yet, before we came to speech, we made shift to light our pipes; for the bo'sun had discovered a case of tobacco in the captain's cabin, and after this we came to the consideration of our position.

We had provender, so the bo'sun calculated, to last us for the better part of two months, and this without any great stint; but we had yet to prove if the brig held water in her casks, for that in the creek was brackish, even so far as we had penetrated from the sea; else we had not been in need. To the charge of this, the bo'sun set Josh, along with two of the men. Another, he told to take charge of the galley, so long as we were in the hulk. But for that night, he said we had no need to do aught; for we had sufficient of water in the boats' breakers to last us till the morrow. And so, in a little, the dusk began to fill the cabin; but we talked on, being greatly content with our present ease and the good tobacco which we enjoyed.

In a little while, one of the men cried out suddenly to us to be silent, and, in that minute, all heard it—a far, drawn-out wailing; the same which had come to us in the evening of the first day. At that we looked at one another through the smoke and the growing dark, and, even as we looked, it became plainer heard, until, in a while, it was all about us—aye! it seemed to come floating down through the broken framework of the skylight as though some weariful, unseen thing stood and cried upon the decks above our heads.

Now through all that crying, none moved; none, that is, save Josh and the bo'sun, and they went up into the scuttle to see whether anything was in sight; but they found nothing, and so came down to us; for there was no wisdom in exposing ourselves, unarmed as we were, save for our sheath-knives.

And so, in a little, the night crept down upon the world, and still we sat within the dark cabin, none speaking, and knowing of the rest only by the glows of their pipes.

All at once there came a low, muttered growl, stealing across the land; and immediately the crying was quenched in its sullen thunder. It died away, and there was a full minute of silence; then, once more it came, and it was nearer and more plain to the ear. I took my pipe from my mouth; for I had come again upon the great fear and uneasiness which the happenings of the first night had bred in me, and the taste of the smoke brought me no more pleasure. The muttered growl swept over our heads and died away into the distance, and there was a sudden silence.

Then, in that quietness, came the bo'sun's voice. He was bidding us haste every one into the captain's cabin. As we moved to obey him, he ran to draw over the lid of the scuttle; and Josh went with him, and, together, they had it across; though with difficulty. When we had come into the captain's cabin, we closed and barred the door, piling two great sea chests up against it; and so we felt near safe; for we knew that no thing, man nor beast, could come at us there. Yet, as may be supposed, we felt not altogether secure; for there was that in the growling which now filled the darkness, that seemed demoniac, and we knew not what horrid Powers were abroad.

And so through the night the growling continued, seeming to be mighty near unto us—aye! almost over our heads, and of a loudness far surpassing all that had come to us on the previous night; so that I thanked the Almighty that we had come into shelter in the midst of so much fear.

III.
The Thing That Made Search

Now at times, I fell upon sleep, as did most of the others; but, for the most part, I lay half sleeping and half waking—being unable to attain to true sleep by reason of the everlasting growling above us in the night, and the fear which it bred in me. Thus, it chanced that just after midnight, I caught a sound in the main cabin beyond the door, and immediately I was fully waked. I sat me up and listened, and so became aware that something was fumbling about the deck of the main cabin. At that, I got to my feet and made my way to where the bo'sun lay, meaning to waken him, if he slept; but he caught me by the ankle, as I stooped to shake him, and whispered to me to keep silence; for he too had been aware of that strange noise of something fumbling beyond in the big cabin.

In a little, we crept both of us so close to the door as the chests would allow, and there we crouched, listening; but could not tell what manner of thing it might be which produced so strange a noise. For it was neither shuffling, nor treading of any kind, nor yet was it the whirr of a bat's wings, the which had first occurred to me, knowing how vampires are said to inhabit the nights in dismal places. Nor yet was it the slur of a snake; but rather it seemed to us to be as though a great wet cloth were being rubbed everywhere across the floor and bulkheads. We were the better able to be certain of the truth of this likeness, when, suddenly, it passed across the further side of the door behind which we listened: at which, you may be sure, we drew backwards both of us in fright; though the door, and the chests, stood between us and that which rubbed against it.

Presently, the sound ceased, and, listen as we might, we could no longer distinguish it. Yet, until the morning, we dozed no more; being troubled in mind as to what manner of thing it was which had made search in the big cabin.

Then in time the day came, and the growling ceased. For a mournful while the sad crying filled our ears, and then at last the eternal silence that fills the day hours of that dismal land fell upon us.

So, being at last in quietness, we slept, being greatly awearied. About seven in the morning, the bo'sun waked me, and I found that they had opened the door into the big cabin; but though the bo'sun and I made careful search, we could nowhere come upon anything to tell us aught concerning the thing which had put us so in fright. Yet, I know not if I am right in saying that we came upon nothing; for, in several places, the bulkheads had a *chafed* look; but whether this had been there before that night, we had no means of telling.

Of that which we had heard, the bo'sun bade me make no mention, for he would not have the men put more in fear than need be. This I conceived to be wisdom, and so held my peace. Yet I was much troubled in my mind to know what manner of thing it was which we had need to fear, and more—I desired greatly to know whether we should be free of it in the daylight hours; for there was always with me, as I went hither and thither, the thought that IT—for that is how I designated it in my mind—might come upon us to our destruction.

Now after breakfast, at which we had each a portion of salt pork, besides rum and biscuit (for by now the fire in the caboose had been set going), we turned-to at various matters, under the directing of the bo'sun. Josh and two of the men made examination of the water casks, and the rest of us lifted the main hatch-covers, to make inspection of her cargo; but lo! we found nothing, save some three feet of water in her hold.

By this time, Josh had drawn some water off from the casks; but it was most unsuitable for drinking, being vile of smell and taste. Yet the bo'sun bade him draw some into buckets, so that the air might haply purify it; but though this was done, and the water allowed to stand through the morning, it was but little better.

At this, as might be imagined, we were exercised in our minds as to the manner in which we should come upon suitable water; for by now we were beginning to be in need of it. Yet though one said one thing, and another said another, no one had wit enough to call to mind any method by which our need should be satisfied. Then, when we had made an end of dining, the bo'sun sent Josh, with four of the men, upstream, perchance after a mile or two the water should prove of sufficient freshness to meet our purpose. Yet they returned a little before sundown having no water; for everywhere it was salt.

Now the bo'sun, foreseeing that it might be impossible to come upon water, had set the man whom he had ordained to be our cook, to boiling the creek water in three great kettles. This he had ordered to be done soon after the boat left; and over the spout of each, he had hung a great pot of iron, filled with cold water from the hold—this being cooler than that from the creek—so that the steam from each kettle impinged upon the cold surface of the iron pots, and being by this means condensed, was caught in three buckets placed beneath them upon the floor of the caboose. In this way, enough water was collected to supply us for the evening and the following morning; yet it was but a slow method, and we had sore need of a speedier, were we to leave the hulk so soon as I, for one, desired.

We made our supper before sunset, so as to be free of the crying which we had reason to expect. After that, the bo'sun shut the scuttle, and we went every one of us into the captain's cabin, after which we barred the door, as on the previous night; and well was it for us that we acted with this prudence.

By the time that we had come into the captain's cabin, and secured the door, it was upon sunsetting, and as the dusk came on, so did the melancholy wailing pass over the land; yet, being by now somewhat inured to so much strangeness, we lit our pipes, and smoked; though I observed that none talked; for the crying without was not to be forgotten.

Now, as I have said, we kept silence; but this was only for a time, and our reason for breaking it was a discovery made by George, the younger apprentice. This lad, being no smoker, was fain to do something to while away the time, and with this intent, he had raked out the contents of a small box, which had lain upon the deck at the side of the forrard bulkhead.

The box had appeared filled with odd small lumber of which a part was a dozen or so grey paper wrappers, such as are used, I believe, for carrying samples of corn; though I have seen them put to other purposes, as, indeed, was now the case. At first George had tossed these aside; but it growing darker the bo'sun lit one of the candles which we had found in the lazarette. Thus, George, who was proceeding to tidy back the rubbish which was cumbering the place, discovered something which caused him to cry out to us his astonishment.

Now, upon hearing George call out, the bo'sun bade him keep silence, thinking it was but a piece of boyish restlessness; but George drew the candle to him, and bade us to listen; for the wrappers were covered with fine handwriting after the fashion of a woman's.

Even as George told us of that which he had found we became aware that the night was upon us; for suddenly the crying ceased, and in place thereof there came out of the far distance the low thunder of the night-growling, that had tormented us through the past two nights. For a space, we ceased to smoke, and sat—listening; for it was a very fearsome sound. In a very little while it seemed to surround the ship, as on the previous nights; but at length, using ourselves to it, we resumed our smoking, and bade George to read out to us from the writing upon the paper wrappers.

Then George, though shaking somewhat in his voice, began to decipher that which was upon the wrappers, and a strange and awesome story it was, and bearing much upon our own concerns:—

"Now, when they discovered the spring among the trees that crown the bank, there was much rejoicing; for we had come to have much need of water. And some, being in fear of the ship (declaring, because of all our misfortune and the strange disappearances of their messmates and the brother of my lover, that she was haunted by a devil), declared their intention of taking their gear up to the spring, and there making a camp. This they conceived and carried out in the space of one afternoon; though our Captain, a good and true man, begged of them, as they valued life, to stay within the shelter of their living-place. Yet, as I have remarked, they would none of them hark to his counseling, and, because the Mate and the bo'sun were gone he had no means of compelling them to wisdom —"

At this point, George ceased to read, and began to rustle among the wrappers, as though in search for the continuation of the story.

Presently he cried out that he could not find it, and dismay was upon his face.

But the bo'sun told him to read on from such sheets as were left; for, as he observed, we had no knowledge if more existed; and we were fain to know further of that spring, which, from the story, appeared to be over the bank near to the vessel.

George, being thus adjured, picked up the topmost sheet; for they were, as I heard him explain to the bo'sun, all oddly numbered, and having but little reference one to the other. Yet we were mightily keen to know even so much as such odd scraps might tell unto us. Whereupon, George read from the next wrapper, which ran thus:—

"Now, suddenly, I heard the Captain cry out that there was something in the main cabin, and immediately my lover's voice calling to me to lock my door, and on no condition to open it. Then the door of the Captain's cabin slammed, and there came a silence, and the silence was broken by a *sound*. Now, this was the first time that I had heard the Thing make search through the big cabin; but, afterwards, my lover told me it had happened aforetime, and they had told me naught, fearing to frighten me needlessly; though now I understood why my lover had bidden me never to leave my stateroom door unbolted in the nighttime. I remember also, wondering if the noise of breaking glass that had waked me somewhat from my dreams a night or two previously, had been the work of this indescribable Thing; for on the morning following that night, the glass in the skylight had been smashed. Thus it was that my thoughts wandered out to trifles, while yet my soul seemed ready to leap out from my bosom with fright.

"I had, by reason of usage, come to ability to sleep despite of the fearsome growling; for I had conceived its cause to be the mutter of spirits in the night, and had not allowed myself to be unnecessarily frightened with doleful thoughts; for my lover had assured me of our safety, and that we should yet come to our home. And now, beyond my door, I could hear that fearsome sound of the Thing searching—"

George came to a sudden pause; for the bo'sun had risen and put a great hand upon his shoulder. The lad made to speak; but the bo'sun beckoned to him to say no word, and at that we, who had grown to nervousness through the happenings in the story, began every one to listen. Thus we heard a sound which had escaped us in the noise of the growling without the vessel, and the interest of the reading.

For a space we kept very silent, no man doing more than let the breath go in and out of his body, and so each one of us knew that something moved without, in the big cabin. In a little, something touched upon our door, and it was, as I have mentioned earlier, as though a great swab rubbed and scrubbed at the woodwork. At this, the men nearest unto the door came backwards in a surge, being put in sudden fear by reason of the Thing being so near; but the bo'sun held up a hand, bidding them, in a low voice, to make no unneedful noise. Yet, as though the sounds of their moving had been heard, the door was shaken with such violence that we waited, everyone, expecting to see it torn from its hinges; but it stood, and we hasted to brace it by means of the bunk boards, which we placed between it and the two great chests, and upon these we set a third chest, so that the door was quite hid.

Now, I have no remembrance whether I have put down that when we came first to the ship, we had found the stern window upon the larboard side to be shattered; but so it was, and the bo'sun had closed it by means of a teak-wood cover which was made to go over it in stormy weather, with stout battens across, which were set tight with wedges. This he had done upon the first night, having fear that some evil thing might come upon us through the opening, and very prudent was this same action of his, as shall be seen. Then George cried out that something was at the cover of the larboard window, and we stood back, growing ever more fearful because that some evil creature was so eager to come at us. But the bo'sun, who was a very courageous man, and calm withal, walked over to the closed window, and saw to it that the battens were secure; for he had knowledge sufficient to be sure, if this were so, that no creature with strength less than that of a whale could break it down, and in such case its bulk would assure us from being molested.

Then, even as he made sure of the fastenings, there came a cry of fear from some of the men; for there had come at the glass of the unbroken window, a reddish mass, which plunged up against it, sucking upon it, as it were. Then Josh, who was nearest to the table, caught up the candle, and held it towards the Thing; thus I saw that it had the appearance of a many-flapped thing shaped as it might be, out of raw beef—*but it was alive.*

At this, we stared, everyone being too bemused with terror to do aught to protect ourselves, even had we been possessed of weapons. And as we remained thus, an instant, like silly sheep awaiting the butcher, I heard the framework creak and crack, and there ran splits all across the glass. In another moment, the whole thing would have been torn away, and the cabin undefended, but that the bo'sun, with a great curse at us for our landlubberly lack of use, seized the other cover, and clapped it over the window. At that, there was more help than could be made to avail, and the battens and wedges were in place in a trice. That this was no sooner accomplished than need be, we had immediate proof; for there came a rending of wood and a splintering of glass, and after that a strange yowling out in the dark, and the yowling rose above and drowned the continuous growling that filled the night. In a little, it died away, and in the brief silence that seemed to ensue, we heard a slobby fumbling at the teak cover; but it was well secured, and we had no immediate cause for fear.

IV.
The Two Faces

Of the remainder of that night, I have but a confused memory. At times we heard the door shaken behind the great chests; but no harm came to it. And, odd whiles, there was a soft thudding and rubbing upon the decks over our heads, and once, as I recollect, the Thing made a final try at the teak covers across the windows; but the day came at last, and found me sleeping. Indeed, we had slept beyond the noon, but that the bo'sun, mindful of our needs, waked us, and we removed the chests. Yet, for perhaps the space of a minute, none durst open the door, until the bo'sun bid us stand to one side. We faced about at him then, and saw that he held a great cutlass in his right hand.

He called to us that there were four more of the weapons, and made a backward motion with his left hand towards an open locker. At that, as might be supposed, we made some haste to the place to which he pointed, and found that, among some other gear, there were three more weapons such as he held; but the fourth was a straight cut-and-thrust, and this I had the good fortune to secure.

Being now armed, we ran to join the bo'sun; for by this he had the door open, and was scanning the main cabin. I would remark here how a good weapon doth seem to put heart into a man; for I, who but a few, short hours since had feared for my life, was now right full of lustiness and fight; which, mayhap, was no matter for regret.

From the main cabin, the bo'sun led up on to the deck, and I remember some surprise at finding the lid of the scuttle even as we had left it the previous night; but then I recollected that the skylight was broken, and there was access to the big cabin that way. Yet, I questioned within myself as to what manner of thing it could be which ignored the convenience of the scuttle, and descended by way of the broken skylight.

We made a search of the decks and fo'cas'le, but found nothing, and, after that, the bo'sun stationed two of us on guard, whilst the rest went about such duties as were needful. In a little, we came to breakfast, and, after that, we prepared to test the story upon the sample wrappers and see perchance whether there was indeed a spring of fresh water among the trees.

Now between the vessel and the trees, lay a slope of the thick mud, against which the vessel rested. To have scrambled up this bank had been next to impossible, by reason of its fat richness; for, indeed, it looked fit to crawl; but that

Josh called out to the bo'sun that he had come upon a ladder, lashed across the fo'cas'le head. This was brought, also several hatch covers. The latter were placed first upon the mud, and the ladder laid upon them; by which means we were enabled to pass up to the top of the bank without contact with the mud.

Here, we entered at once among the trees; for they grew right up to the edge; but we had no trouble in making a way; for they were nowhere close together; but standing, rather, each one in a little open space by itself.

We had gone a little way among the trees, when, suddenly, one who was with us cried out that he could see something away on our right, and we clutched everyone his weapon the more determinedly, and went towards it. Yet it proved to be but a seaman's chest, and a space further off, we discovered another. And so, after a little walking, we found the camp; but there was small semblance of a camp about it; for the sail of which the tent had been formed, was all torn and stained, and lay muddy upon the ground. Yet the spring was all we had wished, clear and sweet, and so we knew we might dream of deliverance.

Now, upon our discovery of the spring, it might be thought that we should set up a shout to those upon the vessel; but this was not so; for there was something in the air of the place which cast a gloom upon our spirits, and we had no disinclination to return unto the vessel.

Upon coming to the brig, the bo'sun called to four of the men to go down into the boats, and pass up the breakers: also, he collected all the buckets belonging to the brig, and forthwith each of us was set to our work. Some, those with the weapons, entered into the wood, and gave down the water to those stationed upon the bank, and these, in turn, passed it to those in the vessel. To the man in the galley, the bo'sun gave command to fill a boiler with some of the most select pieces of the pork and beef from the casks and get them cooked so soon as might be, and so we were kept at it; for it had been determined—now that we had come upon water—that we should stay not an hour longer in that monster-ridden craft, and we were all agog to get the boats revictualled, and put back to the sea, from which we had too gladly escaped.

So we worked through all that remainder of the morning, and right on into the afternoon; for we were in mortal fear of the coming dark. Towards four o'clock, the bo'sun sent the man, who had been set to do our cooking, up to us with slices of salt meat upon biscuits, and we ate as we worked, washing our throats with water from the spring, and so, before the evening, we had filled our breakers, and near every vessel which was convenient for us to take in the boats. More, some of us snatched the chance to wash our bodies; for we were sore with brine, having dipped in the sea to keep down thirst as much as might be.

Now, though it had not taken us so great a while to make a finish of our water-carrying if matters had been more convenient; yet because of the softness of the ground under our feet, and the care with which we had to pick our steps, and some little distance between us and the brig, it had grown later than we desired, before we had made an end. Therefore, when the bo'sun sent word that we should come aboard, and bring our gear, we made all haste. Thus, as it chanced, I found that I had left my sword beside the spring, having placed it there to have two hands for the carrying of one of the breakers. At my remarking my loss, George, who stood near, cried out that he would run for it, and was gone in a moment, being greatly curious to see the spring.

Now, at this moment, the bo'sun came up, and called for George; but I informed him that he had run to the spring to bring me my sword. At this, the bo'sun stamped his foot, and swore a great oath, declaring that he had kept the lad by him all the day; having a wish to keep him from any danger which the wood might hold, and knowing the lad's desire to adventure there. At this, a matter which I should have known, I reproached myself for so gross a piece of stupidity, and hastened after the bo'sun, who had disappeared over the top of the bank. I saw his back as he passed into the wood, and ran until I was up with him; for, suddenly, as it were, I found that a sense of chilly dampness had come among the trees; though a while before the place had been full of the warmth of the sun. This, I put to the account of evening, which was drawing on apace; and also, it must be borne in mind, that there were but the two of us.

We came to the spring; but George was not to be seen, and I saw no sign of my sword. At this, the bo'sun raised his voice, and cried out the lad's name. Once he called, and again; then at the second shout we heard the boy's shrill halloo, from some distance ahead among the trees. At that, we ran towards the sound, plunging heavily across the ground, which was everywhere covered with a thick scum, that clogged the feet in walking. As we ran, we hallooed, and so came upon the boy, and I saw that he had my sword.

The bo'sun ran towards him, and caught him by the arm, speaking with anger, and commanding him to return with us immediately to the vessel.

But the lad, for reply, pointed with my sword, and we saw that he pointed at what appeared to be a bird against the trunk of one of the trees. This, as I moved closer, I perceived to be a part of the tree, and no bird; but it had a very wondrous likeness to a bird; so much so that I went up to it, to see if my eyes had deceived me. Yet it seemed no more than a freak of nature, though most wondrous in its fidelity; being but an excrescence upon the trunk. With a sudden thought that it would make me a curio, I reached up to see whether I could break it away from the tree; but it was above my reach, so that I had to leave it. Yet, one thing I discovered; for, in stretching towards the protuberance, I had placed a hand upon the tree, and its trunk was soft as pulp under my fingers, much after the fashion of a mushroom.

As we turned to go, the bo'sun inquired of George his reason for going beyond the spring, and George told him that he had seemed to hear someone calling to him among the trees, and there had been so much pain in the voice that he had run towards it; but been unable to discover the owner. Immediately afterwards he had seen the curious, bird-like excrescence upon a tree nearby. Then we had called, and of the rest we had knowledge.

We had come nigh to the spring on our return journey, when a sudden low whine seemed to run among the trees. I glanced towards the sky, and realized that the evening was upon us. I was about to remark upon this to the bo'sun, when, abruptly, he came to a stand, and bent forward to stare into the shadows to our right. At that, George and I turned ourselves about to perceive what matter it was which had attracted the attention of the bo'sun; thus we made out a tree some twenty yards away, which had all its branches wrapped about its trunk, much as the lash of a whip is wound about its stock. Now this seemed to us a very strange sight, and we made all of us toward it, to learn the reason of so extraordinary a happening.

Yet, when we had come close upon it, we had no means of arriving at a knowledge of that which it portended; but walked each of us around the tree, and were more astonished, after our circumnavigation of the great vegetable than before.

Now, suddenly, and in the distance, I caught the far wailing that came before the night, and abruptly, as it seemed to me, the tree wailed at us. At that I was vastly astonished and frightened; yet, though I retreated, I could not withdraw my gaze from the tree; but scanned it the more intently; and, suddenly, I saw a brown, human face peering at us from between the wrapped branches. At this, I stood very still, being seized with that fear which renders one shortly incapable of movement. Then, before I had possession of myself, I saw that it was of a part with the trunk of the tree; for I could not tell where it ended and the tree began.

Then I caught the bo'sun by the arm, and pointed; for whether it was a part of the tree or not, it was a work of the devil; but the bo'sun, on seeing it, ran straightway so close to the tree that he might have touched it with his hand, and I found myself beside him. Now, George, who was on the bo'sun's other side, whispered that there was another face, not unlike to a woman's, and, indeed, so soon as I perceived it, I saw that the tree had a second excrescence, most strangely after the face of a woman. Then the bo'sun cried out with an oath, at the strangeness of the thing, and I felt the arm, which I held, shake somewhat, as it might be with a deep emotion. Then, far away, I heard again the sound of the wailing and, immediately, from among the trees about us, there came answering wails and a great sighing. And before I had time to be more than aware of these things, the tree wailed again at us. And at that, the bo'sun cried out suddenly that he knew; though of what it was that he *knew* I had at that time no knowledge. And, immediately, he began with his cutlass to strike at the tree before us, and to cry upon God to blast it; and lo! at his smiting a very fearsome thing happened, for the tree did bleed like any live creature. Thereafter, a great yowling came from it, and it began to writhe. And, suddenly, I became aware that all about us the trees were a-quiver.

Then George cried out, and ran round upon my side of the bo'sun, and I saw that one of the great cabbage-like things pursued him upon its stem, even as an evil serpent; and very dreadful it was, for it had become blood red in color; but I smote it with the sword, which I had taken from the lad, and it fell to the ground.

Now from the brig I heard them hallooing, and the trees had become like live things, and there was a vast growling in the air, and hideous trumpetings. Then I caught the bo'sun again by the arm, and shouted to him that we must run for our lives; and this we did, smiting with our swords as we ran; for there came things at us, out from the growing dusk.

Thus we made the brig, and, the boats being ready, I scrambled after the bo'sun into his, and we put straightway into the creek, all of us, pulling with so much haste as our loads would allow. As we went I looked back at the brig, and it seemed to me that a multitude of things hung over the bank above her, and there seemed a flicker of things moving hither and thither aboard of her. And then we were in the great creek up which we had come, and so, in a little, it was night.

All that night we rowed, keeping very strictly to the center of the big creek, and all about us bellowed the vast growling, being more fearsome than ever I had heard it, until it seemed to me that we had waked all that land of terror to a knowledge of our presence. But, when the morning came, so good a speed had we made, what with our fear, and the current being with us, that we were nigh upon the open sea; whereat each one of us raised a shout, feeling like freed prisoners.

And so, full of thankfulness to the Almighty, we rowed outward to the sea.

V.
The Great Storm

Now, as I have said, we came at last in safety to the open sea, and so for a time had some degree of peace; though it was long ere we threw off all of the terror which the Land of Lonesomeness had cast over our hearts.

And one more matter there is regarding that land, which my memory recalls. It will be remembered that George found certain wrappers upon which there was writing. Now, in the haste of our leaving, he had given no thought to take them with him; yet a portion of one he found within the side pocket of his jacket, and it ran somewhat thus:—

"But I hear my lover's voice wailing in the night, and I go to find him; for my loneliness is not to be borne. May God have mercy upon me!"

And that was all.

For a day and a night we stood out from the land towards the North, having a steady breeze to which we set our lug sails, and so made very good way, the sea being quiet, though with a slow, lumbering swell from the Southward.

It was on the morning of the second day of our escape that we met with the beginnings of our adventure into the Silent Sea, the which I am about to make as clear as I am able.

The night had been quiet, and the breeze steady until near on to the dawn, when the wind slacked away to nothing, and we lay there waiting, perchance the sun should bring the breeze with it. And this it did; but no such wind as we did desire; for when the morning came upon us, we discovered all that part of the sky to be full of a fiery redness, which presently spread away down to the South, so that an entire quarter of the heavens was, as it seemed to us, a mighty arc of blood-colored fire.

Now, at the sight of these omens, the bo'sun gave orders to prepare the boats for the storm which we had reason to expect, looking for it in the South, for it was from that direction that the swell came rolling upon us. With this intent, we roused out so much heavy canvas as the boats contained, for we had gotten a bolt and a half from the hulk in the creek; also the boat covers which we could lash down to the brass studs under the gunnels of the boats. Then, in each boat, we mounted the whaleback—which had been stowed along the tops of the thwarts—also its supports, lashing the same to the thwarts below the knees. Then we laid two lengths of the stout canvas the full length of the boat over the whaleback, overlapping and nailing them to the same, so that they sloped away down over the gunnels upon each side as though they had formed a roof to us. Here, whilst some stretched the canvas, nailing its lower edges to the gunnels, others were employed in lashing together the oars and the mast, and to this bundle they secured a considerable length of new three-and-a-half-inch hemp rope, which we had brought away from the hulk along with the canvas. This rope was then passed over the bows and in through the painter ring, and thence to the forrard thwarts, where it was made fast, and we gave attention to parcel it with odd strips of canvas against danger of chafe. And the same was done in both of the boats, for we could not put our trust in the painters, besides which they had not sufficient length to secure safe and easy riding.

Now by this time we had the canvas nailed down to the gunnels around our boat, after which we spread the boat-cover over it, lacing it down to the brass studs beneath the gunnel. And so we had all the boat covered in, save a place in the stern where a man might stand to wield the steering oar, for the boats were double bowed. And in each boat we made the same preparation, lashing all movable articles, and preparing to meet so great a storm as might well fill the heart with terror; for the sky cried out to us that it would be no light wind, and further, the great swell from the South grew more huge with every hour that passed; though as yet it was without virulence, being slow and oily and black against the redness of the sky.

Presently we were ready, and had cast over the bundle of oars and the mast, which was to serve as our sea anchor, and so we lay waiting. It was at this time that the bo'sun called over to Josh certain advice with regard to that which lay before us. And after that the two of them sculled the boats a little apart; for there might be a danger of their being dashed together by the first violence of the storm.

And so came a time of waiting, with Josh and the bo'sun each of them at the steering oars, and the rest of us stowed away under the coverings. From where I crouched near the bo'sun, I had sight of Josh away upon our port side: he was standing up black as a shape of night against the mighty redness, when the boat came to the foamless crowns of the swells, and then gone from sight in the hollows between.

Now midday had come and gone, and we had made shift to eat so good a meal as our appetites would allow; for we had no knowledge how long it might be ere we should have chance of another, if, indeed, we had ever need to think more of such. And then, in the middle part of the afternoon, we heard the first cryings of the storm—a far-distant moaning, rising and falling most solemnly.

Presently, all the Southern part of the horizon so high up, maybe, as some seven to ten degrees, was blotted out by a great black wall of cloud, over which the red glare came down upon the great swells as though from the light of some vast and unseen fire. It was about this time, I observed that the sun had the appearance of a great full moon, being pale and clearly defined, and seeming to have no warmth nor brilliancy; and this, as may be imagined, seemed most strange to us, the more so because of the redness in the South and East.

And all this while the swells increased most prodigiously; though without making broken water: yet they informed us that we had done well to take so much precaution; for surely they were raised by a very great storm. A little before evening, the moaning came again, and then a space of silence; after which there rose a very sudden bellowing, as of wild beasts, and then once more the silence.

About this time, the bo'sun making no objection, I raised my head above the cover until I was in a standing position; for, until now, I had taken no more than occasional peeps; and I was very glad of the chance to stretch my limbs; for I had grown mightily cramped. Having stirred the sluggishness of my blood, I sat me down again; but in such position that I could see every part of the horizon without difficulty. Ahead of us, that is to the South, I saw now that the great wall of cloud had risen some further degrees, and there was something less of the redness; though, indeed, what there was left of it was sufficiently terrifying; for it appeared to crest the black cloud like red foam, seeming, it might be, as though a mighty sea made ready to break over the world.

Towards the West, the sun was sinking behind a curious red-tinted haze, which gave it the appearance of a dull red disk. To the North, seeming very high in the sky, were some flecks of cloud lying motionless, and of a very pretty rose color. And here I may remark that all the sea to the North of us appeared as a very ocean of dull red fire; though, as might be expected, the swells, coming up from the South, against the light were so many exceeding great hills of blackness.

It was just after I had made these observations that we heard again the distant roaring of the storm, and I know not how to convey the exceeding terror of that sound. It was as though some mighty beast growled far down towards the South; and it seemed to make very clear to me that we were but two small craft in a very lonesome place. Then, even while the roaring lasted, I saw a sudden light flare up, as it were from the edge of the Southern horizon. It had somewhat the appearance of lightning; yet vanished not immediately, as is the wont of lightning; and more, it had not been my experience to witness such spring up from out of the sea, but, rather, down from the heavens. Yet I have little doubt but that it was a form of lightning; for it came many times after this, so that I had chance to observe it minutely. And frequently, as I watched, the storm would shout at us in a most fearsome manner.

Then, when the sun was low upon the horizon, there came to our ears a very shrill, screaming noise, most penetrating and distressing, and, immediately afterwards the bo'sun shouted out something in a hoarse voice, and commenced to sway furiously upon the steering oar. I saw his stare fixed upon a point a little on our larboard bow, and perceived that in that direction the sea was all blown up into vast clouds of dust-like froth, and I knew that the storm was upon us. Immediately afterwards a cold blast struck us; but we suffered no harm, for the bo'sun had gotten the boat bows-on by this. The wind passed us, and there was an instant of calm. And now all the air above us was full of a continuous roaring, so very loud and intense that I was like to be deafened. To windward, I perceived an enormous wall of spray bearing down upon us, and I heard again the shrill screaming, pierce through the roaring. Then, the bo'sun whipped in his oar under the cover, and, reaching forward, drew the canvas aft, so that it covered the entire boat, and he held it down against the gunnel upon the starboard side, shouting in my ear to do likewise upon the larboard. Now had it not been for this forethought on the part of the bo'sun we had been all dead men; and this may be the better believed when I explain that we felt the water falling upon the stout canvas overhead, tons and tons, though so beaten to froth as to lack solidity to sink or crush us. I have said "felt"; for I would make it so clear as may be, here once and for all, that so intense was the roaring and screaming of the elements, there could no sound have penetrated to us, no! not the pealing of mighty thunders. And so for the space of maybe a full minute the boat quivered and shook most vilely, so that she seemed like to have been shaken in pieces, and from a dozen places between the gunnel and the covering canvas, the water spurted in upon us. And here one other thing I would make mention of: During that minute, the boat had ceased to rise and fall upon the great swell, and whether this was because the sea was flattened by the first rush of the wind, or that the excess of the storm held her steady, I am unable to tell; and can put down only that which we felt.

Now, in a little, the first fury of the blast being spent, the boat began to sway from side to side, as though the wind blew now upon the one beam, and now upon the other; and several times we were stricken heavily with the blows of solid water. But presently this ceased, and we returned once again to the rise and fall of the swell, only that now we received a cruel jerk every time that the boat came upon the top of a sea. And so a while passed.

Towards midnight, as I should judge, there came some mighty flames of lightning, so bright that they lit up the boat through the double covering of canvas; yet no man of us heard aught of the thunder; for the roaring of the storm made all else a silence.

And so to the dawn, after which, finding that we were still, by the mercy of God, possessed of our lives, we made shift to eat and drink; after which we slept.

Now, being extremely wearied by the stress of the past night, I slumbered through many hours of the storm, waking at some time between noon and evening. Overhead, as I lay looking upwards, the canvas showed of a dull leadenish color, blackened completely at whiles by the dash of spray and water. And so, presently, having eaten again, and feeling that all things lay in the hands of the Almighty, I came once more upon sleep.

Twice through the following night was I wakened by the boat being hurled upon her beam-ends by the blows of the seas; but she righted easily, and took scarce any water, the canvas proving a very roof of safety. And so the morning came again.

Being now rested, I crawled after to where the bo'sun lay, and, the noise of the storm lulling odd instants, shouted in his ear to know whether the wind was easing at whiles. To this he nodded, whereat I felt a most joyful sense of hope pulse through me, and ate such food as could be gotten, with a very good relish.

In the afternoon, the sun broke out suddenly, lighting up the boat most gloomily through the wet canvas; yet a very welcome light it was, and bred in us a hope that the storm was near to breaking. In a little, the sun disappeared; but, presently, it coming again, the bo'sun beckoned to me to assist him, and we removed such temporary nails as we had used to fasten down the after part of the canvas, and pushed back the covering a space sufficient to allow our heads to go through into the daylight. On looking out, I discovered the air to be full of spray, beaten as fine as dust, and then, before I could note aught else, a little gout of water took me in the face with such force as to deprive me of breath; so that I had to descend beneath the canvas for a little while.

So soon as I was recovered, I thrust forth my head again, and now I had some sight of the terrors around us. As each huge sea came towards us, the boat shot up to meet it, right up to its very crest, and there, for the space of some instants, we would seem to be swamped in a very ocean of foam, boiling up on each side of the boat to the height of many feet. Then, the sea passing from under us, we would go swooping dizzily down the great, black, froth-splotched back of the wave, until the oncoming sea caught us up most mightily. Odd whiles, the crest of a sea would hurl forward before we had reached the top, and though the boat shot upward like a veritable feather, yet the water would swirl right over us, and we would have to draw in our heads most suddenly; in such cases the wind flapping the cover down so soon as our hands were removed. And, apart from the way in which the boat met the seas, there was a very sense of terror in the air; the continuous roaring and howling of the storm; the *screaming* of the foam, as the frothy summits of the briny mountains hurled past us, and the wind that tore the breath out of our weak human throats, are things scarce to be conceived.

Presently, we drew in our heads, the sun having vanished again, and nailed down the canvas once more, and so prepared for the night.

From here on until the morning, I have very little knowledge of any happenings; for I slept much of the time, and, for the rest, there was little to know, cooped up beneath the cover. Nothing save the interminable, thundering swoop of the boat downwards, and then the halt and upward hurl, and the occasional plunges and surges to larboard or starboard, occasioned, I can only suppose, by the indiscriminate might of the seas.

I would make mention here, how that I had little thought all this while for the peril of the other boat, and, indeed, I was so very full of our own that it is no matter at which to wonder. However, as it proved, and as this is a most suitable place in which to tell it, the boat that held Josh and the rest of the crew came through the storm with safety; though it was not until many years afterwards that I had the good fortune to hear from Josh himself how that, after the storm, they were picked up by a homeward-bound vessel, and landed in the Port of London.

And now, to our own happenings.

VI.
The Weed-Choked Sea

It was some little while before midday that we grew conscious that the sea had become very much less violent; and this despite the wind roaring with scarce abated noise. And, presently, everything about the boat, saving the wind, having grown indubitably calmer, and no great water breaking over the canvas, the bo'sun beckoned me again to assist him lift the after part of the cover. This we did, and put forth our heads to inquire the reason of the unexpected quietness of the sea; not knowing but that we had come suddenly under the lee of some unknown land. Yet, for a space, we could see nothing, beyond the surrounding billows; for the sea was still very furious, though no matter to cause us concern, after that through which we had come.

Presently, however, the bo'sun, raising himself, saw something, and, bending cried in my ear that there was a low bank which broke the force of the sea; but he was full of wonder to know how that we had passed it without shipwreck. And whilst he was still pondering the matter I raised myself, and took a look on all sides of us, and so I discovered that there lay another great bank upon our larboard side, and this I pointed out to him. Immediately afterwards, we came upon a great mass of seaweed swung up on the crest of a sea, and, presently, another. And so we drifted on, and the seas grew less with astonishing rapidity, so that, in a little, we stripped off the cover so far as the midship thwart; for the rest of the men were sorely in need of the fresh air, after so long a time below the canvas covering.

It was after we had eaten, that one of them made out that there was another low bank astern upon which we were drifting. At that, the bo'sun stood up and made an examination of it, being much exercised in his mind to know how we might come clear of it with safety. Presently, however, we had come so near to it that we discovered it to be composed of seaweed, and so we let the boat drive upon it, making no doubt but that the other banks, which we had seen, were of a similar nature.

In a little, we had driven in among the weed; yet, though our speed was greatly slowed, we made some progress, and so in time came out upon the other side, and now we found the sea to be near quiet, so that we hauled in our sea anchor—which had collected a great mass of weed about it—and removed the whaleback and canvas coverings, after which we stepped the mast, and set a tiny storm-foresail upon the boat; for we wished to have her under control, and could set no more than this, because of the violence of the breeze.

Thus we drove on before the wind, the bo'sun steering, and avoiding all such banks as showed ahead, and ever the sea grew calmer. Then, when it was near on to evening, we discovered a huge stretch of the weed that seemed to block all the sea ahead, and, at that, we hauled down the foresail, and took to our oars, and began to pull, broadside on to it, towards the West. Yet so strong was the breeze, that we were being driven down rapidly upon it. And then, just before sunset, we opened out the end of it, and drew in our oars, very thankful to set the little foresail, and run off again before the wind.

And so, presently, the night came down upon us, and the bo'sun made us take turn and turn about to keep a lookout; for the boat was going some knots through the water, and we were among strange seas; but *he* took no sleep all that night, keeping always to the steering oar.

I have memory, during my time of watching, of passing odd floating masses, which I make no doubt were weed, and once we drove right atop of one; but drew clear without much trouble. And all the while, through the dark to starboard, I could make out the dim outline of that enormous weed extent lying low upon the sea, and seeming without end. And so, presently, my time to watch being at an end, I returned to my slumber, and when next I waked it was morning.

Now the morning discovered to me that there was no end to the weed upon our starboard side; for it stretched away into the distance ahead of us so far as we could see; while all about us the sea was full of floating masses of the stuff. And then, suddenly, one of the men cried out that there was a vessel in among the weed. At that, as may be imagined, we were very greatly excited, and stood upon the thwarts that we might get better view of her. Thus I saw her a great way in from the edge of the weed, and I noted that her foremast was gone near to the deck, and she had no main topmast; though, strangely enough, her mizzen stood unharmed. And beyond this, I could make out but little, because of the distance; though the sun, which was upon our larboard side, gave me some sight of her hull, but not much, because of the weed in which she was deeply embedded; yet it seemed to me that her sides were very weather-worn, and in one place some glistening brown object, which may have been a fungus, caught the rays of the sun, sending off a wet sheen.

There we stood, all of us, upon the thwarts, staring and exchanging opinions, and were like to have overset the boat; but that the bo'sun ordered us down. And after this we made our breakfast, and had much discussion regarding the stranger, as we ate.

Later, towards midday, we were able to set our mizzen; for the storm had greatly modified, and so, presently, we hauled away to the West, to escape a great bank of the weed which ran out from the main body. Upon rounding this, we let the boat off again, and set the main lug, and thus made very good speed before the wind. Yet though we ran all that afternoon parallel with the weed to starboard, we came not to its end. And three separate times we saw the hulks of rotting vessels, some of them having the appearance of a previous age, so ancient did they seem.

Now, towards evening, the wind dropped to a very little breeze, so that we made but slow way, and thus we had better chance to study the weed. And now we saw that it was full of crabs; though for the most part so very minute as to escape the casual glance; yet they were not all small, for in a while I discovered a swaying among the weed, a little way in from the edge, and immediately I saw the mandible of a very great crab stir amid the weed. At that, hoping to obtain it for food, I pointed it out to the bo'sun, suggesting that we should try and capture it. And so, there being by now scarce any wind, he bade us get out a couple of the oars, and back the boat up to the weed. This we did, after which he made fast a piece of salt meat to a bit of spun yarn, and bent this onto the boat hook. Then he made a running bowline, and slipped the loop onto the shaft of the boat hook, after which he held out the boat hook, after the fashion of a fishing rod, over the place where I had seen the crab. Almost immediately, there swept up an enormous claw, and grasped the meat, and at that, the bo'sun cried out to me to take an oar and slide the bowline along the boat-hook, so that it should fall over the claw, and this I did, and immediately some of us hauled upon the line, taughtening it about the great claw. Then the bo'sun sung out to us to haul the crab aboard, that we had it most securely; yet on the instant we had reason to wish that we had been less successful; for the creature, feeling the tug of our pull upon it, tossed the weed in all directions, and thus we had full sight of it, and discovered it to be so great a crab as is scarce conceivable—a very monster. And further, it was apparent to us that the brute had no fear of us, nor intention to escape; but rather made to come at us; whereat the bo'sun, perceiving our danger, cut the line, and bade us put weight upon the oars, and so in a moment we were in safety, and very determined to have no more meddlings with such creatures.

Presently, the night came upon us, and, the wind remaining low, there was everywhere about us a great stillness, most solemn after the continuous roaring of the storm which had beset us in the previous days. Yet now and again a little wind would rise and blow across the sea, and where it met the weed, there would come a low, damp rustling, so that I could hear the passage of it for no little time after the calm had come once more all about us.

Now it is a strange thing that I, who had slept amid the noise of the past days, should find sleeplessness amid so much calm; yet so it was, and presently I took the steering oar, proposing that the rest should sleep, and to this the bo'sun agreed, first warning me, however, most particularly to have care that I kept the boat off the weed (for we had still a little way on us), and, further, to call him should anything unforeseen occur. And after that, almost immediately he fell asleep, as indeed did the most of the men.

From the time that I relieved the bo'sun, until midnight, I sat upon the gunnel of the boat, with the steering oar under my arm, and watched and listened, most full of a sense of the strangeness of the seas into which we had come. It is true that I had heard tell of seas choked up with weed—seas that were full of stagnation, having no tides; but I had not thought to come upon such an one in my wanderings; having, indeed, set down such tales as being bred of imagination, and without reality in fact.

Then, a little before the dawn, and when the sea was yet full of darkness, I was greatly startled to hear a prodigious splash amid the weed, mayhaps at a distance of some hundred yards from the boat. Then, as I stood full of alertness, and knowing not what the next moment might bring forth, there came to me across the immense waste of weed, a long, mournful cry, and then again the silence. Yet, though I kept very quiet, there came no further sound, and I was about to re-seat myself, when, afar off in that strange wilderness, there flashed out a sudden flame of fire.

Now upon seeing fire in the midst of so much lonesomeness, I was as one amazed, and could do naught but stare. Then, my judgment returning to me, I stooped and waked the bo'sun; for it seemed to me that this was a matter for his attention. He, after staring at it awhile, declared that he could see the shape of a vessel's hull beyond the flame; but, immediately, he was in doubt, as, indeed, I had been all the while. And then, even as we peered, the light vanished, and though we waited for the space of some minutes; watching steadfastly, there came no further sight of that strange illumination.

From now until the dawn, the bo'sun remained awake with me, and we talked much upon that which we had seen; yet could come to no satisfactory conclusion; for it seemed impossible to us that a place of so much desolation could contain any living being. And then, just as the dawn was upon us, there loomed up a fresh wonder—the hull of a great vessel maybe a couple or three score fathoms in from the edge of the weed. Now the wind was still very light, being no more than an occasional breath, so that we went past her at a drift, thus the dawn had strengthened sufficiently to give to us a clear sight of the stranger, before we had gone more than a little past her. And now I perceived that she lay full broadside on to us, and that her three masts were gone close down to the deck. Her side was streaked in places with rust, and in others a green scum overspread her; but it was no more than a glance that I gave at any of those matters; for I had spied something which drew all my attention—great leathery arms splayed all across her side, some of them crooked inboard over the rail, and then, low down, seen just above the weed, the huge, brown, glistening bulk of so great a monster as ever I had conceived. The bo'sun saw it in the same instant and cried out in a hoarse whisper that it was a mighty devilfish, and then, even as he spoke, two of the arms flickered up into the cold light of the dawn, as though the creature had been asleep, and we had waked it. At that, the bo'sun seized an oar, and I did likewise, and, so swiftly as we dared, for fear of making any unneedful noise, we pulled the boat to a safer distance. From there and until the vessel had become indistinct by reason of the space we put between us, we watched that great creature clutched to the old hull, as it might be a limpet to a rock.

Presently, when it was broad day, some of the men began to rouse up, and in a little we broke our fast, which was not displeasing to me, who had spent the night watching. And so through the day we sailed with a very light wind upon our larboard quarter. And all the while we kept the great waste of weed upon our starboard side, and apart from the mainland of the weed, as it were, there were scattered about an uncountable number of weed islets and banks, and there were thin patches of it that appeared scarce above the water, and through these later we let the boat sail; for they had not sufficient density to impede our progress more than a little.

And then, when the day was far spent, we came in sight of another wreck amid the weeds. She lay in from the edge perhaps so much as the half of a mile, and she had all three of her lower masts in, and her lower yards squared. But what took our eyes more than aught else was a great superstructure which had been built upward from her rails, almost halfway to her main tops, and this, as we were able to perceive, was supported by ropes let down from the yards; but of what material the superstructure was composed, I have no knowledge; for it was so over-grown with some form of green stuff—as was so much of the hull as showed above the weed—as to defy our guesses. And because of this growth, it was borne upon us that the ship must have been lost to the world a very great age ago. At this suggestion, I grew full of solemn thought; for it seemed to me that we had come upon the cemetery of the oceans.

Now, in a little while after we had passed this ancient craft, the night came down upon us, and we prepared for sleep, and because the boat was making some little way through the water, the bo'sun gave out that each of us should stand our turn at the steering-oar, and that he was to be called should any fresh matter transpire. And so we settled down for the night, and owing to my previous sleeplessness, I was full weary, so that I knew nothing until the one whom I was to relieve shook me into wakefulness. So soon as I was fully waked, I perceived that a low moon hung above the horizon, and shed a very ghostly light across the great weed world to starboard. For the rest, the night was exceeding quiet, so that no sound came to me in all that ocean, save the rippling of the water upon our bends as the boat forged slowly along. And so I settled down to pass the time ere I should be allowed to sleep; but first I asked the man whom I had relieved, how long a time had passed since moon-rise; to which he replied that it was no more than the half of an hour, and after that I questioned whether he had seen aught strange amid the weed during his time at the oar; but he had seen nothing, except that once he had fancied a light had shown in the midst of the waste; yet it could have been naught save a humor of the imagination; though apart from this, he had heard a strange crying a little after midnight, and twice there had been great splashes among the weed. And after that he fell asleep, being impatient at my questioning.

Now it so chanced that my watch had come just before the dawn; for which I was full of thankfulness, being in that frame of mind when the dark breeds strange and unwholesome fancies. Yet, though I was so near to the dawn, I was not to escape free of the eerie influence of that place; for, as I sat, running my gaze to and fro over its grey immensity, it came to me that there were strange movements among the weed, and I seemed to see vaguely, as one may see things in dreams, dim white faces peer out at me here and there; yet my common sense assured me that I was but deceived by the uncertain light and the sleep in my eyes; yet for all that, it put my nerves on the quiver.

A little later, there came to my ears the noise of a very great splash amid the weed; but though I stared with intentness, I could nowhere discern aught as likely to be the cause thereof. And then, suddenly, between me and the moon, there drove up from out of that great waste a vast bulk, flinging huge masses of weed in all directions. It seemed to be no more than a hundred fathoms distant, and, against the moon, I saw the outline of it most clearly—a mighty devilfish. Then it had fallen back once more with a prodigious splash, and so the quiet fell again, finding me sore afraid, and no little bewildered that so monstrous a creature could leap with such agility. And then (in my fright I had let the boat come near to the edge of the weed) there came a subtle stir opposite to our starboard bow, and something slid down into the water. I swayed upon the oar to turn the boat's head outward, and with the same movement leant forward and sideways to peer, bringing my face near to the boat's rail. In the same instant, I found myself looking down into a white demoniac face, human save that the mouth and nose had greatly the appearance of a beak. The thing was gripping at the side of the boat with two flickering hands—gripping the bare, smooth outer surface, in a way that woke in my mind a sudden memory of the great devilfish which had clung to the side of the wreck we had passed in the previous dawn. I saw the face come up towards me, and one misshapen hand fluttered almost to my throat, and there came a sudden, hateful reek in my nostrils—foul and abominable. Then, I came into possession of my faculties, and drew back with great haste and a wild cry of fear. And then I had the steering-oar by the middle, and was smiting downward with the loom over the side of the boat; but the thing was gone from my sight. I remember shouting out to the bo'sun and to the men to awake, and then the bo'sun had me by the shoulder, was calling in my ear to know what dire thing had come about. At that, I cried out that I did not know, and, presently, being somewhat calmer, I told them of the thing that I had seen;

but even as I told of it, there seemed to be no truth in it, so that they were all at a loss to know whether I had fallen asleep, or that I had indeed seen a devil.

And presently the dawn was upon us.

VII.
The Island in the Weed

It was as we were all discussing the matter of the devil face that had peered up at me out of the water, that Job, the ordinary seaman, discovered the island in the light of the growing dawn, and, seeing it, sprang to his feet, with so loud a cry that we were like for the moment to have thought he had seen a second demon. Yet when we made discovery of that which he had already perceived, we checked our blame at his sudden shout; for the sight of land, after so much desolation, made us very warm in our hearts.

Now at first the island seemed but a very small matter; for we did not know at that time that we viewed it from its end; yet despite this, we took to our oars and rowed with all haste towards it, and so, coming nearer, were able to see that it had a greater size than we had imagined. Presently, having cleared the end of it, and keeping to that side which was further from the great mass of the weed-continent, we opened out a bay that curved inward to a sandy beach, most seductive to our tired eyes. Here, for the space of a minute, we paused to survey the prospect, and I saw that the island was of a very strange shape, having a great hump of black rock at either end, and dipping down into a steep valley between them. In this valley there seemed to be a deal of a strange vegetation that had the appearance of mighty toadstools; and down nearer the beach there was a thick grove of a kind of very tall reed, and these we discovered afterwards to be exceeding tough and light, having something of the qualities of the bamboo.

Regarding the beach, it might have been most reasonably supposed that it would be very thick with the driftweed; but this was not so, at least, not at that time; though a projecting horn of the black rock which ran out into the sea from the upper end of the island, was thick with it.

And now, the bo'sun having assured himself that there was no appearance of any danger, we bent to our oars, and presently had the boat aground upon the beach, and here, finding it convenient, we made our breakfast. During this meal, the bo'sun discussed with us the most proper thing to do, and it was decided to push the boat off from the shore, leaving Job in her, whilst the remainder of us made some exploration of the island.

And so, having made an end of eating, we proceeded as we had determined, leaving Job in the boat, ready to scull ashore for us if we were pursued by any savage creature, while the rest of us made our way towards the nearer hump, from which, as it stood some hundred feet above the sea, we hoped to get a very good idea of the remainder of the island. First, however, the bo'sun handed out to us the two cutlasses and the cut-and-thrust (the other two cutlasses being in Josh's boat), and, taking one himself, he passed me the cut-and-thrust, and gave the other cutlass to the biggest of the men. Then he bade the others keep their sheath knives handy, and was proceeding to lead the way, when one of them called out to us to wait a moment, and, with that, ran quickly to the clump of reeds. Here, he took one with both his hands and bent upon it; but it would not break, so that he had to notch it about with his knife, and thus, in a little, he had it clear. After this, he cut off the upper part, which was too thin and lissome for his purpose, and then thrust the handle of his knife into the end of the portion which he had retained, and in this wise he had a most serviceable lance or spear. For the reeds were very strong, and hollow after the fashion of bamboo, and when he had bound some yarn about the end into which he had thrust his knife, so as to prevent it splitting, it was a fit enough weapon for any man.

Now the bo'sun, perceiving the happiness of the fellow's idea, bade the rest make to themselves similar weapons, and whilst they were busy thus, he commended the man very warmly. And so, in a little, being now most comfortably armed, we made inland towards the nearer black hill, in very good spirits. Presently, we were come to the rock which formed the hill, and found that it came up out of the sand with great abruptness, so that we could not climb it on the seaward side. At that, the bo'sun led us round a space towards that side where lay the valley, and here there was under-foot neither sand nor rock; but ground of strange and spongy texture, and then suddenly, rounding a jutting spur of the rock, we came upon the first of the vegetation—an incredible mushroom; nay, I should say toadstool; for it had no healthy look about it, and gave out a heavy, mouldy odor. And now we perceived that the valley was filled with them, all, that is, save a great circular patch where nothing appeared to be growing; though we were not yet at a sufficient height to ascertain the reason of this.

Presently, we came to a place where the rock was split by a great fissure running up to the top, and showing many ledges and convenient shelves upon which we might obtain hold and footing. And so we set-to about climbing, helping one another so far as we had ability, until, in about the space of some ten minutes, we reached the top, and from thence had a very fine view. We perceived now that there was a beach upon that side of the island which was opposed to the weed; though, unlike that upon which we had landed, it was greatly choked with weed which had drifted ashore. After that, I gave notice to see what space of water lay between the island and the edge of the great weed-continent, and guessed it to be no more than maybe some ninety yards, at which I fell to wishing that it had been greater, for I was grown much in awe of the weed and the strange things which I conceived it to contain.

Abruptly, the bo'sun clapped me upon the shoulder, and pointed to some object that lay out in the weed at a distance of not much less than the half of a mile from where we stood. Now, at first, I could not conceive what manner of thing it was at which I stared, until the bo'sun, remarking my bewilderment, informed me that it was a vessel all covered in, no doubt as a protection against the devil-fish and other strange creatures in the weed. And now I began to trace the hull of her amid all that hideous growth; but of her masts, I could discern nothing; and I doubted not but that they had been carried away by some storm ere she was caught by the weed; and then the thought came to me of the end of those who had built up that protection against the horrors which the weed-world held hidden amid its slime.

Presently, I turned my gaze once more upon the island, which was very plain to see from where we stood. I conceived, now that I could see so much of it, that its length would be near to half a mile, though its breadth was something under four hundred yards; thus it was very long in proportion to its width. In the middle part it had less breadth than at the ends, being perhaps three hundred yards at its narrowest, and a hundred yards wider at its broadest.

Upon both sides of the island, as I have made already a mention, there was a beach, though this extended no great distance along the shore, the remainder being composed of the black rock of which the hills were formed. And now, having a closer regard to the beach upon the weed-side of the island, I discovered amid the wrack that had been cast ashore, a portion of the lower mast and topmast of some great ship, with rigging attached; but the yards were all gone. This find, I pointed out to the bo'sun, remarking that it might prove of use for firing; but he smiled at me, telling me that the dried weed would make a very abundant fire, and this without going to the labor of cutting the mast into suitable logs.

And now, he, in turn, called my attention to the place where the huge fungi had come to a stop in their growing, and I saw that in the center of the valley there was a great circular opening in the earth, like to the mouth of a prodigious pit, and it appeared to be filled to within a few feet of the mouth with water, over which spread a brown and horrid scum. Now, as may be supposed, I stared with some intentness at this; for it had the look of having been made with labor, being very symmetrical, yet I could not conceive but that I was deluded by the distance, and that it would have a rougher appearance when viewed from a nearer standpoint.

From contemplating this, I looked down upon the little bay in which our boat floated. Job was sitting in the stern, sculling gently with the steering oar and watching us. At that, I waved my hand to him in friendly fashion, and he waved back, and then, even as I looked, I saw something in the water under the boat—something dark colored that was all of a-move. The boat appeared to be floating over it as over a mass of sunk weed, and then I saw that, whatever it was, it was rising to the surface. At this a sudden horror came over me, and I clutched the bo'sun by the arm, and pointed, crying out that there was something under the boat. Now the bo'sun, so soon as he saw the thing, ran forward to the brow of the hill and, placing his hands to his mouth after the fashion of a trumpet, sang out to the boy to bring the boat to the shore and make fast the painter to a large piece of rock. At the bo'sun's hail, the lad called out "I, I," and, standing up, gave a sweep with his oar that brought the boat's head round towards the beach. Fortunately for him he was no more than some thirty yards from the shore at this time, else he had never come to it in this life; for the next moment the moving brown mass beneath the boat shot out a great tentacle and the oar was torn out of Job's hands with such power as to throw him right over on to the starboard gunnel of the boat. The oar itself was drawn down out of sight, and for the minute the boat was left untouched. Now the bo'sun cried out to the boy to take another oar, and get ashore while still he had chance, and at that we all called out various things, one advising one thing, and another recommending some other; yet our advice was vain, for the boy moved not, at which some cried out that he was stunned. I looked now to where the brown thing had been, for the boat had moved a few fathoms from the spot, having got some way upon her before the oar was snatched, and thus I discovered that the monster had disappeared, having, I conceived, sunk again into the depths from which it had risen; yet it might re-appear at any moment, and in that case the boy would be taken before our eyes.

At this juncture, the bo'sun called to us to follow him, and led the way to the great fissure up which we had climbed, and so, in a minute, we were, each of us, scrambling down with what haste we could make towards the valley. And all the while as I dropped from ledge to ledge, I was full of torment to know whether the monster had returned.

The bo'sun was the first man to reach the bottom of the cleft, and he set off immediately round the base of the rock to the beach, the rest of us following him as we made safe our footing in the valley. I was the third man down; but, being light and fleet of foot, I passed the second man and caught up with the bo'sun just as he came upon the sand. Here, I found that the boat was within some five fathoms of the beach, and I could see Job still lying insensible; but of the monster there was no sign.

And so matters were, the boat nearly a dozen yards from the shore, and Job lying insensible in her; with, somewhere near under her keel (for all that we knew) a great monster, and we helpless upon the beach.

Now I could not imagine how to save the lad, and indeed I fear he had been left to destruction—for I had deemed it madness to try to reach the boat by swimming—but for the extraordinary bravery of the bo'sun, who, without hesitating, dashed into the water and swam boldly out to the boat, which, by the grace of God, he reached without mishap, and climbed in over the bows.

Immediately, he took the painter and hove it to us, bidding us tail on to it and bring the boat to shore without delay, and by this method of gaining the beach he showed wisdom; for in this wise he escaped attracting the attention of the monster by unneedful stirring of the water, as he would surely have done had he made use of an oar.

Yet, despite his care, we had not finished with the creature; for, just as the boat grounded, I saw the lost steering oar shoot up half its length out of the sea, and immediately there was a mighty splather in the water astern, and the next instant the air seemed full of huge, whirling arms. At that, the bo'sun gave one look behind, and, seeing the thing upon him, snatched the boy into his arms, and sprang over the bows on to the sand. Now, at sight of the devil-fish, we had all made for the back of the beach at a run, none troubling even to retain the painter, and because of this, we were like to have lost the boat; for the great cuttlefish had its arms all splayed about it, seeming to have a mind to drag it down into the deep water from whence it had risen, and it had possibly succeeded, but that the bo'sun brought us all to our senses; for, having laid Job out of harm's way, he was the first to seize the painter, which lay trailed upon the sand, and, at that, we got back our courage and ran to assist him.

Now there happened to be convenient a great spike of rock, the same, indeed, to which the bo'sun had bidden Job tie the boat, and to this we ran the painter, taking a couple of turns about it and two half-hitches, and now, unless the rope carried away, we had no reason to fear the loss of the boat; though there seemed to us to be a danger of the creature's crushing it. Because of this, and because of a feeling of natural anger against the thing, the bo'sun took up from the sand one of the spears which had been cast down when we hauled the boat ashore. With this, he went down so far as seemed safe, and prodded the creature in one of its tentacles—the weapon entering easily, at which I was surprised, for I had understood that these monsters were near to invulnerable in all parts save their eyes. At receiving this stab, the great fish appeared to feel no hurt for it showed no signs of pain, and, at that, the bo'sun was further emboldened to go nearer, so that he might deliver a more deadly wound; yet scarce had he taken two steps before the hideous thing was upon him, and, but for an agility wonderful in so great a man, he had been destroyed. Yet, spite of so narrow an escape from death, he was not the less determined to wound or destroy the creature, and, to this end, he dispatched some of us to the grove of reeds to get half a dozen of the strongest, and when we returned with these, he bade two of the men lash their spears securely to them, and by this means they had now spears of a length of between thirty and forty feet. With these, it was possible to attack the devilfish without coming within reach of its tentacles. And now being ready, he took one of the spears, telling the biggest of the men to take the other. Then he directed him to aim for the right eye of the huge fish whilst he would attack the left.

Now since the creature had so nearly captured the bo'sun, it had ceased to tug at the boat, and lay silent, with its tentacles spread all about it, and its great eyes appearing just over the stern, so that it presented an appearance of watching our movements; though I doubt if it saw us with any clearness; for it must have been dazed with the brightness of the sunshine.

And now the bo'sun gave the signal to attack, at which he and the man ran down upon the creature with their lances, as it were in rest. The bo'sun's spear took the monster truly in its left eye; but the one wielded by the man was too bendable, and sagged so much that it struck the stern-post of the boat, the knife blade snapping off short. Yet it mattered not; for the wound inflicted by the bo'sun's weapon was so frightful, that the giant cuttlefish released the boat, and slid back into deep water, churning it into foam, and gouting blood.

For some minutes we waited to make sure that the monster had indeed gone, and after that, we hastened to the boat, and drew her up so far as we were able; after which we unloaded the heaviest of her contents, and so were able to get her right clear of the water.

And for an hour afterwards the sea all about the little beach was stained black, and in places red.

VIII.
The Noises in the Valley

Now, so soon as we had gotten the boat into safety, the which we did with a most feverish haste, the bo'sun gave his attention to Job; for the boy had not yet recovered from the blow which the loom of the oar had dealt him beneath the chin when the monster snatched at it. For awhile, his attentions produced no effect; but presently, having bathed the lad's face with water from the sea, and rubbed rum into his chest over the heart, the youth began to show signs of life, and soon opened his eyes, whereupon the bo'sun gave him a stiff jorum of the rum, after which he asked him how he seemed in himself. To this Job replied in a weak voice that he was dizzy and his head and neck ached badly, on hearing which, the bo'sun bade him keep lying until he had come more to himself. And so we left him in quietness under a little shade of canvas and reeds; for the air was warm and the sand dry, and he was not like to come to any harm there.

At a little distance, under the directing of the bo'sun, we made to prepare dinner, for we were now very hungry, it seeming a great while since we had broken our fast. To this end, the bo'sun sent two of the men across the island to gather some of the dry seaweed; for we intended to cook some of the salt meat, this being the first cooked meal since ending the meat which we had boiled before leaving the ship in the creek.

In the meanwhile, and until the return of the men with the fuel, the bo'sun kept us busied in various ways. Two he sent to cut a bundle of the reeds, and another couple to bring the meat and the iron boiler, the latter being one that we had taken from the old brig.

Presently, the men returned with the dried seaweed, and very curious stuff it seemed, some of it being in chunks near as thick as a man's body; but exceeding brittle by reason of its dryness. And so in a little, we had a very good fire going, which we fed with the seaweed and pieces of the reeds, though we found the latter to be but indifferent fuel, having too much sap, and being troublesome to break into convenient size.

Now when the fire had grown red and hot, the bo'sun half filled the boiler with sea water, in which he placed the meat; and the pan, having a stout lid, he did not scruple to place it in the very heart of the fire, so that soon we had the contents boiling merrily.

Having gotten the dinner underway, the bo'sun set about preparing our camp for the night, which we did by making a rough framework with the reeds, over which we spread the boat's sails and the cover, pegging the canvas down with tough splinters of the reed. When this was completed, we set-to and carried there all our stores, after which the bo'sun took us over to the other side of the island to gather fuel for the night, which we did, each man bearing a great double armful.

Now by the time that we had brought over, each of us, two loads of the fuel, we found the meat to be cooked, and so, without more to-do, set ourselves down and made a very good meal off it and some biscuits, after which we had each of us a sound tot of the rum. Having made an end of eating and drinking, the bo'sun went over to where Job lay, to inquire how he felt, and found him lying very quiet, though his breathing had a heavy touch about it. However, we could conceive of nothing by which he might be bettered, and so left him, being more hopeful that Nature would bring him to health than any skill of which we were possessed.

By this time it was late afternoon, so that the bo'sun declared we might please ourselves until sunset, deeming that we had earned a very good right to rest; but that from sunset till the dawn we should, he told us, have each of us to take turn and turn about to watch; for though we were no longer upon the water, none might say whether we were out of danger or not, as witness the happening of the morning; though, certainly, he apprehended no danger from the devil-fish so long as we kept well away from the water's edge.

And so from now until dark most of the men slept; but the bo'sun spent much of that time in overhauling the boat, to see how it might chance to have suffered during the storm, and also whether the struggles of the devil-fish had strained it in any way. And, indeed, it was speedily evident that the boat would need some attention; for the plank in her bottom next but one to the keel, upon the starboard side, had been burst inwards; this having been done, it would seem, by some rock in the beach hidden just beneath the water's edge, the devil-fish having, no doubt, ground the boat down upon it. Happily, the damage was not great; though it would most certainly have to be carefully repaired before the boat would be again seaworthy. For the rest, there seemed to be no other part needing attention.

Now I had not felt any call to sleep, and so had followed the bo'sun to the boat, giving him a hand to remove the bottom-boards, and finally to slue her bottom a little upwards, so that he might examine the leak more closely. When he had made an end with the boat, he went over to the stores, and looked closely into their condition, and also to see how they were lasting. And, after that, he sounded all the water-breakers; having done which, he remarked that it would be well for us if we could discover any fresh water upon the island.

By this time it was getting on towards evening, and the bo'sun went across to look at Job, finding him much as he had been when we visited him after dinner. At that, the bo'sun asked me to bring across one of the longer of the bottom-boards, which I did, and we made use of it as a stretcher to carry the lad into the tent. And afterwards, we carried all the loose woodwork of the boat into the tent, emptying the lockers of their contents, which included some oakum, a small boat's hatchet, a coil of one-and-a-half-inch hemp line, a good saw, an empty colza-oil tin, a bag of copper nails, some bolts and washers, two fishing-lines, three spare tholes, a three-pronged grain without the shaft, two balls of spun yarn, three hanks of roping-twine, a piece of canvas with four roping-needles stuck in it, the boat's lamp, a spare plug, and a roll of light duck for making boat's sails.

And so, presently, the dark came down upon the island, at which the bo'sun waked the men, and bade them throw more fuel onto the fire, which had burned down to a mound of glowing embers much shrouded in ash. After that, one of them part filled the boiler with fresh water, and soon we were occupied most pleasantly upon a supper of cold, boiled salt-meat, hard biscuits, and rum mixed with hot water. During supper, the bo'sun made clear to the men regarding the watches, arranging how they should follow, so that I found I was set down to take my turn from midnight until one of the clock. Then, he explained to them about the burst plank in the bottom of the boat, and how that it would have to be put right before we could hope to leave the island, and that after that night we should have to go most strictly with the victuals; for there seemed to be nothing upon the island, that we had up till then discovered, fit to satisfy our bellies. More than this, if we could find no fresh water, he should have to distill some to make up for that which we had drunk, and this must be done before leaving the island.

Now by the time that the bo'sun had made an end of explaining these matters, we had ceased from eating, and soon after this we made each one of us a comfortable place in the sand within the tent, and lay down to sleep. For a while, I found myself very wakeful, which may have been because of the warmth of the night, and, indeed, at last I got up and went out of the tent, conceiving that I might the better find sleep in the open air. And so it proved; for, having lain down at the side of the tent, a little way from the fire, I fell soon into a deep slumber, which at first was dreamless. Presently, however, I came upon a very strange and unsettling dream; for I dreamed that I had been left alone on the island, and was sitting very desolate upon the edge of the brown-scummed pit. Then I was aware suddenly that it was very dark and very silent, and I began to shiver; for it seemed to me that something which repulsed my whole being had come quietly behind me. At that I tried mightily to turn and look into the shadows among the great fungi that stood all about me; but I had no power to turn. And the thing was coming nearer, though never a sound came to me, and I gave out a scream, or tried to; but my voice made no stir in the rounding quiet; and then something wet and cold touched my face, and slithered down and covered my mouth, and paused there for a vile, breathless moment. It passed onward and fell to my throat—and stayed there ...

Someone stumbled and fell over my feet, and at that, I was suddenly awake. It was the man on watch making a walk round the back of the tent, and he had not known of my presence till he fell over my boots. He was somewhat shaken and startled, as might be supposed; but steadied himself on learning that it was no wild creature crouched there in the shadow; and all the time, as I answered his inquiries, I was full of a strange, horrid feeling that something had left me at the moment of my awakening. There was a slight, hateful odor in my nostrils that was not altogether unfamiliar, and then, suddenly, I was aware that my face was damp and that there was a curious sense of tingling at my throat. I put up my hand and felt my face, and the hand when I brought it away was slippery with slime, and at that, I put up my other hand, and touched my throat, and there it was the same, only, in addition, there was a slight swelled place a little to one side of the wind-pipe, the sort of place that the bite of a mosquito will make; but I had no thought to blame any mosquito.

Now the stumbling of the man over me, my awakening, and the discovery that my face and throat were be-slimed, were but the happenings of some few, short instants; and then I was upon my feet, and following him round to the fire; for I had a sense of chilliness and a great desire not to be alone. Now, having come to the fire, I took some of the water that had been left in the boiler, and washed my face and neck, after which I felt more my own man. Then I asked the man to look at my throat, so that he might give me some idea of what manner of place the swelling seemed, and he, lighting a piece of the dry seaweed to act as a torch, made examination of my neck; but could see little, save a number of small ring-like marks, red inwardly, and white at the edges, and one of them was bleeding slightly. After that, I asked him whether he had seen anything moving round the tent; but he had seen nothing during all the time that he had been on watch; though it was true that he had heard odd noises; but nothing very near at hand. Of the places on my throat he seemed to think but little, suggesting that I had been bitten by some sort of sand-fly; but at that, I shook my head, and told him of my dream, and after that, he was as anxious to keep near me as I to him. And so the night passed onward, until my turn came to watch.

For a little while, the man whom I had relieved sat beside me; having, I conceived, the kindly intent of keeping me company; but so soon as I perceived this, I entreated him to go and get his sleep, assuring him that I had no longer any feelings of fear—such as had been mine upon awakening and discovering the state of my face and throat—and, upon this, he consented to leave me, and so, in a little, I sat alone beside the fire.

For a certain space, I kept very quiet, listening; but no sound came to me out of the surrounding darkness, and so, as though it were a fresh thing, it was borne in upon me how that we were in a very abominable place of lonesomeness and desolation. And I grew very solemn.

Thus as I sat, the fire, which had not been replenished for a while, dwindled steadily until it gave but a dullish glow around. And then, in the direction of the valley, I heard suddenly the sound of a dull thud, the noise coming to me through the stillness with a very startling clearness. At that, I perceived that I was not doing my duty to the rest, nor to myself, by sitting and allowing the fire to cease from flaming; and immediately reproaching myself, I seized and cast a mass of the dry weed upon the fire, so that a great blaze shot up into the night, and afterwards I glanced quickly to right and to left, holding my cut-and-thrust very readily, and most thankful to the Almighty that I had brought no harm to any by reason of my carelessness, which I incline me to believe was that strange inertia which is bred by fear. And then, even as I looked about me, there came to me across the silence of the beach a fresh noise, a continual soft slithering to and fro in the bottom of the valley, as though a multitude of creatures moved stealthily. At this, I threw yet more fuel upon the fire, and after that I fixed my gaze in the direction of the valley: thus in the following instant it seemed to me that I saw a certain thing, as it might be a shadow, move on the outer borders of the firelight. Now the man who had kept watch before me had left his spear stuck upright in the sand convenient to my grasp, and, seeing something moving, I seized the weapon and hurled it with all my strength in its direction; but there came no answering cry to tell that I had struck anything living, and immediately afterwards there fell once more a great silence upon the island, being broken only by a far splash out upon the weed.

It may be conceived with truth that the above happenings had put a very considerable strain upon my nerves, so that I looked to and fro continually, with ever and anon a quick glance behind me; for it seemed to me that I might expect some demoniac creature to rush upon me at any moment. Yet, for the space of many minutes, there came to me neither any sight nor sound of living creature; so that I knew not what to think, being near to doubting if I had heard aught beyond the common.

And then, even as I made halt upon the threshold of doubt, I was assured that I had not been mistaken; for, abruptly, I was aware that all the valley was full of a rustling, scampering sort of noise, through which there came to me occasional soft thuds, and anon the former slithering sounds. And at that, thinking a host of evil things to be upon us, I cried out to the bo'sun and the men to awake.

Immediately upon my shout, the bo'sun rushed out from the tent, the men following, and everyone with his weapon, save the man who had left his spear in the sand, and that lay now somewhere beyond the light of the fire. Then the bo'sun shouted, to know what thing had caused me to cry out; but I replied nothing, only held up my hand for quietness, yet when this was granted, the noises in the valley had ceased; so that the bo'sun turned to me, being in need of some explanation; but I begged him to hark a little longer, which he did, and, the sounds re-commencing almost immediately, he heard sufficient to know that I had not waked them all without due cause. And then, as we stood each one of us staring into the darkness where lay the valley, I seemed to see again some shadowy thing upon the boundary of the firelight; and, in the same instant, one of the men cried out and cast his spear into the darkness. But the bo'sun turned upon him with a very great anger; for in throwing his weapon, the man had left himself without, and thus brought danger to the whole; yet, as will be remembered, I had done likewise but a little since.

Presently, there coming again a quietness within the valley, and none knowing what might be toward, the bo'sun caught up a mass of the dry weed, and, lighting it at the fire, ran with it towards that portion of the beach which lay between us and the valley. Here he cast it upon the sand, singing out to some of the men to bring more of the weed, so that we might have a fire there, and thus be able to see if anything made to come at us out of the deepness of the hollow.

Presently, we had a very good fire, and by the light of this the two spears were discovered, both of them stuck in the sand, and no more than a yard one from the other, which seemed to me a very strange thing.

Now, for a while after the lighting of the second fire, there came no further sounds from the direction of the valley; nothing indeed to break the quietness of the island, save the occasional lonely splashes that sounded from time to time out in the vastness of the weed-continent. Then, about an hour after I had waked the bo'sun, one of the men who had been tending the fires came up to him to say that we had come to the end of our supply of weed-fuel. At that, the bo'sun looked very blank, the which did the rest of us, as well we might; yet there was no help for it, until one of the men bethought him of the remainder of the bundle of reeds which we had cut, and which, burning but poorly, we had discarded for the weed. This was discovered at the back of the tent, and with it we fed the fire that burned between us and the valley; but the other we suffered to die out, for the reeds were not sufficient to support even the one until the dawn.

At last, and whilst it was still dark, we came to the end of our fuel, and as the fire died down, so did the noises in the valley recommence. And there we stood in the growing dark, each one keeping a very ready weapon, and a more ready glance. And at times the island would be mightily quiet, and then again the sounds of things crawling in the valley. Yet, I think the silences tried us the more.

And so at last came the dawn.

IX.
What Happened in the Dusk

Now with the coming of the dawn, a lasting silence stole across the island and into the valley, and, conceiving that we had nothing more to fear, the bo'sun bade us get some rest, whilst he kept watch. And so I got at last a very substantial little spell of sleep, which made me fit enough for the day's work.

Presently, after some hours had passed, the bo'sun roused us to go with him to the further side of the island to gather fuel, and soon we were back with each a load, so that in a little we had the fire going right merrily.

Now for breakfast, we had a hash of broken biscuit, salt meat and some shellfish which the bo'sun had picked up from the beach at the foot of the further hill; the whole being right liberally flavored with some of the vinegar, which the bo'sun said would help keep down any scurvy that might be threatening us. And at the end of the meal he served out to us each a little of the molasses, which we mixed with hot water, and drank.

The meal being ended, he went into the tent to take a look at Job, the which he had done already in the early morning; for the condition of the lad preyed somewhat upon him; he being, for all his size and top-roughness, a man of surprisingly tender heart. Yet the boy remained much as on the previous evening, so that we knew not what to do with him to bring him into better health. One thing we tried, knowing that no food had passed his lips since the previous morning, and that was to get some little quantity of hot water, rum and molasses down his throat; for it seemed to us he might die from very lack of food; but though we worked with him for more than the half of an hour, we could not get him to come-to sufficiently to take anything, and without that we had fear of suffocating him. And so, presently, we had perforce to leave him within the tent, and go about our business; for there was very much to be done.

Yet, before we did aught else, the bo'sun led us all into the valley, being determined to make a very thorough exploration of it, perchance there might be any lurking beast or devil-thing waiting to rush out and destroy us as we worked, and more, he would make search that he might discover what manner of creatures had disturbed our night.

Now in the early morning, when we had gone for the fuel, we had kept to the upper skirt of the valley where the rock of the nearer hill came down into the spongy ground, but now we struck right down into the middle part of the vale, making a way amid the mighty fungi to the pit-like opening that filled the bottom of the valley. Now though the ground was very soft, there was in it so much of springiness that it left no trace of our steps after we had gone on a little way, none, that is, save that in odd places, a wet patch followed upon our treading. Then, when we got ourselves near to the pit, the ground became softer, so that our feet sank into it, and left very real impressions; and here we found tracks most curious and bewildering; for amid the slush that edged the pit—which I would mention here had less the look of a pit now that I had come near to it—were multitudes of markings which I can liken to nothing so much as the tracks of mighty slugs amid the mud, only that they were not altogether like to that of slugs; for there were other markings such as might have been made by bunches of eels cast down and picked up continually, at least, this is what they suggested to me, and I do but put it down as such.

Apart from the markings which I have mentioned, there was everywhere a deal of slime, and this we traced all over the valley among the great toadstool plants; but, beyond that which I have already remarked, we found nothing. Nay, but I was near to forgetting, we found a quantity of this thin slime upon those fungi which filled the end of the little valley nearest to our encampment, and here also we discovered many of them fresh broken or uprooted, and there was the same mark of the beast upon them all, and now I remember the dull thuds that I had heard in the night, and made little doubt but that the creatures had climbed the great toadstools so that they might spy us out; and it may be that many climbed upon one, so that their weight broke the fungi, or uprooted them. At least, so the thought came to me.

And so we made an end of our search, and after that, the bo'sun set each one of us to work. But first he had us all back to the beach to give a hand to turn over the boat, so that he might get to the damaged part. Now, having the bottom of the boat full to his view, he made discovery that there was other damage beside that of the burst plank; for the bottom plank of all had come away from the keel, which seemed to us a very serious matter; though it did not show when the boat was upon her bilges. Yet the bo'sun assured us that he had no doubts but that she could be made seaworthy, though it would take a greater while than hitherto he had thought needful.

Having concluded his examination of the boat, the bo'sun sent one of the men to bring the bottom-boards out of the tent; for he needed some planking for the repair of the damage. Yet when the boards had been brought, he needed still something which they could not supply, and this was a length of very sound wood of some three inches in breadth each way, which he intended to bolt against the starboard side of the keel, after he had gotten the planking replaced so far as was possible. He had hopes that by means of this device he would be able to nail the bottom plank to this, and then caulk it with oakum, so making the boat almost so sound as ever.

Now hearing him express his need for such a piece of timber, we were all adrift to know from whence such a thing could be gotten, until there came suddenly to me a memory of the mast and topmast upon the other side of the island, and at once I made mention of them. At that, the bo'sun nodded, saying that we might get the timber out of it, though it would be a work requiring some considerable labor, in that we had only a hand-saw and a small hatchet. Then he sent us across to be getting it clear of the weed, promising to follow when he had made an end of trying to get the two displaced planks back into position.

Having reached the spars, we set-to with a very good will to shift away the weed and wrack that was piled over them, and very much entangled with the rigging. Presently we had laid them bare, and so we discovered them to be in remarkably sound condition, the lower-mast especially being a fine piece of timber. All the lower and topmast standing rigging was still attached, though in places the lower rigging was stranded so far as halfway up the shrouds; yet there remained much that was good and all of it quite free from rot, and of the very finest quality of white hemp, such as is to be seen only in the best found vessels.

About the time that we had finished clearing the weed, the bo'sun came over to us, bringing with him the saw and the hatchet. Under his directions, we cut the lanyards of the topmast rigging, and after that sawed through the topmast just above the cap. Now this was a very tough piece of work, and employed us a great part of the morning, even though we took turn and turn at the saw, and when it was done we were mightily glad that the bo'sun bade one of the men go over with some weed and make up the fire for dinner, after which he was to put on a piece of the salt meat to boil.

In the meanwhile, the bo'sun had started to cut through the topmast, about fifteen feet beyond the first cut, for that was the length of the batten he required; yet so wearisome was the work, that we had not gotten more than half through with it before the man whom the bo'sun had sent, returned to say that the dinner was ready. When this was dispatched, and we had rested a little over our pipes, the bo'sun rose and led us back; for he was determined to get through with the topmast before dark.

Presently, relieving each other frequently, we completed the second cut, and after that the bo'sun set us to saw a block about twelve inches deep from the remaining portion of the topmast. From this, when we had cut it, he proceeded to hew wedges with the hatchet. Then he notched the end of the fifteen-foot log, and into the notch he drove the wedges, and so, towards evening, as much, maybe, by good luck as good management, he had divided the log into two halves—the split running very fairly down the center.

Now, perceiving how that it drew near to sundown, he bade the men haste and gather weed and carry it across to our camp; but one he sent along the shore to make a search for shell-fish among the weed; yet he himself ceased not to work at the divided log, and kept me with him as helper. Thus, within the next hour, we had a length, maybe some four inches in diameter, split off the whole length of one of the halves, and with this he was very well content; though it seemed but a very little result for so much labor.

By this time the dusk was upon us, and the men, having made an end of weed carrying, were returned to us, and stood about, waiting for the bo'sun to go into camp. At this moment, the man the bo'sun had sent to gather shellfish, returned, and he had a great crab upon his spear, which he had spitted through the belly. This creature could not have been less than a foot across the back, and had a very formidable appearance; yet it proved to be a most tasty matter for our supper, when it had been placed for a while in boiling water.

Now so soon as this man was returned, we made at once for the camp, carrying with us the piece of timber which we had hewn from the topmast. By this time it was quite dusk, and very strange amid the great fungi as we struck across the upper edge of the valley to the opposite beach. Particularly, I noticed that the hateful, moldy odor of these monstrous vegetables was more offensive than I had found it to be in the daytime; though this may be because I used my nose the more, in that I could not use my eyes to any great extent.

We had gotten halfway across the top of the valley, and the gloom was deepening steadily, when there stole to me upon the calmness of the evening air, a faint smell; something quite different from that of the surrounding fungi. A moment later I got a great whiff of it, and was near sickened with the abomination of it; but the memory of that foul thing which had come to the side of the boat in the dawn-gloom, before we discovered the island, roused me to a terror beyond that of the sickness of my stomach; for, suddenly, I knew what manner of thing it was that had beslimed my face and throat upon the previous night, and left its hideous stench lingering in my nostrils. And with the knowledge, I cried out to the bo'sun to make haste, for there were demons with us in the valley. And at that, some of the men made to run; but he bade them, in a very grim voice, stay where they were, and keep well together, else would they be attacked and overcome, straggled all among the fungi in the dark. And this, being, I doubt not, as much in fear of the rounding dark as of the bo'sun, they did, and so we came safely out of the valley; though there seemed to follow us a little lower down the slope an uncanny slithering.

Now so soon as we reached the camp, the bo'sun ordered four fires to be lit—one on each side of the tent, and this we did, lighting them at the embers of our old fire, which we had most foolishly allowed to die down. When the fires had been got going, we put on the boiler, and treated the great crab as I have already mentioned, and so fell-to upon a very hearty supper; but, as we ate, each man had his weapon stuck in the sand beside him; for we had knowledge that the valley held some devilish thing, or maybe many; though the knowing did not spoil our appetites.

And so, presently, we came to an end of eating, whereat each man pulled out his pipe, intending to smoke; but the bo'sun told one of the men to get him upon his feet and keep watch, else might we be in danger of surprise, with every man lolling upon the sand; and this seemed to me very good sense; for it was easy to see that the men, too readily, deemed themselves secure, by reason of the brightness of the fires about them.

Now, whilst the men were taking their ease within the circle of the fires, the bo'sun lit one of the dips which we had out of the ship in the creek, and went in to see how Job was, after the day's rest. At that, I rose up, reproaching myself for having forgotten the poor lad, and followed the bo'sun into the tent. Yet, I had but reached the opening, when he gave out a loud cry, and held the candle low down to the sand. At that, I saw the reason for his agitation, for, in the place where we had left Job, there was nothing. I stepped into the tent, and, in the same instant, there came to my nostrils the faint odor of the horrible stench which had come to me in the valley, and before then from the thing that came to the side of the boat. And, suddenly, I knew that Job had fallen prey of those foul things, and, knowing this, I called out to the bo'sun that *they* had taken the boy, and then my eyes caught the smear of slime upon the sand, and I had proof that I was not mistaken.

Now, so soon as the bo'sun knew all that was in my mind; though indeed it did but corroborate that which had come to his own, he came swiftly out from the tent, bidding the men to stand back; for they had come all about the entrance, being very much discomposed at that which the bo'sun had discovered. Then the bo'sun took from a bundle of the reeds, which they had cut at the time when he had bidden them gather fuel, several of the thickest, and to one of these he bound a great mass of the dry weed; whereupon the men, divining his intention, did likewise with the others, and so we had each of us the wherewithal for a mighty torch.

So soon as we had completed our preparations, we took each man his weapon and, plunging our torches into the fires, set off along the track which had been made by the devil-things and the body of poor Job; for now that we had suspicion that harm had come to him, the marks in the sand, and the slime, were very plain to be seen, so that it was a wonder that we had not discovered them earlier.

Now the bo'sun led the way, and, finding the marks led direct to the valley, he broke into a run, holding his torch well above his head. At that, each of us did likewise; for we had a great desire to be together, and further than this, I think with truth I may say, we were all fierce to avenge Job, so that we had less of fear in our hearts than otherwise had been the case.

In less than the half of a minute we had reached the end of the valley; but here, the ground being of a nature not happy in the revealing of tracks, we were at fault to know in which direction to continue. At that, the bo'sun set up a loud shout to Job, perchance he might be yet alive; but there came no answer to us, save a low and uncomfortable echo. Then the bo'sun, desiring to waste no more time, ran straight down towards the center of the valley, and we followed, and kept our eyes very open about us. We had gotten perhaps halfway, when one of the men shouted that he saw something ahead; but the bo'sun had seen it earlier; for he was running straight down upon it, holding his torch high and swinging his great cutlass. Then, instead of smiting, he fell upon his knees beside it, and the following instant we were up with him, and in that same moment it seemed to me that I saw a number of white shapes melt swiftly into the shadows further ahead: but I had no thought for these when I perceived that by which the bo'sun knelt; for it was the stark body of Job, and no inch of it but was covered with the little ringed marks that I had discovered upon my throat, and from every place there ran a trickle of blood, so that he was a most horrid and fearsome sight.

At the sight of Job so mangled and be-bled, there came over us the sudden quiet of a mortal terror, and in that space of silence, the bo'sun placed his hand over the poor lad's heart; but there was no movement, though the body was still warm. Immediately upon that, he rose to his feet, a look of vast wrath upon his great face. He plucked his torch from the ground, into which he had plunged the haft, and stared round into the silence of the valley; but there was no living thing in sight, nothing save the giant fungi and the strange shadows cast by our great torches, and the loneliness.

At this moment, one of the men's torches, having burnt near out, fell all to pieces, so that he held nothing but the charred support, and immediately two more came to a like end. Upon this, we became afraid that they would not last us back to the camp, and we looked to the bo'sun to know his wish; but the man was very silent, and peering everywhere into the shadows. Then a fourth torch fell to the ground in a shower of embers, and I turned to look. In the same instant there came a great flare of light behind me, accompanied by the dull thud of a dry matter set suddenly alight. I glanced swiftly back to the bo'sun, and he was staring up at one of the giant toadstools which was in flames all along its nearer edge, and burning with an incredible fury, sending out spirits of flame, and anon giving out sharp reports, and at each report, a fine powder was belched in thin streams; which, getting into our throats and nostrils, set us sneezing and coughing most lamentably; so that I am convinced, had any enemy come upon us at that moment, we had been undone by reason of our uncouth helplessness.

Now whether it had come to the bo'sun to set alight this first of the fungi, I know not; for it may be that his torch coming by chance against it, set it afire. However it chanced, the bo'sun took it as a veritable hint from Providence, and was already setting his torch to one a little further off, whilst the rest of us were near to choking with our coughings and sneezings. Yet, that we were so suddenly overcome by the potency of the powder, I doubt if a full minute passed before we were each one busied after the manner of the bo'sun; and those whose torches had burned out, knocked flaming pieces from the burning fungus, and with these impaled upon their torch-sticks, did so much execution as any.

And thus it happened that within five minutes of this discovery of Job's body, the whole of that hideous valley sent up to heaven the reek of its burning; whilst we, filled with murderous desires, ran hither and thither with our weapons, seeking to destroy the vile creatures that had brought the poor lad to so unholy a death. Yet nowhere could we discover any brute or creature upon which to ease our vengeance, and so, presently, the valley becoming impassable by reason of the heat, the flying sparks and the abundance of the acrid dust, we made back to the body of the boy, and bore him thence to the shore.

And during all that night no man of us slept, and the burning of the fungi sent up a mighty pillar of flame out of the valley, as out of the mouth of a monstrous pit and when the morning came it still burned. Then when it was daylight, some of us slept, being greatly awearied; but some kept watch.

And when we waked there was a great wind and rain upon the island.

X.
The Light in the Weed

Now the wind was very violent from the sea, and threatened to blow down our tent, the which, indeed, it achieved at last as we made an end of a cheerless breakfast. Yet, the bo'sun bade us not trouble to put it up again; but spread it out with the edges raised upon props made from the reeds, so that we might catch some of the rainwater; for it was become imperative that we should renew our supply before putting out again to sea. And whilst some of us were busied about this, he took the others and set up a small tent made of the spare canvas, and under this he sheltered all of our matters like to be harmed by the rain.

In a little, the rain continuing very violent, we had near a breaker-full of water collected in the canvas, and were about to run it off into one of the breakers, when the bo'sun cried out to us to hold, and first taste the water before we mixed it with that which we had already. At that, we put down our hands and scooped up some of the water to taste, and thus we discovered it to be brackish and quite undrinkable, at which I was amazed, until the bo'sun reminded us that the canvas had been saturated for many days with salt water, so that it would take a great quantity of fresh before all the salt was washed out. Then he told us to lay it flat upon the beach, and scour it well on both sides with the sand, which we did, and afterwards let the rain rinse it well, whereupon the next water that we caught we found to be near fresh; though not sufficiently so for our purpose. Yet when we had rinsed it once more, it became clear of the salt, so that we were able to keep all that we caught further.

And then, something before noon, the rain ceased to fall, though coming again at odd times in short squalls; yet the wind died not, but blew steadily, and continued so from that quarter during the remainder of the time that we were upon the island.

Upon the ceasing of the rain, the bo'sun called us all together, that we might make a decent burial of the unfortunate lad, whose remains had lain during the night upon one of the bottom-boards of the boat. After a little discussion, it was decided to bury him in the beach; for the only part where there was soft earth was in the valley, and none of us had a stomach for that place. Moreover, the sand was soft and easy to dig, and as we had no proper tools, this was a great consideration. Presently, using the bottom-boards and the oars and the hatchet, we had a place large and deep enough to hold the boy, and into this we placed him. We made no prayer over him; but stood about the grave for a little space, in silence. Then, the bo'sun signed to us to fill in the sand; and, therewith, we covered up the poor lad, and left him to his sleep.

And, presently, we made our dinner, after which the bo'sun served out to each one of us a very sound tot of the rum; for he was minded to bring us back again to a cheerful state of mind.

After we had sat awhile, smoking, the bo'sun divided us into two parties to make a search through the island among the rocks, perchance we should find water, collected from the rain, among the hollows and crevasses; for though we had gotten some, through our device with the sail, yet we had by no means caught sufficient for our needs. He was especially anxious for haste, in that the sun had come out again; for he was feared that such small pools as we should find would be speedily dried up by its heat.

Now the bo'sun headed one party, and set the big seaman over the other, bidding all to keep their weapons very handy. Then he set out to the rocks about the base of the nearer hill, sending the others to the farther and greater one, and in each party we carried an empty breaker slung from a couple of the stout reeds, so that we might put all such driblets as we should find, straight away into it, before they had time to vanish into the hot air; and for the purpose of bailing up the water, we had brought with us our tin pannikins, and one of the boat's bailers.

In a while, and after much scrambling amid the rocks, we came upon a little pool of water that was remarkably sweet and fresh, and from this we removed near three gallons before it became dry; and after that we came across, maybe, five or six others; but not one of them near so big as the first; yet we were not displeased; for we had near three parts filled the breaker, and so we made back to the camp, having some wonder as to the luck of the other party.

When we came near the camp, we found the others returned before us, and seeming in a very high content with themselves; so that we had no need to call to them as to whether they had filled their breaker. When they saw us, they set out to us at a run to tell us that they had come upon a great basin of fresh water in a deep hollow a third of the distance up the side of the far hill, and at this the bo'sun bade us put down our breaker and make all of us to the hill, so that he might examine for himself whether their news was so good as it seemed.

Presently, being guided by the other party, we passed around to the back of the far hill, and discovered it to go upward to the top at an easy slope, with many ledges and broken places, so that it was scarce more difficult than a stair to climb. And so, having climbed perhaps ninety or a hundred feet, we came suddenly upon the place which held the water, and found that they had not made too much of their discovery; for the pool was near twenty feet long by twelve broad, and so clear as though it had come from a fountain; yet it had considerable depth, as we discovered by thrusting a spear shaft down into it.

Now the bo'sun, having seen for himself how good a supply of water there was for our needs, seemed very much relieved in his mind, and declared that within three days at the most we might leave the island, at which we felt none of us any regret. Indeed, had the boat escaped harm, we had been able to leave that same day; but this could not be; for there was much to be done before we had her seaworthy again.

Having waited until the bo'sun had made complete his examination, we turned to descend, thinking that this would be the bo'sun's intention; but he called to us to stay, and, looking back, we saw that he made to finish the ascent of the hill. At that, we hastened to follow him; though we had no notion of his reason for going higher. Presently, we were come to the top, and here we found a very spacious place, nicely level save that in one or two parts it was crossed by deepish cracks, maybe half a foot to a foot wide, and perhaps three to six fathoms long; but, apart from these and some great boulders, it was, as I have mentioned, a spacious place; moreover it was bone dry and pleasantly firm under one's feet, after so long upon the sand.

I think, even thus early, I had some notion of the bo'sun's design; for I went to the edge that overlooked the valley, and peered down, and, finding it nigh a sheer precipice, found myself nodding my head, as though it were in accordance with some part formed wish. Presently, looking about me, I discovered the bo'sun to be surveying that part which looked over towards the weed, and I made across to join him. Here, again, I saw that the hill fell away very sheer, and after that we went across to the seaward edge, and there it was near as abrupt as on the weed side.

Then, having by this time thought a little upon the matter, I put it straight to the bo'sun that here would make indeed a very secure camping place, with nothing to come at us upon our sides or back; and our front, where was the slope, could be watched with ease. And this I put to him with great warmth; for I was mortally in dread of the coming night.

Now when I had made an end of speaking, the bo'sun disclosed to me that this was, as I had suspicion, his intent, and immediately he called to the men that we should haste down, and ship our camp to the top of the hill. At that, the men expressed their approbation, and we made haste every one of us to the camp, and began straightway to move our gear to the hilltop.

In the meanwhile, the bo'sun, taking me to assist him, set-to again upon the boat, being intent to get his batten nicely shaped and fit to the side of the keel, so that it would bed well to the keel, but more particularly to the plank which had sprung outward from its place. And at this he labored the greater part of that afternoon, using the little hatchet to shape the wood, which he did with surprising skill; yet when the evening was come, he had not brought it to his liking. But it must not be thought that he did naught but work at the boat; for he had the men to direct, and once he had to make his way to the top of the hill to fix the place for the tent. And after the tent was up, he set them to carry the dry weed to the new camp, and at this he kept them until near dusk; for he had vowed never again to be without a sufficiency of fuel. But two of the men he sent to collect shell-fish—putting two of them to the task, because he would not have one alone upon the island, not knowing but that there might be danger, even though it were bright day; and a most happy ruling it proved; for, a little past the middle of the afternoon, we heard them shouting at the other end of the valley, and, not knowing but that they were in need of assistance, we ran with all haste to discover the reason of their calling, passing along the right-hand side of the blackened and sodden vale. Upon reaching the further beach, we saw a most incredible sight; for the two men were running towards us through the thick masses of the weed, while, no more than four or five fathoms behind, they were pursued by an enormous crab. Now I had thought the crab we had tried to capture before coming to the island, a prodigy unsurpassed; but this creature was more than treble its size, seeming as though a prodigious table were a-chase of them, and moreover, spite of its monstrous bulk, it made better way over the weed than I should have conceived to be possible—running almost sideways, and with one enormous claw raised near a dozen feet into the air.

Now whether, omitting accidents, the men would have made good their escape to the firmer ground of the valley, where they could have attained to a greater speed, I do not know; but suddenly one of them tripped over a loop of the weed, and the next instant lay helpless upon his face. He had been dead the following moment, but for the pluck of his companion, who faced round manfully upon the monster, and ran at it with his twenty-foot spear. It seemed to me that the spear took it about a foot below the overhanging armor of the great back shell, and I could see that it penetrated some distance into the creature, the man having, by the aid of Providence, stricken it in a vulnerable part. Upon receiving this thrust, the mighty crab ceased at once its pursuit, and clipped at the haft of the spear with its great mandible, snapping the weapon more easily than I had done the same thing to a straw. By the time we had raced up to the men, the one who had stumbled was again upon his feet, and turning to assist his comrade; but the bo'sun snatched his spear from him, and leapt forward himself; for the crab was making now at the other man. Now the bo'sun did not attempt to thrust the spear into the monster; but instead he made two swift blows at the great protruding eyes, and in a moment the creature had curled itself up, helpless, save that the huge claw waved about aimlessly. At that, the bo'sun drew us off, though the man who had attacked the crab desired to make an end of it, averring that we should get some very good eating out of it; but to this the bo'sun would not listen, telling him that it was yet capable of very deadly mischief, did any but come within reach of its prodigious mandible.

And after this, he bade them look no more for shellfish; but take out the two fishing-lines which we had, and see if they could catch aught from some safe ledge on the further side of the hill upon which we had made our camp. Then he returned to his mending of the boat.

It was a little before the evening came down upon the island, that the bo'sun ceased work; and, after that, he called to the men, who, having made an end of their fuel carrying, were standing near, to place the full breakers—which we had not thought needful to carry to the new camp on account of their weight—under the upturned boat, some holding up the gunnel whilst the others pushed them under. Then the bo'sun laid the unfinished batten along with them, and we lowered the boat again over all, trusting to its weight to prevent any creature from meddling with aught.

After that, we made at once to the camp, being wearifully tired, and with a hearty anticipation of supper. Upon reaching the hilltop, the men whom the bo'sun had sent with the lines, came to show him a very fine fish, something like to a huge king-fish, which they had caught a few minutes earlier. This, the bo'sun, after examining, did not hesitate to pronounce fit for food; whereupon they set-to and opened and cleaned it. Now, as I have said, it was not unlike a great king-fish, and like it, had a mouth full of very formidable teeth; the use of which I understood the better when I saw the contents of its stomach, which seemed to consist of nothing but the coiled tentacles of squid or cuttlefish, with which, as I have shown, the weed-continent swarmed. When these were upset upon the rock, I was confounded to perceive the length and thickness of some of them; and could only conceive that this particular fish must be a very desperate enemy to them, and able successfully to attack monsters of a bulk infinitely greater than its own.

After this, and whilst the supper was preparing, the bo'sun called to some of the men to put up a piece of the spare canvas upon a couple of the reeds, so as to make a screen against the wind, which up there was so fresh that it came near at times to scattering the fire abroad. This they found not difficult; for a little on the windward side of the fire there ran one of the cracks of which I have made previous mention, and into this they jammed the supports, and so in a very little time had the fire screened.

Presently, the supper was ready, and I found the fish to be very fair eating; though somewhat coarse; but this was no great matter for concern with so empty a stomach as I contained. And here I would remark, that we made our fishing save our provisions through all our stay on the island. Then, after we had come to an end of our eating, we lay down to a most comfortable smoke; for we had no fear of attack, at that height, and with precipices upon all sides save that which lay in front. Yet, so soon as we had rested and smoked a while, the bo'sun set the watches; for he would run no risk through carelessness.

By this time the night was drawing on apace; yet it was not so dark but that one could perceive matters at a very reasonable distance. Presently, being in a mood that tended to thoughtfulness, and feeling a desire to be alone for a little, I strolled away from the fire to the leeward edge of the hilltop. Here, I paced up and down awhile, smoking and meditating. Anon, I would stare out across the immensity of the vast continent of weed and slime that stretched its incredible desolation out beyond the darkening horizon, and there would come the thought to me of the terror of men whose vessels had been entangled among its strange growths, and so my thoughts came to the lone derelict that lay out there in the dusk, and I fell to wondering what had been the end of her people, and at that I grew yet more solemn in my heart. For it seemed to me that they must have died at last by starvation, and if not by that, then by the act of some one of the devil-creatures which inhabited that lonely weed-world. And then, even as I fell upon this thought, the bo'sun clapped me upon the shoulder, and told me in a very hearty way to come to the light of the fire, and banish all melancholy thoughts; for he had a very penetrating discernment, and had followed me quietly from the camping place, having had reason once or twice before to chide me for gloomy meditations. And for this, and many other matters, I had grown to like the man, the which I could almost believe at times, was his regarding of me; but his words were too few for me to gather his feelings; though I had hope that they were as I surmised.

And so I came back to the fire, and presently, it not being my time to watch until after midnight, I turned into the tent for a spell of sleep, having first arranged a comfortable spread of some of the softer portions of the dry weed to make me a bed.

Now I was very full of sleep, so that I slept heavily, and in this wise heard not the man on watch call the bo'sun; yet the rousing of the others waked me, and so I came to myself and found the tent empty, at which I ran very hurriedly to the doorway, and so discovered that there was a clear moon in the sky, the which, by reason of the cloudiness that had prevailed, we had been without for the past two nights. Moreover, the sultriness had gone, the wind having blown it away with the clouds; yet though, maybe, I appreciated this, it was but in a half-conscious manner; for I was put about to discover the whereabouts of the men, and the reason of their leaving the tent. With this purpose, I stepped out from the entrance, and the following instant discovered them all in a clump beside the leeward edge of the hilltop. At that, I held my tongue; for I knew not but that silence might be their desire; but I ran hastily over to them, and inquired of the bo'sun what manner of thing it was which called them from their sleep, and he, for answer, pointed out into the greatness of the weed-continent.

At that, I stared out over the breadth of the weed, showing very ghostly in the moonlight; but, for the moment, I saw not the thing to which he purposed to draw my attention. Then, suddenly, it fell within the circle of my gaze—a little light out in the lonesomeness. For the space of some moments, I stared with bewildered eyes; then it came to me with abruptness that the light shone from the lone derelict lying out in the weed, the same that upon that very evening, I had looked with sorrow and awe, because of the end of those who had been in her—and now, behold, a light burning, seemingly within one of her after cabins; though the moon was scarce powerful enough to enable the outline of the hulk to be seen clear of the rounding wilderness.

And from this time, until the day, we had no more sleep; but made up the fire, and sat round it, full of excitement and wonder, and getting up continually to discover if the light still burned. This it ceased to do about an hour after I had first seen it; but it was the more proof that some of our kind were no more than the half of a mile from our camp.

And at last the day came.

XI.
The Signals from the Ship

Now so soon as it was clearly light, we went all of us to the leeward brow of the hill to stare upon the derelict, which now we had cause to believe no derelict, but an inhabited vessel. Yet though we watched her for upwards of two hours, we could discover no sign of any living creature, the which, indeed, had we been in cooler minds, we had not thought strange, seeing that she was all so shut in by the great superstructure; but we were hot to see a fellow creature, after so much lonesomeness and terror in strange lands and seas, and so could not by any means contain ourselves in patience until those aboard the hulk should choose to discover themselves to us.

And so, at last, being wearied with watching, we made it up together to shout when the bo'sun should give us the signal, by this means making a good volume of sound which we conceived the wind might carry down to the vessel. Yet though we raised many shouts, making as it seemed to us a very great noise, there came no response from the ship, and at last we were fain to cease from our calling, and ponder some other way of bringing ourselves to the notice of those within the hulk.

For a while we talked, some proposing one thing, and some another; but none of them seeming like to achieve our purpose. And after that we fell to marveling that the fire which we had lit in the valley had not awakened them to the fact that some of their fellow creatures were upon the island; for, had it, we could not suppose but that they would have kept a perpetual watch upon the island until such time as they should have been able to attract our notice. Nay! More than this, it was scarce credible that they should not have made an answering fire, or set some of their bunting above the superstructure, so that our gaze should be arrested upon the instant we chanced to glance towards the hulk. But so far from this, there appeared even a purpose to shun our attention; for that light which we had viewed in the past night was more in the way of an accident, than of the nature of a purposeful exhibition.

And so, presently, we went to breakfast, eating heartily; our night of wakefulness having given us mighty appetites; but, for all that, we were so engrossed by the mystery of the lonesome craft, that I doubt if any of us knew what manner of food it was with which we filled our bellies. For first one view of the matter would be raised, and when this had been combated, another would be broached, and in this wise it came up finally that some of the men were falling in doubt whether the ship was inhabited by anything human, saying rather that it might be held by some demoniac creature of the great weed-continent. At this proposition, there came among us a very uncomfortable silence; for not only did it chill the warmth of our hopes; but seemed like to provide us with a fresh terror, who were already acquainted with too much. Then the bo'sun spoke, laughing with a hearty contempt at our sudden fears, and pointed out that it was just as like that they aboard the ship had been put in fear by the great blaze from the valley, as that they should take it for a sign that fellow creatures and friends were at hand. For, as he put it to us, who of us could say what fell brutes and demons the weed-continent did hold, and if we had reason to know that there were very dread things among the weed, how much the more must they, who had, for all that we knew, been many years beset around by such. And so, as he went on to make clear, we might suppose that they were very well aware there had come some creatures to the island; yet, maybe, they desired not to make themselves known until they had been given sight of them, and because of this, we must wait until they chose to discover themselves to us.

Now when the bo'sun had made an end, we felt each one of us greatly cheered; for his discourse seemed very reasonable. Yet still there were many matters that troubled our company; for, as one put it, was it not mightily strange that we had not had previous sight of their light, or, in the day, of the smoke from their galley fire? But to this the bo'sun replied that our camp hitherto had lain in a place where we had not sight, even of the great world of weed, leaving alone any view of the derelict. And more, that at such times as we had crossed to the opposite beach, we had been occupied too sincerely to have much thought to watch the hulk, which, indeed, from that position showed only her great superstructure. Further, that, until the preceding day, we had but once climbed to any height; and that from our present camp the derelict could not be viewed, and to do so, we had to go near to the leeward edge of the hilltop.

And so, breakfast being ended, we went all of us to see if there were yet any signs of life in the hulk; but when an hour had gone, we were no wiser. Therefore, it being folly to waste further time, the bo'sun left one man to watch from the brow of the hill, charging him very strictly to keep in such position that he could be seen by any aboard the silent craft, and so took the rest down to assist him in the repairing of the boat. And from thence on, during the day, he gave the men a turn each at watching, telling them to wave to him should there come any sign from the hulk. Yet, excepting the watch, he kept every man so busy as might be, some bringing weed to keep up a fire which he had lit near the boat; one to help him turn and hold the batten upon which he labored; and two he sent across to the wreck of the mast, to detach one of the futtock shrouds, which (as is most rare) were made of iron rods. This, when they brought it, he bade me heat in the fire, and afterwards beat out straight at one end, and when this was done, he set me to burn holes with it through the keel of the boat, at such places as he had marked, these being for the bolts with which he had determined to fasten on the batten.

In the meanwhile, he continued to shape the batten until it was a very good and true fit according to his liking. And all the while he cried out to this man and to that one to do this or that; and so I perceived that, apart from the necessity of getting the boat into a seaworthy condition, he was desirous to keep the men busied; for they were become so excited at the thought of fellow creatures almost within hail, that he could not hope to keep them sufficiently in hand without some matter upon which to employ them.

Now, it must not be supposed that the bo'sun had no share of our excitement; for I noticed that he gave ever and anon a glance to the crown of the far hill, perchance the watchman had some news for us. Yet the morning went by, and no signal came to tell us that the people in the ship had design to show themselves to the man upon watch, and so we came to dinner. At this meal, as might be supposed, we had a second discussion upon the strangeness of the behavior of those aboard the hulk; yet none could give any more reasonable explanation than the bo'sun had given in the morning, and so we left it at that.

Presently, when we had smoked and rested very comfortably, for the bo'sun was no tyrant, we rose at his bidding to descend once more to the beach. But at this moment, one of the men having run to the edge of the hill to take a short look at the hulk, cried out that a part of the great superstructure over the quarter had been removed, or pushed back, and that there was a figure there, seeming, so far as his unaided sight could tell, to be looking through a spy-glass at the island. Now it would be difficult to tell of all our excitement at this news, and we ran eagerly to see for ourselves if it could be as he informed us. And so it was; for we could see the person very clearly; though remote and small because of the distance. That he had seen us, we discovered in a moment; for he began suddenly to wave something, which I judged to be the spy-glass, in a very wild manner, seeming also to be jumping up and down. Yet, I doubt not but that we were as much excited; for suddenly I discovered myself to be shouting with the rest in a most insane fashion, and moreover I was waving my hands and running to and fro upon the brow of the hill. Then, I observed that the figure on the hulk had disappeared; but it was for no more than a moment, and then it was back and there were near a dozen with it, and it seemed to me that some of them were females; but the distance was over great for surety. Now these, all of them, seeing us upon the brow of the hill, where we must have shown up plain against the sky, began at once to wave in a very frantic way, and we, replying in like manner, shouted ourselves hoarse with vain greetings. But soon we grew wearied of the unsatisfactoriness of this method of showing our excitement, and one took a piece of the square canvas, and let it stream out into the wind, waving it to them, and another took a second piece and did likewise, while a third man rolled up a short bit into a cone and made use of it as a speaking trumpet; though I doubt if his voice carried any the further because of it. For my part, I had seized one of the long bamboo-like reeds which were lying about near the fire, and with this I was making a very brave show. And so it may be seen how very great and genuine was our exaltation upon our discovery of these poor people shut off from the world within that lonesome craft.

Then, suddenly, it seemed to come to us to realize that *they* were among the weed, and *we* upon the hilltop, and that we had no means of bridging that which lay between. And at this we faced one another to discuss what we should do to effect the rescue of those within the hulk. Yet it was little that we could even suggest; for though one spoke of how he had seen a rope cast by means of a mortar to a ship that lay offshore, yet this helped us not, for we had no mortar; but here the same man cried out that they in the ship might have such a thing, so that they would be able to shoot the rope to us, and at this we thought more upon his saying; for if they had such a weapon, then might our difficulties be solved. Yet we were greatly at a loss to know how we should discover whether they were possessed of one, and further to explain our design to them. But here the bo'sun came to our help, and bade one man go quickly and char some of the reeds in the fire, and whilst this was doing he spread out upon the rock one of the spare lengths of canvas; then he sung out to the man to bring him one of the pieces of charred reed, and with this he wrote our question upon the canvas, calling for fresh charcoal as he required it. Then, having made an end of writing, he bade two of the men take hold of the canvas by the ends and expose it to the view of those in the ship, and in this manner we got them to understand our desires. For, presently, some of them went away, and came back after a little, and held up for us to see, a very great square of white, and upon it a great "NO," and at this were we again at our wits' ends to know how it would be possible to rescue those within the ship; for, suddenly, our whole desire to leave the island, was changed into a determination to rescue the people in the hulk, and, indeed, had our intentions not been such we had been veritable curs; though I am happy to tell that we had no thought at this juncture but for those who were now looking to us to restore them once more to the world to which they had been so long strangers.

Now, as I have said, we were again at our wits' ends to know how to come at those within the hulk, and there we stood all of us, talking together, perchance we should hit upon some plan, and anon we would turn and wave to those who watched us so anxiously. Yet, a while passed, and we had come no nearer to a method of rescue. Then a thought came to me (waked perchance by the mention of shooting the rope over to the hulk by means of a mortar) how that I had read once in a book, of a fair maid whose lover effected her escape from a castle by a similar artifice, only that in his case he made use of a bow in place of a mortar, and a cord instead of a rope, his sweetheart hauling up the rope by means of the cord.

Now it seemed to me a possible thing to substitute a bow for the mortar, if only we could find the material with which to make such a weapon, and with this in view, I took up one of the lengths of the bamboo-like reed, and tried the spring of it, which I found to be very good; for this curious growth, of which I have spoken hitherto as a reed, had no resemblance to that plant, beyond its appearance; it being extraordinarily tough and woody, and having considerably more nature than a bamboo. Now, having tried the spring of it, I went over to the tent and cut a piece of sampsonline which I found among the gear, and with this and the reed I contrived a rough bow. Then I looked about until I came upon a very young and slender reed which had been cut with the rest, and from this I fashioned some sort of an arrow, feathering it with a piece of one of the broad, stiff leaves, which grew upon the plant, and after that I went forth to the crowd about the leeward edge of the hill. Now when they saw me thus armed, they seemed to think that I intended a jest, and some of them laughed, conceiving that it was a very odd action on my part; but when I explained that which was in my mind, they ceased from laughter, and shook their heads, making that I did but waste time; for, as they said, nothing save gunpowder could cover so great a distance. And after that they turned again to the bo'sun with whom some of them seemed to be in argument. And so for a little space I held my peace, and listened; thus I discovered that certain of the men advocated the taking of the boat—so soon as it was sufficiently repaired—and making a passage through the weed to the ship, which they proposed to do by cutting a narrow canal. But the bo'sun shook his head, and reminded them of the great devil-fish and crabs, and the worse things which the weed concealed, saying that those in the ship would have done it long since had it been possible, and at that the men were silenced, being robbed of their unreasoning ardor by his warnings.

Now just at this point there happened a thing which proved the wisdom of that which the bo'sun contended; for, suddenly, one of the men cried out to us to look, and at that we turned quickly, and saw that there was a great commotion among those who were in the open place in the superstructure; for they were running this way and that, and some were pushing to the slide which filled the opening. And then, immediately, we saw the reason for their agitation and haste; for there was a stir in the weed near to the stem of the ship, and the next instant, monstrous tentacles were reached up to the place where had been the opening; but the door was shut, and those aboard the hulk in safety. At this manifestation, the men about me who had proposed to make use of the boat, and the others also, cried out their horror of the vast creature, and, I am convinced, had the rescue depended upon their use of the boat, then had those in the hulk been forever doomed.

Now, conceiving that this was a good point at which to renew my importunities, I began once again to explain the probabilities of my plan succeeding, addressing myself more particularly to the bo'sun. I told how that I had read that the ancients made mighty weapons, some of which could throw a great stone so heavy as two men, over a distance surpassing a quarter of a mile; moreover, that they compassed huge catapults which threw a lance, or great arrow, even further. On this, he expressed much surprise, never having heard of the like; but doubted greatly that we should be able to construct such a weapon. Yet, I told him that I was prepared; for I had the plan of one clearly in my mind, and further I pointed out to him that we had the wind in our favor, and that we were a great height up, which would allow the arrow to travel the farther before it came so low as the weed.

Then I stepped to the edge of the hill, and, bidding him watch, fitted my arrow to the string, and, having bent the bow, loosed it, whereupon, being aided by the wind and the height on which I stood, the arrow plunged into the weed at a distance of near two hundred yards from where we stood, that being about a quarter of the distance on the road to the derelict. At that, the bo'sun was won over to my idea; though, as he remarked, the arrow had fallen nearer had it been drawing a length of yarn after it, and to this I assented; but pointed out that my bow and arrow was but a rough affair, and, more, that I was no archer; yet I promised him, with the bow that I should make, to cast a shaft clean over the hulk, did he but give me his assistance, and bid the men to help.

Now, as I have come to regard it in the light of greater knowledge, my promise was exceeding rash; but I had faith in my conception, and was very eager to put it to the test; the which, after much discussion at supper, it was decided I should be allowed to do.

XII.
The Making of the Great Bow

The fourth night upon the island was the first to pass without incident. It is true that a light showed from the hulk out in the weed; but now that we had made some acquaintance with her inmates, it was no longer a cause for excitement, so much as contemplation. As for the valley where the vile things had made an end of Job, it was very silent and desolate under the moonlight; for I made a point to go and view it during my time on watch; yet, for all that it lay empty, it was very eerie, and a place to conjure up uncomfortable thoughts, so that I spent no great time pondering it.

This was the second night on which we had been free from the terror of the devil-things, and it seemed to me that the great fire had put them in fear of us and driven them away; but of the truth or error of this idea, I was to learn later.

Now it must be admitted that, apart from a short look into the valley, and occasional starings at the light out in the weed, I gave little attention to aught but my plans for the great bow, and to such use did I put my time, that when I was relieved, I had each particular and detail worked out, so that I knew very well just what to set the men doing so soon as we should make a start in the morning.

Presently, when the morning had come, and we had made an end of breakfast, we turned-to upon the great bow, the bo'sun directing the men under my supervision. Now, the first matter to which I bent attention, was the raising, to the top of the hill, of the remaining half of that portion of the topmast which the bo'sun had split in twain to procure the batten for the boat. To this end, we went down, all of us, to the beach where lay the wreckage, and, getting about the portion which I intended to use, carried it to the foot of the hill; then we sent a man to the top to let down the rope by which we had moored the boat to the sea anchor, and when we had bent this on securely to the piece of timber, we returned to the hilltop, and tailed on to the rope, and so, presently, after much wearifil pulling, had it up.

The next thing I desired was that the split face of the timber should be rubbed straight, and this the bo'sun understood to do, and whilst he was about it, I went with some of the men to the grove of reeds, and here, with great care, I made a selection of some of the finest, these being for the bow, and after that I cut some which were very clean and straight, intending them for the great arrows. With these we returned once more to the camp, and there I set-to and trimmed them of their leaves, keeping these latter, for I had a use for them. Then I took a dozen reeds and cut them each to a length of twenty-five feet, and afterwards notched them for the strings. In the meanwhile, I had sent two men down to the wreckage of the masts to cut away a couple of the hempen shrouds and bring them to the camp, and they, appearing about this time, I set to work to unlay the shrouds, so that they might get out the fine white yarns which lay beneath the outer covering of tar and blacking. These, when they had come at them, we found to be very good and sound, and this being so, I bid them make three-yarn sennit; meaning it for the strings of the bows. Now, it will be observed that I have said bows, and this I will explain. It had been my original intention to make one great bow, lashing a dozen of the reeds together for the purpose; but this, upon pondering it, I conceived to be but a poor plan; for there would be much life and power lost in the rendering of each piece through the lashings, when the bow was released. To obviate this, and further, to compass the bending of the bow, the which had, at first, been a source of puzzlement to me as to how it was to be accomplished, I had determined to make twelve separate bows, and these I intended to fasten at the end of the stock one above the other, so that they were all in one plane vertically, and because of this conception, I should be able to bend the bows one at a time, and slip each string over the catch-notch, and afterwards frap the twelve strings together in the middle part so that they would be but one string to the butt of the arrow. All this, I explained to the bo'sun, who, indeed, had been exercised in his own mind as to how we should be able to bend such a bow as I intended to make, and he was mightily pleased with my method of evading this difficulty, and also one other, which, else, had been greater than the bending, and that was the *stringing* of the bow, which would have proved a very awkward work.

Presently, the bo'sun called out to me that he had got the surface of the stock sufficiently smooth and nice; and at that I went over to him; for now I wished him to burn a slight groove down the center, running from end to end, and this I desired to be done very exactly; for upon it depended much of the true flight of the arrow. Then I went back to my own work; for I had not yet finished notching the bows. Presently, when I had made an end of this, I called for a length of the sennit, and, with the aid of another man, contrived to string one of the bows. This, when I had finished, I found to be very springy, and so stiff to bend that I had all that I could manage to do so, and at this I felt very satisfied.

Presently, it occurred to me that I should do well to set some of the men to work upon the line which the arrow was to carry; for I had determined that this should be made also from the white hemp yarns, and, for the sake of lightness, I conceived that one thickness of yarn would be sufficient; but so that it might compass enough of strength, I bid them split the yarns and lay the two halves up together, and in this manner they made me a very light and sound line; though it must not be supposed that it was finished at once; for I needed over half a mile of it, and thus it was later finished than the bow itself.

Having now gotten all things in train, I set me down to work upon one of the arrows; for I was anxious to see what sort of a fist I should make of them, knowing how much would depend upon the balance and truth of the missile. In the end, I made a very fair one, feathering it with its own leaves, and truing and smoothing it with my knife; after which I inserted a small bolt in the forrard end, to act as a head, and, as I conceived, give it balance; though whether I was right in this latter, I am unable to say. Yet, before I had finished my arrow, the bo'sun had made the groove, and called me over to him, that I might admire it, the which I did; for it was done with a wonderful neatness.

Now I have been so busy with my description of how we made the great bow, that I have omitted to tell of the flight of time, and how we had eaten our dinner this long while since, and how that the people in the hulk had waved to us, and we had returned their signals, and then written upon a length of the canvas the one word, "WAIT." And, besides all this, some had gathered our fuel for the coming night.

And so, presently, the evening came upon us; but we ceased not to work; for the bo'sun bade the men to light a second great fire, beside our former one, and by the light of this we worked another long spell; though it seemed short enough, by reason of the interest of the work. Yet, at last, the bo'sun bade us to stop and make supper, which we did, and after that, he set the watches, and the rest of us turned in; for we were very weary.

In spite of my previous weariness, when the man whom I relieved called me to take my watch, I felt very fresh and wide awake, and spent a great part of the time, as on the preceding night, in studying over my plans for completing the great bow, and it was then that I decided finally in what manner I would secure the bows athwart the end of the stock; for until then I had been in some little doubt, being divided between several methods. Now, however, I concluded to make twelve grooves across the sawn end of the stock, and fit the middles of the bows into these, one above the other, as I have already mentioned; and then to lash them at each side to bolts driven into the sides of the stock. And with this idea I was very well pleased; for it promised to make them secure, and this without any great amount of work.

Now, though I spent much of my watch in thinking over the details of my prodigious weapon, yet it must not be supposed that I neglected to perform my duty as watchman; for I walked continually about the top of the hill, keeping my cut-and-thrust ready for any sudden emergency. Yet my time passed off quietly enough; though it is true that I witnessed one thing which brought me a short spell of disquiet thought. It was in this wise:—I had come to that part of the hilltop which overhung the valley, and it came to me, abruptly, to go near to the edge and look over. Thus, the moon being very bright, and the desolation of the valley reasonably clear to the eye, it appeared to me, as I looked that I saw a movement among certain of the fungi which had not burnt, but stood up shriveled and blackened in the valley. Yet by no means could I be sure that it was not a sudden fancy, born of the eeriness of that desolate-looking vale; the more so as I was like to be deceived because of the uncertainty which the light of the moon gives. Yet, to prove my doubts, I went back until I had found a piece of rock easy to throw, and this, taking a short run, I cast into the valley, aiming at the spot where it had seemed to me that there had been a movement. Immediately upon this, I caught a glimpse of some moving thing, and then, more to my right, something else stirred, and at this, I looked towards it; but could discover nothing. Then, looking back at the clump at which I had aimed my missile, I saw that the slime-covered pool, which lay near, was all a-quiver, or so it seemed. Yet the next instant I was just as full of doubt; for, even as I watched it, I perceived that it was quite still. And after that, for some time, I kept a very strict gaze into the valley; yet could nowhere discover aught to prove my suspicions, and, at last, I ceased from watching it; for I feared to grow fanciful, and so wandered to that part of the hill which overlooked the weed.

Presently, when I had been relieved, I returned to sleep, and so till the morning. Then, when we had made each of us a hasty breakfast—for all were grown mightily keen to see the great bow completed—we set-to upon it, each at our appointed task. Thus, the bo'sun and I made it our work to make the twelve grooves athwart the flat end of the stock, into which I proposed to fit and lash the bows, and this we accomplished by means of the iron futtock-shroud, which we heated in its middle part, and then, each taking an end (protecting our hands with canvas), we went one on each side and applied the iron until at length we had the grooves burnt out very nicely and accurately. This work occupied us all the morning; for the grooves had to be deeply burnt; and in the meantime the men had completed near enough sennit for the stringing of the bows; yet those who were at work on the line which the arrow was to carry, had scarce made more than half, so that I called off one man from the sennit to turn-to, and give them a hand with the making of the line.

When dinner was ended, the bo'sun and I set-to about fitting the bows into their places, which we did, and lashed them to twenty-four bolts, twelve a side, driven into the timber of the stock, about twelve inches in from the end. After this, we bent and strung the bows, taking very great care to have each bent exactly as the one below it; for we started at the bottom. And so, before sunset, we had that part of our work ended.

Now, because the two fires which we had lit on the previous night had exhausted our fuel, the bo'sun deemed it prudent to cease work, and go down all of us to bring up a fresh supply of the dry seaweed and some bundles of the reeds. This we did, making an end of our journeyings just as the dusk came over the island. Then, having made a second fire, as on the preceding night, we had first our supper, and after that another spell of work, all the men turning to upon the line which the arrow was to carry, whilst the bo'sun and I set-to, each of us, upon the making of a fresh arrow; for I had realized that we should have to make one or two flights before we could hope to find our range and make true our aim.

Later, maybe about nine of the night, the bo'sun bade us all to put away our work, and then he set the watches, after which the rest of us went into the tent to sleep; for the strength of the wind made the shelter a very pleasant thing.

That night, when it came my turn to watch, I minded me to take a look into the valley; but though I watched at intervals through the half of an hour, I saw nothing to lead me to imagine that I had indeed seen aught on the previous night, and so I felt more confident in my mind that we should be troubled no further by the devil-things which had destroyed poor Job. Yet I must record one thing which I saw during my watch; though this was from the edge of the hilltop which overlooked the weed-continent, and was not in the valley, but in the stretch of clear water which lay between the island and the weed. As I saw it, it seemed to me that a number of great fish were swimming across from the island, diagonally towards the great continent of weed: they were swimming in one wake, and keeping a very regular line; but not breaking the water after the manner of porpoises or black fish. Yet, though I have mentioned this, it must not be supposed that I saw any very strange thing in such a sight, and indeed, I thought nothing more of it than to wonder what sort of fish they might be; for, as I saw them indistinctly in the moonlight, they made a queer appearance, seeming each of them to be possessed of two tails, and further, I could have thought I perceived a flicker as of tentacles just beneath the surface; but of this I was by no means sure.

Upon the following morning, having hurried our breakfast, each of us set-to again upon our tasks; for we were in hopes to have the great bow at work before dinner. Soon, the bo'sun had finished his arrow, and mine was completed very shortly after, so that there lacked nothing now to the completion of our work, save the finishing of the line, and the getting of the bow into position. This latter, assisted by the men, we proceeded now to effect, making a level bed of rocks near the edge of the hill which overlooked the weed. Upon this we placed the great bow, and then, having sent the men back to their work at the line, we proceeded to the aiming of the huge weapon. Now, when we had gotten the instrument pointed, as we conceived, straight over the hulk, the which we accomplished by squinting along the groove which the bo'sun had burnt down the center of the stock, we turned-to upon the arranging of the notch and trigger, the notch being to hold the strings when the weapon was set, and the trigger—a board bolted on loosely at the side just below the notch—to push them upwards out of this place when we desired to discharge the bow. This part of the work took up no great portion of our time, and soon we had all ready for our first flight. Then we commenced to set the bows, bending the bottom one first, and then those above in turn, until all were set; and, after that, we laid the arrow very carefully in the groove. Then I took two pieces of spun yarn and frapped the strings together at each end of the notch, and by this means I was assured that all the strings would act in unison when striking the butt of the arrow. And so we had all things ready for the discharge; whereupon, I placed my foot upon the trigger, and, bidding the bo'sun watch carefully the flight of the arrow, pushed downwards. The next instant, with a mighty twang, and a quiver that made the great stock stir on its bed of rocks, the bow sprang to its lesser tension, hurling the arrow outwards and upwards in a vast arc. Now, it may be conceived with what mortal interest we watched its flight, and so in a minute discovered that we had aimed too much to the right, for the arrow struck the weed ahead of the hulk—but *beyond* it. At that, I was filled near to bursting with pride and joy, and the men who had come forward to witness the trial, shouted to acclaim my success, whilst the bo'sun clapped me twice upon the shoulder to signify his regard, and shouted as loud as any.

And now it seemed to me that we had but to get the true aim, and the rescue of those in the hulk would be but a matter of another day or two; for, having once gotten a line to the hulk, we should haul across a thin rope by its means, and with this a thicker one; after which we should set this up so taut as possible, and then bring the people in the hulk to the island by means of a seat and block which we should haul to and fro along the supporting line.

Now, having realized that the bow would indeed carry so far as the wreck, we made haste to try our second arrow, and at the same time we bade the men go back to their work upon the line; for we should have need of it in a very little while. Presently, having pointed the bow more to the left, I took the frappings off the strings, so that we could bend the bows singly, and after that we set the great weapon again. Then, seeing that the arrow was straight in the groove, I replaced the frappings, and immediately discharged it. This time, to my very great pleasure and pride, the arrow went with a wonderful straightness towards the ship, and, clearing the superstructure, passed out of our sight as it fell behind it. At this, I was all impatience to try to get the line to the hulk before we made our dinner; but the men had not yet laid-up sufficient; there being then only four hundred and fifty fathoms (which the bo'sun measured off by stretching it along his arms and across his chest). This being so, we went to dinner, and made very great haste through it; and, after that, every one of us worked at the line, and so in about an hour we had sufficient; for I had estimated that it would not be wise to make the attempt with a less length than five hundred fathoms.

Having now completed a sufficiency of the line, the bo'sun set one of the men to flake it down very carefully upon the rock beside the bow, whilst he himself tested it at all such parts as he thought in any way doubtful, and so, presently, all was ready. Then I bent it on to the arrow, and, having set the bow whilst the men were flaking down the line, I was prepared immediately to discharge the weapon.

Now, all the morning, a man upon the hulk had observed us through a spy-glass, from a position that brought his head just above the edge of the superstructure, and, being aware of our intentions—having watched the previous flights—he understood the bo'sun, when he beckoned to him, that we had made ready for a third shot, and so, with an answering wave of his spy-glass, he disappeared from our sight. At that, having first turned to see that all were clear of the line, I pressed down the trigger, my heart beating very fast and thick, and so in a moment the arrow was sped. But now, doubtless because of the weight of the line, it made nowhere near so good a flight as on the previous occasion, the arrow striking the weed some two hundred yards short of the hulk, and at this, I could near have wept with vexation and disappointment.

Immediately upon the failure of my shot, the bo'sun called to the men to haul in the line very carefully, so that it should not be parted through the arrow catching in the weed; then he came over to me, and proposed that we should set-to at once to make a heavier arrow, suggesting that it had been lack of weight in the missile which had caused it to fall short. At that, I felt once more hopeful, and turned-to at once to prepare a new arrow; the bo'sun doing likewise; though in his case he intended to make a lighter one than that which had failed; for, as he put it, though the heavier one fell short, yet might the lighter succeed, and if neither, then we could only suppose that the bow lacked power to carry the line, and in that case, we should have to try some other method.

Now, in about two hours, I had made my arrow, the bo'sun having finished his a little earlier, and so (the men having hauled in all the line and flaked it down ready) we prepared to make another attempt to cast it over the hulk. Yet, a second time we failed, and by so much that it seemed hopeless to think of success; but, for all that it appeared useless, the bo'sun insisted on making a last try with the light arrow, and, presently, when we had gotten the line ready again, we loosed upon the wreck; but in this case so lamentable was our failure, that I cried out to the bo'sun to set the useless thing upon the fire and burn it; for I was sorely irked by its failure, and could scarce abide to speak civilly of it.

Now the bo'sun, perceiving how I felt, sung out that we would cease troubling about the hulk for the present, and go down all of us to gather reeds and weed for the fire; for it was drawing nigh to evening. And this we did, though all in a disconsolate condition of mind; for we had seemed so near to success, and now it appeared to be further than ever from us. And so, in a while, having brought up a sufficiency of fuel, the bo'sun sent two of the men down to one of the ledges which overhung the sea, and bade them see whether they could not secure a fish for our supper. Then, taking our places about the fire, we fell-to upon a discussion as to how we should come at the people in the hulk.

Now, for a while there came no suggestion worthy of notice, until at last there occurred to me a notable idea, and I called out suddenly that we should make a small fire balloon, and float off the line to them by such means. At that, the men about the fire were silent a moment; for the idea was new to them, and moreover they needed to comprehend just what I meant. Then, when they had come fully at it, the one who had proposed that they should make spears of their knives, cried out to know why a kite would not do, and at that I was confounded, in that so simple an expedient had not occurred to any before; for, surely, it would be but a little matter to float a line to them by means of a kite, and, further, such a thing would take no great making.

And so, after a space of talk, it was decided that upon the morrow we should build some sort of kite, and with it fly a line over the hulk, the which should be a task of no great difficulty with so good a breeze as we had continually with us.

And, presently, having made our supper off a very fine fish, which the two fishermen had caught whilst we talked, the bo'sun set the watches, and the rest turned-in.

XIII.
The Weed Men

Now, on that night, when I came to my watch, I discovered that there was no moon, and, save for such light as the fire threw, the hilltop was in darkness; yet this was no great matter to trouble me; for we had been unmolested since the burning of the fungi in the valley, and thus I had lost much of the haunting fear which had beset me upon the death of Job. Yet, though I was not so much afraid as I had been, I took all precautions that suggested themselves to me, and built up the fire to a goodly height, after which I took my cut-and-thrust, and made the round of the camping place. At the edges of the cliffs which protected us on three sides, I made some pause, staring down into the darkness, and listening; though this latter was of but small use because of the strength of the wind which roared continually in my ears. Yet though I neither saw nor heard anything, I was presently possessed of a strange uneasiness, which made me return twice or thrice to the edge of the cliffs; but always without seeing or hearing anything to justify my superstitions. And so, presently, being determined to give way to no fancifulness, I avoided the boundary of cliffs, and kept more to that part which commanded the slope, up and down which we made our journeys to and from the island below.

Then, it would be near halfway through my time of watching, there came to me out of the immensity of weed that lay to leeward, a far distant sound that grew upon my ear, rising and rising into a fearsome screaming and shrieking, and then dying away into the distance in queer sobs, and so at last to a note below that of the wind's. At this, as might be supposed, I was somewhat shaken in myself to hear so dread a noise coming out of all that desolation, and then, suddenly, the thought came to me that the screaming was from the ship to leeward of us, and I ran immediately to the edge of the cliff overlooking the weed, and stared into the darkness; but now I perceived, by a light which burned in the hulk, that the screaming had come from some place a great distance to the right of her, and more, as my sense assured me, it could by no means have been possible for those in her to have sent their voices to me against such a breeze as blew at that time.

And so, for a space, I stood nervously pondering, and peering away into the blackness of the night; thus, in a little, I perceived a dull glow upon the horizon, and, presently, there rose into view the upper edge of the moon, and a very welcome sight it was to me; for I had been upon the point of calling the bo'sun to inform him regarding the sound which I had heard; but I had hesitated, being afraid to seem foolish if nothing should befall. Then, even as I stood watching the moon rise into view, there came again to me the beginning of that screaming, somewhat like to the sound of a woman sobbing with a giant's voice, and it grew and strengthened until it pierced through the roar of the wind with an amazing clearness, and then slowly, and seeming to echo and echo, it sank away into the distance, and there was again in my ears no sound beyond that of the wind.

At this, having looked fixedly in the direction from which the sound had proceeded, I ran straightway to the tent and roused the bo'sun; for I had no knowledge of what the noise might portend, and this second cry had shaken from me all my bashfulness. Now the bo'sun was upon his feet almost before I had made an end of shaking him, and catching up his great cutlass which he kept always by his side, he followed me swiftly out on to the hilltop. Here, I explained to him that I had heard a very fearsome sound which had appeared to proceed out of the vastness of the weed-continent, and that, upon a repetition of the noise, I had decided to call him; for I knew not but that it might signal to us of some coming danger. At that, the bo'sun commended me; though chiding me in that I had hesitated to call him at the first occurrence of the crying, and then, following me to the edge of the leeward cliff, he stood there with me, waiting and listening, perchance there might come again a recurrence of the noise.

For perhaps something over an hour we stood there very silent and listening; but there came to us no sound beyond the continuous noise of the wind, and so, by that time, having grown somewhat impatient of waiting, and the moon being well risen, the bo'sun beckoned to me to make the round of the camp with him. Now, just as I turned away, chancing to look downward at the clear water directly below, I was amazed to see that an innumerable multitude of great fish, like unto those which I had seen on the previous night, were swimming from the weed-continent towards the island. At that, I stepped nearer the edge; for they came so directly towards the island that I expected to see them close inshore; yet I could not perceive one; for they seemed all of them to vanish at a point some thirty yards distant from the beach, and at that, being amazed both by the numbers of the fish and their strangeness, and the way in which they came on continually, yet never reached the shore, I called to the bo'sun to come and see; for he had gone on a few paces. Upon hearing my call, he came running back; whereat I pointed into the sea below. At that, he stooped forward and peered very intently, and I with him; yet neither one of us could discover the meaning of so curious an exhibition, and so for a while we watched, the bo'sun being quite so much interested as I.

Presently, however, he turned away, saying that we did foolishly to stand here peering at every curious sight, when we should be looking to the welfare of the camp, and so we began to go the round of the hilltop. Now, whilst we had been watching and listening, we had suffered the fire to die down to a most unwise lowness, and consequently, though the moon was rising, there was by no means the same brightness that should have made the camp light. On perceiving this, I went forward to throw some fuel on to the fire, and then, even as I moved, it seemed to me that I saw something stir in the shadow of the tent. And at that, I ran towards the place, uttering a shout, and waving my cut-and-thrust; yet I found nothing, and so, feeling somewhat foolish, I turned to make up the fire, as had been my intention, and whilst I was thus busied, the bo'sun came running over to me to know what I had seen, and in the same instant there ran three of the men out of the tent, all of them waked by my sudden cry. But I had naught to tell them, save that my fancy had played me a trick, and had shown me something where my eyes could find nothing, and at that, two of the men went back to resume their sleep; but the third, the big fellow to whom the bo'sun had given the other cutlass, came with us, bringing his weapon; and, though he kept silent, it seemed to me that he had gathered something of our uneasiness; and for my part I was not sorry to have his company.

Presently, we came to that portion of the hill which overhung the valley, and I went to the edge of the cliff, intending to peer over; for the valley had a very unholy fascination for me. Yet, no sooner had I glanced down than I started, and ran back to the bo'sun and plucked him by the sleeve, and at that, perceiving my agitation, he came with me in silence to see what matter had caused me so much quiet excitement. Now, when he looked over, he also was astounded, and drew back instantly; then, using great caution, he bent forward once more, and stared down, and, at that, the big seaman came up behind, walking upon his toes, and stooped to see what manner of thing we had discovered. Thus we each of us stared down upon a most unearthly sight; for the valley all beneath us was a-swarm with moving creatures, white and unwholesome in the moonlight, and their movements were somewhat like the movements of monstrous slugs, though the things themselves had no resemblance to such in their contours; but minded me of naked humans, very fleshy and crawling upon their stomachs; yet their movements lacked not a surprising rapidity. And now, looking a little over the bo'sun's shoulder, I discovered that these hideous things were coming up out from the pit-like pool in the bottom of the valley, and, suddenly, I was minded of the multitudes of strange fish which we had seen swimming towards the island; but which had all disappeared before reaching the shore, and I had no doubt but that they entered the pit through some natural passage known to them beneath the water. And now I was made to understand my thought of the previous night, that I had seen the flicker of tentacles; for these things below us had each two short and stumpy arms; but the ends appeared divided into hateful and wriggling masses of small tentacles, which slid hither and thither as the creatures moved about the bottom of the valley, and at their hinder ends, where they should have grown feet, there seemed other flickering bunches; but it must not be supposed that we saw these things clearly.

Now it is scarcely possible to convey the extraordinary disgust which the sight of these human slugs bred in me; nor, could I, do I think I would; for were I successful, then would others be like to retch even as I did, the spasm coming on without premonition, and born of very horror. And then, suddenly, even as I stared, sick with loathing and apprehension, there came into view, not a fathom below my feet, a face like to the face which had peered up into my own on that night, as we drifted beside the weed-continent. At that, I could have screamed, had I been in less terror; for the great eyes, so big as crown pieces, the bill like to an inverted parrot's, and the slug-like undulating of its white and slimy body, bred in me the dumbness of one mortally stricken. And, even as I stayed there, my helpless body bent and rigid, the bo'sun spat a mighty curse into my ear, and, leaning forward, smote at the thing with his cutlass; for in the instant that I had seen it, it had advanced upward by so much as a yard. Now, at this action of the bo'sun's, I came suddenly into possession of myself, and thrust downward with so much vigor that I was like to have followed the brute's carcass; for I overbalanced, and danced giddily for a moment upon the edge of eternity; and then the bo'sun had me by the waistband, and I was back in safety; but in that instant through which I had struggled for my balance, I had discovered that the face of the cliff was near hid with the number of the things which were making up to us, and I turned to the bo'sun, crying out to him that there were thousands of them swarming up to us. Yet, he was gone already from me, running towards the fire, and shouting to the men in the tent to haste to our help for their very lives, and then he came racing back with a great armful of the weed, and after him came the big seaman, carrying a burning tuft from the camp fire, and so in a few moments we had a blaze, and the men were bringing more weed; for we had a very good stock upon the hilltop; for which the Almighty be thanked.

Now, scarce had we lit one fire, when the bo'sun cried out to the big seaman to make another, further along the edge of the cliff, and, in the same instant, I shouted, and ran over to that part of the hill which lay towards the open sea; for I had seen a number of moving things about the edge of the seaward cliff. Now here there was a deal of shadow; for there were scattered certain large masses of rock about this part of the hill, and these held off both the light of the moon, and that from the fires. Here, I came abruptly upon three great shapes moving with stealthiness towards the camp, and, behind these, I saw dimly that there were others. Then, with a loud cry for help, I made at the three, and, as I charged, they rose up on end at me, and I found that they overtopped me, and their vile tentacles were reached out at me. Then I was smiting, and gasping, sick with a sudden stench, the stench of the creatures which I had come already to know. And then something clutched at me, something slimy and vile, and great mandibles champed in my face; but I stabbed upward, and the thing fell from me, leaving me dazed and sick, and smiting weakly. Then there came a rush of feet behind, and a sudden blaze, and the bo'sun crying out encouragement, and, directly, he and the big seaman thrust themselves in front of me, hurling from them great masses of burning weed, which they had borne, each of them, up a long reed. And immediately the things were gone, slithering hastily down over the cliff edge.

And so, presently, I was more my own man, and made to wipe from my throat the slime left by the clutch of the monster: and afterwards I ran from fire to fire with weed, feeding them, and so a space passed, during which we had safety; for by that time we had fires all about the top of the hill, and the monsters were in mortal dread of fire, else had we been dead, all of us, that night.

Now, a while before the dawn, we discovered, for the second time since we had been upon the island, that our fuel could not last us the night at the rate at which we were compelled to burn it, and so the bo'sun told the men to let out every second fire, and thus we staved off for a while the time when we should have to face a spell of darkness, and the things which, at present, the fires held off from us. And so at last, we came to the end of the weed and the reeds, and the bo'sun called out to us to watch the cliff edges very carefully, and smite on the instant that anything showed; but that, should he call, all were to gather by the central fire for a last stand. And, after that, he blasted the moon which had passed behind a great bank of cloud. And thus matters were, and the gloom deepened as the fires sank lower and lower. Then I heard a man curse, on that part of the hill which lay towards the weed-continent, his cry coming up to me against the wind, and the bo'sun shouted to us to all have a care, and directly afterwards I smote at something that rose silently above the edge of the cliff opposite to where I watched.

Perhaps a minute passed, and then there came shouts from all parts of the hilltop, and I knew that the weed men were upon us, and in the same instant there came two above the edge near me, rising with a ghostly quietness, yet moving lithely. Now the first, I pierced somewhere in the throat, and it fell backward; but the second, though I thrust it through, caught my blade with a bunch of its tentacles, and was like to have snatched it from me; but that I kicked it in the face, and at that, being, I believe, more astonished than hurt, it loosed my sword, and immediately fell away out of sight. Now this had taken, in all, no more than some ten seconds; yet already I perceived so many as four others coming into view a little to my right, and at that it seemed to me that our deaths must be very near, for I knew not how we were to cope with the creatures, coming as they were so boldly and with such rapidity. Yet, I hesitated not, but ran at them, and now I thrust not; but cut at their faces, and found this to be very effectual; for in this wise disposed I of three in as many strokes; but the fourth had come right over the cliff edge, and rose up at me upon its hinder parts, as had done those others when the bo'sun had succored me. At that, I gave way, having a very lively dread; but, hearing all about me the cries of conflict, and knowing that I could expect no help, I made at the brute: then as it stooped and reached out one of its bunches of tentacles, I sprang back, and slashed at them, and immediately I followed this up by a thrust in the stomach, and at that it collapsed into a writhing white ball, that rolled this way and that, and so, in its agony, coming to the edge of the cliff, it fell over, and I was left, sick and near helpless with the hateful stench of the brutes.

Now by this time all the fires about the edges of the hill were sunken into dull glowing mounds of embers; though that which burnt near to the entrance of the tent was still of a good brightness; yet this helped us but little, for we fought too far beyond the immediate circle of its beams to have benefit of it. And still the moon, at which now I threw a despairing glance, was no more than a ghostly shape behind the great bank of cloud which was passing over it. Then, even as I looked upward, glancing as it might be over my left shoulder, I saw, with a sudden horror, that something had come anigh me, and upon the instant, I caught the reek of the thing, and leapt fearfully to one side, turning as I sprang. Thus was I saved in the very moment of my destruction; for the creature's tentacles smeared the back of my neck as I leapt, and then I had smitten, once and again, and conquered.

Immediately after this, I discovered something to be crossing the dark space that lay between the dull mound of the nearest fire, and that which lay further along the hilltop, and so, wasting no moment of time, I ran towards the thing, and cut it twice across the head before ever it could get upon its hind parts, in which position I had learned greatly to dread them. Yet, no sooner had I slain this one, than there came a rush of maybe a dozen upon me; these having climbed silently over the cliff edge in the meanwhile. At this, I dodged, and ran madly towards the glowing mound of the nearest fire, the brutes following me almost so quick as I could run; but I came to the fire the first, and then, a sudden thought coming to me, I thrust the point of my cut-and-thrust among the embers and switched a great shower of them at the creatures, and at that I had a momentary clear vision of many white, hideous faces stretched out towards me, and brown, champing mandibles which had the upper beak shutting into the lower; and the clumped, wriggling tentacles were all a-flutter. Then the gloom came again; but immediately, I switched another and yet another shower of the burning embers towards them, and so, directly, I saw them give back, and then they were gone. At this, all about the edges of the hilltop, I saw the fires being scattered in like manner; for others had adopted this device to help them in their sore straits.

For a little after this, I had a short breathing space, the brutes seeming to have taken fright; yet I was full of trembling, and I glanced hither and thither, not knowing when some one or more of them would come upon me. And ever I glanced towards the moon, and prayed the Almighty that the clouds would pass quickly, else should we be all dead men; and then, as I prayed, there rose a sudden very terrible scream from one of the men, and in the same moment there came something over the edge of the cliff fronting me; but I cleft it or ever it could rise higher, and in my ears there echoed still the sudden scream which had come from that part of the hill which lay to the left of me: yet I dared not to leave my station; for to have done so would have been to have risked all, and so I stayed, tortured by the strain of ignorance, and my own terror.

Again, I had a little spell in which I was free from molestation; nothing coming into sight so far as I could see to right or left of me; though others were less fortunate, as the curses and sounds of blows told to me, and then, abruptly, there came another cry of pain, and I looked up again to the moon, and prayed aloud that it might come out to show some light before we were all destroyed; but it remained hid. Then a sudden thought came into my brain, and I shouted at the top of my voice to the bo'sun to set the great cross-bow upon the central fire; for thus we should have a big blaze—the wood being very nice and dry. Twice I shouted to him, saying:—"Burn the bow! Burn the bow!" And immediately he replied, shouting to all the men to run to him and carry it to the fire; and this we did and bore it to the center fire, and then ran back with all speed to our places. Thus in a minute we had some light, and the light grew as the fire took hold of the great log, the wind fanning it to a blaze. And so I faced outwards, looking to see if any vile face showed above the edge before me, or to my right or left. Yet, I saw nothing, save, as it seemed to me, once a fluttering tentacle came up, a little to my right; but nothing else for a space.

Perhaps it was near five minutes later, that there came another attack, and, in this, I came near to losing my life, through my folly in venturing too near to the edge of the cliff; for, suddenly, there shot up out from the darkness below, a clump of tentacles, and caught me about the left ankle, and immediately I was pulled to a sitting posture, so that both my feet were over the edge of the precipice, and it was only by the mercy of God that I had not plunged head foremost into the valley. Yet, as it was, I suffered a mighty peril; for the brute that had my foot, put a vast strain upon it, trying to pull me down; but I resisted, using my hands and seat to sustain me, and so, discovering that it could not compass my end in this wise, it slacked somewhat of the stress, and bit at my boot, shearing through the hard leather, and nigh destroying my small toe; but now, being no longer compelled to use both hands to retain my position, I slashed down with great fury, being maddened by the pain and the mortal fear which the creature had put upon me; yet I was not immediately free of the brute; for it caught my sword blade; but I snatched it away before it could take a proper hold, mayhaps cutting its feelers somewhat thereby; though of this I cannot be sure, for they seemed not to grip around a thing, but to *suck* to it; then, in a moment, by a lucky blow, I maimed it, so that it loosed me, and I was able to get back into some condition of security.

And from this onwards, we were free from molestation; though we had no knowledge but that the quietness of the weed men did but portend a fresh attack, and so, at last, it came to the dawn; and in all this time the moon came not to our help, being quite hid by the clouds which now covered the whole arc of the sky, making the dawn of a very desolate aspect.

And so soon as there was a sufficiency of light, we examined the valley; but there were nowhere any of the weed men, no! nor even any of their dead for it seemed that they had carried off all such and their wounded, and so we had no opportunity to make an examination of the monsters by daylight. Yet, though we could not come upon their dead, all about the edges of the cliffs was blood and slime, and from the latter there came ever the hideous stench which marked the brutes; but from this we suffered little, the wind carrying it far away to leeward, and filling our lungs with sweet and wholesome air.

Presently, seeing that the danger was past, the bo'sun called us to the center fire, on which burnt still the remnants of the great bow, and here we discovered for the first time that one of the men was gone from us. At that, we made search about the hilltop, and afterwards in the valley and about the island; but found him not.

XIV.
In Communication

Now of the search which we made through the valley for the body of Tompkins, that being the name of the lost man, I have some doleful memories. But first, before we left the camp, the bo'sun gave us all a very sound tot of the rum, and also a biscuit apiece, and thereafter we hasted down, each man holding his weapon readily. Presently, when we were come to the beach which ended the valley upon the seaward side, the bo'sun led us along to the bottom of the hill, where the precipices came down into the softer stuff which covered the valley, and here we made a careful search, perchance he had fallen over, and lay dead or wounded near to our hands. But it was not so, and after that, we went down to the mouth of the great pit, and here we discovered the mud all about it to be covered with multitudes of tracks, and in addition to these and the slime, we found many traces of blood; but nowhere any signs of Tompkins. And so, having searched all the valley, we came out upon the weed which strewed the shore nearer to the great weed-continent; but discovered nothing until we had made up towards the foot of the hill, where it came down sheer into the sea. Here, I climbed on to a ledge—the same from which the men had caught their fish—, thinking that, if Tompkins had fallen from above, he might lie in the water at the foot of the cliff, which was here, maybe, some ten to twenty feet deep; but, for a little space, I saw nothing. Then, suddenly, I discovered that there was something white, down in the sea away to my left, and, at that, I climbed farther out along the ledge.

In this wise I perceived that the thing which had attracted my notice was the dead body of one of the weed men. I could see it but dimly, catching odd glimpses of it as the surface of the water smoothed at whiles. It appeared to me to be lying curled up, and somewhat upon its right side, and in proof that it was dead, I saw a mighty wound that had come near to shearing away the head; and so, after a further glance, I came in, and told what I had seen. At that, being convinced by this time that Tompkins was indeed done to death, we ceased our search; but first, before we left the spot, the bo'sun climbed out to get a sight of the dead weed man and after him the rest of the men, for they were greatly curious to see clearly what manner of creature it was that had attacked us in the night. Presently, having seen so much of the brute as the water would allow, they came in again to the beach, and afterwards were returned to the opposite side of the island, and so, being there, we crossed over to the boat, to see whether it had been harmed; but found it to be untouched. Yet, that the creatures had been all about it, we could perceive by the marks of slime upon the sand, and also by the strange trail which they had left in the soft surface. Then one of the men called out that there had been something at Job's grave, which, as will be remembered, had been made in the sand some little distance from the place of our first camp. At that, we looked all of us, and it was easy to see that it had been disturbed, and so we ran hastily to it, knowing not what to fear; thus we found it to be empty; for the monsters had dug down to the poor lad's body, and of it we could discover no sign. Upon this, we came to a greater horror of the weed men than ever; for we knew them now to be foul ghouls who could not let even the dead body rest in the grave.

Now after this, the bo'sun led us all back to the hilltop, and there he looked to our hurts; for one man had lost two fingers in the night's fray; another had been bitten savagely in the left arm; whilst a third had all the skin of his face raised in wheals where one of the brutes had fixed its tentacles. And all of these had received but scant attention, because of the stress of the fight, and, after that, through the discovery that Tompkins was missing. Now, however, the bo'sun set-to upon them, washing and binding them up, and for dressings he made use of some of the oakum which we had with us, binding this on with strips torn from the roll of spare duck, which had been in the locker of the boat.

For my part, seizing this chance to make some examination of my wounded toe, the which, indeed, was causing me to limp, I found that I had endured less harm than seemed to me; for the bone of the toe was untouched, though showing bare; yet when it was cleansed, I had not overmuch pain with it; though I could not suffer to have the boot on, and so bound some canvas about my foot, until such time as it should be healed.

Presently, when our wounds were all attended to, the which had taken time, for there was none of us altogether untouched, the bo'sun bade the man whose fingers were damaged, to lie down in the tent, and the same order he gave also to him that was bitten in the arm. Then, the rest of us he directed to go down with him and carry up fuel; for that the night had shown him how our very lives depended upon a sufficiency of this; and so all that morning we brought fuel to the hilltop, both weed and reeds, resting not until midday, when he gave us a further tot of the rum, and after that set one of the men upon the dinner. Then he bade the man, Jessop by name, who had proposed to fly a kite over the vessel in the weed, to say whether he had any craft in the making of such a matter. At that, the fellow laughed, and told the bo'sun that he would make him a kite that would fly very steadily and strongly, and this without the aid of a tail. And so the bo'sun bade him set-to without delay, for that we should do well to deliver the people in the hulk, and afterwards make all haste from the island, which was no better than a nesting place of ghouls.

Now hearing the man say that his kite would fly without a tail, I was mightily curious to see what manner of thing he would make; for I had never seen the like, nor heard that such was possible. Yet he spoke of no more than he could accomplish; for he took two of the reeds and cut them to a length of about six feet; then he bound them together in the middle so that they formed a Saint Andrew's cross, and after that he made two more such crosses, and when these were completed, he took four reeds maybe a dozen feet long, and bade us stand them upright in the shape of a square, so that they formed the four corners, and after that he took one of the crosses, and laid it in the square so that its four ends touched the four uprights, and in this position he lashed it. Then he took the second cross and lashed it midway between the top and bottom of the uprights, and after that he lashed the third at the top, so that the three of them acted as spreaders to keep the four longer reeds in their places as though they were for the uprights of a little square tower. Now, when he had gotten so far as that, the bo'sun called out to us to make our dinners, and this we did, and afterwards had a short time in which to smoke, and whilst we were thus at our ease the sun came out, the which it had not done all the day, and at that we felt vastly brighter; for the day had been very gloomy with clouds until that time, and what with the loss of Tompkins, and our own fears and hurts, we had been exceeding doleful, but now, as I have said, we became more cheerful, and went very alertly to the finishing of the kite.

At this point it came suddenly to the bo'sun that we had made no provision of cord for the flying of the kite, and he called out to the man to know what strength the kite would require, at which Jessop answered him that maybe ten-yarn sennit would do, and this being so, the bo'sun led three of us down to the wrecked mast upon the further beach, and from this we stripped all that was left of the shrouds, and carried them to the top of the hill, and so, presently, having unlaid them, we set-to upon the sennit, using ten yarns; but plaiting two as one, by which means we progressed with more speed than if we had taken them singly.

Now, as we worked, I glanced occasionally towards Jessop, and saw that he stitched a band of the light duck around each end of the framework which he had made, and these bands I judged to be about four feet wide, in this wise leaving an open space between the two, so that now the thing looked something like to a Punchinello show, only that the opening was in the wrong place, and there was too much of it. After that he bent on a bridle to two of the uprights, making this of a piece of good hemp rope which he found in the tent, and then he called out to the bo'sun that the kite was finished. At that, the bo'sun went over to examine it, the which did all of us; for none of us had seen the like of such a thing, and, if I misdoubt not, few of us had much faith that it would fly; for it seemed so big and unwieldy. Now, I think that Jessop gathered something of our thoughts; for, calling to one of us to hold the kite, lest it should blow away, he went into the tent, and brought out the remainder of the hemp line, the same from which he had cut the bridle. This, he bent on to it, and, giving the end into our hands, bade us go back with it until all the slack was taken up, he, in the meanwhile, steadying the kite. Then, when we had gone back to the extent of the line, he shouted to us to take a very particular hold upon it, and then, stooping, caught the kite by the bottom, and threw it into the air, whereupon, to our amazement, having swooped somewhat to one side, it steadied and mounted upwards into the sky like a very bird.

Now at this, as I have made mention, we were astonished, for it appeared like a miracle to us to see so cumbrous a thing fly with so much grace and persistence, and further, we were mightily surprised at the manner in which it pulled upon the rope, tugging with such heartiness that we were like to have loosed it in our first astonishment, had it not been for the warning which Jessop called to us.

And now, being well assured of the properness of the kite, the bo'sun bade us to draw it in, the which we did only with difficulty, because of its bigness and the strength of the breeze. And when we had it back again upon the hilltop, Jessop moored it very securely to a great piece of rock, and, after that, having received our approbation, he turned-to with us upon the making of the sennit.

Presently, the evening drawing near, the bo'sun set us to the building of fires about the hilltop, and after that, having waved our goodnights to the people in the hulk, we made our suppers, and lay down to smoke, after which, we turned-to again at our plaiting of the sennit, the which we were in very great haste to have done. And so, later, the dark having come down upon the island, the bo'sun bade us take burning weed from the center fire, and set light to the heaps of weed that we had stacked round the edges of the hill for that purpose, and so in a few minutes the whole of the hilltop was very light and cheerful, and afterwards, having put two of the men to keep watch and attend to the fires, he sent the rest of us back to our sennit making, keeping us at it until maybe about ten of the clock, after which he arranged that two men at a time should be on watch throughout the night, and then he bade the rest of us turn in, so soon as he had looked to our various hurts.

Now, when it came to my turn to watch, I discovered that I had been chosen to accompany the big seaman, at which I was by no means displeased; for he was a most excellent fellow, and moreover a very lusty man to have near, should anything come upon one unawares. Yet, we were happy in that the night passed off without trouble of any sort, and so at last came the morning.

So soon as we had made our breakfast, the bo'sun took us all down to the carrying of fuel; for he saw very clearly that upon a good supply of this depended our immunity from attack. And so for the half of the morning we worked at the gathering of weed and reeds for our fires. Then, when we had obtained a sufficiency for the coming night, he set us all to work again upon the sennit, and so until dinner, after which we turned-to once more upon our plaiting. Yet it was plain that it would take several days to make a sufficient line for our purpose, and because of this, the bo'sun cast about in his mind for some way in which he could quicken its production. Presently, as a result of some little thought, he brought out from the tent the long piece of hemp rope with which we had moored the boat to the sea anchor, and proceeded to unlay it, until he had all three strands separate. Then he bent the three together, and so had a very rough line of maybe some hundred and eighty fathoms in length, yet, though so rough, he judged it strong enough, and thus we had this much the less sennit to make.

Now, presently, we made our dinner, and after that for the rest of the day we kept very steadily to our plaiting, and so, with the previous day's work, had near two hundred fathoms completed by the time that the bo'sun called us to cease and come to supper. Thus it will be seen that counting all, including the piece of hemp line from which the bridle had been made, we may be said to have had at this time about four hundred fathoms towards the length which we needed for our purpose, this having been reckoned at five hundred fathoms.

After supper, having lit all the fires, we continued to work at the plaiting, and so, until the bo'sun set the watches, after which we settled down for the night, first, however, letting the bo'sun see to our hurts. Now this night, like to the previous, brought us no trouble; and when the day came, we had first our breakfast, and then set-to upon our collecting of fuel, after which we spent the rest of the day at the sennit, having manufactured a sufficiency by the evening, the which the bo'sun celebrated by a very rousing tot of the rum. Then, having made our supper, we lit the fires, and had a very comfortable evening, after which, as on the preceding nights, having let the bo'sun attend our wounds, we settled for the night, and on this occasion the bo'sun let the man who had lost his fingers, and the one who had been bitten so badly in the arm, take their first turn at the watching since the night of the attack.

Now when the morning came we were all of us very eager to come to the flying of the kite; for it seemed possible to us that we might effect the rescue of the people in the hulk before the evening. And, at the thought of this, we experienced a very pleasurable sense of excitement; yet, before the bo'sun would let us touch the kite, he insisted that we should gather our usual supply of fuel, the which order, though full of wisdom, irked us exceedingly, because of our eagerness to set about the rescue. But at last this was accomplished, and we made to get the line ready, testing the knots, and seeing that it was all clear for running. Yet, before setting the kite off, the bo'sun took us down to the further beach to bring up the foot of the royal and t'gallant mast, which remained fast to the topmast, and when we had this upon the hilltop, he set its ends upon two rocks, after which he piled a heap of great pieces around them, leaving the middle part clear. Round this he passed the kite line a couple or three times, and then gave the end to Jessop to bend onto the bridle of the kite, and so he had all ready for paying out to the wreck.

And now, having nothing to do, we gathered round to watch, and, immediately, the bo'sun giving the signal, Jessop cast the kite into the air, and, the wind catching it, lifted it strongly and well, so that the bo'sun could scarce pay out fast enough. Now, before the kite had been let go, Jessop had bent to the forward end of it a great length of the spun yarn, so that those in the wreck could catch it as it trailed over them, and, being eager to witness whether they would secure it without trouble, we ran all of us to the edge of the hill to watch. Thus, within five minutes from the time of the loosing of the kite, we saw the people in the ship wave to us to cease veering, and immediately afterwards the kite came swiftly downwards, by which we knew that they had the tripping-line, and were hauling upon it, and at that we gave out a great cheer, and afterwards we sat about and smoked, waiting until they had read our instructions, which we had written upon the covering of the kite.

Presently, maybe the half of an hour afterwards, they signaled to us to haul upon our line, which we proceeded to do without delay, and so, after a great space, we had hauled in all of our rough line, and come upon the end of theirs, which proved to be a fine piece of three-inch hemp, new and very good; yet we could not conceive that this would stand the stress necessary to lift so great a length clear of the weed, as would be needful, or ever we could hope to bring the people of the ship over it in safety. And so we waited some little while, and, presently, they signaled again to us to haul, which we did, and found that they had bent on a much greater rope to the bight of the three-inch hemp, having merely intended the latter for a hauling-line by which to get the heavier rope across the weed to the island. Thus, after a weariful time of pulling, we got the end of the bigger rope up to the hilltop, and discovered it to be an extraordinarily sound rope of some four inches diameter, and smoothly laid of fine yarns round and very true and well spun, and with this we had every reason to be satisfied.

Now to the end of the big rope they had tied a letter, in a bag of oilskin, and in it they said some very warm and grateful things to us, after which they set out a short code of signals by which we should be able to understand one another on certain general matters, and at the end they asked if they should send us any provision ashore; for, as they explained, it would take some little while to get the rope set taut enough for our purpose, and the carrier fixed and in working order. Now, upon reading this letter, we called out to the bo'sun that he should ask them if they would send us some soft bread; the which he added thereto a request for lint and bandages and ointment for our hurts. And this he bade me write upon one of the great leaves from off the reeds, and at the end he told me to ask if they desired us to send them any fresh water. And all of this, I wrote with a sharpened splinter of reed, cutting the words into the surface of the leaf. Then, when I had made an end of writing, I gave the leaf to the bo'sun, and he enclosed it in the oilskin bag, after which he gave the signal for those in the hulk to haul on the smaller line, and this they did.

Presently, they signed to us to pull in again, the which we did, and so, when we had hauled in a great length of their line, we came to the little oilskin bag, in which we found lint and bandages and ointment, and a further letter, which set out that they were baking bread, and would send us some so soon as it was out from the oven.

Now, in addition to the matters for the healing of our wounds, and the letter, they had included a bundle of paper in loose sheets, some quills and an inkhorn, and at the end of their epistle, they begged very earnestly of us to send them some news of the outer world; for they had been shut up in that strange continent of weed for something over seven years. They told us then that there were twelve of them in the hulk, three of them being women, one of whom had been the captain's wife; but he had died soon after the vessel became entangled in the weed, and along with him more than half of the ship's company, having been attacked by giant devil-fish, as they were attempting to free the vessel from the weed, and afterwards they who were left had built the superstructure as a protection against the devil-fish, and the *devil-men*, as they termed them; for, until it had been built, there had been no safety about the decks, neither day nor night.

To our question as to whether they were in need of water, the people in the ship replied that they had a sufficiency, and, further, that they were very well supplied with provisions; for the ship had sailed from London with a general cargo, among which there was a vast quantity of food in various shapes and forms. At this news we were greatly pleased, seeing that we need have no more anxiety regarding a lack of victuals, and so in the letter which I went into the tent to write, I put down that we were in no great plentitude of provisions, at which hint I guessed they would add somewhat to the bread when it should be ready. And after that I wrote down such chief events as my memory recalled as having occurred in the course of the past seven years, and then, a short account of our own adventures, up to that time, telling them of the attack which we had suffered from the weed men, and asking such questions as my curiosity and wonder prompted.

Now whilst I had been writing, sitting in the mouth of the tent, I had observed, from time to time, how that the bo'sun was busied with the men in passing the end of the big rope round a mighty boulder, which lay about ten fathoms in from the edge of the cliff which overlooked the hulk. This he did, parceling the rope where the rock was in any way sharp, so as to protect it from being cut; for which purpose he made use of some of the canvas. And by the time that I had the letter completed, the rope was made very secure to the great piece of rock, and, further, they had put a large piece of chafing gear under that part of the rope where it took the edge of the cliff.

Now having, as I have said, completed the letter, I went out with it to the bo'sun; but, before placing it in the oilskin bag he bade me add a note at the bottom, to say that the big rope was all fast, and that they could heave on it so soon as it pleased them, and after that we dispatched the letter by means of the small line, the men in the hulk hauling it off to them so soon as they perceived our signals.

By this, it had come well on to the latter part of the afternoon, and the bo'sun called us to make some sort of a meal, leaving one man to watch the hulk, perchance they should signal to us. For we had missed our dinner in the excitement of the day's work, and were come now to feel the lack of it. Then, in the midst of it, the man upon the lookout cried out that they were signaling to us from the ship, and, at that, we ran all of us to see what they desired, and so, by the code which we had arranged between us, we found that they waited for us to haul upon the small line. This did we, and made out presently that we were hauling something across the weed, of a very fair bulk, at which we warmed to our work, guessing that it was the bread which they had promised us, and so it proved, and done up with great neatness in a long roll of tarpaulin, which had been wrapped around both the loaves and the rope, and lashed very securely at the ends, thus producing a taper shape convenient for passing over the weed without catching. Now, when we came to open this parcel, we discovered that my hint had taken very sound effect; for there were in the parcel, besides the loaves, a boiled ham, a Dutch cheese, two bottles of port well padded from breakage, and four pounds of tobacco in plugs. And at this coming of good things, we stood all of us upon the edge of the hill, and waved our thanks to those in the ship, they waving back in all goodwill, and after that we went back to our meal, at which we sampled the new victuals with very lusty appetites.

There was in the parcel, one other matter, a letter, most neatly indited, as had been the former epistles, in a feminine handwriting, so that I guessed they had one of the women to be their scribe. This epistle answered some of my queries, and, in particular, I remember that it informed me as to the probable cause of the strange crying which preceded the attack by the weed men, saying that on each occasion when they in the ship had suffered their attacks, there had been always this same crying, being evidently a summoning call or signal to the attack, though how given, the writer had not discovered; for the weed *devils*—this being how they in the ship spoke always of them—made never a sound when attacking, not even when wounded to the death, and, indeed, I may say here, that we never learned the way in which that lonesome sobbing was produced, nor, indeed, did they, or we, discover more than the merest tithe of the mysteries which that great continent of weed holds in its silence.

Another matter to which I had referred was the consistent blowing of the wind from one quarter, and this the writer told me happened for as much as six months in the year, keeping up a very steady strength. A further thing there was which gave me much interest; it was that the ship had not been always where we had discovered her; for at one time they had been so far within the weed, that they could scarce discern the open sea upon the far horizon; but that at times the weed opened in great gulfs that went yawning through the continent for scores of miles, and in this way the shape and coasts of the weed were being constantly altered; these happenings being for the most part at the change of the wind.

And much more there was that they told us then and afterwards, how that they dried weed for their fuel, and how the rains, which fell with great heaviness at certain periods, supplied them with fresh water; though, at times, running short, they had learnt to distill sufficient for their needs until the next rains.

Now, near to the end of the epistle, there came some news of their present actions, and thus we learnt that they in the ship were busy at staying the stump of the mizzen-mast, this being the one to which they proposed to attach the big rope, taking it through a great iron-bound snatch-block, secured to the head of the stump, and then down to the mizzen-capstan, by which, and a strong tackle, they would be able to heave the line so taut as was needful.

Now, having finished our meal, the bo'sun took out the lint, bandages and ointment, which they had sent us from the hulk, and proceeded to dress our hurts, beginning with him who had lost his fingers, which, happily, were making a very healthy heal. And afterwards we went all of us to the edge of the cliff, and sent back the lookout to fill such crevices in his stomach as remained yet empty; for we had passed him already some sound hunks of the bread and ham and cheese, to eat whilst he kept watch, and so he had suffered no great harm.

It may have been near an hour after this, that the bo'sun pointed out to me that they in the ship had commenced to heave upon the great rope, and so I perceived, and stood watching it; for I knew that the bo'sun had some anxiety as to whether it would take-up sufficiently clear of the weed to allow those in the ship to be hauled along it, free from molestation by the great devil-fish.

Presently, as the evening began to draw on, the bo'sun bade us go and build our fires about the hilltop, and this we did, after which we returned to learn how the rope was lifting, and now we perceived that it had come clear of the weed, at which we felt mightily rejoiced, and waved encouragement, chance there might be any who watched us from the hulk. Yet, though the rope was up clear of the weed, the bight of it had to rise to a much greater height, or ever it would do for the purpose for which we intended it, and already it suffered a vast strain, as I discovered by placing my hand upon it; for, even to lift the slack of so great a length of line meant the stress of some tons. And later I saw that the bo'sun was growing anxious; for he went over to the rock around which he had made fast the rope, and examined the knots, and those places where he had parceled it, and after that he walked to the place where it went over the edge of the cliff, and here he made a further scrutiny; but came back presently, seeming not dissatisfied.

Then, in a while, the darkness came down upon us, and we lighted our fires and prepared for the night, having the watches arranged as on the preceding nights.

XV.
Aboard the Hulk

Now when it came to my watch, the which I took in company with the big seaman, the moon had not yet risen, and all the island was vastly dark, save the hilltop, from which the fires blazed in a score of places, and very busy they kept us, supplying them with fuel. Then, when maybe the half of our watch had passed, the big seaman, who had been to feed the fires upon the weed side of the hilltop, came across to me, and bade me come and put my hand upon the lesser rope; for that he thought they in the ship were anxious to haul it in so that they might send some message across to us. At his words, I asked him very anxiously whether he had perceived them waving a light, the which we had arranged to be our method of signaling in the night, in the event of such being needful; but, to this, he said that he had seen naught; and, by now, having come near the edge of the cliff, I could see for myself, and so perceived that there was none signaling to us from the hulk. Yet, to please the fellow, I put my hand upon the line, which we had made fast in the evening to a large piece of rock, and so, immediately, I discovered that something was pulling upon it, hauling and then slackening, so that it occurred to me that the people in the vessel might be indeed wishful to send us some message, and at that, to make sure, I ran to the nearest fire, and, lighting a tuft of weed, waved it thrice; but there came not any answering signal from those in the ship, and at that I went back to feel at the rope, to assure myself that it had not been the pluck of the wind upon it; but I found that it was something very different from the wind, something that plucked with all the sharpness of a hooked fish, only that it had been a mighty great fish to have given such tugs, and so I knew that some vile thing out in the darkness of the weed was fast to the rope, and at this there came the fear that it might break it, and then a second thought that something might be climbing up to us along the rope, and so I bade the big seaman stand ready with his great cutlass, whilst I ran and waked the bo'sun. And this I did, and explained to him how that something meddled with the lesser rope, so that he came immediately to see for himself how this might be, and when he had put his hand upon it, he bade me go and call the rest of the men, and let them stand round by the fires; for that there was something abroad in the night, and we might be in danger of attack; but he and the big seaman stayed by the end of the rope, watching, so far as the darkness would allow, and ever and anon feeling the tension upon it.

Then, suddenly, it came to the bo'sun to look to the second line, and he ran, cursing himself for his thoughtlessness; but because of its greater weight and tension, he could not discover for certain whether anything meddled with it or not; yet he stayed by it, arguing that if aught touched the smaller rope then might something do likewise with the greater, only that the small line lay along the weed, whilst the greater one had been some feet above it when the darkness had fallen over us, and so might be free from any prowling creatures.

And thus, maybe, an hour passed, and we kept watch and tended the fires, going from one to another, and, presently, coming to that one which was nearest to the bo'sun, I went over to him, intending to pass a few minutes in talk; but as I drew nigh to him, I chanced to place my hand upon the big rope, and at that I exclaimed in surprise; for it had become much slacker than when last I had felt it in the evening, and I asked the bo'sun whether he had noticed it, whereat he felt the rope, and was almost more amazed than I had been; for when last he had touched it, it had been taut, and humming in the wind. Now, upon this discovery, he was in much fear that something had bitten through it, and called to the men to come all of them and pull upon the rope, so that he might discover whether it was indeed parted; but when they came and hauled upon it, they were unable to gather in any of it, whereat we felt all of us mightily relieved in our minds; though still unable to come at the cause of its sudden slackness.

And so, a while later, there rose the moon, and we were able to examine the island and the water between it and the weed-continent, to see whether there was anything stirring; yet neither in the valley, nor on the faces of the cliffs, nor in the open water could we perceive aught living, and as for anything among the weed, it was small use trying to discover it among all that shaggy blackness. And now, being assured that nothing was coming at us, and that, so far as our eyes could pierce, there climbed nothing upon the ropes, the bo'sun bade us get turned-in, all except those whose time it was to watch. Yet, before I went into the tent, I made a careful examination of the big rope, the which did also the bo'sun, but could perceive no cause for its slackness; though this was quite apparent in the moonlight, the rope going down with greater abruptness than it had done in the evening. And so we could but conceive that they in the hulk had slacked it for some reason; and after that we went to the tent and a further spell of sleep.

In the early morning we were waked by one of the watchmen, coming into the tent to call the bo'sun; for it appeared that the hulk had moved in the night, so that its stern was now pointed somewhat towards the island. At this news, we ran all of us from the tent to the edge of the hill, and found it to be indeed as the man had said, and now I understood the reason of that sudden slackening of the rope; for, after withstanding the stress upon it for some hours, the vessel had at last yielded, and slewed its stern towards us, moving also to some extent bodily in our direction.

And now we discovered that a man in the lookout place in the top of the structure was waving a welcome to us, at which we waved back, and then the bo'sun bade me haste and write a note to know whether it seemed to them likely that they might be able to heave the ship clear of the weed, and this I did, greatly excited within myself at this new thought, as, indeed, was the bo'sun himself and the rest of the men. For could they do this, then how easily solved were every problem of coming to our own country. But it seemed too good a thing to have come true, and yet I could but hope. And so, when my letter was completed, we put it up in the little oilskin bag, and signaled to those in the ship to haul in upon the line. Yet, when they went to haul, there came a mighty splather amid the weed, and they seemed unable to gather in any of the slack, and then, after a certain pause, I saw the man in the lookout point something, and immediately afterwards there belched out in front of him a little puff of smoke, and, presently, I caught the report of a musket, so that I knew that he was firing at something in the weed. He fired again, and yet once more, and after that they were able to haul in upon the line, and so I perceived that his fire had proved effectual; yet we had no knowledge of the thing at which he had discharged his weapon.

Now, presently, they signaled to us to draw back the line, the which we could do only with great difficulty, and then the man in the top of the super-structure signed to us to vast hauling, which we did, whereupon he began to fire again into the weed; though with what effect we could not perceive. Then, in a while he signaled to us to haul again, and now the rope came more easily; yet still with much labor, and a commotion in the weed over which it lay and, in places, sank. And so, at last, as it cleared the weed because of the lift of the cliff, we saw that a great crab had clutched it, and that we hauled it towards us; for the creature had too much obstinacy to let go.

Perceiving this, and fearing that the great claws of the crab might divide the rope, the bo'sun caught up one of the men's lances, and ran to the cliff edge, calling to us to pull in gently, and put no more strain upon the line than need be. And so, hauling with great steadiness, we brought the monster near to the edge of the hill, and there, at a wave from the bo'sun, stayed our pulling. Then he raised the spear, and smote at the creature's eyes, as he had done on a previous occasion, and immediately it loosed its hold, and fell with a mighty splash into the water at the foot of the cliff. Then the bo'sun bade us haul in the rest of the rope, until we should come to the packet, and, in the meantime, he examined the line to see whether it had suffered harm through the mandibles of the crab; yet, beyond a little chafe, it was quite sound.

And so we came to the letter, which I opened and read, finding it to be written in the same feminine hand which had indited the others. From it we gathered that the ship had burst through a very thick mass of the weed which had compacted itself about her, and that the second mate, who was the only officer remaining to them, thought there might be good chance to heave the vessel out; though it would have to be done with great slowness, so as to allow the weed to part gradually, otherwise the ship would but act as a gigantic rake to gather up weed before it, and so form its own barrier to clear water. And after this there were kind wishes and hopes that we had spent a good night, the which I took to be prompted by the feminine heart of the writer, and after that I fell to wondering whether it was the captain's wife who acted as scribe. Then I was waked from my pondering, by one of the men crying out that they in the ship had commenced to heave again upon the big rope, and, for a time, I stood and watched it rise slowly, as it came to tautness.

I had stood there awhile, watching the rope, when, suddenly, there came a commotion amid the weed, about two-thirds of the way to the ship, and now I saw that the rope had freed itself from the weed, and clutching it, were, maybe, a score of giant crabs. At this sight, some of the men cried out their astonishment, and then we saw that there had come a number of men into the lookout place in the top of the superstructure, and, immediately, they opened a very brisk fire upon the creatures, and so, by ones and twos they fell back into the weed, and after that, the men in the hulk resumed their heaving, and so, in a while, had the rope some feet clear of the surface.

Now, having tautened the rope so much as they thought proper, they left it to have its due effect upon the ship, and proceeded to attach a great block to it; then they signaled to us to slack away on the little rope until they had the middle part of it, and this they hitched around the neck of the block, and to the eye in the strop of the block they attached a bo'sun's chair, and so they had ready a carrier, and by this means we were able to haul stuff to and from the hulk without having to drag it across the surface of the weed; being, indeed, the fashion in which we had intended to haul ashore the people in the ship. But now we had the bigger project of salvaging the ship herself, and, further, the big rope, which acted as support for the carrier, was not yet of a sufficient height above the weed-continent for it to be safe to attempt to bring any ashore by such means; and now that we had hopes of saving the ship, we did not intend to risk parting the big rope, by trying to attain such a degree of tautness as would have been necessary at this time to have raised its bight to the desired height.

Now, presently, the bo'sun called out to one of the men to make breakfast, and when it was ready we came to it, leaving the man with the wounded arm to keep watch; then when we had made an end, he sent him, that had lost his fingers, to keep a lookout whilst the other came to the fire and ate his breakfast. And in the meanwhile, the bo'sun took us down to collect weed and reeds for the night, and so we spent the greater part of the morning, and when we had made an end of this, we returned to the top of the hill, to discover how matters were going forward; thus we found, from the one at the lookout, that they, in the hulk, had been obliged to heave twice upon the big rope to keep it off the weed, and by this we knew that the ship was indeed making a slow sternway towards the island—

slipping steadily through the weed, and as we looked at her, it seemed almost that we could perceive that she was nearer; but this was no more than imagination; for, at most, she could not have moved more than some odd fathoms. Yet it cheered us greatly, so that we waved our congratulations to the man who stood in the lookout in the superstructure, and he waved back.

Later, we made dinner, and afterwards had a very comfortable smoke, and then the bo'sun attended to our various hurts. And so through the afternoon we sat about upon the crest of the hill overlooking the hulk, and thrice had they in the ship to heave upon the big rope, and by evening they had made near thirty fathoms towards the island, the which they told us in reply to a query which the bo'sun desired me to send them, several messages having passed between us in the course of the afternoon, so that we had the carrier upon our side. Further than this, they explained that they would tend the rope during the night, so that the strain would be kept up, and, more, this would keep the ropes off the weed.

And so, the night coming down upon us, the bo'sun bade us light the fires about the top of the hill, the same having been laid earlier in the day, and thus, our supper having been dispatched, we prepared for the night. And all through it there burned lights aboard the hulk, the which proved very companionable to us in our times of watching; and so, at last came the morning, the darkness having passed without event. And now, to our huge pleasure, we discovered that the ship had made great progress in the night; being now so much nearer that none could suppose it a matter of imagination; for she must have moved nigh sixty fathoms nearer to the island, so that now we seemed able almost to recognize the face of the man in the lookout; and many things about the hulk we saw with greater clearness, so that we scanned her with a fresh interest. Then the man in the lookout waved a morning greeting to us, the which we returned very heartily, and, even as we did so, there came a second figure beside the man, and waved some white matter, perchance a handkerchief, which is like enough, seeing that it was a woman, and at that, we took off our head coverings, all of us, and shook them at her, and after this we went to our breakfast; having finished which, the bo'sun dressed our hurts, and then, setting the man, who had lost his fingers, to watch, he took the rest of us, excepting him that was bitten in the arm, down to collect fuel, and so the time passed until near dinner.

When we returned to the hilltop, the man upon the lookout told us that they in the ship had heaved not less than four separate times upon the big rope, the which, indeed, they were doing at that present minute; and it was very plain to see that the ship had come nearer even during the short space of the morning. Now, when they had made an end of tautening the rope, I perceived that it was, at last, well clear of the weed through all its length, being at its lowest part nigh twenty feet above the surface, and, at that, a sudden thought came to me which sent me hastily to the bo'sun; for it had occurred to me that there existed no reason why we should not pay a visit to those aboard the hulk. But when I put the matter to him, he shook his head, and, for awhile, stood out against my desire; but, presently, having examined the rope, and considering that I was the lightest of any in the island, he consented, and at that I ran to the carrier which had been hauled across to our side, and got me into the chair. Now, the men, so soon as they perceived my intention, applauded me very heartily, desiring to follow; but the bo'sun bade them be silent, and, after that, he lashed me into the chair, with his own hands, and then signaled to those in the ship to haul upon the small rope; he, in the meanwhile, checking my descent towards the weeds, by means of our end of the hauling-line.

And so, presently, I had come to the lowest part, where the bight of the rope dipped downward in a bow towards the weed, and rose again to the mizzenmast of the hulk. Here I looked downward with somewhat fearful eyes; for my weight on the rope made it sag somewhat lower than seemed to me comfortable, and I had a very lively recollection of some of the horrors which that quiet surface hid. Yet I was not long in this place; for they in the ship, perceiving how the rope let me nearer to the weed than was safe, pulled very heartily upon the hauling-line, and so I came quickly to the hulk.

Now, as I drew nigh to the ship, the men crowded upon a little platform which they had built in the superstructure somewhat below the broken head of the mizzen, and here they received me with loud cheers and very open arms, and were so eager to get me out of the bo'sun's chair, that they cut the lashings, being too impatient to cast them loose. Then they led me down to the deck, and here, before I had knowledge of aught else, a very buxom woman took me into her arms, kissing me right heartily, at which I was greatly taken aback; but the men about me did naught but laugh, and so, in a minute, she loosed me, and there I stood, not knowing whether to feel like a fool or a hero; but inclining rather to the latter. Then, at this minute, there came a second woman, who bowed to me in a manner most formal, so that we might have been met in some fashionable gathering, rather than in a cast-away hulk in the lonesomeness and terror of that weed-choked sea; and at her coming all the mirth of the men died out of them, and they became very sober, whilst the buxom woman went backward for a piece, and seemed somewhat abashed. Now, at all this, I was greatly puzzled, and looked from one to another to learn what it might mean; but in the same moment the woman bowed again, and said something in a low voice touching the weather, and after that she raised her glance to my face, so that I saw her eyes, and they were so strange and full of melancholy, that I knew on the instant why she spoke and acted in so unmeaning a way; for the poor creature was out of her mind, and when I learned afterwards that she was the captain's wife, and had seen him die in the arms of a mighty devil-fish, I grew to understand how she had come to such a pass.

Now for a minute after I had discovered the woman's madness, I was so taken aback as to be unable to answer her remark; but for this there appeared no necessity; for she turned away and went aft towards the saloon stairway, which stood open, and here she was met by a maid very bonny and fair, who led her tenderly down from my sight. Yet, in a minute, this same maid appeared, and ran along the decks to me, and caught my two hands, and shook them, and looked up at me with such roguish, playful eyes, that she warmed my heart, which had been strangely chilled by the greeting of the poor mad woman. And she said many hearty things regarding my courage, to which I knew in my heart I had no claim; but I let her run on, and so, presently, coming more to possession of herself, she discovered that she was still holding my hands, the which, indeed, I had been conscious of the while with a very great pleasure; but at her discovery she dropped them with haste, and stood back from me a space, and so there came a little coolness into her talk: yet this lasted not long; for we were both of us young, and, I think, even thus early we attracted one the other; though, apart from this, there was so much that we desired each to learn, that we could not but talk freely, asking question for question, and giving answer for answer. And thus a time passed, in which the men left us alone, and went presently to the capstan, about which they had taken the big rope, and at this they toiled awhile; for already the ship had moved sufficiently to let the line fall slack.

Presently, the maid, whom I had learnt was niece to the captain's wife, and named Mary Madison, proposed to take me the round of the ship, to which proposal I agreed very willingly; but first I stopped to examine the mizzen stump, and the manner in which the people of the ship had stayed it, the which they had done very cunningly, and I noted how that they had removed some of the superstructure from about the head of the mast, so as to allow passage for the rope, without putting a strain upon the superstructure itself. Then when I had made an end upon the poop, she led me down on to the main-deck, and here I was very greatly impressed by the prodigious size of the structure which they had built about the hulk, and the skill with which it had been carried out, the supports crossing from side to side and to the decks in a manner calculated to give great solidity to that which they upheld. Yet, I was very greatly puzzled to know where they had gotten a sufficiency of timber to make so large a matter; but upon this point she satisfied me by explaining that they had taken up the 'tween decks, and used all such bulkheads as they could spare, and, further, that there had been a good deal among the dunnage which had proved usable.

And so we came at last to the galley, and here I discovered the buxom woman to be installed as cook, and there were in with her a couple of fine children, one of whom I guessed to be a boy of maybe some five years, and the second a girl, scarce able to do more than toddle. At this I turned and asked Mistress Madison whether these were her cousins; but in the next moment I remembered that they could not be; for, as I knew, the captain had been dead some seven years; yet it was the woman in the galley who answered my question; for she turned and, with something of a red face, informed me that they were hers, at which I felt some surprise; but supposed that she had taken passage in the ship with her husband; yet in this I was not correct; for she proceeded to explain that, thinking they were cut off from the world for the rest of this life, and falling very fond of the carpenter, they had made it up together to make a sort of marriage, and had gotten the second mate to read the service over them. She told me then, how that she had taken passage with her mistress, the captain's wife, to help her with her niece, who had been but a child when the ship sailed; for she had been very attached to them both, and they to her. And so she came to an end of her story, expressing a hope that she had done no wrong by her marriage, as none had been intended. And to this I made answer, assuring her that no decent-minded man could think the worse of her; but that I, for my part, thought rather the better, seeing that I liked the pluck which she had shown. At that she cast down the soup ladle, which she had in her fist, and came towards me, wiping her hands; but I gave back, for I shamed to be hugged again, and before Mistress Mary Madison, and at that she came to a stop and laughed very heartily; but, all the same, called down a very warm blessing upon my head; for which I had no cause to feel the worse. And so I passed on with the captain's niece.

Presently, having made the round of the hulk, we came aft again to the poop, and discovered that they were heaving once more upon the big rope, the which was very heartening, proving, as it did, that the ship was still a-move. And so, a little later, the girl left me, having to attend to her aunt. Now whilst she was gone, the men came all about me, desiring news of the world beyond the weed-continent, and so for the next hour I was kept very busy, answering their questions. Then the second mate called out to them to take another heave upon the rope, and at that they turned to the capstan, and I with them, and so we hove it taut again, after which they got about me once more, questioning; for so much seemed to have happened in the seven years in which they had been imprisoned. And then, after a while, I turned-to and questioned them on such points as I had neglected to ask Mistress Madison, and they discovered to me their terror and sickness of the weed-continent, its desolation and horror, and the dread which had beset them at the thought that they should all of them come to their ends without sight of their homes and countrymen.

Now, about this time, I became conscious that I had grown very empty; for I had come off to the hulk before we had made our dinner, and had been in such interest since, that the thought of food had escaped me; for I had seen none eating in the hulk, they, without doubt, having dined earlier than my coming. But now, being made aware of my state by the grumbling of my stomach, I inquired whether there was any food to be had at such a time, and, at that, one of the men ran to tell the woman in the galley that I had missed my dinner, at which she made much ado, and set-to and prepared me a very good meal, which she carried aft and set out for me in the saloon, and after that she sent me down to it.

Presently, when I had come near to being comfortable, there chanced a lightsome step upon the floor behind me, and, turning, I discovered that Mistress Madison was surveying me with a roguish and somewhat amused air. At that, I got hastily to my feet; but she bade me sit down, and therewith she took a seat opposite, and so bantered me with a gentle playfulness that was not displeasing to me, and at which I played so good a second as I had ability. Later, I fell to questioning her, and, among other matters, discovered that it was she who acted as scribe for the people in the hulk, at which I told her that I had done likewise for those on the island. After that, our talk became somewhat personal, and I learnt that she was near on to nineteen years of age, whereat I told her that I had passed my twenty-third. And so we chatted on, until, presently, it occurred to me that I had better be preparing to return to the island, and I rose to my feet with this intention; yet feeling that I had been very much happier to have stayed, the which I thought, for a moment, had not been displeasing to her, and this I imagined, noting somewhat in her eyes when I made mention that I must be gone. Yet it may be that I flattered myself.

Now when I came out on deck, they were busied again in heaving taut the rope, and, until they had made an end, Mistress Madison and I filled the time with such chatter as is wholesome between a man and maid who have not long met, yet find one another pleasing company. Then, when at last the rope was taut, I went up to the mizzen staging, and climbed into the chair, after which some of the men lashed me in very securely. Yet when they gave the signal to haul me to the island, there came for awhile no response, and then signs that we could not understand; but no movement to haul me across the weed. At that, they unlashed me from the chair, bidding me get out, whilst they sent a message to discover what might be wrong. And this they did, and, presently, there came back word that the big rope had stranded upon the edge of the cliff, and that they must slacken it somewhat at once, the which they did, with many expressions of dismay. And so, maybe an hour passed, during which we watched the men working at the rope, just where it came down over the edge of the hill, and Mistress Madison stood with us and watched; for it was very terrible, this sudden thought of failure (though it were but temporary) when they were so near to success. Yet, at last there came a signal from the island for us to loose the hauling-line, the which we did, allowing them to haul across the carrier, and so, in a little while, they signaled back to us to pull in, which, having done, we found a letter in the bag lashed to the carrier, in which the bo'sun made it plain that he had strengthened the rope, and placed fresh chafing gear about it, so that he thought it would be so safe as ever to heave upon; but to put it to a less strain. Yet he refused to allow me to venture across upon it, saying that I must stay in the ship until we were clear of the weed; for if the rope had stranded in one place, then had it been so cruelly tested that there might be some other points at which it was ready to give. And this final note of the bo'sun's made us all very serious;

for, indeed, it seemed possible that it was as he suggested; yet they reassured themselves by pointing out that, like enough, it had been the chafe upon the cliff edge which had frayed the strand, so that it had been weakened before it parted; but I, remembering the chafing gear which the bo'sun had put about it in the first instance, felt not so sure; yet I would not add to their anxieties.

And so it came about that I was compelled to spend the night in the hulk; but, as I followed Mistress Madison into the big saloon, I felt no regret, and had near forgotten already my anxiety regarding the rope.

And out on deck there sounded most cheerily the clack of the capstan.

XVI.
Freed

Now, when Mistress Madison had seated herself, she invited me to do likewise, after which we fell into talk, first touching upon the matter of the stranding of the rope, about which I hastened to assure her, and later to other things, and so, as is natural enough with a man and maid, to ourselves, and here we were very content to let it remain.

Presently, the second mate came in with a note from the bo'sun, which he laid upon the table for the girl to read, the which she beckoned me to do also, and so I discovered that it was a suggestion, written very rudely and ill-spelled, that they should send us a quantity of reeds from the island, with which we might be able to ease the weed somewhat from around the stern of the hulk, thus aiding her progress. And to this the second mate desired the girl to write a reply, saying that we should be very happy for the reeds, and would endeavor to act upon his hint, and this Mistress Madison did, after which she passed the letter to me, perchance I desired to send any message. Yet I had naught that I wished to say, and so handed it back, with a word of thanks, and, at once, she gave it to the second mate, who went, forthwith, and dispatched it.

Later, the stout woman from the galley came aft to set out the table, which occupied the center of the saloon, and whilst she was at this, she asked for information on many things, being very free and unaffected in her speech, and seeming with less of deference to my companion, than a certain motherliness; for it was very plain that she loved Mistress Madison, and in this my heart did not blame her. Further, it was plain to me that the girl had a very warm affection for her old nurse, which was but natural, seeing that the old woman had cared for her through all the past years, besides being companion to her, and a good and cheerful one, as I could guess.

Now awhile I passed in answering the buxom woman's questions, and odd times such occasional ones as were slipped in by Mistress Madison; and then, suddenly there came the clatter of men's feet overhead, and, later, the thud of something being cast down upon the deck, and so we knew that the reeds had come. At that, Mistress Madison cried out that we should go and watch the men try them upon the weed; for that if they proved of use in easing that which lay in our path, then should we come the more speedily to the clear water, and this without the need of putting so great a strain upon the hawser, as had been the case hitherto.

When we came to the poop, we found the men removing a portion of the superstructure over the stern, and after that they took some of the stronger reeds, and proceeded to work at the weed that stretched away in a line with our taffrail. Yet that they anticipated danger, I perceived; for there stood by them two of the men and the second mate, all armed with muskets, and these three kept a very strict watch upon the weed, knowing, through much experience of its terrors, how that there might be a need for their weapons at any moment. And so a while passed, and it was plain that the men's work upon the weed was having effect; for the rope grew slack visibly, and those at the capstan had all that they could do, taking fleet and fleet with the tackle, to keep it anywhere near to tautness, and so, perceiving that they were kept so hard at it, I ran to give a hand, the which did Mistress Madison, pushing upon the capstan-bars right merrily and with heartiness. And thus a while passed, and the evening began to come down upon the lonesomeness of the weed-continent. Then there appeared the buxom woman, and bade us come to our suppers, and her manner of addressing the two of us was the manner of one who might have mothered us; but Mistress Madison cried out to her to wait, that we had found work to do, and at that the big woman laughed, and came towards us threateningly, as though intending to remove us hence by force.

And now, at this moment, there came a sudden interruption which checked our merriment; for, abruptly, there sounded the report of a musket in the stern, and then came shouts, and the noise of the two other weapons, seeming like thunder, being pent by the over-arching superstructure. And, directly, the men about the taffrail gave back, running here and there, and so I saw that great arms had come all about the opening which they had made in the superstructure, and two of these flickered in-board, searching hither and thither; but the stout woman took a man near to her, and thrust him out of danger, and after that, she caught Mistress Madison up in her big arms, and ran down on to the main-deck with her, and all this before I had come to a full knowledge of our danger. But now I perceived that I should do well to get further back from the stern, the which I did with haste, and, coming to a safe position, I stood and stared at the huge creature, its great arms, vague in the growing dusk, writhing about in vain search for a victim. Then returned the second mate, having been for more weapons, and now I observed that he armed all the men, and had brought up a spare musket for my use, and so we commenced, all of us, to fire at the monster, whereat it began to lash about most furiously, and so, after some minutes, it slipped away from the opening and slid down into the weed. Upon that several of the men rushed to replace those parts of the superstructure which had been removed, and I with them; yet there were sufficient for the job, so that I had no need to do aught; thus, before they had made up the opening, I had been given chance to look out upon the weed, and so discovered that all the surface which lay between our stern and the island, was moving in vast ripples, as though mighty fish were swimming beneath it, and then, just before the men put back the last of the great panels, I saw the weed all tossed up like to a vast pot a-boil, and then a vague glimpse of thousands of monstrous arms that filled the air, and came towards the ship.

And then the men had the panel back in its place, and were hasting to drive the supporting struts into their positions. And when this was done, we stood awhile and listened; but there came no sound above that of the wail of the wind across the extent of the weed-continent. And at that, I turned to the men, asking how it was that I could hear no sounds of the creatures attacking us, and so they took me up into the lookout place, and from there I stared down at the weed; but it was without movement, save for the stirring of the wind, and there was nowhere any sign of the devil-fish. Then, seeing me amazed, they told me how that anything which moved the weed seemed to draw them from all parts; but that they seldom touched the hulk unless there was something visible to them which had movement. Yet, as they went on to explain, there would be hundreds and hundreds of them lying all about the ship, hiding in the weed; but that if we took care not to show ourselves within their reach, they would have gone most of them by the morning. And this the men told me in a very matter-of-fact way; for they had become inured to such happenings.

Presently, I heard Mistress Madison calling to me by name, and so descended out of the growing darkness, to the interior of the superstructure, and here they had lit a number of rude slush-lamps, the oil for which, as I learned later, they obtained from a certain fish which haunted the sea, beneath the weed, in very large schools, and took near any sort of bait with great readiness. And so, when I had climbed down into the light, I found the girl waiting for me to come to supper, for which I discovered myself to be in a mightily agreeable humor.

Presently, having made an end of eating, she leaned back in her seat and commenced once more to bait me in her playful manner, the which appeared to afford her much pleasure, and in which I joined with no less, and so we fell presently to more earnest talk, and in this wise we passed a great space of the evening. Then there came to her a sudden idea, and what must she do but propose that we should climb to the lookout, and to this I agreed with a very happy willingness. And to the lookout we went. Now when we had come there, I perceived her reason for this freak; for away in the night, astern the hulk, there blazed halfway between the heaven and the sea, a mighty glow, and suddenly, as I stared, being dumb with admiration and surprise, I knew that it was the blaze of our fires upon the crown of the bigger hill; for, all the hill being in shadow, and hidden by the darkness, there showed only the glow of the fires, hung, as it were, in the void, and a very striking and beautiful spectacle it was. Then, as I watched, there came, abruptly a figure into view upon the edge of the glow, showing black and minute, and this I knew to be one of the men come to the edge of the hill to take a look at the hulk, or test the strain on the hawser. Now, upon my expressing admiration of the sight to Mistress Madison, she seemed greatly pleased, and told me that she had been up many times in the darkness to view it. And after that we went down again into the interior of the superstructure, and here the men were taking a further heave upon the big rope, before settling the watches for the night, the which they managed, by having one man at a time to keep awake and call the rest whenever the hawser grew slack.

Later Mistress Madison showed me where I was to sleep, and so, having bid one another a very warm good-night, we parted, she going to see that her aunt was comfortable, and I out on to the main-deck to have a chat with the man on watch. In this way, I passed the time until midnight, and in that while we had been forced to call the men thrice to heave upon the hawser, so quickly had the ship begun to make way through the weed. Then, having grown sleepy, I said goodnight, and went to my berth, and so had my first sleep upon a mattress, for some weeks.

Now when the morning was come, I waked, hearing Mistress Madison calling upon me from the other side of my door, and rating me very saucily for a lie-a-bed, and at that I made good speed at dressing, and came quickly into the saloon, where she had ready a breakfast that made me glad I had waked. But first, before she would do aught else, she had me out to the lookout place, running up before me most merrily and singing in the fullness of her glee, and so, when I had come to the top of the superstructure, I perceived that she had very good reason for so much merriment, and the sight which came to my eyes, gladdened me most mightily, yet at the same time filling me with a great amazement; for, behold! in the course of that one night, we had made near unto two hundred fathoms across the weed, being now, with what we had made previously, no more than some thirty fathoms in from the edge of the weed. And there stood Mistress Madison beside me, doing somewhat of a dainty step-dance upon the flooring of the lookout, and singing a quaint old lilt that I had not heard that dozen years, and this little thing, I think, brought back more clearly to me than aught else how that this winsome maid had been lost to the world for so many years, having been scarce of the age of twelve when the ship had been lost in the weed-continent. Then, as I turned to make some remark, being filled with many feelings, there came a hail, from far above in the air, as it might be, and, looking up, I discovered the man upon the hill to be standing along the edge, and waving to us, and now I perceived how that the hill towered a very great way above us, seeming, as it were, to overhang the hulk though we were yet some seventy fathoms distant from the sheer sweep of its nearer precipice. And so, having waved back our greeting, we made down to breakfast, and, having come to the saloon, set-to upon the good victuals, and did very sound justice thereto.

Presently, having made an end of eating, and hearing the clack of the capstan-pawls, we hurried out on deck, and put our hands upon the bars, intending to join in that last heave which should bring the ship free out of her long captivity, and so for a time we moved round about the capstan, and I glanced at the girl beside me; for she had become very solemn, and indeed it was a strange and solemn time for her; for she, who had dreamed of the world as her childish eyes had seen it, was now, after many hopeless years, to go forth once more to it—to live in it, and to learn how much had been dreams, and how much real; and with all these thoughts I credited her; for they seemed such as would have come to me at such a time, and, presently, I made some blundering effort to show to her that I had understanding of the tumult which possessed her, and at that she smiled up at me with a sudden queer flash of sadness and merriment, and our glances met, and I saw something in hers, which was but newborn, and though I was but a young man, my heart interpreted it for me, and I was all hot suddenly with the pain and sweet delight of this new thing; for I had not dared to think upon that which already my heart had made bold to whisper to me, so that even thus soon I was miserable out of her presence. Then she looked downward at her hands upon the bar; and, in the same instant, there came a loud, abrupt cry from the second mate, to vast heaving, and at that all the men pulled out their bars and cast them upon the deck, and ran, shouting, to the ladder that led to the lookout, and we followed, and so came to the top, and discovered that at last the ship was clear of the weed, and floating in the open water between it and the island.

Now at the discovery that the hulk was free, the men commenced to cheer and shout in a very wild fashion, as, indeed, is no cause for wonder, and we cheered with them. Then, suddenly, in the midst of our shouting, Mistress Madison plucked me by the sleeve and pointed to the end of the island where the foot of the bigger hill jutted out in a great spur, and now I perceived a boat, coming round into view, and in another moment I saw that the bo'sun stood in the stern, steering; thus I knew that he must have finished repairing her whilst I had been on the hulk. By this, the men about us had discovered the nearness of the boat, and commenced shouting afresh, and they ran down, and to the bows of the vessel, and got ready a rope to cast. Now when the boat came near, the men in her scanned us very curiously, but the bo'sun took off his head-gear, with a clumsy grace that well became him; at which Mistress Madison smiled very kindly upon him, and, after that, she told me with great frankness that he pleased her, and, more, that she had never seen so great a man, which was not strange seeing that she had seen but few since she had come to years when men become of interest to a maid.

After saluting us the bo'sun called out to the second mate that he would tow us round to the far side of the island, and to this the officer agreed, being, I surmised, by no means sorry to put some solid matter between himself and the desolation of the great weed-continent; and so, having loosed the hawser, which fell from the hilltop with a prodigious splash, we had the boat head, towing. In this wise we opened out, presently, the end of the hill; but feeling now the force of the breeze, we bent a kedge to the hawser, and, the bo'sun carrying it seawards, we warped ourselves to windward of the island, and here, in forty fathoms, we vast heaving, and rode to the kedge.

Now when this was accomplished they called to our men to come aboard, and this they did, and spent all of that day in talk and eating; for those in the ship could scarce make enough of our fellows. And then, when it had come to night, they replaced that part of the superstructure which they had removed from about the head of the mizzen-stump, and so, all being secure, each one turned-in and had a full night's rest, of the which, indeed, many of them stood in sore need.

The following morning, the second mate had a consultation with the bo'sun, after which he gave the order to commence upon the removal of the great superstructure, and to this each one of us set himself with vigor. Yet it was a work requiring some time, and near five days had passed before we had the ship stripped clear. When this had been accomplished, there came a busy time of routing out various matter of which we should have need in jury-rigging her; for they had been so long in disuse, that none remembered where to look for them. At this a day and a half was spent, and after that we set-to about fitting her with such jury-masts as we could manage from our material.

Now, after the ship had been dismasted, all those seven years gone, the crew had been able to save many of her spars, these having remained attached to her, through their inability to cut away all of the gear; and though this had put them in sore peril at the time, of being sent to the bottom with a hole in their side, yet now had they every reason to be thankful; for, by this accident, we had now a foreyard, a topsail-yard, a main t'gallant-yard, and the fore-topmast. They had saved more than these; but had made use of the smaller spars to shore up the superstructure, sawing them into lengths for that purpose. Apart from such spars as they had managed to secure, they had a spare topmast lashed along under the larboard bulwarks, and a spare t'gallant and royal mast lying along the starboard side.

Now, the second mate and the bo'sun set the carpenter to work upon the spare topmast, bidding him make for it some trestle-trees and bolsters, upon which to lay the eyes of the rigging; but they did not trouble him to shape it. Further, they ordered the same to be fitted to the foretopmast and the spare t'gallant and royal mast. And in the meanwhile, the rigging was prepared, and when this was finished, they made ready the shears to hoist the spare topmast, intending this to take the place of the main lower-mast. Then, when the carpenter had carried out their orders, he was set to make three partners with a step cut in each, these being intended to take the heels of the three masts, and when these were completed, they bolted them securely to the decks at the fore part of each one of the stumps of the three lower-masts. And so, having all ready, we hove the mainmast into position, after which we proceeded to rig it. Now, when we had made an end of this, we set-to upon the foremast, using for this the foretopmast which they had saved, and after that we hove the mizzenmast into place, having for this the spare t'gallant and royal mast.

Now the manner in which we secured the masts, before ever we came to the rigging of them, was by lashing them to the stumps of the lower-masts, and after we had lashed them, we drove dunnage and wedges between the masts and the lashings, thus making them very secure. And so, when we had set up the rigging, we had confidence that they would stand all such sail as we should be able to set upon them. Yet, further than this, the bo'sun bade the carpenter make wooden caps of six inch oak, these caps to fit over the *squared* heads of the lower-mast stumps, and having a hole, each of them, to embrace the jury-mast, and by making these caps in two halves, they were able to bolt them on after the masts had been hove into position.

And so, having gotten in our three jury lower-masts, we hoisted up the foreyard to the main, to act as our mainyard, and did likewise with the topsail-yard to the fore, and after that, we sent up the t'gallant-yard to the mizzen. Thus we had her sparred, all but a bowsprit and jibboom; yet this we managed by making a stumpy, spike bowsprit from one of the smaller spars which they had used to shore up the superstructure, and because we feared that it lacked strength to bear the strain of our fore and aft stays, we took down two hawsers from the fore, passing them in through the hawse-holes and setting them up there. And so we had her rigged, and, after that, we bent such sail as our gear abled us to carry, and in this wise had the hulk ready for sea.

Now, the time that it took us to rig the ship, and fit her out, was seven weeks, saving one day. And in all this time we suffered no molestation from any of the strange habitants of the weed-continent; though this may have been because we kept fires of dried weed going all the night about the decks, these fires being lit on big flat pieces of rock which we had gotten from the island. Yet, for all that we had not been troubled, we had more than once discovered strange things in the water swimming near to the vessel; but a flare of weed, hung over the side, on the end of a reed, had sufficed always to scare away such unholy visitants.

And so at last we came to the day on which we were in so good a condition that the bo'sun and the second mate considered the ship to be in a fit state to put to sea—the carpenter having gone over so much of her hull as he could get at and found her everywhere very sound; though her lower parts were hideously overgrown with weed, barnacles and other matters; yet this we could not help, and it was not wise to attempt to scrape her, having consideration to the creatures which we knew to abound in those waters.

Now in those seven weeks, Mistress Madison and I had come very close to one another, so that I had ceased to call her by any name save Mary, unless it were a dearer one than that; though this would be one of my own invention, and would leave my heart too naked did I put it down here.

Of our love one for the other, I think yet, and ponder how that mighty man, the bo'sun, came so quickly to a knowledge of the state of our hearts; for he gave me a very sly hint one day that he had a sound idea of the way in which the wind blew, and yet, though he said it with a half-jest, methought there was something wistful in his voice, as he spoke, and at that I just clapped my hand in his, and he gave it a very huge grip. And after that he ceased from the subject.

XVII.
How We Came to Our Own Country

Now, when the day came on which we made to leave the nearness of the island, and the waters of that strange sea, there was great lightness of heart among us, and we went very merrily about such tasks as were needful. And so, in a little, we had the kedge tripped, and had cast the ship's head to starboard, and presently, had her braced up upon the larboard tack, the which we managed very well; though our gear worked heavily, as might be expected. And after that we had gotten under way, we went to the lee side to witness the last of that lonesome island, and with us came the men of the ship, and so, for a space, there was a silence among us; for they were very quiet, looking astern and saying naught; but we had sympathy with them, knowing somewhat of those past years.

And now the bo'sun came to the break of the poop, and called down to the men to muster aft, the which they did, and I with them; for I had come to regard them as my very good comrades; and rum was served out to each of them, and to me along with the rest, and it was Mistress Madison herself who dipped it out to us from the wooden bucket; though it was the buxom woman who had brought it up from the lazarette. Now, after the rum, the bo'sun bade the crew to clear up the gear about the decks, and get matters secured, and at that I turned to go with the men, having become so used to work with them; but he called to me to come up to him upon the poop, the which I did, and there he spoke respectfully, remonstrating with me, and reminding me that now there was need no longer for me to toil; for that I was come back to my old position of passenger, such as I had been in the *Glen Carrig*, ere she foundered. But to this talk of his, I made reply that I had as good a right to work my passage home as any other among us; for though I had paid for a passage in the *Glen Carrig*, I had done no such thing regarding the *Seabird*—this being the name of the hulk—and to this, my reply, the bo'sun said little; but I perceived that he liked my spirit, and so from thence until we reached the Port of London, I took my turn and part in all seafaring matters, having become by this quite proficient in the calling. Yet, in one matter, I availed myself of my former position; for I chose to live aft, and by this was abled to see much of my sweetheart, Mistress Madison.

Now after dinner upon the day on which we left the island, the bo'sun and the second mate picked the watches, and thus I found myself chosen to be in the bo'sun's, at which I was mightly pleased. And when the watches had been picked, they had all hands to 'bout ship, the which, to the pleasure of all, she accomplished; for under such gear and with so much growth upon her bottom, they had feared that we should have to veer, and by this we should have lost much distance to leeward, whereas we desired to edge so much to windward as we could, being anxious to put space between us and the weed-continent. And twice more that day we put the ship about, though the second time it was to avoid a great bank of weed that lay floating athwart our bows; for all the sea to windward of the island, so far as we had been able to see from the top of the higher hill, was studded with floating masses of the weed, like unto thousands of islets, and in places like to far-spreading reefs. And, because of these, the sea all about the island remained very quiet and unbroken, so that there was never any surf, no, nor scarce a broken wave upon its shore, and this, for all that the wind had been fresh for many days.

When the evening came, we were again upon the larboard tack, making, perhaps, some four knots in the hour; though, had we been in proper rig, and with a clean bottom, we had been making eight or nine, with so good a breeze and so calm a sea. Yet, so far, our progress had been very reasonable; for the island lay, maybe, some five miles to leeward, and about fifteen astern. And so we prepared for the night. Yet, a little before dark, we discovered that the weed-continent trended out towards us; so that we should pass it, maybe, at a distance of something like half a mile, and, at that, there was talk between the second mate and the bo'sun as to whether it was better to put the ship about, and gain a greater sea-room before attempting to pass this promontory of weed; but at last they decided that we had naught to fear; for we had fair way through the water, and further, it did not seem reasonable to suppose that we should have aught to fear from the habitants of the weed-continent, at so great a distance as the half of a mile. And so we stood on; for, once past the point, there was much likelihood of the weed trending away to the Eastward, and if this were so, we could square-in immediately and get the wind upon our quarter, and so make better way.

Now it was the bo'sun's watch from eight of the evening until midnight, and I, with another man, had the lookout until four bells. Thus it chanced that, coming abreast of the point during our time of watching, we peered very earnestly to leeward; for the night was dark, having no moon until nearer the morning; and we were full of unease in that we had come so near again to the desolation of that strange continent. And then, suddenly, the man with me clutched my shoulder, and pointed into the darkness upon our bow, and thus I discovered that we had come nearer to the weed than the bo'sun and the second mate had intended; they, without doubt, having miscalculated our leeway. At this, I turned and sang out to the bo'sun that we were near to running upon the weed, and, in the same moment, he shouted to the helmsman to luff, and directly afterwards our starboard side was brushing against the great outlying tufts of the point, and so, for a breathless minute, we waited. Yet the ship drew clear, and so into the open water beyond the point; but I had seen something as we scraped against the weed, a sudden glimpse of white, gliding among the growth, and then I saw others, and, in a moment, I was down on the main-deck, and running aft to the bo'sun; yet midway along the deck a horrid shape came above the starboard rail, and I gave out a loud cry of warning. Then I had a capstan-bar from the rack near, and smote with it at the thing, crying all the while for help, and at my blow the thing went from my sight, and the bo'sun was with me, and some of the men.

Now the bo'sun had seen my stroke, and so sprang upon the t'gallant rail, and peered over; but gave back on the instant, shouting to me to run and call the other watch, for that the sea was full of the monsters swimming off to the ship, and at that I was away at a run, and when I had waked the men, I raced aft to the cabin and did likewise with the second mate, and so returned in a minute, bearing the bo'sun's cutlass, my own cut-and-thrust, and the lantern that hung always in the saloon. Now when I had gotten back, I found all things in a mighty scurry—men running about in their shirts and drawers, some in the galley bringing fire from the stove, and others lighting a fire of dry weed to leeward of the galley, and along the starboard rail there was already a fierce fight, the men using capstan-bars, even as I had done. Then I thrust the bo'sun's cutlass into his hand, and at that he gave a great shout, part of joy, and part of approbation, and after that he snatched the lantern from me, and had run to the larboard side of the deck, before I was well aware that he had taken the light; but now I followed him, and happy it was for all of us in the ship that he had thought to go at that moment; for the light of the lantern showed me the vile faces of three of the weed men climbing over the larboard rail; yet the bo'sun had cleft them or ever I could come near; but in a moment I was full busy; for there came nigh a dozen heads above the rail a little aft of where I was, and at that I ran at them, and did good execution; but some had been aboard, if the bo'sun had not come to my help. And now the decks were full of light, several fires having been lit, and the second mate having brought out fresh lanterns; and now the men had gotten their cutlasses, the which were more handy than the capstan-bars; and so the fight went forward, some having come over to our side to help us, and a very wild sight it must have seemed to any onlooker; for all about the decks burned the fires and the lanterns, and along the rails ran the men, smiting at hideous faces that rose in dozens into the wild glare of our fighting lights. And everywhere drifted the stench of the brutes. And up on the poop, the fight was as brisk as elsewhere; and here, having been drawn by a cry for help, I discovered the buxom woman smiting with a gory meat-axe at a vile thing which had gotten a clump of its tentacles upon her dress; but she had dispatched it, or ever my sword could help her, and then, to my astonishment, even at that time of peril, I discovered the captain's wife, wielding a small sword, and the face of her was like to the face of a tiger; for her mouth was drawn, and showed her teeth clenched; but she uttered no word nor cry, and I doubt not but that she had some vague idea that she worked her husband's vengeance.

Then, for a space, I was as busy as any, and afterwards I ran to the buxom woman to demand the whereabouts of Mistress Madison, and she, in a very breathless voice, informed me that she had locked her in her room out of harm's way, and at that I could have embraced the woman; for I had been sorely anxious to know that my sweetheart was safe.

And, presently, the fight diminished, and so, at last, came to an end, the ship having drawn well away from the point, and being now in the open. And after that I ran down to my sweetheart, and opened her door, and thus, for a space, she wept, having her arms about my neck; for she had been in sore terror for me, and for all the ship's company. But, soon, drying her tears, she grew very indignant with her nurse for having locked her into her room, and refused to speak to that good woman for near an hour. Yet I pointed out to her that she could be of very great use in dressing such wounds as had been received, and so she came back to her usual brightness, and brought out bandages, and lint, and ointment, and thread, and was presently very busy.

Now it was later that there rose a fresh commotion in the ship; for it had been discovered that the captain's wife was a-missing. At this, the bo'sun and the second mate instituted a search; but she was nowhere to be found, and, indeed, none in the ship ever saw her again, at which it was presumed that she had been dragged over by some of the weed men, and so come upon her death. And at this, there came a great prostration to my sweetheart so that she would not be comforted for the space of nigh three days, by which time the ship had come clear of those strange seas, having left the incredible desolation of the weed-continent far under our starboard counter.

And so, after a voyage which lasted for nine and seventy days since getting underway, we came to the Port of London, having refused all offers of assistance on the way.

Now here, I had to say farewell to my comrades of so many months and perilous adventures; yet, being a man not entirely without means, I took care that each of them should have a certain gift by which to remember me.

And I placed monies in the hands of the buxom woman, so that she could have no reason to stint my sweetheart, and she having—for the comfort of her conscience—taken her good man to the church, set up a little house upon the borders of my estate; but this was not until Mistress Madison had come to take her place at the head of my hall in the County of Essex.

Now one further thing there is of which I must tell. Should any, chancing to trespass upon my estate, come upon a man of very mighty proportions, albeit somewhat bent by age, seated comfortably at the door of his little cottage, then shall they know him for my friend the bo'sun; for to this day do he and I foregather, and let our talk drift to the desolate places of this earth, pondering upon that which we have seen—the weed-continent, where reigns desolation and the terror of its strange habitants. And, after that, we talk softly of the land where God hath made monsters after the fashion of trees. Then, maybe, my children come about me, and so we change to other matters; for the little ones love not terror.

/

THE HOUSE ON THE BORDERLAND

1908

From the Manuscript discovered in 1877 by Messrs. Tonnison and Berreggnog in the Ruins that lie to the South of the Village of Kraighten, in the West of Ireland. Set out here, with Notes.

To My Father

(Whose feet tread the lost eons)

Open the door,
  And listen!
Only the wind's muffled roar,
  And the glisten
Of tears 'round the moon.
  And, in fancy, the tread
Of vanishing shoon—
  Out in the night with the Dead.

"Hush! And hark
  To the sorrowful cry
Of the wind in the dark.
  Hush and hark, without murmur or sigh,
    To shoon that tread the lost eons:
  To the sound that bids you to die.
Hush and hark! Hush and Hark!"

Shoon of the Dead

AUTHOR'S INTRODUCTION TO THE MANUSCRIPT

Many are the hours in which I have pondered upon the story that is set forth in the following pages. I trust that my instincts are not awry when they prompt me to leave the account, in simplicity, as it was handed to me.

And the MS. itself—You must picture me, when first it was given into my care, turning it over, curiously, and making a swift, jerky examination. A small book it is; but thick, and all, save the last few pages, filled with a quaint but legible handwriting, and writ very close. I have the queer, faint, pit-water smell of it in my nostrils now as I write, and my fingers have subconscious memories of the soft, "cloggy" feel of the long-damp pages.

I read, and, in reading, lifted the Curtains of the Impossible that blind the mind, and looked out into the unknown. Amid stiff, abrupt sentences I wandered; and, presently, I had no fault to charge against their abrupt tellings; for, better far than my own ambitious phrasing, is this mutilated story capable of bringing home all that the old Recluse, of the vanished house, had striven to tell.

Of the simple, stiffly given account of weird and extraordinary matters, I will say little. It lies before you. The inner story must be uncovered, personally, by each reader, according to ability and desire. And even should any fail to see, as now I see, the shadowed picture and conception of that to which one may well give the accepted titles of Heaven and Hell; yet can I promise certain thrills, merely taking the story as a story.

WILLIAM HOPE HODGSON

DECEMBER 17, 1907

I.
The Finding of the Manuscript

Right away in the west of Ireland lies a tiny hamlet called Kraighten. It is situated, alone, at the base of a low hill. Far around there spreads a waste of bleak and totally inhospitable country; where, here and there at great intervals, one may come upon the ruins of some long desolate cottage—unthatched and stark. The whole land is bare and unpeopled, the very earth scarcely covering the rock that lies beneath it, and with which the country abounds, in places rising out of the soil in wave-shaped ridges.

Yet, in spite of its desolation, my friend Tonnison and I had elected to spend our vacation there. He had stumbled on the place by mere chance the year previously, during the course of a long walking tour, and discovered the possibilities for the angler in a small and unnamed river that runs past the outskirts of the little village.

I have said that the river is without name; I may add that no map that I have hitherto consulted has shown either village or stream. They seem to have entirely escaped observation: indeed, they might never exist for all that the average guide tells one. Possibly this can be partly accounted for by the fact that the nearest railway station (Ardrahan) is some forty miles distant.

It was early one warm evening when my friend and I arrived in Kraighten. We had reached Ardrahan the previous night, sleeping there in rooms hired at the village post office, and leaving in good time on the following morning, clinging insecurely to one of the typical jaunting cars.

It had taken us all day to accomplish our journey over some of the roughest tracks imaginable, with the result that we were thoroughly tired and somewhat bad tempered. However, the tent had to be erected and our goods stowed away before we could think of food or rest. And so we set to work, with the aid of our driver, and soon had the tent up upon a small patch of ground just outside the little village, and quite near to the river.

Then, having stored all our belongings, we dismissed the driver, as he had to make his way back as speedily as possible, and told him to come across to us at the end of a fortnight. We had brought sufficient provisions to last us for that space of time, and water we could get from the stream. Fuel we did not need, as we had included a small oil-stove among our outfit, and the weather was fine and warm.

It was Tonnison's idea to camp out instead of getting lodgings in one of the cottages. As he put it, there was no joke in sleeping in a room with a numerous family of healthy Irish in one corner and the pigsty in the other, while overhead a ragged colony of roosting fowls distributed their blessings impartially, and the whole place so full of peat smoke that it made a fellow sneeze his head off just to put it inside the doorway.

Tonnison had got the stove lit now and was busy cutting slices of bacon into the frying pan; so I took the kettle and walked down to the river for water. On the way, I had to pass close to a little group of the village people, who eyed me curiously, but not in any unfriendly manner, though none of them ventured a word.

As I returned with my kettle filled, I went up to them and, after a friendly nod, to which they replied in like manner, I asked them casually about the fishing; but, instead of answering, they just shook their heads silently, and stared at me. I repeated the question, addressing more particularly a great, gaunt fellow at my elbow; yet again I received no answer. Then the man turned to a comrade and said something rapidly in a language that I did not understand; and, at once, the whole crowd of them fell to jabbering in what, after a few moments, I guessed to be pure Irish. At the same time they cast many glances in my direction. For a minute, perhaps, they spoke among themselves thus; then the man I had addressed faced 'round at me and said something. By the expression of his face I guessed that he, in turn, was questioning me; but now I had to shake my head, and indicate that I did not comprehend what it was they wanted to know; and so we stood looking at one another, until I heard Tonnison calling to me to hurry up with the kettle. Then, with a smile and a nod, I left them, and all in the little crowd smiled and nodded in return, though their faces still betrayed their puzzlement.

It was evident, I reflected as I went toward the tent, that the inhabitants of these few huts in the wilderness did not know a word of English; and when I told Tonnison, he remarked that he was aware of the fact, and, more, that it was not at all uncommon in that part of the country, where the people often lived and died in their isolated hamlets without ever coming in contact with the outside world.

"I wish we had got the driver to interpret for us before he left," I remarked, as we sat down to our meal. "It seems so strange for the people of this place not even to know what we've come for."

Tonnison grunted an assent, and thereafter was silent for a while.

Later, having satisfied our appetites somewhat, we began to talk, laying our plans for the morrow; then, after a smoke, we closed the flap of the tent, and prepared to turn in.

"I suppose there's no chance of those fellows outside taking anything?" I asked, as we rolled ourselves in our blankets.

Tonnison said that he did not think so, at least while we were about; and, as he went on to explain, we could lock up everything, except the tent, in the big chest that we had brought to hold our provisions. I agreed to this, and soon we were both asleep.

Next morning, early, we rose and went for a swim in the river; after which we dressed and had breakfast. Then we roused out our fishing tackle and overhauled it, by which time, our breakfasts having settled somewhat, we made all secure within the tent and strode off in the direction my friend had explored on his previous visit.

During the day we fished happily, working steadily upstream, and by evening we had one of the prettiest creels of fish that I had seen for a long while. Returning to the village, we made a good feed off our day's spoil, after which, having selected a few of the finer fish for our breakfast, we presented the remainder to the group of villagers who had assembled at a respectful distance to watch our doings. They seemed wonderfully grateful, and heaped mountains of what I presumed to be Irish blessings upon our heads.

Thus we spent several days, having splendid sport, and first-rate appetites to do justice upon our prey. We were pleased to find how friendly the villagers were inclined to be, and that there was no evidence of their having ventured to meddle with our belongings during our absences.

It was on a Tuesday that we arrived in Kraighten, and it would be on the Sunday following that we made a great discovery. Hitherto we had always gone up-stream; on that day, however, we laid aside our rods, and, taking some provisions, set off for a long ramble in the opposite direction. The day was warm, and we trudged along leisurely enough, stopping about mid-day to eat our lunch upon a great flat rock near the riverbank. Afterward we sat and smoked awhile, resuming our walk only when we were tired of inaction.

For perhaps another hour we wandered onward, chatting quietly and comfortably on this and that matter, and on several occasions stopping while my companion—who is something of an artist—made rough sketches of striking bits of the wild scenery.

And then, without any warning whatsoever, the river we had followed so confidently, came to an abrupt end—vanishing into the earth.

"Good Lord!" I said, "who ever would have thought of this?"

And I stared in amazement; then I turned to Tonnison. He was looking, with a blank expression upon his face, at the place where the river disappeared.

In a moment he spoke.

"Let us go on a bit; it may reappear again—anyhow, it is worth investigating."

I agreed, and we went forward once more, though rather aimlessly; for we were not at all certain in which direction to prosecute our search. For perhaps a mile we moved onward; then Tonnison, who had been gazing about curiously, stopped and shaded his eyes.

"See!" he said, after a moment, "isn't that mist or something, over there to the right—away in a line with that great piece of rock?" And he indicated with his hand.

I stared, and, after a minute, seemed to see something, but could not be certain, and said so.

"Anyway," my friend replied, "we'll just go across and have a glance." And he started off in the direction he had suggested, I following. Presently, we came among bushes, and, after a time, out upon the top of a high, boulder-strewn bank, from which we looked down into a wilderness of bushes and trees.

"Seems as though we had come upon an oasis in this desert of stone," muttered Tonnison, as he gazed interestedly. Then he was silent, his eyes fixed; and I looked also; for up from somewhere about the center of the wooded lowland there rose high into the quiet air a great column of hazelike spray, upon which the sun shone, causing innumerable rainbows.

"How beautiful!" I exclaimed.

"Yes," answered Tonnison, thoughtfully. "There must be a waterfall, or something, over there. Perhaps it's our river come to light again. Let's go and see."

Down the sloping bank we made our way, and entered among the trees and shrubberies. The bushes were matted, and the trees overhung us, so that the place was disagreeably gloomy; though not dark enough to hide from me the fact that many of the trees were fruit trees, and that, here and there, one could trace indistinctly, signs of a long departed cultivation. Thus it came to me that we were making our way through the riot of a great and ancient garden. I said as much to Tonnison, and he agreed that there certainly seemed reasonable grounds for my belief.

What a wild place it was, so dismal and somber! Somehow, as we went forward, a sense of the silent loneliness and desertion of the old garden grew upon me, and I felt shivery. One could imagine things lurking among the tangled bushes; while, in the very air of the place, there seemed something uncanny. I think Tonnison was conscious of this also, though he said nothing.

Suddenly, we came to a halt. Through the trees there had grown upon our ears a distant sound. Tonnison bent forward, listening. I could hear it more plainly now; it was continuous and harsh—a sort of droning roar, seeming to come from far away. I experienced a queer, indescribable, little feeling of nervousness. What sort of place was it into which we had got? I looked at my companion, to see what he thought of the matter; and noted that there was only puzzlement in his face; and then, as I watched his features, an expression of comprehension crept over them, and he nodded his head.

"That's a waterfall," he exclaimed, with conviction. "I know the sound now." And he began to push vigorously through the bushes, in the direction of the noise.

As we went forward, the sound became plainer continually, showing that we were heading straight toward it. Steadily, the roaring grew louder and nearer, until it appeared, as I remarked to Tonnison, almost to come from under our feet —and still we were surrounded by the trees and shrubs.

"Take care!" Tonnison called to me. "Look where you're going." And then, suddenly, we came out from among the trees, on to a great open space, where, not six paces in front of us, yawned the mouth of a tremendous chasm, from the depths of which the noise appeared to rise, along with the continuous, mistlike spray that we had witnessed from the top of the distant bank.

For quite a minute we stood in silence, staring in bewilderment at the sight; then my friend went forward cautiously to the edge of the abyss. I followed, and, together, we looked down through a boil of spray at a monster cataract of frothing water that burst, spouting, from the side of the chasm, nearly a hundred feet below.

"Good Lord!" said Tonnison.

I was silent, and rather awed. The sight was so unexpectedly grand and eerie; though this latter quality came more upon me later.

Presently, I looked up and across to the further side of the chasm. There, I saw something towering up among the spray: it looked like a fragment of a great ruin, and I touched Tonnison on the shoulder. He glanced 'round, with a start, and I pointed toward the thing. His gaze followed my finger, and his eyes lighted up with a sudden flash of excitement, as the object came within his field of view.

"Come along," he shouted above the uproar. "We'll have a look at it. There's something queer about this place; I feel it in my bones." And he started off, 'round the edge of the craterlike abyss. As we neared this new thing, I saw that I had not been mistaken in my first impression. It was undoubtedly a portion of some ruined building; yet now I made out that it was not built upon the edge of the chasm itself, as I had at first supposed; but perched almost at the extreme end of a huge spur of rock that jutted out some fifty or sixty feet over the abyss. In fact, the jagged mass of ruin was literally suspended in midair.

Arriving opposite it, we walked out on to the projecting arm of rock, and I must confess to having felt an intolerable sense of terror as I looked down from that dizzy perch into the unknown depths below us—into the deeps from which there rose ever the thunder of the falling water and the shroud of rising spray.

Reaching the ruin, we clambered 'round it cautiously, and, on the further side, came upon a mass of fallen stones and rubble. The ruin itself seemed to me, as I proceeded now to examine it minutely, to be a portion of the outer wall of some prodigious structure, it was so thick and substantially built; yet what it was doing in such a position I could by no means conjecture. Where was the rest of the house, or castle, or whatever there had been?

I went back to the outer side of the wall, and thence to the edge of the chasm, leaving Tonnison rooting systematically among the heap of stones and rubbish on the outer side. Then I commenced to examine the surface of the ground, near the edge of the abyss, to see whether there were not left other remnants of the building to which the fragment of ruin evidently belonged. But though I scrutinized the earth with the greatest care, I could see no signs of anything to show that there had ever been a building erected on the spot, and I grew more puzzled than ever.

Then, I heard a cry from Tonnison; he was shouting my name, excitedly, and without delay I hurried along the rocky promontory to the ruin. I wondered whether he had hurt himself, and then the thought came, that perhaps he had found something.

I reached the crumbled wall and climbed 'round. There I found Tonnison standing within a small excavation that he had made among the *débris*: he was brushing the dirt from something that looked like a book, much crumpled and dilapidated; and opening his mouth, every second or two, to bellow my name. As soon as he saw that I had come, he handed his prize to me, telling me to put it into my satchel so as to protect it from the damp, while he continued his explorations. This I did, first, however, running the pages through my fingers, and noting that they were closely filled with neat, old-fashioned writing which was quite legible, save in one portion, where many of the pages were almost destroyed, being muddied and crumpled, as though the book had been doubled back at that part. This, I found out from Tonnison, was actually as he had discovered it, and the damage was due, probably, to the fall of masonry upon the opened part. Curiously enough, the book was fairly dry, which I attributed to its having been so securely buried among the ruins.

Having put the volume away safely, I turned-to and gave Tonnison a hand with his self-imposed task of excavating; yet, though we put in over an hour's hard work, turning over the whole of the upheaped stones and rubbish, we came upon nothing more than some fragments of broken wood, that might have been parts of a desk or table; and so we gave up searching, and went back along the rock, once more to the safety of the land.

The next thing we did was to make a complete tour of the tremendous chasm, which we were able to observe was in the form of an almost perfect circle, save for where the ruin-crowned spur of rock jutted out, spoiling its symmetry.

The abyss was, as Tonnison put it, like nothing so much as a gigantic well or pit going sheer down into the bowels of the earth.

For some time longer, we continued to stare about us, and then, noticing that there was a clear space away to the north of the chasm, we bent our steps in that direction.

Here, distant from the mouth of the mighty pit by some hundreds of yards, we came upon a great lake of silent water—silent, that is, save in one place where there was a continuous bubbling and gurgling.

Now, being away from the noise of the spouting cataract, we were able to hear one another speak, without having to shout at the tops of our voices, and I asked Tonnison what he thought of the place—I told him that I didn't like it, and that the sooner we were out of it the better I should be pleased.

He nodded in reply, and glanced at the woods behind furtively. I asked him if he had seen or heard anything. He made no answer; but stood silent, as though listening, and I kept quiet also.

Suddenly, he spoke.

"Hark!" he said, sharply. I looked at him, and then away among the trees and bushes, holding my breath involuntarily. A minute came and went in strained silence; yet I could hear nothing, and I turned to Tonnison to say as much; and then, even as I opened my lips to speak, there came a strange wailing noise out of the wood on our left... It appeared to float through the trees, and there was a rustle of stirring leaves, and then silence.

All at once, Tonnison spoke, and put his hand on my shoulder. "Let us get out of here," he said, and began to move slowly toward where the surrounding trees and bushes seemed thinnest. As I followed him, it came to me suddenly that the sun was low, and that there was a raw sense of chilliness in the air.

Tonnison said nothing further, but kept on steadily. We were among the trees now, and I glanced around, nervously; but saw nothing, save the quiet branches and trunks and the tangled bushes. Onward we went, and no sound broke the silence, except the occasional snapping of a twig under our feet, as we moved forward. Yet, in spite of the quietness, I had a horrible feeling that we were not alone; and I kept so close to Tonnison that twice I kicked his heels clumsily, though he said nothing. A minute, and then another, and we reached the confines of the wood coming out at last upon the bare rockiness of the countryside. Only then was I able to shake off the haunting dread that had followed me among the trees.

Once, as we moved away, there seemed to come again a distant sound of wailing, and I said to myself that it was the wind—yet the evening was breathless.

Presently, Tonnison began to talk.

"Look you," he said with decision, "I would not spend the night in *that* place for all the wealth that the world holds. There is something unholy—diabolical—about it. It came to me all in a moment, just after you spoke. It seemed to me that the woods were full of vile things—you know!"

"Yes," I answered, and looked back toward the place; but it was hidden from us by a rise in the ground.

"There's the book," I said, and I put my hand into the satchel.

"You've got it safely?" he questioned, with a sudden access of anxiety.

"Yes," I replied.

"Perhaps," he continued, "we shall learn something from it when we get back to the tent. We had better hurry, too; we're a long way off still, and I don't fancy, now, being caught out here in the dark."

It was two hours later when we reached the tent; and, without delay, we set to work to prepare a meal; for we had eaten nothing since our lunch at midday.

Supper over, we cleared the things out of the way, and lit our pipes. Then Tonnison asked me to get the manuscript out of my satchel. This I did, and then, as we could not both read from it at the same time, he suggested that I should read the thing out loud. "And mind," he cautioned, knowing my propensities, "don't go skipping half the book."

Yet, had he but known what it contained, he would have realized how needless such advice was, for once at least. And there seated in the opening of our little tent, I began the strange tale of *The House on the Borderland* (for such was the title of the MS.); this is told in the following pages.

II.
The Plain of Silence

I am an old man. I live here in this ancient house, surrounded by huge, unkempt gardens.

The peasantry, who inhabit the wilderness beyond, say that I am mad. That is because I will have nothing to do with them. I live here alone with my old sister, who is also my housekeeper. We keep no servants—I hate them. I have one friend, a dog; yes, I would sooner have old Pepper than the rest of Creation together. He, at least, understands me—and has sense enough to leave me alone when I am in my dark moods.

I have decided to start a kind of diary; it may enable me to record some of the thoughts and feelings that I cannot express to anyone; but, beyond this, I am anxious to make some record of the strange things that I have heard and seen, during many years of loneliness, in this weird old building.

For a couple of centuries, this house has had a reputation, a bad one, and, until I bought it, for more than eighty years no one had lived here; consequently, I got the old place at a ridiculously low figure.

I am not superstitious; but I have ceased to deny that things happen in this old house—things that I cannot explain; and, therefore, I must needs ease my mind, by writing down an account of them, to the best of my ability; though, should this, my diary, ever be read when I am gone, the readers will but shake their heads, and be the more convinced that I was mad.

This house, how ancient it is! though its age strikes one less, perhaps, than the quaintness of its structure, which is curious and fantastic to the last degree. Little curved towers and pinnacles, with outlines suggestive of leaping flames, predominate; while the body of the building is in the form of a circle.

I have heard that there is an old story, told amongst the country people, to the effect that the devil built the place. However, that is as may be. True or not, I neither know nor care, save as it may have helped to cheapen it, ere I came.

I must have been here some ten years before I saw sufficient to warrant any belief in the stories, current in the neighborhood, about this house. It is true that I had, on at least a dozen occasions, seen, vaguely, things that puzzled me, and, perhaps, had felt more than I had seen. Then, as the years passed, bringing age upon me, I became often aware of something unseen, yet unmistakably present, in the empty rooms and corridors. Still, it was as I have said many years before I saw any real manifestations of the so-called supernatural.

It was not Halloween. If I were telling a story for amusement's sake, I should probably place it on that night of nights; but this is a true record of my own experiences, and I would not put pen to paper to amuse anyone. No. It was after midnight on the morning of the twenty-first day of January. I was sitting reading, as is often my custom, in my study. Pepper lay, sleeping, near my chair.

Without warning, the flames of the two candles went low, and then shone with a ghastly green effulgence. I looked up, quickly, and as I did so I saw the lights sink into a dull, ruddy tint; so that the room glowed with a strange, heavy, crimson twilight that gave the shadows behind the chairs and tables a double depth of blackness; and wherever the light struck, it was as though luminous blood had been splashed over the room.

Down on the floor, I heard a faint, frightened whimper, and something pressed itself in between my two feet. It was Pepper, cowering under my dressing gown. Pepper, usually as brave as a lion!

It was this movement of the dog's, I think, that gave me the first twinge of *real* fear. I had been considerably startled when the lights burnt first green and then red; but had been momentarily under the impression that the change was due to some influx of noxious gas into the room. Now, however, I saw that it was not so; for the candles burned with a steady flame, and showed no signs of going out, as would have been the case had the change been due to fumes in the atmosphere.

I did not move. I felt distinctly frightened; but could think of nothing better to do than wait. For perhaps a minute, I kept my glance about the room, nervously. Then I noticed that the lights had commenced to sink, very slowly; until presently they showed minute specks of red fire, like the gleamings of rubies in the darkness. Still, I sat watching; while a sort of dreamy indifference seemed to steal over me; banishing altogether the fear that had begun to grip me.

Away in the far end of the huge old-fashioned room, I became conscious of a faint glow. Steadily it grew, filling the room with gleams of quivering green light; then they sank quickly, and changed—even as the candle flames had done—into a deep, somber crimson that strengthened, and lit up the room with a flood of awful glory.

The light came from the end wall, and grew ever brighter until its intolerable glare caused my eyes acute pain, and involuntarily I closed them. It may have been a few seconds before I was able to open them. The first thing I noticed was that the light had decreased, greatly; so that it no longer tried my eyes. Then, as it grew still duller, I was aware, all at once, that, instead of looking at the redness, I was staring through it, and through the wall beyond.

Gradually, as I became more accustomed to the idea, I realized that I was looking out on to a vast plain, lit with the same gloomy twilight that pervaded the room. The immensity of this plain scarcely can be conceived. In no part could I perceive its confines. It seemed to broaden and spread out, so that the eye failed to perceive any limitations. Slowly, the details of the nearer portions began to grow clear; then, in a moment almost, the light died away, and the vision—if vision it were—faded and was gone.

Suddenly, I became conscious that I was no longer in the chair. Instead, I seemed to be hovering above it, and looking down at a dim something, huddled and silent. In a little while, a cold blast struck me, and I was outside in the night, floating, like a bubble, up through the darkness. As I moved, an icy coldness seemed to enfold me, so that I shivered.

After a time, I looked to right and left, and saw the intolerable blackness of the night, pierced by remote gleams of fire. Onward, outward, I drove. Once, I glanced behind, and saw the earth, a small crescent of blue light, receding away to my left. Further off, the sun, a splash of white flame, burned vividly against the dark.

An indefinite period passed. Then, for the last time, I saw the earth—an enduring globule of radiant blue, swimming in an eternity of ether. And there I, a fragile flake of soul dust, flickered silently across the void, from the distant blue, into the expanse of the unknown.

A great while seemed to pass over me, and now I could nowhere see anything. I had passed beyond the fixed stars and plunged into the huge blackness that waits beyond. All this time I had experienced little, save a sense of lightness and cold discomfort. Now however the atrocious darkness seemed to creep into my soul, and I became filled with fear and despair. What was going to become of me? Where was I going? Even as the thoughts were formed, there grew against the impalpable blackness that wrapped me a faint tinge of blood. It seemed extraordinarily remote, and mistlike; yet, at once, the feeling of oppression was lightened, and I no longer despaired.

Slowly, the distant redness became plainer and larger; until, as I drew nearer, it spread out into a great, somber glare—dull and tremendous. Still, I fled onward, and, presently, I had come so close, that it seemed to stretch beneath me, like a great ocean of somber red. I could see little, save that it appeared to spread out interminably in all directions.

In a further space, I found that I was descending upon it; and, soon, I sank into a great sea of sullen, red-hued clouds. Slowly, I emerged from these, and there, below me, I saw the stupendous plain that I had seen from my room in this house that stands upon the borders of the Silences.

Presently, I landed, and stood, surrounded by a great waste of loneliness. The place was lit with a gloomy twilight that gave an impression of indescribable desolation.

Afar to my right, within the sky, there burnt a gigantic ring of dull-red fire, from the outer edge of which were projected huge, writhing flames, darted and jagged. The interior of this ring was black, black as the gloom of the outer night. I comprehended, at once, that it was from this extraordinary sun that the place derived its doleful light.

From that strange source of light, I glanced down again to my surroundings. Everywhere I looked, I saw nothing but the same flat weariness of interminable plain. Nowhere could I descry any signs of life; not even the ruins of some ancient habitation.

Gradually, I found that I was being borne forward, floating across the flat waste. For what seemed an eternity, I moved onward. I was unaware of any great sense of impatience; though some curiosity and a vast wonder were with me continually. Always, I saw around me the breadth of that enormous plain; and, always, I searched for some new thing to break its monotony; but there was no change—only loneliness, silence, and desert.

Presently, in a half-conscious manner, I noticed that there was a faint mistiness, ruddy in hue, lying over its surface. Still, when I looked more intently, I was unable to say that it was really mist; for it appeared to blend with the plain, giving it a peculiar unrealness, and conveying to the senses the idea of unsubstantiality.

Gradually, I began to weary with the sameness of the thing. Yet, it was a great time before I perceived any signs of the place, toward which I was being conveyed.

"At first, I saw it, far ahead, like a long hillock on the surface of the Plain. Then, as I drew nearer, I perceived that I had been mistaken; for, instead of a low hill, I made out, now, a chain of great mountains, whose distant peaks towered up into the red gloom, until they were almost lost to sight."

III.
The House in the Arena

And so, after a time, I came to the mountains. Then, the course of my journey was altered, and I began to move along their bases, until, all at once, I saw that I had come opposite to a vast rift, opening into the mountains. Through this, I was borne, moving at no great speed. On either side of me, huge, scarped walls of rocklike substance rose sheer. Far overhead, I discerned a thin ribbon of red, where the mouth of the chasm opened, among inaccessible peaks. Within, was gloom, deep and somber, and chilly silence. For a while, I went onward steadily, and then, at last, I saw, ahead, a deep, red glow, that told me I was near upon the further opening of the gorge.

A minute came and went, and I was at the exit of the chasm, staring out upon an enormous amphitheater of mountains. Yet, of the mountains, and the terrible grandeur of the place, I recked nothing; for I was confounded with amazement to behold, at a distance of several miles and occupying the center of the arena, a stupendous structure built apparently of green jade. Yet, in itself, it was not the discovery of the building that had so astonished me; but the fact, which became every moment more apparent, that in no particular, save in color and its enormous size, did the lonely structure vary from this house in which I live.

For a while, I continued to stare, fixedly. Even then, I could scarcely believe that I saw aright. In my mind, a question formed, reiterating incessantly: "What does it mean?" "What does it mean?" and I was unable to make answer, even out of the depths of my imagination. I seemed capable only of wonder and fear. For a time longer, I gazed, noting continually some fresh point of resemblance that attracted me. At last, wearied and sorely puzzled, I turned from it, to view the rest of the strange place on to which I had intruded.

Hitherto, I had been so engrossed in my scrutiny of the House, that I had given only a cursory glance 'round. Now, as I looked, I began to realize upon what sort of a place I had come. The arena, for so I have termed it, appeared a perfect circle of about ten to twelve miles in diameter, the House, as I have mentioned before, standing in the center. The surface of the place, like to that of the Plain, had a peculiar, misty appearance, that was yet not mist.

From a rapid survey, my glance passed quickly upward along the slopes of the circling mountains. How silent they were. I think that this same abominable stillness was more trying to me than anything that I had so far seen or imagined.

I was looking up, now, at the great crags, towering so loftily. Up there, the impalpable redness gave a blurred appearance to everything.

And then, as I peered, curiously, a new terror came to me; for away up among the dim peaks to my right, I had descried a vast shape of blackness, giantlike. It grew upon my sight. It had an enormous equine head, with gigantic ears, and seemed to peer steadfastly down into the arena. There was that about the pose that gave me the impression of an eternal watchfulness—of having warded that dismal place, through unknown eternities. Slowly, the monster became plainer to me; and then, suddenly, my gaze sprang from it to something further off and higher among the crags. For a long minute, I gazed, fearfully. I was strangely conscious of something not altogether unfamiliar—as though something stirred in the back of my mind. The thing was black, and had four grotesque arms. The features showed indistinctly, 'round the neck, I made out several light-colored objects. Slowly, the details came to me, and I realized, coldly, that they were skulls. Further down the body was another circling belt, showing less dark against the black trunk. Then, even as I puzzled to know what the thing was, a memory slid into my mind, and straightway, I knew that I was looking at a monstrous representation of Kali, the Hindu goddess of death.

Other remembrances of my old student days drifted into my thoughts. My glance fell back upon the huge beast-headed Thing. Simultaneously, I recognized it for the ancient Egyptian god Set, or Seth, the Destroyer of Souls. With the knowledge, there came a great sweep of questioning—"Two of the—!" I stopped, and endeavored to think. Things beyond my imagination peered into my frightened mind. I saw, obscurely. "The old gods of mythology!" I tried to comprehend to what it was all pointing. My gaze dwelt, flickeringly, between the two. "If—"

An idea came swiftly, and I turned, and glanced rapidly upward, searching the gloomy crags, away to my left. Something loomed out under a great peak, a shape of greyness. I wondered I had not seen it earlier, and then remembered I had not yet viewed that portion. I saw it more plainly now. It was, as I have said, grey. It had a tremendous head; but no eyes. That part of its face was blank.

Now, I saw that there were other things up among the mountains. Further off, reclining on a lofty ledge, I made out a livid mass, irregular and ghoulish. It seemed without form, save for an unclean, half-animal face, that looked out, vilely, from somewhere about its middle. And then I saw others—there were hundreds of them. They seemed to grow out of the shadows. Several I recognized almost immediately as mythological deities; others were strange to me, utterly strange, beyond the power of a human mind to conceive.

On each side, I looked, and saw more, continually. The mountains were full of strange things—Beast-gods, and Horrors so atrocious and bestial that possibility and decency deny any further attempt to describe them. And I—I was filled with a terrible sense of overwhelming horror and fear and repugnance; yet, spite of these, I wondered exceedingly. Was there then, after all, something in the old heathen worship, something more than the mere deifying of men, animals, and elements? The thought gripped me—was there?

Later, a question repeated itself. What were they, those Beast-gods, and the others? At first, they had appeared to me just sculptured Monsters placed indiscriminately among the inaccessible peaks and precipices of the surrounding mountains. Now, as I scrutinized them with greater intentness, my mind began to reach out to fresh conclusions. There was something about them, an indescribable sort of silent vitality that suggested, to my broadening consciousness, a state of life-in-death—a something that was by no means life, as we understand it; but rather an inhuman form of existence, that well might be likened to a deathless trance—a condition in which it was possible to imagine their continuing, eternally. "Immortal!" the word rose in my thoughts unbidden; and, straightway, I grew to wondering whether this might be the immortality of the gods.

And then, in the midst of my wondering and musing, something happened. Until then, I had been staying just within the shadow of the exit of the great rift. Now, without volition on my part, I drifted out of the semi-darkness and began to move slowly across the arena—toward the House. At this, I gave up all thoughts of those prodigious Shapes above me—and could only stare, frightenedly, at the tremendous structure toward which I was being conveyed so remorselessly. Yet, though I searched earnestly, I could discover nothing that I had not already seen, and so became gradually calmer.

Presently, I had reached a point more than halfway between the House and the gorge. All around was spread the stark loneliness of the place, and the unbroken silence. Steadily, I neared the great building. Then, all at once, something caught my vision, something that came 'round one of the huge buttresses of the House, and so into full view. It was a gigantic thing, and moved with a curious lope, going almost upright, after the manner of a man. It was quite unclothed, and had a remarkable luminous appearance. Yet it was the face that attracted and frightened me the most. It was the face of a swine.

Silently, intently, I watched this horrible creature, and forgot my fear, momentarily, in my interest in its movements. It was making its way, cumbrously 'round the building, stopping as it came to each window to peer in and shake at the bars, with which—as in this house—they were protected; and whenever it came to a door, it would push at it, fingering the fastening stealthily. Evidently, it was searching for an ingress into the House.

I had come now to within less than a quarter of a mile of the great structure, and still I was compelled forward. Abruptly, the Thing turned and gazed hideously in my direction. It opened its mouth, and, for the first time, the stillness of that abominable place was broken, by a deep, booming note that sent an added thrill of apprehension through me. Then, immediately, I became aware that it was coming toward me, swiftly and silently. In an instant, it had covered half the distance that lay between. And still, I was borne helplessly to meet it. Only a hundred yards, and the brutish ferocity of the giant face numbed me with a feeling of unmitigated horror. I could have screamed, in the supremeness of my fear; and then, in the very moment of my extremity and despair, I became conscious that I was looking down upon the arena, from a rapidly increasing height. I was rising, rising. In an inconceivably short while, I had reached an altitude of many hundred feet. Beneath me, the spot that I had just left, was occupied by the foul Swine-creature. It had gone down on all fours and was snuffing and rooting, like a veritable hog, at the surface of the arena. A moment and it rose to its feet, clutching upward, with an expression of desire upon its face such as I have never seen in this world.

Continually, I mounted higher. A few minutes, it seemed, and I had risen above the great mountains—floating, alone, afar in the redness. At a tremendous distance below, the arena showed, dimly; with the mighty House looking no larger than a tiny spot of green. The Swine-thing was no longer visible.

Presently, I passed over the mountains, out above the huge breadth of the plain. Far away, on its surface, in the direction of the ring-shaped sun, there showed a confused blur. I looked toward it, indifferently. It reminded me, somewhat, of the first glimpse I had caught of the mountain-amphitheater.

With a sense of weariness, I glanced upward at the immense ring of fire. What a strange thing it was! Then, as I stared, out from the dark center, there spurted a sudden flare of extraordinary vivid fire. Compared with the size of the black center, it was as naught; yet, in itself, stupendous. With awakened interest, I watched it carefully, noting its strange boiling and glowing. Then, in a moment, the whole thing grew dim and unreal, and so passed out of sight. Much amazed, I glanced down to the Plain from which I was still rising. Thus, I received a fresh surprise. The Plain—everything had vanished, and only a sea of red mist was spread far below me. Gradually as I stared this grew remote, and died away into a dim far mystery of red against an unfathomable night. A while, and even this had gone, and I was wrapped in an impalpable, lightless gloom.

IV.
The Earth

Thus I was, and only the memory that I had lived through the dark, once before, served to sustain my thoughts. A great time passed—ages. And then a single star broke its way through the darkness. It was the first of one of the outlying clusters of this universe. Presently, it was far behind, and all about me shone the splendor of the countless stars. Later, years it seemed, I saw the sun, a clot of flame. Around it, I made out presently several remote specks of light—the planets of the Solar system. And so I saw the earth again, blue and unbelievably minute. It grew larger, and became defined.

A long space of time came and went, and then at last I entered into the shadow of the world—plunging headlong into the dim and holy earth night. Overhead were the old constellations, and there was a crescent moon. Then, as I neared the earth's surface, a dimness swept over me, and I appeared to sink into a black mist.

For a while, I knew nothing. I was unconscious. Gradually, I became aware of a faint, distant whining. It became plainer. A desperate feeling of agony possessed me. I struggled madly for breath, and tried to shout. A moment, and I got my breath more easily. I was conscious that something was licking my hand. Something damp swept across my face. I heard a panting, and then again the whining. It seemed to come to my ears, now, with a sense of familiarity, and I opened my eyes. All was dark; but the feeling of oppression had left me. I was seated, and something was whining piteously, and licking me. I felt strangely confused, and, instinctively, tried to ward off the thing that licked. My head was curiously vacant, and, for the moment, I seemed incapable of action or thought. Then, things came back to me, and I called 'Pepper,' faintly. I was answered by a joyful bark, and renewed and frantic caresses.

In a little while, I felt stronger, and put out my hand for the matches. I groped about, for a few moments, blindly; then my hands lit upon them, and I struck a light, and looked confusedly around. All about me, I saw the old, familiar things. And there I sat, full of dazed wonders, until the flame of the match burnt my finger, and I dropped it; while a hasty expression of pain and anger, escaped my lips, surprising me with the sound of my own voice.

After a moment, I struck another match, and, stumbling across the room, lit the candles. As I did so, I observed that they had not burned away, but had been put out.

As the flames shot up, I turned, and stared about the study; yet there was nothing unusual to see; and, suddenly, a gust of irritation took me. What had happened? I held my head, with both hands, and tried to remember. Ah! the great, silent Plain, and the ring-shaped sun of red fire. Where were they? Where had I seen them? How long ago? I felt dazed and muddled. Once or twice, I walked up and down the room, unsteadily. My memory seemed dulled, and, already, the thing I had witnessed came back to me with an effort.

I have a remembrance of cursing, peevishly, in my bewilderment. Suddenly, I turned faint and giddy, and had to grasp at the table for support. During a few moments, I held on, weakly; and then managed to totter sideways into a chair. After a little time, I felt somewhat better, and succeeded in reaching the cupboard where, usually, I keep brandy and biscuits. I poured myself out a little of the stimulant, and drank it off. Then, taking a handful of biscuits, I returned to my chair, and began to devour them, ravenously. I was vaguely surprised at my hunger. I felt as though I had eaten nothing for an uncountably long while.

As I ate, my glance roved about the room, taking in its various details, and still searching, though almost unconsciously, for something tangible upon which to take hold, among the invisible mysteries that encompassed me. 'Surely,' I thought, 'there must be something—' And, in the same instant, my gaze dwelt upon the face of the clock in the opposite corner. Therewith, I stopped eating, and just stared. For, though its ticking indicated most certainly that it was still going, the hands were pointing to a little *before* the hour of midnight; whereas it was, as well I knew, considerably *after* that time when I had witnessed the first of the strange happenings I have just described.

For perhaps a moment I was astounded and puzzled. Had the hour been the same as when I had last seen the clock, I should have concluded that the hands had stuck in one place, while the internal mechanism went on as usual; but that would, in no way, account for the hands having traveled backward. Then, even as I turned the matter over in my wearied brain, the thought flashed upon me that it was now close upon the morning of the twenty-second, and that I had been unconscious to the visible world through the greater portion of the last twenty-four hours. The thought occupied my attention for a full minute; then I commenced to eat again. I was still very hungry.

During breakfast, next morning, I inquired casually of my sister regarding the date, and found my surmise correct. I had, indeed, been absent—at least in spirit—for nearly a day and a night.

My sister asked me no questions; for it is not by any means the first time that I have kept to my study for a whole day, and sometimes a couple of days at a time, when I have been particularly engrossed in my books or work.

And so the days pass on, and I am still filled with a wonder to know the meaning of all that I saw on that memorable night. Yet, well I know that my curiosity is little likely to be satisfied.

V.
The Thing in the Pit

This house is, as I have said before, surrounded by a huge estate, and wild and uncultivated gardens.

Away at the back, distant some three hundred yards, is a dark, deep ravine—spoken of as the "Pit," by the peasantry. At the bottom runs a sluggish stream so overhung by trees as scarcely to be seen from above.

In passing, I must explain that this river has a subterranean origin, emerging suddenly at the East end of the ravine, and disappearing, as abruptly, beneath the cliffs that form its Western extremity.

It was some months after my vision (if vision it were) of the great Plain that my attention was particularly attracted to the Pit.

I happened, one day, to be walking along its Southern edge, when, suddenly, several pieces of rock and shale were dislodged from the face of the cliff immediately beneath me, and fell with a sullen crash through the trees. I heard them splash in the river at the bottom; and then silence. I should not have given this incident more than a passing thought, had not Pepper at once begun to bark savagely; nor would he be silent when I bade him, which is most unusual behavior on his part.

Feeling that there must be someone or something in the Pit, I went back to the house, quickly, for a stick. When I returned, Pepper had ceased his barks and was growling and smelling, uneasily, along the top.

Whistling to him to follow me, I started to descend cautiously. The depth to the bottom of the Pit must be about a hundred and fifty feet, and some time as well as considerable care was expended before we reached the bottom in safety.

Once down, Pepper and I started to explore along the banks of the river. It was very dark there due to the overhanging trees, and I moved warily, keeping my glance about me and my stick ready.

Pepper was quiet now and kept close to me all the time. Thus, we searched right up one side of the river, without hearing or seeing anything. Then, we crossed over—by the simple method of jumping—and commenced to beat our way back through the underbrush.

We had accomplished perhaps half the distance, when I heard again the sound of falling stones on the other side—the side from which we had just come. One large rock came thundering down through the treetops, struck the opposite bank, and bounded into the river, driving a great jet of water right over us. At this, Pepper gave out a deep growl; then stopped, and pricked up his ears. I listened, also.

A second later, a loud, half-human, half-piglike squeal sounded from among the trees, apparently about halfway up the South cliff. It was answered by a similar note from the bottom of the Pit. At this, Pepper gave a short, sharp bark, and, springing across the little river, disappeared into the bushes.

Immediately afterward, I heard his barks increase in depth and number, and in between there sounded a noise of confused jabbering. This ceased, and, in the succeeding silence, there rose a semi-human yell of agony. Almost immediately, Pepper gave a long-drawn howl of pain, and then the shrubs were violently agitated, and he came running out with his tail down, and glancing as he ran over his shoulder. As he reached me, I saw that he was bleeding from what appeared to be a great claw wound in the side that had almost laid bare his ribs.

Seeing Pepper thus mutilated, a furious feeling of anger seized me, and, whirling my staff, I sprang across, and into the bushes from which Pepper had emerged. As I forced my way through, I thought I heard a sound of breathing. Next instant, I had burst into a little clear space, just in time to see something, livid white in color, disappear among the bushes on the opposite side. With a shout, I ran toward it; but, though I struck and probed among the bushes with my stick, I neither saw nor heard anything further; and so returned to Pepper. There, after bathing his wound in the river, I bound my wetted handkerchief 'round his body; having done which, we retreated up the ravine and into the daylight again.

On reaching the house, my sister inquired what had happened to Pepper, and I told her he had been fighting with a wildcat, of which I had heard there were several about.

I felt it would be better not to tell her how it had really happened; though, to be sure, I scarcely knew myself; but this I did know, that the thing I had seen run into the bushes was no wildcat. It was much too big, and had, so far as I had observed, a skin like a hog's, only of a dead, unhealthy white color. And then—it had run upright, or nearly so, upon its hind feet, with a motion somewhat resembling that of a human being. This much I had noticed in my brief glimpse, and, truth to tell, I felt a good deal of uneasiness, besides curiosity as I turned the matter over in my mind.

It was in the morning that the above incident had occurred.

Then, it would be after dinner, as I sat reading, that, happening to look up suddenly, I saw something peering in over the window ledge the eyes and ears alone showing.

"A pig, by Jove!" I said, and rose to my feet. Thus, I saw the thing more completely; but it was no pig—God alone knows what it was. It reminded me, vaguely, of the hideous Thing that had haunted the great arena. It had a grotesquely human mouth and jaw; but with no chin of which to speak. The nose was prolonged into a snout; thus it was that with the little eyes and queer ears, gave it such an extraordinarily swinelike appearance. Of forehead there was little, and the whole face was of an unwholesome white color.

For perhaps a minute, I stood looking at the thing with an ever growing feeling of disgust, and some fear. The mouth kept jabbering, inanely, and once emitted a half-swinish grunt. I think it was the eyes that attracted me the most; they seemed to glow, at times, with a horribly human intelligence, and kept flickering away from my face, over the details of the room, as though my stare disturbed it.

It appeared to be supporting itself by two clawlike hands upon the windowsill. These claws, unlike the face, were of a clayey brown hue, and bore an indistinct resemblance to human hands, in that they had four fingers and a thumb; though these were webbed up to the first joint, much as are a duck's. Nails it had also, but so long and powerful that they were more like the talons of an eagle than aught else.

As I have said, before, I felt some fear; though almost of an impersonal kind. I may explain my feeling better by saying that it was more a sensation of abhorrence; such as one might expect to feel, if brought in contact with something superhumanly foul; something unholy—belonging to some hitherto undreamt of state of existence.

I cannot say that I grasped these various details of the brute at the time. I think they seemed to come back to me, afterward, as though imprinted upon my brain. I imagined more than I saw as I looked at the thing, and the material details grew upon me later.

For perhaps a minute I stared at the creature; then as my nerves steadied a little I shook off the vague alarm that held me, and took a step toward the window. Even as I did so, the thing ducked and vanished. I rushed to the door and looked 'round hurriedly; but only the tangled bushes and shrubs met my gaze.

I ran back into the house, and, getting my gun, sallied out to search through the gardens. As I went, I asked myself whether the thing I had just seen was likely to be the same of which I had caught a glimpse in the morning. I inclined to think it was.

I would have taken Pepper with me; but judged it better to give his wound a chance to heal. Besides, if the creature I had just seen was, as I imagined, his antagonist of the morning, it was not likely that he would be of much use.

I began my search, systematically. I was determined, if it were possible, to find and put an end to that swine-thing. This was, at least, a material Horror!

At first, I searched, cautiously; with the thought of Pepper's wound in my mind; but, as the hours passed, and not a sign of anything living, showed in the great, lonely gardens, I became less apprehensive. I felt almost as though I would welcome the sight of it. Anything seemed better than this silence, with the ever-present feeling that the creature might be lurking in every bush I passed. Later, I grew careless of danger, to the extent of plunging right through the bushes, probing with my gun barrel as I went.

At times, I shouted; but only the echoes answered back. I thought thus perhaps to frighten or stir the creature to showing itself; but only succeeded in bringing my sister Mary out, to know what was the matter. I told her, that I had seen the wildcat that had wounded Pepper, and that I was trying to hunt it out of the bushes. She seemed only half satisfied, and went back into the house, with an expression of doubt upon her face. I wondered whether she had seen or guessed anything. For the rest of the afternoon, I prosecuted the search anxiously. I felt that I should be unable to sleep, with that bestial thing haunting the shrubberies, and yet, when evening fell, I had seen nothing. Then, as I turned homeward, I heard a short, unintelligible noise, among the bushes to my right. Instantly, I turned, and, aiming quickly, fired in the direction of the sound. Immediately afterward, I heard something scuttling away among the bushes. It moved rapidly, and in a minute had gone out of hearing. After a few steps I ceased my pursuit, realizing how futile it must be in the fast gathering gloom; and so, with a curious feeling of depression, I entered the house.

That night, after my sister had gone to bed, I went 'round to all the windows and doors on the ground floor; and saw to it that they were securely fastened. This precaution was scarcely necessary as regards the windows, as all of those on the lower storey are strongly barred; but with the doors—of which there are five—it was wisely thought, as not one was locked.

Having secured these, I went to my study, yet, somehow, for once, the place jarred upon me; it seemed so huge and echoey. For some time I tried to read; but at last finding it impossible I carried my book down to the kitchen where a large fire was burning, and sat there.

I dare say, I had read for a couple of hours, when, suddenly, I heard a sound that made me lower my book, and listen, intently. It was a noise of something rubbing and fumbling against the back door. Once the door creaked, loudly; as though force were being applied to it. During those few, short moments, I experienced an indescribable feeling of terror, such as I should have believed impossible. My hands shook; a cold sweat broke out on me, and I shivered violently.

Gradually, I calmed. The stealthy movements outside had ceased.

Then for an hour I sat silent and watchful. All at once the feeling of fear took me again. I felt as I imagine an animal must, under the eye of a snake. Yet now I could hear nothing. Still, there was no doubting that some unexplained influence was at work.

Gradually, imperceptibly almost, something stole on my ear—a sound that resolved itself into a faint murmur. Quickly it developed and grew into a muffled but hideous chorus of bestial shrieks. It appeared to rise from the bowels of the earth.

I heard a thud, and realized in a dull, half comprehending way that I had dropped my book. After that, I just sat; and thus the daylight found me, when it crept wanly in through the barred, high windows of the great kitchen.

With the dawning light, the feeling of stupor and fear left me; and I came more into possession of my senses.

Thereupon I picked up my book, and crept to the door to listen. Not a sound broke the chilly silence. For some minutes I stood there; then, very gradually and cautiously, I drew back the bolt and opening the door peeped out.

My caution was unneeded. Nothing was to be seen, save the grey vista of dreary, tangled bushes and trees, extending to the distant plantation.

With a shiver, I closed the door, and made my way, quietly, up to bed.

VI.
The Swine-Things

It was evening, a week later. My sister sat in the garden, knitting. I was walking up and down, reading. My gun leant up against the wall of the house; for, since the advent of that strange thing in the gardens, I had deemed it wise to take precautions. Yet, through the whole week, there had been nothing to alarm me, either by sight or sound; so that I was able to look back, calmly, to the incident; though still with a sense of unmitigated wonder and curiosity.

I was, as I have just said, walking up and down, and somewhat engrossed in my book. Suddenly, I heard a crash, away in the direction of the Pit. With a quick movement, I turned and saw a tremendous column of dust rising high into the evening air.

My sister had risen to her feet, with a sharp exclamation of surprise and fright.

Telling her to stay where she was, I snatched up my gun, and ran toward the Pit. As I neared it, I heard a dull, rumbling sound, that grew quickly into a roar, split with deeper crashes, and up from the Pit drove a fresh volume of dust.

The noise ceased, though the dust still rose, tumultuously.

I reached the edge, and looked down; but could see nothing save a boil of dust clouds swirling hither and thither. The air was so full of the small particles, that they blinded and choked me; and, finally, I had to run out from the smother, to breathe.

Gradually, the suspended matter sank, and hung in a panoply over the mouth of the Pit.

I could only guess at what had happened.

That there had been a land-slip of some kind, I had little doubt; but the cause was beyond my knowledge; and yet, even then, I had half imaginings; for, already, the thought had come to me, of those falling rocks, and that Thing in the bottom of the Pit; but, in the first minutes of confusion, I failed to reach the natural conclusion, to which the catastrophe pointed.

Slowly, the dust subsided, until, presently, I was able to approach the edge, and look down.

For a while, I peered impotently, trying to see through the reek. At first, it was impossible to make out anything. Then, as I stared, I saw something below, to my left, that moved. I looked intently toward it, and, presently, made out another, and then another—three dim shapes that appeared to be climbing up the side of the Pit. I could see them only indistinctly. Even as I stared and wondered, I heard a rattle of stones, somewhere to my right. I glanced across; but could see nothing. I leant forward, and peered over, and down into the Pit, just beneath where I stood; and saw no further than a hideous, white swine-face, that had risen to within a couple of yards of my feet. Below it, I could make out several others. As the Thing saw me, it gave a sudden, uncouth squeal, which was answered from all parts of the Pit. At that, a gust of horror and fear took me, and, bending down, I discharged my gun right into its face. Straightway, the creature disappeared, with a clatter of loose earth and stones.

There was a momentary silence, to which, probably, I owe my life; for, during it, I heard a quick patter of many feet, and, turning sharply, saw a troop of the creatures coming toward me, at a run. Instantly, I raised my gun and fired at the foremost, who plunged head-long, with a hideous howling. Then, I turned to run. More than halfway from the house to the Pit, I saw my sister—she was coming toward me. I could not see her face, distinctly, as the dusk had fallen; but there was fear in her voice as she called to know why I was shooting.

"Run!" I shouted in reply. "Run for your life!"

Without more ado, she turned and fled—picking up her skirts with both hands. As I followed, I gave a glance behind. The brutes were running on their hind legs—at times dropping on all fours.

I think it must have been the terror in my voice, that spurred Mary to run so; for I feel convinced that she had not, as yet, seen those hell creatures that pursued.

On we went, my sister leading.

Each moment, the nearing sounds of the footsteps, told me that the brutes were gaining on us, rapidly. Fortunately, I am accustomed to live, in some ways, an active life. As it was, the strain of the race was beginning to tell severely upon me.

Ahead, I could see the back door—luckily it was open. I was some half-dozen yards behind Mary, now, and my breath was sobbing in my throat. Then, something touched my shoulder. I wrenched my head 'round, quickly, and saw one of those monstrous, pallid faces close to mine. One of the creatures, having outrun its companions, had almost overtaken me. Even as I turned, it made a fresh grab. With a sudden effort, I sprang to one side, and, swinging my gun by the barrel, brought it crashing down upon the foul creature's head. The Thing dropped, with an almost human groan.

Even this short delay had been nearly sufficient to bring the rest of the brutes down upon me; so that, without an instant's waste of time, I turned and ran for the door.

Reaching it, I burst into the passage; then, turning quickly, slammed and bolted the door, just as the first of the creatures rushed against it, with a sudden shock.

My sister sat, gasping, in a chair. She seemed in a fainting condition; but I had no time then to spend on her. I had to make sure that all the doors were fastened. Fortunately, they were. The one leading from my study into the gardens, was the last to which I went. I had just had time to note that it was secured, when I thought I heard a noise outside. I stood perfectly silent, and listened. Yes! Now I could distinctly hear a sound of whispering, and something slithered over the panels, with a rasping, scratchy noise. Evidently, some of the brutes were feeling with their claw-hands, about the door, to discover whether there were any means of ingress.

That the creatures should so soon have found the door was—to me—a proof of their reasoning capabilities. It assured me that they must not be regarded, by any means, as mere animals. I had felt something of this before, when that first Thing peered in through my window. Then I had applied the term superhuman to it, with an almost instinctive knowledge that the creature was something different from the brute-beast. Something beyond human; yet in no good sense; but rather as something foul and hostile to the *great* and *good* in humanity. In a word, as something intelligent, and yet inhuman. The very thought of the creatures filled me with revulsion.

Now, I bethought me of my sister, and, going to the cupboard, I got out a flask of brandy, and a wine-glass. Taking these, I went down to the kitchen, carrying a lighted candle with me. She was not sitting in the chair, but had fallen out, and was lying upon the floor, face downward.

Very gently, I turned her over, and raised her head somewhat. Then, I poured a little of the brandy between her lips. After a while, she shivered slightly. A little later, she gave several gasps, and opened her eyes. In a dreamy, unrealizing way, she looked at me. Then her eyes closed, slowly, and I gave her a little more of the brandy. For, perhaps a minute longer, she lay silent, breathing quickly. All at once, her eyes opened again, and it seemed to me, as I looked, that the pupils were dilated, as though fear had come with returning consciousness. Then, with a movement so unexpected that I started backward, she sat up. Noticing that she seemed giddy, I put out my hand to steady her. At that, she gave a loud scream, and, scrambling to her feet, ran from the room.

For a moment, I stayed there—kneeling and holding the brandy flask. I was utterly puzzled and astonished.

Could she be afraid of me? But no! Why should she? I could only conclude that her nerves were badly shaken, and that she was temporarily unhinged. Upstairs, I heard a door bang, loudly, and I knew that she had taken refuge in her room. I put the flask down on the table. My attention was distracted by a noise in the direction of the back door. I went toward it, and listened. It appeared to be shaken, as though some of the creatures struggled with it, silently; but it was far too strongly constructed and hung to be easily moved.

Out in the gardens rose a continuous sound. It might have been mistaken, by a casual listener, for the grunting and squealing of a herd of pigs. But, as I stood there, it came to me that there was sense and meaning to all those swinish noises. Gradually, I seemed able to trace a semblance in it to human speech—glutinous and sticky, as though each articulation were made with difficulty: yet, nevertheless, I was becoming convinced that it was no mere medley of sounds; but a rapid interchange of ideas.

By this time, it had grown quite dark in the passages, and from these came all the varied cries and groans of which an old house is so full after nightfall. It is, no doubt, because things are then quieter, and one has more leisure to hear. Also, there may be something in the theory that the sudden change of temperature, at sundown, affects the structure of the house, somewhat—causing it to contract and settle, as it were, for the night. However, this is as may be; but, on that night in particular, I would gladly have been quit of so many eerie noises. It seemed to me, that each crack and creak was the coming of one of those Things along the dark corridors; though I knew in my heart that this could not be, for I had seen, myself, that all the doors were secure.

Gradually, however, these sounds grew on my nerves to such an extent that, were it only to punish my cowardice, I felt I must make the 'round of the basement again, and, if anything were there, face it. And then, I would go up to my study, for I knew sleep was out of the question, with the house surrounded by creatures, half beasts, half something else, and entirely unholy.

Taking the kitchen lamp down from its hook, I made my way from cellar to cellar, and room to room; through pantry and coal-hole—along passages, and into the hundred-and-one little blind alleys and hidden nooks that form the basement of the old house. Then, when I knew I had been in every corner and cranny large enough to conceal aught of any size, I made my way to the stairs.

With my foot on the first step, I paused. It seemed to me, I heard a movement, apparently from the buttery, which is to the left of the staircase. It had been one of the first places I searched, and yet, I felt certain my ears had not deceived me. My nerves were strung now, and, with hardly any hesitation, I stepped up to the door, holding the lamp above my head. In a glance, I saw that the place was empty, save for the heavy, stone slabs, supported by brick pillars; and I was about to leave it, convinced that I had been mistaken; when, in turning, my light was flashed back from two bright spots outside the window, and high up. For a few moments, I stood there, staring. Then they moved—revolving slowly, and throwing out alternate scintillations of green and red; at least, so it appeared to me. I knew then that they were eyes.

Slowly, I traced the shadowy outline of one of the Things. It appeared to be holding on to the bars of the window, and its attitude suggested climbing. I went nearer to the window, and held the light higher. There was no need to be afraid of the creature; the bars were strong, and there was little danger of its being able to move them. And then, suddenly, in spite of the knowledge that the brute could not reach to harm me, I had a return of the horrible sensation of fear, that had assailed me on that night, a week previously. It was the same feeling of helpless, shuddering fright. I realized, dimly, that the creature's eyes were looking into mine with a steady, compelling stare. I tried to turn away; but could not. I seemed, now, to see the window through a mist. Then, I thought other eyes came and peered, and yet others; until a whole galaxy of malignant, staring orbs seemed to hold me in thrall.

My head began to swim, and throb violently. Then, I was aware of a feeling of acute physical pain in my left hand. It grew more severe, and forced, literally forced, my attention. With a tremendous effort, I glanced down; and, with that, the spell that had held me was broken. I realized, then, that I had, in my agitation, unconsciously caught hold of the hot lamp-glass, and burnt my hand, badly. I looked up to the window, again. The misty appearance had gone, and, now, I saw that it was crowded with dozens of bestial faces. With a sudden access of rage, I raised the lamp, and hurled it, full at the window. It struck the glass (smashing a pane), and passed between two of the bars, out into the garden, scattering burning oil as it went. I heard several loud cries of pain, and, as my sight became accustomed to the dark, I discovered that the creatures had left the window.

Pulling myself together, I groped for the door, and, having found it, made my way upstairs, stumbling at each step. I felt dazed, as though I had received a blow on the head. At the same time, my hand smarted badly, and I was full of a nervous, dull rage against those Things.

Reaching my study, I lit the candles. As they burnt up, their rays were reflected from the rack of firearms on the sidewall. At the sight, I remembered that I had there a power, which, as I had proved earlier, seemed as fatal to those monsters as to more ordinary animals; and I determined I would take the offensive.

First of all, I bound up my hand; for the pain was fast becoming intolerable. After that, it seemed easier, and I crossed the room, to the rifle stand. There, I selected a heavy rifle—an old and tried weapon; and, having procured ammunition, I made my way up into one of the small towers, with which the house is crowned.

From there, I found that I could see nothing. The gardens presented a dim blur of shadows—a little blacker, perhaps, where the trees stood. That was all, and I knew that it was useless to shoot down into all that darkness. The only thing to be done, was to wait for the moon to rise; then, I might be able to do a little execution.

In the meantime, I sat still, and kept my ears open. The gardens were comparatively quiet now, and only an occasional grunt or squeal came up to me. I did not like this silence; it made me wonder on what devilry the creatures were bent. Twice, I left the tower, and took a walk through the house; but everything was silent.

Once, I heard a noise, from the direction of the Pit, as though more earth had fallen. Following this, and lasting for some fifteen minutes, there was a commotion among the denizens of the gardens. This died away, and, after that all was again quiet.

About an hour later, the moon's light showed above the distant horizon. From where I sat, I could see it over the trees; but it was not until it rose clear of them, that I could make out any of the details in the gardens below. Even then, I could see none of the brutes; until, happening to crane forward, I saw several of them lying prone, up against the wall of the house. What they were doing, I could not make out. It was, however, a chance too good to be ignored; and, taking aim, I fired at the one directly beneath. There was a shrill scream, and, as the smoke cleared away, I saw that it had turned on its back, and was writhing, feebly. Then, it was quiet. The others had disappeared.

Immediately after this, I heard a loud squeal, in the direction of the Pit. It was answered, a hundred times, from every part of the garden. This gave me some notion of the number of the creatures, and I began to feel that the whole affair was becoming even more serious than I had imagined.

As I sat there, silent and watchful, the thought came to me—Why was all this? What were these Things? What did it mean? Then my thoughts flew back to that vision (though, even now, I doubt whether it was a vision) of the Plain of Silence. What did that mean? I wondered—And that Thing in the arena? Ugh! Lastly, I thought of the house I had seen in that faraway place. That house, so like this in every detail of external structure, that it might have been modeled from it; or this from that. I had never thought of that—

At this moment, there came another long squeal, from the Pit, followed, a second later, by a couple of shorter ones. At once, the garden was filled with answering cries. I stood up, quickly, and looked over the parapet. In the moonlight, it seemed as though the shrubberies were alive. They tossed hither and thither, as though shaken by a strong, irregular wind; while a continuous rustling, and a noise of scampering feet, rose up to me. Several times, I saw the moonlight gleam on running, white figures among the bushes, and, twice, I fired. The second time, my shot was answered by a short squeal of pain.

A minute later, the gardens lay silent. From the Pit, came a deep, hoarse Babel of swine-talk. At times, angry cries smote the air, and they would be answered by multitudinous gruntings. It occurred to me, that they were holding some kind of a council, perhaps to discuss the problem of entering the house. Also, I thought that they seemed much enraged, probably by my successful shots.

It occurred to me, that now would be a good time to make a final survey of our defenses. This, I proceeded to do at once; visiting the whole of the basement again, and examining each of the doors. Luckily, they are all, like the back one, built of solid, iron-studded oak. Then, I went upstairs to the study. I was more anxious about this door. It is, palpably, of a more modern make than the others, and, though a stout piece of work, it has little of their ponderous strength.

I must explain here, that there is a small, raised lawn on this side of the house, upon which this door opens—the windows of the study being barred on this account. All the other entrances—excepting the great gateway which is never opened—are in the lower storey.

VII.
The Attack

I spent some time, puzzling how to strengthen the study door. Finally, I went down to the kitchen, and with some trouble, brought up several heavy pieces of timber. These, I wedged up, slantwise, against it, from the floor, nailing them top and bottom. For half an hour, I worked hard, and, at last, got it shored to my mind.

Then, feeling easier, I resumed my coat, which I had laid aside, and proceeded to attend to one or two matters before returning to the tower. It was whilst thus employed, that I heard a fumbling at the door, and the latch was tried. Keeping silence, I waited. Soon, I heard several of the creatures outside. They were grunting to one another, softly. Then, for a minute, there was quietness. Suddenly, there sounded a quick, low grunt, and the door creaked under a tremendous pressure. It would have burst inward; but for the supports I had placed. The strain ceased, as quickly as it had begun, and there was more talk.

Presently, one of the Things squealed, softly, and I heard the sound of others approaching. There was a short confabulation; then again, silence; and I realized that they had called several more to assist. Feeling that now was the supreme moment, I stood ready, with my rifle presented. If the door gave, I would, at least, slay as many as possible.

Again came the low signal; and, once more, the door cracked, under a huge force. For, a minute perhaps, the pressure was kept up; and I waited, nervously; expecting each moment to see the door come down with a crash. But no; the struts held, and the attempt proved abortive. Then followed more of their horrible, grunting talk, and, whilst it lasted, I thought I distinguished the noise of fresh arrivals.

After a long discussion, during which the door was several times shaken, they became quiet once more, and I knew that they were going to make a third attempt to break it down. I was almost in despair. The props had been severely tried in the two previous attacks, and I was sorely afraid that this would prove too much for them.

At that moment, like an inspiration, a thought flashed into my troubled brain. Instantly, for it was no time to hesitate, I ran from the room, and up stair after stair. This time, it was not to one of the towers, that I went; but out on to the flat, leaded roof itself. Once there, I raced across to the parapet, that walls it 'round, and looked down. As I did so, I heard the short, grunted signal, and, even up there, caught the crying of the door under the assault.

There was not a moment to lose, and, leaning over, I aimed, quickly, and fired. The report rang sharply, and, almost blending with it, came the loud splud of the bullet striking its mark. From below, rose a shrill wail; and the door ceased its groaning. Then, as I took my weight from off the parapet, a huge piece of the stone coping slid from under me, and fell with a crash among the disorganized throng beneath. Several horrible shrieks quavered through the night air, and then I heard a sound of scampering feet. Cautiously, I looked over. In the moonlight, I could see the great copingstone, lying right across the threshold of the door. I thought I saw something under it—several things, white; but I could not be sure.

And so a few minutes passed.

As I stared, I saw something come 'round, out of the shadow of the house. It was one of the Things. It went up to the stone, silently, and bent down. I was unable to see what it did. In a minute it stood up. It had something in its talons, which it put to its mouth and tore at…

For the moment, I did not realize. Then, slowly, I comprehended. The Thing was stooping again. It was horrible. I started to load my rifle. When I looked again, the monster was tugging at the stone—moving it to one side. I leant the rifle on the coping, and pulled the trigger. The brute collapsed, on its face, and kicked, slightly.

Simultaneously, almost, with the report, I heard another sound—that of breaking glass. Waiting, only to recharge my weapon, I ran from the roof, and down the first two flights of stairs.

Here, I paused to listen. As I did so, there came another tinkle of falling glass. It appeared to come from the floor below. Excitedly, I sprang down the steps, and, guided by the rattle of the window-sash, reached the door of one of the empty bedrooms, at the back of the house. I thrust it open. The room was but dimly illuminated by the moonlight; most of the light being blotted out by moving figures at the window. Even as I stood, one crawled through, into the room. Leveling my weapon, I fired point-blank at it—filling the room with a deafening bang. When the smoke cleared, I saw that the room was empty, and the window free. The room was much lighter. The night air blew in, coldly, through the shattered panes. Down below, in the night, I could hear a soft moaning, and a confused murmur of swine-voices.

Stepping to one side of the window, I reloaded, and then stood there, waiting. Presently, I heard a scuffling noise. From where I stood in the shadow, I could see, without being seen.

Nearer came the sounds, and then I saw something come up above the sill, and clutch at the broken window-frame. It caught a piece of the woodwork; and, now, I could make out that it was a hand and arm. A moment later, the face of one of the Swine-creatures rose into view. Then, before I could use my rifle, or do anything, there came a sharp crack—cr-ac-k; and the window-frame gave way under the weight of the Thing. Next instant, a squashing thud, and a loud outcry, told me that it had fallen to the ground. With a savage hope that it had been killed, I went to the window. The moon had gone behind a cloud, so that I could see nothing; though a steady hum of jabbering, just beneath where I stood, indicated that there were several more of the brutes close at hand.

As I stood there, looking down, I marveled how it had been possible for the creatures to climb so far; for the wall is comparatively smooth, while the distance to the ground must be, at least, eighty feet.

All at once, as I bent, peering, I saw something, indistinctly, that cut the grey shadow of the house-side, with a black line. It passed the window, to the left, at a distance of about two feet. Then, I remembered that it was a gutter-pipe, that had been put there some years ago, to carry off the rainwater. I had forgotten about it. I could see, now, how the creatures had managed to reach the window. Even as the solution came to me, I heard a faint slithering, scratching noise, and knew that another of the brutes was coming. I waited some odd moments; then leant out of the window and felt the pipe. To my delight, I found that it was quite loose, and I managed, using the rifle-barrel as a crowbar, to lever it out from the wall. I worked quickly. Then, taking hold with both bands, I wrenched the whole concern away, and hurled it down—with the Thing still clinging to it—into the garden.

For a few minutes longer, I waited there, listening; but, after the first general outcry, I heard nothing. I knew, now, that there was no more reason to fear an attack from this quarter. I had removed the only means of reaching the window, and, as none of the other windows had any adjacent water pipes, to tempt the climbing powers of the monsters, I began to feel more confident of escaping their clutches.

Leaving the room, I made my way down to the study. I was anxious to see how the door had withstood the test of that last assault. Entering, I lit two of the candles, and then turned to the door. One of the large props had been displaced, and, on that side, the door had been forced inward some six inches.

It was Providential that I had managed to drive the brutes away just when I did! And that copingstone! I wondered, vaguely, how I had managed to dislodge it. I had not noticed it loose, as I took my shot; and then, as I stood up, it had slipped away from beneath me ... I felt that I owed the dismissal of the attacking force, more to its timely fall than to my rifle. Then the thought came, that I had better seize this chance to shore up the door, again. It was evident that the creatures had not returned since the fall of the copingstone; but who was to say how long they would keep away?

There and then, I set-to, at repairing the door—working hard and anxiously. First, I went down to the basement, and, rummaging 'round, found several pieces of heavy oak planking. With these, I returned to the study, and, having removed the props, placed the planks up against the door. Then, I nailed the heads of the struts to these, and, driving them well home at the bottoms, nailed them again there.

Thus, I made the door stronger than ever; for now it was solid with the backing of boards, and would, I felt convinced, stand a heavier pressure than hitherto, without giving way.

After that, I lit the lamp which I had brought from the kitchen, and went down to have a look at the lower windows.

Now that I had seen an instance of the strength the creatures possessed, I felt considerable anxiety about the windows on the ground floor—in spite of the fact that they were so strongly barred.

I went first to the buttery, having a vivid remembrance of my late adventure there. The place was chilly, and the wind, soughing in through the broken glass, produced an eerie note. Apart from the general air of dismalness, the place was as I had left it the night before. Going up to the window, I examined the bars, closely; noting, as I did so, their comfortable thickness. Still, as I looked more intently, it seemed to me, that the middle bar was bent slightly from the straight; yet it was but trifling, and it might have been so for years. I had never, before, noticed them particularly.

I put my hand through the broken window, and shook the bar. It was as firm as a rock. Perhaps the creatures had tried to 'start' it, and, finding it beyond their power, ceased from the effort. After that, I went 'round to each of the windows, in turn; examining them with careful attention; but nowhere else could I trace anything to show that there had been any tampering. Having finished my survey, I went back to the study, and poured myself out a little brandy. Then to the tower to watch.

VIII.
After the Attack

It was now about three a.m., and, presently, the Eastern sky began to pale with the coming of dawn. Gradually, the day came, and, by its light, I scanned the gardens, earnestly; but nowhere could I see any signs of the brutes. I leant over, and glanced down to the foot of the wall, to see whether the body of the Thing I had shot the night before was still there. It was gone. I supposed that others of the monsters had removed it during the night.

Then, I went down on to the roof, and crossed over to the gap from which the coping stone had fallen. Reaching it, I looked over. Yes, there was the stone, as I had seen it last; but there was no appearance of anything beneath it; nor could I see the creatures I had killed, after its fall. Evidently, they also had been taken away. I turned, and went down to my study. There, I sat down, wearily. I was thoroughly tired. It was quite light now; though the sun's rays were not, as yet, perceptibly hot. A clock chimed the hour of four.

I awoke, with a start, and looked 'round, hurriedly. The clock in the corner, indicated that it was three o'clock. It was already afternoon. I must have slept for nearly eleven hours.

With a jerky movement, I sat forward in the chair, and listened. The house was perfectly silent. Slowly, I stood up, and yawned. I felt desperately tired, still, and sat down again; wondering what it was that had waked me.

It must have been the clock striking, I concluded, presently; and was commencing to doze off, when a sudden noise brought me back, once more, to life. It was the sound of a step, as of a person moving cautiously down the corridor, toward my study. In an instant, I was on my feet, and grasping my rifle. Noiselessly, I waited. Had the creatures broken in, whilst I slept? Even as I questioned, the steps reached my door, halted momentarily, and then continued down the passage. Silently, I tiptoed to the doorway, and peeped out. Then, I experienced such a feeling of relief, as must a reprieved criminal—it was my sister. She was going toward the stairs.

I stepped into the hall, and was about to call to her, when it occurred to me, that it was very queer she should have crept past my door, in that stealthy manner. I was puzzled, and, for one brief moment, the thought occupied my mind, that it was not she, but some fresh mystery of the house. Then, as I caught a glimpse of her old petticoat, the thought passed as quickly as it had come, and I half laughed. There could be no mistaking that ancient garment. Yet, I wondered what she was doing; and, remembering her condition of mind, on the previous day, I felt that it might be best to follow, quietly—taking care not to alarm her—and see what she was going to do. If she behaved rationally, well and good; if not, I should have to take steps to restrain her. I could run no unnecessary risks, under the danger that threatened us.

Quickly, I reached the head of the stairs, and paused a moment. Then, I heard a sound that sent me leaping down, at a mad rate—it was the rattle of bolts being unshot. That foolish sister of mine was actually unbarring the back door.

Just as her hand was on the last bolt, I reached her. She had not seen me, and, the first thing she knew, I had hold of her arm. She glanced up quickly, like a frightened animal, and screamed aloud.

"Come, Mary!" I said, sternly, "what's the meaning of this nonsense? Do you mean to tell me you don't understand the danger, that you try to throw our two lives away in this fashion!"

To this, she replied nothing; only trembled, violently, gasping and sobbing, as though in the last extremity of fear.

Through some minutes, I reasoned with her; pointing out the need for caution, and asking her to be brave. There was little to be afraid of now, I explained—and, I tried to believe that I spoke the truth—but she must be sensible, and not attempt to leave the house for a few days.

At last, I ceased, in despair. It was no use talking to her; she was, obviously, not quite herself for the time being. Finally, I told her she had better go to her room, if she could not behave rationally.

Still, she took not any notice. So, without more ado, I picked her up in my arms, and carried her there. At first, she screamed, wildly; but had relapsed into silent trembling, by the time I reached the stairs.

Arriving at her room, I laid her upon the bed. She lay there quietly enough, neither speaking nor sobbing—just shaking in a very ague of fear. I took a rug from a chair near by, and spread it over her. I could do nothing more for her, and so, crossed to where Pepper lay in a big basket. My sister had taken charge of him since his wound, to nurse him, for it had proved more severe than I had thought, and I was pleased to note that, in spite of her state of mind, she had looked after the old dog, carefully. Stooping, I spoke to him, and, in reply, he licked my hand, feebly. He was too ill to do more.

Then, going to the bed, I bent over my sister, and asked her how she felt; but she only shook the more, and, much as it pained me, I had to admit that my presence seemed to make her worse.

And so, I left her—locking the door, and pocketing the key. It seemed to be the only course to take.

The rest of the day, I spent between the tower and my study. For food, I brought up a loaf from the pantry, and on this, and some claret, I lived for that day.

What a long, weary day it was. If only I could have gone out into the gardens, as is my wont, I should have been content enough; but to be cooped in this silent house, with no companion, save a mad woman and a sick dog, was enough to prey upon the nerves of the hardiest. And out in the tangled shrubberies that surrounded the house, lurked—for all I could tell—those infernal Swine-creatures waiting their chance. Was ever a man in such straits?

Once, in the afternoon, and again, later, I went to visit my sister. The second time, I found her tending Pepper; but, at my approach, she slid over, unobtrusively, to the far corner, with a gesture that saddened me beyond belief. Poor girl! her fear cut me intolerably, and I would not intrude on her, unnecessarily. She would be better, I trusted, in a few days; meanwhile, I could do nothing; and I judged it still needful—hard as it seemed—to keep her confined to her room. One thing there was that I took for encouragement: she had eaten some of the food I had taken to her, on my first visit.

And so the day passed.

As the evening drew on, the air grew chilly, and I began to make preparations for passing a second night in the tower—taking up two additional rifles, and a heavy ulster. The rifles I loaded, and laid alongside my other; as I intended to make things warm for any of the creatures who might show, during the night. I had plenty of ammunition, and I thought to give the brutes such a lesson, as should show them the uselessness of attempting to force an entrance.

After that, I made the 'round of the house again; paying particular attention to the props that supported the study door. Then, feeling that I had done all that lay in my power to insure our safety, I returned to the tower; calling in on my sister and Pepper, for a final visit, on the way. Pepper was asleep; but woke, as I entered, and wagged his tail, in recognition. I thought he seemed slightly better. My sister was lying on the bed; though whether asleep or not, I was unable to tell; and thus I left them.

Reaching the tower, I made myself as comfortable as circumstances would permit, and settled down to watch through the night. Gradually, darkness fell, and soon the details of the gardens were merged into shadows. During the first few hours, I sat, alert, listening for any sound that might help to tell me if anything were stirring down below. It was far too dark for my eyes to be of much use.

Slowly, the hours passed; without anything unusual happening. And the moon rose, showing the gardens, apparently empty, and silent. And so, through the night, without disturbance or sound.

Toward morning, I began to grow stiff and cold, with my long vigil; also, I was getting very uneasy, concerning the continued quietness on the part of the creatures. I mistrusted it, and would sooner, far, have had them attack the house, openly. Then, at least, I should have known my danger, and been able to meet it; but to wait like this, through a whole night, picturing all kinds of unknown devilment, was to jeopardize one's sanity. Once or twice, the thought came to me, that, perhaps, they had gone; but, in my heart, I found it impossible to believe that it was so.

IX.
In the Cellars

At last, what with being tired and cold, and the uneasiness that possessed me, I resolved to take a walk through the house; first calling in at the study, for a glass of brandy to warm me. This, I did, and, while there, I examined the door, carefully; but found all as I had left it the night before.

The day was just breaking, as I left the tower; though it was still too dark in the house to be able to see without a light, and I took one of the study candles with me on my 'round. By the time I had finished the ground floor, the daylight was creeping in, wanly, through the barred windows. My search had shown me nothing fresh. Everything appeared to be in order, and I was on the point of extinguishing my candle, when the thought suggested itself to me to have another glance 'round the cellars. I had not, if I remember rightly, been into them since my hasty search on the evening of the attack.

For, perhaps, the half of a minute, I hesitated. I would have been very willing to forego the task—as, indeed, I am inclined to think any man well might—for of all the great, awe-inspiring rooms in this house, the cellars are the hugest and weirdest. Great, gloomy caverns of places, unlit by any ray of daylight. Yet, I would not shirk the work. I felt that to do so would smack of sheer cowardice. Besides, as I reassured myself, the cellars were really the most unlikely places in which to come across anything dangerous; considering that they can be entered, only through a heavy oaken door, the key of which, I carry always on my person.

It is in the smallest of these places that I keep my wine; a gloomy hole close to the foot of the cellar stairs; and beyond which, I have seldom proceeded. Indeed, save for the rummage 'round, already mentioned, I doubt whether I had ever, before, been right through the cellars.

As I unlocked the great door, at the top of the steps, I paused, nervously, a moment, at the strange, desolate smell that assailed my nostrils. Then, throwing the barrel of my weapon forward, I descended, slowly, into the darkness of the underground regions.

Reaching the bottom of the stairs, I stood for a minute, and listened. All was silent, save for a faint drip, drip of water, falling, drop-by-drop, somewhere to my left. As I stood, I noticed how quietly the candle burnt; never a flicker nor flare, so utterly windless was the place.

Quietly, I moved from cellar to cellar. I had but a very dim memory of their arrangement. The impressions left by my first search were blurred. I had recollections of a succession of great cellars, and of one, greater than the rest, the roof of which was upheld by pillars; beyond that my mind was hazy, and predominated by a sense of cold and darkness and shadows. Now, however, it was different; for, although nervous, I was sufficiently collected to be able to look about me, and note the structure and size of the different vaults I entered.

Of course, with the amount of light given by my candle, it was not possible to examine each place, minutely, but I was enabled to notice, as I went along, that the walls appeared to be built with wonderful precision and finish; while here and there, an occasional, massive pillar shot up to support the vaulted roof.

Thus, I came, at last, to the great cellar that I remembered. It is reached, through a huge, arched entrance, on which I observed strange, fantastic carvings, which threw queer shadows under the light of my candle. As I stood, and examined these, thoughtfully, it occurred to me how strange it was, that I should be so little acquainted with my own house. Yet, this may be easily understood, when one realizes the size of this ancient pile, and the fact that only my old sister and I live in it, occupying a few of the rooms, such as our wants decide.

Holding the light high, I passed on into the cellar, and, keeping to the right, paced slowly up, until I reached the further end. I walked quietly, and looked cautiously about, as I went. But, so far as the light showed, I saw nothing unusual.

At the top, I turned to the left, still keeping to the wall, and so continued, until I had traversed the whole of the vast chamber. As I moved along, I noticed that the floor was composed of solid rock, in places covered with a damp mould, in others bare, or almost so, save for a thin coating of light-grey dust.

I had halted at the doorway. Now, however, I turned, and made my way up the center of the place; passing among the pillars, and glancing to right and left, as I moved. About halfway up the cellar, I stubbed my foot against something that gave out a metallic sound. Stooping quickly, I held the candle, and saw that the object I had kicked, was a large, metal ring. Bending lower, I cleared the dust from around it, and, presently, discovered that it was attached to a ponderous trap door, black with age.

Feeling excited, and wondering to where it could lead, I laid my gun on the floor, and, sticking the candle in the trigger guard, took the ring in both hands, and pulled. The trap creaked loudly—the sound echoing, vaguely, through the huge place—and opened, heavily.

Propping the edge on my knee, I reached for the candle, and held it in the opening, moving it to right and left; but could see nothing. I was puzzled and surprised. There were no signs of steps, nor even the appearance of there ever having been any. Nothing; save an empty blackness. I might have been looking down into a bottomless, sideless well. Then, even as I stared, full of perplexity, I seemed to hear, far down, as though from untold depths, a faint whisper of sound. I bent my head, quickly, more into the opening, and listened, intently. It may have been fancy; but I could have sworn to hearing a soft titter, that grew into a hideous, chuckling, faint and distant. Startled, I leapt backward, letting the trap fall, with a hollow clang, that filled the place with echoes. Even then, I seemed to hear that mocking, suggestive laughter; but this, I knew, must be my imagination. The sound, I had heard, was far too slight to penetrate through the cumbrous trap.

For a full minute, I stood there, quivering—glancing, nervously, behind and before; but the great cellar was silent as a grave, and, gradually, I shook off the frightened sensation. With a calmer mind, I became again curious to know into what that trap opened; but could not, then, summon sufficient courage to make a further investigation. One thing I felt, however, was that the trap ought to be secured. This, I accomplished by placing upon it several large pieces of 'dressed' stone, which I had noticed in my tour along the East wall.

Then, after a final scrutiny of the rest of the place, I retraced my way through the cellars, to the stairs, and so reached the daylight, with an infinite feeling of relief, that the uncomfortable task was accomplished.

X.
The Time of Waiting

The sun was now warm, and shining brightly, forming a wondrous contrast to the dark and dismal cellars; and it was with comparatively light feelings, that I made my way up to the tower, to survey the gardens. There, I found everything quiet, and, after a few minutes, went down to Mary's room.

Here, having knocked, and received a reply, I unlocked the door. My sister was sitting, quietly, on the bed; as though waiting. She seemed quite herself again, and made no attempt to move away, as I approached; yet, I observed that she scanned my face, anxiously, as though in doubt, and but half assured in her mind that there was nothing to fear from me.

To my questions, as to how she felt, she replied, sanely enough, that she was hungry, and would like to go down to prepare breakfast, if I did not mind. For a minute, I meditated whether it would be safe to let her out. Finally, I told her she might go, on condition that she promised not to attempt to leave the house, or meddle with any of the outer doors. At my mention of the doors, a sudden look of fright crossed her face; but she said nothing, save to give the required promise, and then left the room, silently.

Crossing the floor, I approached Pepper. He had waked as I entered; but, beyond a slight yelp of pleasure, and a soft rapping with his tail, had kept quiet. Now, as I patted him, he made an attempt to stand up, and succeeded, only to fall back on his side, with a little yowl of pain.

I spoke to him, and bade him lie still. I was greatly delighted with his improvement, and also with the natural kindness of my sister's heart, in taking such good care of him, in spite of her condition of mind. After a while, I left him, and went downstairs, to my study.

In a little time, Mary appeared, carrying a tray on which smoked a hot breakfast. As she entered the room, I saw her gaze fasten on the props that supported the study door; her lips tightened, and I thought she paled, slightly; but that was all. Putting the tray down at my elbow, she was leaving the room, quietly, when I called her back. She came, it seemed, a little timidly, as though startled; and I noted that her hand clutched at her apron, nervously.

"Come, Mary," I said. "Cheer up! Things look brighter. I've seen none of the creatures since yesterday morning, early."

She looked at me, in a curiously puzzled manner; as though not comprehending. Then, intelligence swept into her eyes, and fear; but she said nothing, beyond an unintelligible murmur of acquiescence. After that, I kept silence; it was evident that any reference to the Swine-things, was more than her shaken nerves could bear.

Breakfast over, I went up to the tower. Here, during the greater part of the day, I maintained a strict watch over the gardens. Once or twice, I went down to the basement, to see how my sister was getting along. Each time, I found her quiet, and curiously submissive. Indeed, on the last occasion, she even ventured to address me, on her own account, with regard to some household matter that needed attention. Though this was done with an almost extraordinary timidity, I hailed it with happiness, as being the first word, voluntarily spoken, since the critical moment, when I had caught her unbarring the back door, to go out among those waiting brutes. I wondered whether she was aware of her attempt, and how near a thing it had been; but refrained from questioning her, thinking it best to let well alone.

That night, I slept in a bed; the first time for two nights. In the morning, I rose early, and took a walk through the house. All was as it should be, and I went up to the tower, to have a look at the gardens. Here, again, I found perfect quietness.

At breakfast, when I met Mary, I was greatly pleased to see that she had sufficiently regained command over herself, to be able to greet me in a perfectly natural manner. She talked sensibly and quietly; only keeping carefully from any mention of the past couple of days. In this, I humored her, to the extent of not attempting to lead the conversation in that direction.

Earlier in the morning, I had been to see Pepper. He was mending, rapidly; and bade fair to be on his legs, in earnest, in another day or two. Before leaving the breakfast table, I made some reference to his improvement. In the short discussion that followed, I was surprised to gather, from my sister's remarks, that she was still under the impression that his wound had been given by the wildcat, of my invention. It made me feel almost ashamed of myself for deceiving her. Yet, the lie had been told to prevent her from being frightened. And then, I had been sure that she must have known the truth, later, when those brutes had attacked the house.

During the day, I kept on the alert; spending much of my time, as on the previous day, in the tower; but not a sign could I see of the Swine-creatures, nor hear any sound. Several times, the thought had come to me, that the Things had, at last, left us; but, up to this time, I had refused to entertain the idea, seriously; now, however, I began to feel that there was reason for hope. It would soon be three days since I had seen any of the Things; but still, I intended to use the utmost caution. For all that I could tell, this protracted silence might be a ruse to tempt me from the house—perhaps right into their arms. The thought of such a contingency, was, alone, sufficient to make me circumspect.

So it was, that the fourth, fifth and sixth days went by, quietly, without my making any attempt to leave the house.

On the sixth day, I had the pleasure of seeing Pepper, once more, upon his feet; and, though still very weak, he managed to keep me company during the whole of that day.

XI.
The Searching of the Gardens

How slowly the time went; and never a thing to indicate that any of the brutes still infested the gardens.

It was on the ninth day that, finally, I decided to run the risk, if any there were, and sally out. With this purpose in view, I loaded one of the shotguns, carefully—choosing it, as being more deadly than a rifle, at close quarters; and then, after a final scrutiny of the grounds, from the tower, I called Pepper to follow me, and made my way down to the basement.

At the door, I must confess to hesitating a moment. The thought of what might be awaiting me among the dark shrubberies, was by no means calculated to encourage my resolution. It was but a second, though, and then I had drawn the bolts, and was standing on the path outside the door.

Pepper followed, stopping at the doorstep to sniff, suspiciously; and carrying his nose up and down the jambs, as though following a scent. Then, suddenly, he turned, sharply, and started to run here and there, in semicircles and circles, all around the door; finally returning to the threshold. Here, he began again to nose about.

Hitherto, I had stood, watching the dog; yet, all the time, with half my gaze on the wild tangle of gardens, stretching 'round me. Now, I went toward him, and, bending down, examined the surface of the door, where he was smelling. I found that the wood was covered with a network of scratches, crossing and recrossing one another, in inextricable confusion. In addition to this, I noticed that the doorposts, themselves, were gnawed in places. Beyond these, I could find nothing; and so, standing up, I began to make the tour of the house wall.

Pepper, as soon as I walked away, left the door, and ran ahead, still nosing and sniffing as he went along. At times, he stopped to investigate. Here, it would be a bullet-hole in the pathway, or, perhaps, a powder stained wad. Anon, it might be a piece of torn sod, or a disturbed patch of weedy path; but, save for such trifles, he found nothing. I observed him, critically, as he went along, and could discover nothing of uneasiness, in his demeanor, to indicate that he felt the nearness of any of the creatures. By this, I was assured that the gardens were empty, at least for the present, of those hateful Things. Pepper could not be easily deceived, and it was a relief to feel that he would know, and give me timely warning, if there were any danger.

Reaching the place where I had shot that first creature, I stopped, and made a careful scrutiny; but could see nothing. From there, I went on to where the great copingstone had fallen. It lay on its side, apparently just as it had been left when I shot the brute that was moving it. A couple of feet to the right of the nearer end, was a great dent in the ground; showing where it had struck. The other end was still within the indentation—half in, and half out. Going nearer, I looked at the stone, more closely. What a huge piece of masonry it was! And that creature had moved it, single-handed, in its attempt to reach what lay below.

I went 'round to the further end of the stone. Here, I found that it was possible to see under it, for a distance of nearly a couple of feet. Still, I could see nothing of the stricken creatures, and I felt much surprised. I had, as I have before said, guessed that the remains had been removed; yet, I could not conceive that it had been done so thoroughly as not to leave some certain sign, beneath the stone, indicative of their fate. I had seen several of the brutes struck down beneath it, with such force that they must have been literally driven into the earth; and now, not a vestige of them was to be seen—not even a bloodstain.

I felt more puzzled, than ever, as I turned the matter over in my mind; but could think of no plausible explanation; and so, finally, gave it up, as one of the many things that were unexplainable.

From there, I transferred my attention to the study door. I could see, now, even more plainly, the effects of the tremendous strain, to which it had been subjected; and I marveled how, even with the support afforded by the props, it had withstood the attacks, so well. There were no marks of blows—indeed, none had been given—but the door had been literally riven from its hinges, by the application of enormous, silent force. One thing that I observed affected me profoundly—the head of one of the props had been driven right through a panel. This was, of itself, sufficient to show how huge an effort the creatures had made to break down the door, and how nearly they had succeeded.

Leaving, I continued my tour 'round the house, finding little else of interest; save at the back, where I came across the piece of piping I had torn from the wall, lying among the long grass underneath the broken window.

Then, I returned to the house, and, having re-bolted the back door, went up to the tower. Here, I spent the afternoon, reading, and occasionally glancing down into the gardens. I had determined, if the night passed quietly, to go as far as the Pit, on the morrow. Perhaps, I should be able to learn, then, something of what had happened. The day slipped away, and the night came, and went much as the last few nights had gone.

When I rose the morning had broken, fine and clear; and I determined to put my project into action. During breakfast, I considered the matter, carefully; after which, I went to the study for my shotgun. In addition, I loaded, and slipped into my pocket, a small, but heavy, pistol. I quite understood that, if there were any danger, it lay in the direction of the Pit and I intended to be prepared.

Leaving the study, I went down to the back door, followed by Pepper. Once outside, I took a quick survey of the surrounding gardens, and then set off toward the Pit. On the way, I kept a sharp outlook, holding my gun, handily. Pepper was running ahead, I noticed, without any apparent hesitation. From this, I augured that there was no imminent danger to be apprehended, and I stepped out more quickly in his wake. He had reached the top of the Pit, now, and was nosing his way along the edge.

A minute later, I was beside him, looking down into the Pit. For a moment, I could scarcely believe that it was the same place, so greatly was it changed. The dark, wooded ravine of a fortnight ago, with a foliage-hidden stream, running sluggishly, at the bottom, existed no longer. Instead, my eyes showed me a ragged chasm, partly filled with a gloomy lake of turbid water. All one side of the ravine was stripped of underwood, showing the bare rock.

A little to my left, the side of the Pit appeared to have collapsed altogether, forming a deep V-shaped cleft in the face of the rocky cliff. This rift ran, from the upper edge of the ravine, nearly down to the water, and penetrated into the Pit side, to a distance of some forty feet. Its opening was, at least, six yards across; and, from this, it seemed to taper into about two. But, what attracted my attention, more than even the stupendous split itself, was a great hole, some distance down the cleft, and right in the angle of the V. It was clearly defined, and not unlike an arched doorway in shape; though, lying as it did in the shadow, I could not see it very distinctly.

The opposite side of the Pit, still retained its verdure; but so torn in places, and everywhere covered with dust and rubbish, that it was hardly distinguishable as such.

My first impression, that there had been a land slip, was, I began to see, not sufficient, of itself, to account for all the changes I witnessed. And the water—? I turned, suddenly; for I had become aware that, somewhere to my right, there was a noise of running water. I could see nothing; but, now that my attention had been caught, I distinguished, easily, that it came from somewhere at the East end of the Pit.

Slowly, I made my way in that direction; the sound growing plainer as I advanced, until in a little, I stood right above it. Even then, I could not perceive the cause, until I knelt down, and thrust my head over the cliff. Here, the noise came up to me, plainly; and I saw, below me, a torrent of clear water, issuing from a small fissure in the Pit side, and rushing down the rocks, into the lake beneath. A little further along the cliff, I saw another, and, beyond that again, two smaller ones. These, then, would help to account for the quantity of water in the Pit; and, if the fall of rock and earth had blocked the outlet of the stream at the bottom, there was little doubt but that it was contributing a very large share.

Yet, I puzzled my head to account for the generally *shaken* appearance of the place—these streamlets, and that huge cleft, further up the ravine! It seemed to me, that more than the landslip was necessary to account for these. I could imagine an earthquake, or a great *explosion*, creating some such condition of affairs as existed; but, of these, there had been neither. Then, I stood up, quickly, remembering that crash, and the cloud of dust that had followed, directly, rushing high into the air. But I shook my head, unbelievingly. No! It must have been the noise of the falling rocks and earth, I had heard; of course, the dust would fly, naturally. Still, in spite of my reasoning, I had an uneasy feeling, that this theory did not satisfy my sense of the probable; and yet, was any other, that I could suggest, likely to be half so plausible? Pepper had been sitting on the grass, while I conducted my examination. Now, as I turned up the North side of the ravine, he rose and followed.

Slowly, and keeping a careful watch in all directions, I made the circuit of the Pit; but found little else, that I had not already seen. From the West end, I could see the four waterfalls, uninterruptedly. They were some considerable distance up from the surface of the lake—about fifty feet, I calculated.

For a little while longer, I loitered about; keeping my eyes and ears open, but still, without seeing or hearing anything suspicious. The whole place was wonderfully quiet; indeed, save for the continuous murmur of the water, at the top end, no sound, of any description, broke the silence.

All this while, Pepper had shown no signs of uneasiness. This seemed, to me, to indicate that, for the time being, at least, there was none of the Swine-creatures in the vicinity. So far as I could see, his attention appeared to have been taken, chiefly, with scratching and sniffing among the grass at the edge of the Pit. At times, he would leave the edge, and run along toward the house, as though following invisible tracks; but, in all cases, returning after a few minutes. I had little doubt but that he was really tracing out the footsteps of the Swine-things; and the very fact that each one seemed to lead him back to the Pit, appeared to me, a proof that the brutes had all returned whence they came.

At noon, I went home, for dinner. During the afternoon, I made a partial search of the gardens, accompanied by Pepper; but, without coming upon anything to indicate the presence of the creatures.

Once, as we made our way through the shrubberies, Pepper rushed in among some bushes, with a fierce yelp. At that, I jumped back, in sudden fright, and threw my gun forward, in readiness; only to laugh, nervously, as Pepper reappeared, chasing an unfortunate cat. Toward evening, I gave up the search, and returned to the house. All at once, as we were passing a great clump of bushes, on our right, Pepper disappeared, and I could hear him sniffing and growling among them, in a suspicious manner. With my gun barrel, I parted the intervening shrubbery, and looked inside. There was nothing to be seen, save that many of the branches were bent down, and broken; as though some animal had made a lair there, at no very previous date. It was probably, I thought, one of the places occupied by some of the Swine-creatures, on the night of the attack.

Next day, I resumed my search through the gardens; but without result. By evening, I had been right through them, and now, I knew, beyond the possibility of doubt, that there were no longer any of the Things concealed about the place. Indeed, I have often thought since, that I was correct in my earlier surmise, that they had left soon after the attack.

XII.
The Subterranean Pit

Another week came and went, during which I spent a great deal of my time about the Pit mouth. I had come to the conclusion a few days earlier, that the arched hole, in the angle of the great rift, was the place through which the Swine-things had made their exit, from some unholy place in the bowels of the world. How near the probable truth this went, I was to learn later.

It may be easily understood, that I was tremendously curious, though in a frightened way, to know to what infernal place that hole led; though, so far, the idea had not struck me, seriously, of making an investigation. I was far too much imbued with a sense of horror of the Swine-creatures, to think of venturing, willingly, where there was any chance of coming into contact with them.

Gradually, however, as time passed, this feeling grew insensibly less; so that when, a few days later, the thought occurred to me that it might be possible to clamber down and have a look into the hole, I was not so exceedingly averse to it, as might have been imagined. Still, I do not think, even then, that I really intended to try any such foolhardy adventure. For all that I could tell, it might be certain death, to enter that doleful looking opening. And yet, such is the pertinacity of human curiosity, that, at last, my chief desire was but to discover what lay beyond that gloomy entrance.

Slowly, as the days slid by, my fear of the Swine-things became an emotion of the past—more an unpleasant, incredible memory, than aught else.

Thus, a day came, when, throwing thoughts and fancies adrift, I procured a rope from the house, and, having made it fast to a stout tree, at the top of the rift, and some little distance back from the Pit edge, let the other end down into the cleft, until it dangled right across the mouth of the dark hole.

Then, cautiously, and with many misgivings as to whether it was not a mad act that I was attempting, I climbed slowly down, using the rope as a support, until I reached the hole. Here, still holding on to the rope, I stood, and peered in. All was perfectly dark, and not a sound came to me. Yet, a moment later, it seemed that I could hear something. I held my breath, and listened; but all was silent as the grave, and I breathed freely once more. At the same instant, I heard the sound again. It was like a noise of labored breathing—deep and sharp-drawn. For a short second, I stood, petrified; not able to move. But now the sounds had ceased again, and I could hear nothing.

As I stood there, anxiously, my foot dislodged a pebble, which fell inward, into the dark, with a hollow chink. At once, the noise was taken up and repeated a score of times; each succeeding echo being fainter, and seeming to travel away from me, as though into remote distance. Then, as the silence fell again, I heard that stealthy breathing. For each respiration I made, I could hear an answering breath. The sounds appeared to be coming nearer; and then, I heard several others; but fainter and more distant. Why I did not grip the rope, and spring up out of danger, I cannot say. It was as though I had been paralyzed. I broke out into a profuse sweat, and tried to moisten my lips with my tongue. My throat had gone suddenly dry, and I coughed, huskily. It came back to me, in a dozen, horrible, throaty tones, mockingly. I peered, helplessly, into the gloom; but still nothing showed. I had a strange, choky sensation, and again I coughed, dryly. Again the echo took it up, rising and falling, grotesquely, and dying slowly into a muffled silence.

Then, suddenly, a thought came to me, and I held my breath. The other breathing stopped. I breathed again, and, once more, it re-commenced. But now, I no longer feared. I knew that the strange sounds were not made by any lurking Swine-creature; but were simply the echo of my own respirations.

Yet, I had received such a fright, that I was glad to scramble up the rift, and haul up the rope. I was far too shaken and nervous to think of entering that dark hole then, and so returned to the house. I felt more myself next morning; but even then, I could not summon up sufficient courage to explore the place.

All this time, the water in the Pit had been creeping slowly up, and now stood but a little below the opening. At the rate at which it was rising, it would be level with the floor in less than another week; and I realized that, unless I carried out my investigations soon, I should probably never do so at all; as the water would rise and rise, until the opening, itself, was submerged.

It may have been that this thought stirred me to act; but, whatever it was, a couple of days later, saw me standing at the top of the cleft, fully equipped for the task.

This time, I was resolved to conquer my shirking, and go right through with the matter. With this intention, I had brought, in addition to the rope, a bundle of candles, meaning to use them as a torch; also my double-barreled shotgun. In my belt, I had a heavy horse-pistol, loaded with buckshot.

As before, I fastened the rope to the tree. Then, having tied my gun across my shoulders, with a piece of stout cord, I lowered myself over the edge of the Pit. At this movement, Pepper, who had been eyeing my actions, watchfully, rose to his feet, and ran to me, with a half bark, half wail, it seemed to me, of warning. But I was resolved on my enterprise, and bade him lie down. I would much have liked to take him with me; but this was next to impossible, in the existing circumstances. As my face dropped level with the Pit edge, he licked me, right across the mouth; and then, seizing my sleeve between his teeth, began to pull back, strongly. It was very evident that he did not want me to go. Yet, having made up my mind, I had no intention of giving up the attempt; and, with a sharp word to Pepper, to release me, I continued my descent, leaving the poor old fellow at the top, barking and crying like a forsaken pup.

Carefully, I lowered myself from projection to projection. I knew that a slip might mean a wetting.

Reaching the entrance, I let go the rope, and untied the gun from my shoulders. Then, with a last look at the sky—which I noticed was clouding over, rapidly—I went forward a couple of paces, so as to be shielded from the wind, and lit one of the candles. Holding it above my head, and grasping my gun, firmly, I began to move on, slowly, throwing my glances in all directions.

For the first minute, I could hear the melancholy sound of Pepper's howling, coming down to me. Gradually, as I penetrated further into the darkness, it grew fainter; until, in a little while, I could hear nothing. The path tended downward somewhat, and to the left. Thence it kept on, still running to the left, until I found that it was leading me right in the direction of the house.

Very cautiously, I moved onward, stopping, every few steps, to listen. I had gone, perhaps, a hundred yards, when, suddenly, it seemed to me that I caught a faint sound, somewhere along the passage behind. With my heart thudding heavily, I listened. The noise grew plainer, and appeared to be approaching, rapidly. I could hear it distinctly, now. It was the soft padding of running feet. In the first moments of fright, I stood, irresolute; not knowing whether to go forward or backward. Then, with a sudden realization of the best thing to do, I backed up to the rocky wall on my right, and, holding the candle above my head, waited—gun in hand—cursing my foolhardy curiosity, for bringing me into such a strait.

I had not long to wait, but a few seconds, before two eyes reflected back from the gloom, the rays of my candle. I raised my gun, using my right hand only, and aimed quickly. Even as I did so, something leapt out of the darkness, with a blustering bark of joy that woke the echoes, like thunder. It was Pepper. How he had contrived to scramble down the cleft, I could not conceive. As I brushed my hand, nervously, over his coat, I noticed that he was dripping; and concluded that he must have tried to follow me, and fallen into the water; from which he would not find it very difficult to climb.

Having waited a minute, or so, to steady myself, I proceeded along the way, Pepper following, quietly. I was curiously glad to have the old fellow with me. He was company, and, somehow, with him at my heels, I was less afraid. Also, I knew how quickly his keen ears would detect the presence of any unwelcome creature, should there be such, amid the darkness that wrapped us.

For some minutes we went slowly along; the path still leading straight toward the house. Soon, I concluded, we should be standing right beneath it, did the path but carry far enough. I led the way, cautiously, for another fifty yards, or so. Then, I stopped, and held the light high; and reason enough I had to be thankful that I did so; for there, not three paces forward, the path vanished, and, in place, showed a hollow blackness, that sent sudden fear through me.

Very cautiously, I crept forward, and peered down; but could see nothing. Then, I crossed to the left of the passage, to see whether there might be any continuation of the path. Here, right against the wall, I found that a narrow track, some three feet wide, led onward. Carefully, I stepped on to it; but had not gone far, before I regretted venturing thereon. For, after a few paces, the already narrow way, resolved itself into a mere ledge, with, on the one side the solid, unyielding rock, towering up, in a great wall, to the unseen roof, and, on the other, that yawning chasm. I could not help reflecting how helpless I was, should I be attacked there, with no room to turn, and where even the recoil of my weapon might be sufficient to drive me headlong into the depths below.

To my great relief, a little further on, the track suddenly broadened out again to its original breadth. Gradually, as I went onward, I noticed that the path trended steadily to the right, and so, after some minutes, I discovered that I was not going forward; but simply circling the huge abyss. I had, evidently, come to the end of the great passage.

Five minutes later, I stood on the spot from which I had started; having been completely 'round, what I guessed now to be a vast pit, the mouth of which must be at least a hundred yards across.

For some little time, I stood there, lost in perplexing thought. "What does it all mean?" was the cry that had begun to reiterate through my brain.

A sudden idea struck me, and I searched 'round for a piece of stone. Presently, I found a bit of rock, about the size of a small loaf. Sticking the candle upright in a crevice of the floor, I went back from the edge, somewhat, and, taking a short run, launched the stone forward into the chasm—my idea being to throw it far enough to keep it clear of the sides. Then, I stooped forward, and listened; but, though I kept perfectly quiet, for at least a full minute, no sound came back to me from out of the dark.

I knew, then, that the depth of the hole must be immense; for the stone, had it struck anything, was large enough to have set the echoes of that weird place, whispering for an indefinite period. Even as it was, the cavern had given back the sounds of my footfalls, multitudinously. The place was awesome, and I would willingly have retraced my steps, and left the mysteries of its solitudes unsolved; only, to do so, meant admitting defeat.

Then, a thought came, to try to get a view of the abyss. It occurred to me that, if I placed my candles 'round the edge of the hole, I should be able to get, at least, some dim sight of the place.

I found, on counting, that I had brought fifteen candles, in the bundle—my first intention having been, as I have already said, to make a torch of the lot. These, I proceeded to place 'round the Pit mouth, with an interval of about twenty yards between each.

Having completed the circle, I stood in the passage, and endeavored to get an idea of how the place looked. But I discovered, immediately, that they were totally insufficient for my purpose. They did little more than make the gloom visible. One thing they did, however, and that was, they confirmed my opinion of the size of the opening; and, although they showed me nothing that I wanted to see; yet the contrast they afforded to the heavy darkness, pleased me, curiously. It was as though fifteen tiny stars shone through the subterranean night.

Then, even as I stood, Pepper gave a sudden howl, that was taken up by the echoes, and repeated with ghastly variations, dying away, slowly. With a quick movement, I held aloft the one candle that I had kept, and glanced down at the dog; at the same moment, I seemed to hear a noise, like a diabolical chuckle, rise up from the hitherto, silent depths of the Pit. I started; then, I recollected that it was, probably, the echo of Pepper's howl.

Pepper had moved away from me, up the passage, a few steps; he was nosing along the rocky floor; and I thought I heard him lapping. I went toward him, holding the candle low. As I moved, I heard my boot go sop, sop; and the light was reflected from something that glistened, and crept past my feet, swiftly toward the Pit. I bent lower, and looked; then gave vent to an expression of surprise. From somewhere, higher up the path, a stream of water was running quickly in the direction of the great opening, and growing in size every second.

Again, Pepper gave vent to that deep-drawn howl, and, running at me, seized my coat, and attempted to drag me up the path toward the entrance. With a nervous gesture, I shook him off, and crossed quickly over to the left-hand wall. If anything were coming, I was going to have the wall at my back.

Then, as I stared anxiously up the pathway, my candle caught a gleam, far up the passage. At the same moment, I became conscious of a murmurous roar, that grew louder, and filled the whole cavern with deafening sound. From the Pit, came a deep, hollow echo, like the sob of a giant. Then, I had sprung to one side, on to the narrow ledge that ran 'round the abyss, and, turning, saw a great wall of foam sweep past me, and leap tumultuously into the waiting chasm. A cloud of spray burst over me, extinguishing my candle, and wetting me to the skin. I still held my gun. The three nearest candles went out; but the further ones gave only a short flicker. After the first rush, the flow of water eased down to a steady stream, maybe a foot in depth; though I could not see this, until I had procured one of the lighted candles, and, with it, started to reconnoiter. Pepper had, fortunately, followed me as I leapt for the ledge, and now, very much subdued, kept close behind.

A short examination showed me that the water reached right across the passage, and was running at a tremendous rate. Already, even as I stood there, it had deepened. I could make only a guess at what had happened. Evidently, the water in the ravine had broken into the passage, by some means. If that were the case, it would go on increasing in volume, until I should find it impossible to leave the place. The thought was frightening. It was evident that I must make my exit as hurriedly as possible.

Taking my gun by the stock, I sounded the water. It was a little under knee-deep. The noise it made, plunging down into the Pit, was deafening. Then, with a call to Pepper, I stepped out into the flood, using the gun as a staff. Instantly, the water boiled up over my knees, and nearly to the tops of my thighs, with the speed at which it was racing. For one short moment, I nearly lost my footing; but the thought of what lay behind, stimulated me to a fierce endeavor, and, step-by-step, I made headway.

Of Pepper, I knew nothing at first. I had all I could do to keep on my legs; and was overjoyed, when he appeared beside me. He was wading manfully along. He is a big dog, with longish thin legs, and I suppose the water had less grasp on them, than upon mine. Anyway, he managed a great deal better than I did; going ahead of me, like a guide, and wittingly—or otherwise—helping, somewhat, to break the force of the water. On we went, step by step, struggling and gasping, until somewhere about a hundred yards had been safely traversed. Then, whether it was because I was taking less care, or that there was a slippery place on the rocky floor, I cannot say; but, suddenly, I slipped, and fell on my face. Instantly, the water leapt over me in a cataract, hurling me down, toward that bottomless hole, at a frightful speed. Frantically I struggled; but it was impossible to get a footing. I was helpless, gasping and drowning. All at once, something gripped my coat, and brought me to a standstill. It was Pepper. Missing me, he must have raced back, through the dark turmoil, to find me, and then caught, and held me, until I was able to get to my feet.

I have a dim recollection of having seen, momentarily, the gleams of several lights; but, of this, I have never been quite sure. If my impressions are correct, I must have been washed down to the very brink of that awful chasm, before Pepper managed to bring me to a standstill. And the lights, of course, could only have been the distant flames of the candles, I had left burning. But, as I have said, I am not by any means sure. My eyes were full of water, and I had been badly shaken.

And there was I, without my helpful gun, without light, and sadly confused, with the water deepening; depending solely upon my old friend Pepper, to help me out of that hellish place.

I was facing the torrent. Naturally, it was the only way in which I could have sustained my position a moment; for even old Pepper could not have held me long against that terrific strain, without assistance, however blind, from me.

Perhaps a minute passed, during which it was touch and go with me; then, gradually I re-commenced my tortuous way up the passage. And so began the grimmest fight with death, from which ever I hope to emerge victorious. Slowly, furiously, almost hopelessly, I strove; and that faithful Pepper led me, dragged me, upward and onward, until, at last, ahead I saw a gleam of blessed light. It was the entrance. Only a few yards further, and I reached the opening, with the water surging and boiling hungrily around my loins.

And now I understood the cause of the catastrophe. It was raining heavily, literally in torrents. The surface of the lake was level with the bottom of the opening—nay! more than level, it was above it. Evidently, the rain had swollen the lake, and caused this premature rise; for, at the rate the ravine had been filling, it would not have reached the entrance for a couple more days.

Luckily, the rope by which I had descended, was streaming into the opening, upon the inrushing waters. Seizing the end, I knotted it securely 'round Pepper's body, then, summoning up the last remnant of my strength, I commenced to swarm up the side of the cliff. I reached the Pit edge, in the last stage of exhaustion. Yet, I had to make one more effort, and haul Pepper into safety.

Slowly and wearily, I hauled on the rope. Once or twice, it seemed that I should have to give up; for Pepper is a weighty dog, and I was utterly done. Yet, to let go, would have meant certain death to the old fellow, and the thought spurred me to greater exertions. I have but a very hazy remembrance of the end. I recall pulling, through moments that lagged strangely. I have also some recollection of seeing Pepper's muzzle, appearing over the Pit edge, after what seemed an indefinite period of time. Then, all grew suddenly dark.

XIII.
THE TRAP IN THE GREAT CELLAR

I suppose I must have swooned; for, the next thing I remember, I opened my eyes, and all was dusk. I was lying on my back, with one leg doubled under the other, and Pepper was licking my ears. I felt horribly stiff, and my leg was numb, from the knee, downward. For a few minutes, I lay thus, in a dazed condition; then, slowly, I struggled to a sitting position, and looked about me.

It had stopped raining, but the trees still dripped, dismally. From the Pit, came a continuous murmur of running water. I felt cold and shivery. My clothes were sodden, and I ached all over. Very slowly, the life came back into my numbed leg, and, after a little, I essayed to stand up. This, I managed, at the second attempt; but I was very tottery, and peculiarly weak. It seemed to me, that I was going to be ill, and I made shift to stumble my way toward the house. My steps were erratic, and my head confused. At each step that I took, sharp pains shot through my limbs.

I had gone, perhaps, some thirty paces, when a cry from Pepper, drew my attention, and I turned, stiffly, toward him. The old dog was trying to follow me; but could come no further, owing to the rope, with which I had hauled him up, being still tied 'round his body, the other end not having been unfastened from the tree. For a moment, I fumbled with the knots, weakly; but they were wet and hard, and I could do nothing. Then, I remembered my knife, and, in a minute, the rope was cut.

How I reached the house, I scarcely know, and, of the days that followed, I remember still less. Of one thing, I am certain, that, had it not been for my sister's untiring love and nursing, I had not been writing at this moment.

When I recovered my senses, it was to find that I had been in bed for nearly two weeks. Yet another week passed, before I was strong enough to totter out into the gardens. Even then, I was not able to walk so far as the Pit. I would have liked to ask my sister, how high the water had risen; but felt it was wiser not to mention the subject to her. Indeed, since then, I have made a rule never to speak to her about the strange things, that happen in this great, old house.

It was not until a couple of days later, that I managed to get across to the Pit. There, I found that, in my few weeks' absence, there had been wrought a wondrous change. Instead of the three-parts filled ravine, I looked out upon a great lake, whose placid surface, reflected the light, coldly. The water had risen to within half a dozen feet of the Pit edge. Only in one part was the lake disturbed, and that was above the place where, far down under the silent waters, yawned the entrance to the vast, underground Pit. Here, there was a continuous bubbling; and, occasionally, a curious sort of sobbing gurgle would find its way up from the depth. Beyond these, there was nothing to tell of the things that were hidden beneath. As I stood there, it came to me how wonderfully things had worked out. The entrance to the place whence the Swine-creatures had come, was sealed up, by a power that made me feel there was nothing more to fear from them. And yet, with the feeling, there was a sensation that, now, I should never learn anything further, of the place from which those dreadful Things had come. It was completely shut off and concealed from human curiosity forever.

Strange—in the knowledge of that underground hell-hole—how apposite has been the naming of the Pit. One wonders how it originated, and when. Naturally, one concludes that the shape and depth of the ravine would suggest the name "Pit." Yet, is it not possible that it has, all along, held a deeper significance, a hint —could one but have guessed—of the greater, more stupendous Pit that lies far down in the earth, beneath this old house? Under this house! Even now, the idea is strange and terrible to me. For I have proved, beyond doubt, that the Pit yawns right below the house, which is evidently supported, somewhere above the center of it, upon a tremendous, arched roof, of solid rock.

It happened in this wise, that, having occasion to go down to the cellars, the thought occurred to me to pay a visit to the great vault, where the trap is situated; and see whether everything was as I had left it.

Reaching the place, I walked slowly up the center, until I came to the trap. There it was, with the stones piled upon it, just as I had seen it last. I had a lantern with me, and the idea came to me, that now would be a good time to investigate whatever lay under the great, oak slab. Placing the lantern on the floor, I tumbled the stones off the trap, and, grasping the ring, pulled the door open. As I did so, the cellar became filled with the sound of a murmurous thunder, that rose from far below. At the same time, a damp wind blew up into my face, bringing with it a load of fine spray. Therewith, I dropped the trap, hurriedly, with a half frightened feeling of wonder.

For a moment, I stood puzzled. I was not particularly afraid. The haunting fear of the Swine-things had left me, long ago; but I was certainly nervous and astonished. Then, a sudden thought possessed me, and I raised the ponderous door, with a feeling of excitement. Leaving it standing upon its end, I seized the lantern, and, kneeling down, thrust it into the opening. As I did so, the moist wind and spray drove in my eyes, making me unable to see, for a few moments. Even when my eyes were clear, I could distinguish nothing below me, save darkness, and whirling spray.

Seeing that it was useless to expect to make out anything, with the light so high, I felt in my pockets for a piece of twine, with which to lower it further into the opening. Even as I fumbled, the lantern slipped from my fingers, and hurtled down into the darkness. For a brief instant, I watched its fall, and saw the light shine on a tumult of white foam, some eighty or a hundred feet below me. Then it was gone. My sudden surmise was correct, and now, I knew the cause of the wet and noise. The great cellar was connected with the Pit, by means of the trap, which opened right above it; and the moisture, was the spray, rising from the water, falling into the depths.

In an instant, I had an explanation of certain things, that had hitherto puzzled me. Now, I could understand why the noises—on the first night of the invasion—had seemed to rise directly from under my feet. And the chuckle that had sounded when first I opened the trap! Evidently, some of the Swine-things must have been right beneath me.

Another thought struck me. Were the creatures all drowned? Would they drown? I remembered how unable I had been to find any traces to show that my shooting had been really fatal. Had they life, as we understand life, or were they ghouls? These thoughts flashed through my brain, as I stood in the dark, searching my pockets for matches. I had the box in my hand now, and, striking a light, I stepped to the trap door, and closed it. Then, I piled the stones back upon it; after which, I made my way out from the cellars.

And so, I suppose the water goes on, thundering down into that bottomless hell-pit. Sometimes, I have an inexplicable desire to go down to the great cellar, open the trap, and gaze into the impenetrable, spray-damp darkness. At times, the desire becomes almost overpowering, in its intensity. It is not mere curiosity, that prompts me; but more as though some unexplained influence were at work. Still, I never go; and intend to fight down the strange longing, and crush it; even as I would the unholy thought of self-destruction.

This idea of some intangible force being exerted, may seem reasonless. Yet, my instinct warns me, that it is not so. In these things, reason seems to me less to be trusted than instinct.

One thought there is, in closing, that impresses itself upon me, with ever-growing insistence. It is, that I live in a very strange house; a very awful house. And I have begun to wonder whether I am doing wisely in staying here. Yet, if I left, where could I go, and still obtain the solitude, and the sense of her presence, that alone make my old life bearable?[5]

[5] An apparently unmeaning interpolation. I can find no previous reference in the MS. to this matter. It becomes clearer, however, in the light of succeeding incidents.—Ed.

XIV.
The Sea of Sleep

For a considerable period after the last incident which I have narrated in my diary, I had serious thoughts of leaving this house, and might have done so; but for the great and wonderful thing, of which I am about to write.

How well I was advised, in my heart, when I stayed on here—spite of those visions and sights of unknown and unexplainable things; for, had I not stayed, then I had not seen again the face of her I loved. Yes, though few know it, none now save my sister Mary, I have loved and, ah! me—lost.

I would write down the story of those sweet, old days; but it would be like the tearing of old wounds; yet, after that which has happened, what need have I to care? For she has come to me out of the unknown. Strangely, she warned me; warned me passionately against this house; begged me to leave it; but admitted, when I questioned her, that she could not have come to me, had I been elsewhere. Yet, in spite of this, still she warned me, earnestly; telling me that it was a place, long ago given over to evil, and under the power of grim laws, of which none here have knowledge. And I—I just asked her, again, whether she would come to me elsewhere, and she could only stand, silent.

It was thus, that I came to the place of the Sea of Sleep—so she termed it, in her dear speech with me. I had stayed up, in my study, reading; and must have dozed over the book. Suddenly, I awoke and sat upright, with a start. For a moment, I looked 'round, with a puzzled sense of something unusual. There was a misty look about the room, giving a curious softness to each table and chair and furnishing.

Gradually, the mistiness increased; growing, as it were, out of nothing. Then, slowly, a soft, white light began to glow in the room. The flames of the candles shone through it, palely. I looked from side to side, and found that I could still see each piece of furniture; but in a strangely unreal way, more as though the ghost of each table and chair had taken the place of the solid article.

Gradually, as I looked, I saw them fade and fade; until, slowly, they resolved into nothingness. Now, I looked again at the candles. They shone wanly, and, even as I watched, grew more unreal, and so vanished. The room was filled, now, with a soft, yet luminous, white twilight, like a gentle mist of light. Beyond this, I could see nothing. Even the walls had vanished.

Presently, I became conscious that a faint, continuous sound, pulsed through the silence that wrapped me. I listened intently. It grew more distinct, until it appeared to me that I harked to the breathings of some great sea. I cannot tell how long a space passed thus; but, after a while, it seemed that I could see through the mistiness; and, slowly, I became aware that I was standing upon the shore of an immense and silent sea. This shore was smooth and long, vanishing to right and left of me, in extreme distances. In front, swam a still immensity of sleeping ocean. At times, it seemed to me that I caught a faint glimmer of light, under its surface; but of this, I could not be sure. Behind me, rose up, to an extraordinary height, gaunt, black cliffs.

Overhead, the sky was of a uniform cold grey color—the whole place being lit by a stupendous globe of pale fire, that swam a little above the far horizon, and shed a foamlike light above the quiet waters.

Beyond the gentle murmur of the sea, an intense stillness prevailed. For a long while, I stayed there, looking out across its strangeness. Then, as I stared, it seemed that a bubble of white foam floated up out of the depths, and then, even now I know not how it was, I was looking upon, nay, looking *into* the face of Her—aye! into her face—into her soul; and she looked back at me, with such a commingling of joy and sadness, that I ran toward her, blindly; crying strangely to her, in a very agony of remembrance, of terror, and of hope, to come to me. Yet, spite of my crying, she stayed out there upon the sea, and only shook her head, sorrowfully; but, in her eyes was the old earth-light of tenderness, that I had come to know, before all things, ere we were parted.

"At her perverseness, I grew desperate, and essayed to wade out to her; yet, though I would, I could not. Something, some invisible barrier, held me back, and I was fain to stay where I was, and cry out to her in the fullness of my soul, 'O, my Darling, my Darling—' but could say no more, for very intensity. And, at that, she came over, swiftly, and touched me, and it was as though heaven had opened. Yet, when I reached out my hands to her, she put me from her with tenderly stern hands, and I was abashed—"

THE FRAGMENTS[6]

(*The legible portions of the mutilated leaves.*)

... through tears ... noise of eternity in my ears, we parted ... She whom I love. O, my God ...!

I was a great time dazed, and then I was alone in the blackness of the night. I knew that I journeyed back, once more, to the known universe. Presently, I

[6] Here, the writing becomes undecipherable, owing to the damaged condition of this part of the MS. Below I print such fragments as are legible.—Ed.

emerged from that enormous darkness. I had come among the stars ... vast time ... the sun, far and remote.

I entered into the gulf that separates our system from the outer suns. As I sped across the dividing dark, I watched, steadily, the ever-growing brightness and size of our sun. Once, I glanced back to the stars, and saw them shift, as it were, in my wake, against the mighty background of night, so vast was the speed of my passing spirit.

I drew nigher to our system, and now I could see the shine of Jupiter. Later, I distinguished the cold, blue gleam of the earthlight... I had a moment of bewilderment. All about the sun there seemed to be bright, objects, moving in rapid orbits. Inward, nigh to the savage glory of the sun, there circled two darting points of light, and, further off, there flew a blue, shining speck, that I knew to be the earth. It circled the sun in a space that seemed to be no more than an earth-minute.

... nearer with great speed. I saw the radiances of Jupiter and Saturn, spinning, with incredible swiftness, in huge orbits. And ever I drew more nigh, and looked out upon this strange sight—the visible circling of the planets about the mother sun. It was as though time had been annihilated for me; so that a year was no more to my unfleshed spirit, than is a moment to an earth-bound soul.

The speed of the planets, appeared to increase; and, presently, I was watching the sun, all ringed about with hairlike circles of different colored fire—the paths of the planets, hurtling at mighty speed, about the central flame...

"... the sun grew vast, as though it leapt to meet me... And now I was within the circling of the outer planets, and flitting swiftly, toward the place where the earth, glimmering through the blue splendor of its orbit, as though a fiery mist, circled the sun at a monstrous speed..."[7]

---

[7] NOTE.—The severest scrutiny has not enabled me to decipher more of the damaged portion of the MS. It commences to be legible again with the chapter entitled "The Noise in the Night."—Ed.

XV.
The Noise in the Night

And now, I come to the strangest of all the strange happenings that have befallen me in this house of mysteries. It occurred quite lately—within the month; and I have little doubt but that what I saw was in reality the end of all things. However, to my story.

I do not know how it is; but, up to the present, I have never been able to write these things down, directly they happened. It is as though I have to wait a time, recovering my just balance, and digesting—as it were—the things I have heard or seen. No doubt, this is as it should be; for, by waiting, I see the incidents more truly, and write of them in a calmer and more judicial frame of mind. This by the way.

It is now the end of November. My story relates to what happened in the first week of the month.

It was night, about eleven o'clock. Pepper and I kept one another company in the study—that great, old room of mine, where I read and work. I was reading, curiously enough, the Bible. I have begun, in these later days, to take a growing interest in that great and ancient book. Suddenly, a distinct tremor shook the house, and there came a faint and distant, whirring buzz, that grew rapidly into a far, muffled screaming. It reminded me, in a queer, gigantic way, of the noise that a clock makes, when the catch is released, and it is allowed to run down. The sound appeared to come from some remote height—somewhere up in the night. There was no repetition of the shock. I looked across at Pepper. He was sleeping peacefully.

Gradually, the whirring noise decreased, and there came a long silence.

All at once, a glow lit up the end window, which protrudes far out from the side of the house, so that, from it, one may look both East and West. I felt puzzled, and, after a moment's hesitation, walked across the room, and pulled aside the blind. As I did so, I saw the Sun rise, from behind the horizon. It rose with a steady, perceptible movement. I could see it travel upward. In a minute, it seemed, it had reached the tops of the trees, through which I had watched it. Up, up—It was broad daylight now. Behind me, I was conscious of a sharp, mosquitolike buzzing. I glanced 'round, and knew that it came from the clock. Even as I looked, it marked off an hour. The minute hand was moving 'round the dial, faster than an ordinary second-hand. The hour hand moved quickly from space to space. I had a numb sense of astonishment. A moment later, so it seemed, the two candles went out, almost together. I turned swiftly back to the window; for I had seen the shadow of the window-frames, traveling along the floor toward me, as though a great lamp had been carried up past the window.

I saw now, that the sun had risen high into the heavens, and was still visibly moving. It passed above the house, with an extraordinary sailing kind of motion. As the window came into shadow, I saw another extraordinary thing. The fine-weather clouds were not passing, easily, across the sky—they were scampering, as though a hundred-mile-an-hour wind blew. As they passed, they changed their shapes a thousand times a minute, as though writhing with a strange life; and so were gone. And, presently, others came, and whisked away likewise.

To the West, I saw the sun, drop with an incredible, smooth, swift motion. Eastward, the shadows of every seen thing crept toward the coming greyness. And the movement of the shadows was visible to me—a stealthy, writhing creep of the shadows of the wind-stirred trees. It was a strange sight.

Quickly, the room began to darken. The sun slid down to the horizon, and seemed, as it were, to disappear from my sight, almost with a jerk. Through the greyness of the swift evening, I saw the silver crescent of the moon, falling out of the Southern sky, toward the West. The evening seemed to merge into an almost instant night. Above me, the many constellations passed in a strange, 'noiseless' circling, Westward. The moon fell through that last thousand fathoms of the night-gulf, and there was only the starlight…

About this time, the buzzing in the corner ceased; telling me that the clock had run down. A few minutes passed, and I saw the Eastward sky lighten. A grey, sullen morning spread through all the darkness, and hid the march of the stars. Overhead, there moved, with a heavy, everlasting rolling, a vast, seamless sky of grey clouds—a cloud-sky that would have seemed motionless, through all the length of an ordinary earth-day. The sun was hidden from me; but, from moment to moment, the world would brighten and darken, brighten and darken, beneath waves of subtle light and shadow…

The light shifted ever Westward, and the night fell upon the earth. A vast rain seemed to come with it, and a wind of a most extraordinary loudness—as though the howling of a nightlong gale, were packed into the space of no more than a minute.

This noise passed, almost immediately, and the clouds broke; so that, once more, I could see the sky. The stars were flying Westward, with astounding speed. It came to me now, for the first time, that, though the noise of the wind had passed, yet a constant 'blurred' sound was in my ears. Now that I noticed it, I was aware that it had been with me all the time. It was the world-noise.

And then, even as I grasped at so much comprehension, there came the Eastward light. No more than a few heartbeats, and the sun rose, swiftly. Through the trees, I saw it, and then it was above the trees. Up—up, it soared and all the world was light. It passed, with a swift, steady swing to its highest altitude, and fell thence, Westward. I saw the day roll visibly over my head. A few light clouds flittered Northward, and vanished. The sun went down with one swift, clear plunge, and there was about me, for a few seconds, the darker growing grey of the gloaming.

Southward and Westward, the moon was sinking rapidly. The night had come, already. A minute it seemed, and the moon fell those remaining fathoms of dark sky. Another minute, or so, and the Eastward sky glowed with the coming dawn. The sun leapt upon me with a frightening abruptness, and soared ever more swiftly toward the zenith. Then, suddenly, a fresh thing came to my sight. A black thundercloud rushed up out of the South, and seemed to leap all the arc of the sky, in a single instant. As it came, I saw that its advancing edge flapped, like a monstrous black cloth in the heaven, twirling and undulating rapidly, with a horrid suggestiveness. In an instant, all the air was full of rain, and a hundred lightning flashes seemed to flood downward, as it were in one great shower. In the same second of time, the world-noise was drowned in the roar of the wind, and then my ears ached, under the stunning impact of the thunder.

And, in the midst of this storm, the night came; and then, within the space of another minute, the storm had passed, and there was only the constant 'blur' of the world-noise on my hearing. Overhead, the stars were sliding quickly Westward; and something, mayhaps the particular speed to which they had attained, brought home to me, for the first time, a keen realization of the knowledge that it was the world that revolved. I seemed to see, suddenly, the world—a vast, dark mass—revolving visibly against the stars.

The dawn and the sun seemed to come together, so greatly had the speed of the world-revolution increased. The sun drove up, in one long, steady curve; passed its highest point, and swept down into the Western sky, and disappeared. I was scarcely conscious of evening, so brief was it. Then I was watching the flying constellations, and the Westward hastening moon. In but a space of seconds, so it seemed, it was sliding swiftly downward through the night-blue, and then was gone. And, almost directly, came the morning.

And now there seemed to come a strange acceleration. The sun made one clean, clear sweep through the sky, and disappeared behind the Westward horizon, and the night came and went with a like haste.

As the succeeding day, opened and closed upon the world, I was aware of a sweat of snow, suddenly upon the earth. The night came, and, almost immediately, the day. In the brief leap of the sun, I saw that the snow had vanished; and then, once more, it was night.

Thus matters were; and, even after the many incredible things that I have seen, I experienced all the time a most profound awe. To see the sun rise and set, within a space of time to be measured by seconds; to watch (after a little) the moon leap—a pale, and ever growing orb—up into the night sky, and glide, with a strange swiftness, through the vast arc of blue; and, presently, to see the sun follow, springing out of the Eastern sky, as though in chase; and then again the night, with the swift and ghostly passing of starry constellations, was all too much to view believingly. Yet, so it was—the day slipping from dawn to dusk, and the night sliding swiftly into day, ever rapidly and more rapidly.

The last three passages of the sun had shown me a snow-covered earth, which, at night, had seemed, for a few seconds, incredibly weird under the fast-shifting light of the soaring and falling moon. Now, however, for a little space, the sky was hidden, by a sea of swaying, leaden-white clouds, which lightened and blackened, alternately, with the passage of day and night.

The clouds rippled and vanished, and there was once more before me, the vision of the swiftly leaping sun, and nights that came and went like shadows.

Faster and faster, spun the world. And now each day and night was completed within the space of but a few seconds; and still the speed increased.

It was a little later, that I noticed that the sun had begun to have the suspicion of a trail of fire behind it. This was due, evidently, to the speed at which it, apparently, traversed the heavens. And, as the days sped, each one quicker than the last, the sun began to assume the appearance of a vast, flaming comet flaring across the sky at short, periodic intervals.[8] At night, the moon presented, with much greater truth, a cometlike aspect; a pale, and singularly clear, fast traveling shape of fire, trailing streaks of cold flame. The stars showed now, merely as fine hairs of fire against the dark.

Once, I turned from the window, and glanced at Pepper. In the flash of a day, I saw that he slept, quietly, and I moved once more to my watching.

The sun was now bursting up from the Eastern horizon, like a stupendous rocket, seeming to occupy no more than a second or two in hurling from East to West. I could no longer perceive the passage of clouds across the sky, which seemed to have darkened somewhat. The brief nights, appeared to have lost the proper darkness of night; so that the hairlike fire of the flying stars, showed but dimly. As the speed increased, the sun began to sway very slowly in the sky, from South to North, and then, slowly again, from North to South.

So, amid a strange confusion of mind, the hours passed.

All this while had Pepper slept. Presently, feeling lonely and distraught, I called to him, softly; but he took no notice. Again, I called, raising my voice slightly; still he moved not. I walked over to where he lay, and touched him with my foot, to rouse him. At the action, gentle though it was, he fell to pieces. That is what happened; he literally and actually crumbled into a mouldering heap of bones and dust.

---

[8] The Recluse uses this as an illustration, evidently in the sense of the popular conception of a comet.—Ed.

For the space of, perhaps a minute, I stared down at the shapeless heap, that had once been Pepper. I stood, feeling stunned. What can have happened? I asked myself; not at once grasping the grim significance of that little hill of ash. Then, as I stirred the heap with my foot, it occurred to me that this could only happen in a great space of time. Years—and years.

Outside, the weaving, fluttering light held the world. Inside, I stood, trying to understand what it meant—what that little pile of dust and dry bones, on the carpet, meant. But I could not think, coherently.

I glanced away, 'round the room, and now, for the first time, noticed how dusty and old the place looked. Dust and dirt everywhere; piled in little heaps in the corners, and spread about upon the furniture. The very carpet, itself, was invisible beneath a coating of the same, all pervading, material. As I walked, little clouds of the stuff rose up from under my footsteps, and assailed my nostrils, with a dry, bitter odor that made me wheeze, huskily.

Suddenly, as my glance fell again upon Pepper's remains, I stood still, and gave voice to my confusion—questioning, aloud, whether the years were, indeed, passing; whether this, which I had taken to be a form of vision, was, in truth, a reality. I paused. A new thought had struck me. Quickly, but with steps which, for the first time, I noticed, tottered, I went across the room to the great pier-glass, and looked in. It was too covered with grime, to give back any reflection, and, with trembling hands, I began to rub off the dirt. Presently, I could see myself. The thought that had come to me, was confirmed. Instead of the great, hale man, who scarcely looked fifty, I was looking at a bent, decrepit man, whose shoulders stooped, and whose face was wrinkled with the years of a century. The hair—which a few short hours ago had been nearly coal black—was now silvery white. Only the eyes were bright. Gradually, I traced, in that ancient man, a faint resemblance to my self of other days.

I turned away, and tottered to the window. I knew, now, that I was old, and the knowledge seemed to confirm my trembling walk. For a little space, I stared moodily out into the blurred vista of changeful landscape. Even in that short time, a year passed, and, with a petulant gesture, I left the window. As I did so, I noticed that my hand shook with the palsy of old age; and a short sob choked its way through my lips.

For a little while, I paced, tremulously, between the window and the table; my gaze wandering hither and thither, uneasily. How dilapidated the room was. Everywhere lay the thick dust—thick, sleepy, and black. The fender was a shape of rust. The chains that held the brass clock-weights, had rusted through long ago, and now the weights lay on the floor beneath; themselves two cones of verdigris.

As I glanced about, it seemed to me that I could see the very furniture of the room rotting and decaying before my eyes. Nor was this fancy, on my part; for, all at once, the bookshelf, along the sidewall, collapsed, with a cracking and rending of rotten wood, precipitating its contents upon the floor, and filling the room with a smother of dusty atoms.

How tired I felt. As I walked, it seemed that I could hear my dry joints, creak and crack at every step. I wondered about my sister. Was she dead, as well as Pepper? All had happened so quickly and suddenly. This must be, indeed, the beginning of the end of all things! It occurred to me, to go to look for her; but I felt too weary. And then, she had been so queer about these happenings, of late. Of late! I repeated the words, and laughed, feebly—mirthlessly, as the realization was borne in upon me that I spoke of a time, half a century gone. Half a century! It might have been twice as long!

I moved slowly to the window, and looked out once more across the world. I can best describe the passage of day and night, at this period, as a sort of gigantic, ponderous flicker. Moment by moment, the acceleration of time continued; so that, at nights now, I saw the moon, only as a swaying trail of palish fire, that varied from a mere line of light to a nebulous path, and then dwindled again, disappearing periodically.

The flicker of the days and nights quickened. The days had grown perceptibly darker, and a queer quality of dusk lay, as it were, in the atmosphere. The nights were so much lighter, that the stars were scarcely to be seen, saving here and there an occasional hairlike line of fire, that seemed to sway a little, with the moon.

Quicker, and ever quicker, ran the flicker of day and night; and, suddenly it seemed, I was aware that the flicker had died out, and, instead, there reigned a comparatively steady light, which was shed upon all the world, from an eternal river of flame that swung up and down, North and South, in stupendous, mighty swings.

The sky was now grown very much darker, and there was in the blue of it a heavy gloom, as though a vast blackness peered through it upon the earth. Yet, there was in it, also, a strange and awful clearness, and emptiness. Periodically, I had glimpses of a ghostly track of fire that swayed thin and darkly toward the sun-stream; vanished and reappeared. It was the scarcely visible moon-stream.

Looking out at the landscape, I was conscious again, of a blurring sort of 'flitter,' that came either from the light of the ponderous-swinging sun-stream, or was the result of the incredibly rapid changes of the earth's surface. And every few moments, so it seemed, the snow would lie suddenly upon the world, and vanish as abruptly, as though an invisible giant 'flitted' a white sheet off and on the earth.

Time fled, and the weariness that was mine, grew insupportable. I turned from the window, and walked once across the room, the heavy dust deadening the sound of my footsteps. Each step that I took, seemed a greater effort than the one before. An intolerable ache, knew me in every joint and limb, as I trod my way, with a weary uncertainty.

By the opposite wall, I came to a weak pause, and wondered, dimly, what was my intent. I looked to my left, and saw my old chair. The thought of sitting in it brought a faint sense of comfort to my bewildered wretchedness. Yet, because I was so weary and old and tired, I would scarcely brace my mind to do anything but stand, and wish myself past those few yards. I rocked, as I stood. The floor, even, seemed a place for rest; but the dust lay so thick and sleepy and black. I turned, with a great effort of will, and made toward my chair. I reached it, with a groan of thankfulness. I sat down.

Everything about me appeared to be growing dim. It was all so strange and unthought of. Last night, I was a comparatively strong, though elderly man; and now, only a few hours later—! I looked at the little dust-heap that had once been Pepper. Hours! and I laughed, a feeble, bitter laugh; a shrill, cackling laugh, that shocked my dimming senses.

For a while, I must have dozed. Then I opened my eyes, with a start. Somewhere across the room, there had been a muffled noise of something falling. I looked, and saw, vaguely, a cloud of dust hovering above a pile of debris. Nearer the door, something else tumbled, with a crash. It was one of the cupboards; but I was tired, and took little notice. I closed my eyes, and sat there in a state of drowsy, semi-unconsciousness. Once or twice—as though coming through thick mists—I heard noises, faintly. Then I must have slept.

XVI.
The Awakening

I awoke, with a start. For a moment, I wondered where I was. Then memory came to me…

The room was still lit with that strange light—half-sun, half-moon, light. I felt refreshed, and the tired, weary ache had left me. I went slowly across to the window, and looked out. Overhead, the river of flame drove up and down, North and South, in a dancing semi-circle of fire. As a mighty sleigh in the loom of time it seemed—in a sudden fancy of mine—to be beating home the picks of the years. For, so vastly had the passage of time been accelerated, that there was no longer any sense of the sun passing from East to West. The only apparent movement was the North and South beat of the sun-stream, that had become so swift now, as to be better described as a *quiver*.

As I peered out, there came to me a sudden, inconsequent memory of that last journey among the Outer worlds.[9] I remembered the sudden vision that had come to me, as I neared the Solar System, of the fast whirling planets about the sun—as though the governing quality of time had been held in abeyance, and the Machine of a Universe allowed to run down an eternity, in a few moments or hours. The memory passed, along with a, but partially comprehended, suggestion that I had been permitted a glimpse into further time spaces. I stared out again, seemingly, at the quake of the sun-stream. The speed seemed to increase, even as I looked. Several lifetimes came and went, as I watched.

Suddenly, it struck me, with a sort of grotesque seriousness, that I was still alive. I thought of Pepper, and wondered how it was that I had not followed his fate. He had reached the time of his dying, and had passed, probably through sheer length of years. And here was I, alive, hundreds of thousands of centuries after my rightful period of years.

For, a time, I mused, absently. "Yesterday—" I stopped, suddenly. Yesterday! There was no yesterday. The yesterday of which I spoke had been swallowed up in the abyss of years, ages gone. I grew dazed with much thinking.

Presently, I turned from the window, and glanced 'round the room. It seemed different—strangely, utterly different. Then, I knew what it was that made it

---

[9] Evidently referring to something set forth in the missing and mutilated pages. See Fragments, Chapter 14—Ed.

appear so strange. It was bare: there was not a piece of furniture in the room; not even a solitary fitting of any sort. Gradually, my amazement went, as I remembered, that this was but the inevitable end of that process of decay, which I had witnessed commencing, before my sleep. Thousands of years! Millions of years!

Over the floor was spread a deep layer of dust, that reached half way up to the window-seat. It had grown immeasurably, whilst I slept; and represented the dust of untold ages. Undoubtedly, atoms of the old, decayed furniture helped to swell its bulk; and, somewhere among it all, mouldered the long-ago-dead Pepper.

All at once, it occurred to me, that I had no recollection of wading knee-deep through all that dust, after I awoke. True, an incredible age of years had passed, since I approached the window; but that was evidently as nothing, compared with the countless spaces of time that, I conceived, had vanished whilst I was sleeping. I remembered now, that I had fallen asleep, sitting in my old chair. Had it gone …? I glanced toward where it had stood. Of course, there was no chair to be seen. I could not satisfy myself, whether it had disappeared, after my waking, or before. If it had mouldered under me, surely, I should have been waked by the collapse. Then I remembered that the thick dust, which covered the floor, would have been sufficient to soften my fall; so that it was quite possible, I had slept upon the dust for a million years or more.

As these thoughts wandered through my brain, I glanced again, casually, to where the chair had stood. Then, for the first time, I noticed that there were no marks, in the dust, of my footprints, between it and the window. But then, ages of years had passed, since I had awaked—tens of thousands of years!

My look rested thoughtfully, again upon the place where once had stood my chair. Suddenly, I passed from abstraction to intentness; for there, in its standing place, I made out a long undulation, rounded off with the heavy dust. Yet it was not so much hidden, but that I could tell what had caused it. I knew—and shivered at the knowledge—that it was a human body, ages-dead, lying there, beneath the place where I had slept. It was lying on its right side, its back turned toward me. I could make out and trace each curve and outline, softened, and moulded, as it were, in the black dust. In a vague sort of way, I tried to account for its presence there. Slowly, I began to grow bewildered, as the thought came to me that it lay just about where I must have fallen when the chair collapsed.

Gradually, an idea began to form itself within my brain; a thought that shook my spirit. It seemed hideous and insupportable; yet it grew upon me, steadily, until it became a conviction. The body under that coating, that shroud of dust, was neither more nor less than my own dead shell. I did not attempt to prove it. I knew it now, and wondered I had not known it all along. I was a bodiless thing.

Awhile, I stood, trying to adjust my thoughts to this new problem. In time—how many thousands of years, I know not—I attained to some degree of quietude—sufficient to enable me to pay attention to what was transpiring around me.

Now, I saw that the elongated mound had sunk, collapsed, level with the rest of the spreading dust. And fresh atoms, impalpable, had settled above that mixture of grave-powder, which the eons had ground. A long while, I stood, turned from the window. Gradually, I grew more collected, while the world slipped across the centuries into the future.

Presently, I began a survey of the room. Now, I saw that time was beginning its destructive work, even on this strange old building. That it had stood through all the years was, it seemed to me, proof that it was something different from any other house. I do not think, somehow, that I had thought of its decaying. Though, why, I could not have said. It was not until I had meditated upon the matter, for some considerable time, that I fully realized that the extraordinary space of time through which it had stood, was sufficient to have utterly pulverized the very stones of which it was built, had they been taken from any earthly quarry. Yes, it was undoubtedly moldering now. All the plaster had gone from the walls; even as the woodwork of the room had gone, many ages before.

While I stood, in contemplation, a piece of glass, from one of the small, diamond-shaped panes, dropped, with a dull tap, amid the dust upon the sill behind me, and crumbled into a little heap of powder. As I turned from contemplating it, I saw light between a couple of the stones that formed the outer wall. Evidently, the mortar was falling away…

After awhile, I turned once more to the window, and peered out. I discovered, now, that the speed of time had become enormous. The lateral quiver of the sun-stream, had grown so swift as to cause the dancing semi-circle of flame to merge into, and disappear in, a sheet of fire that covered half the Southern sky from East to West.

From the sky, I glanced down to the gardens. They were just a blur of a palish, dirty green. I had a feeling that they stood higher, than in the old days; a feeling that they were nearer my window, as though they had risen, bodily. Yet, they were still a long way below me; for the rock, over the mouth of the pit, on which this house stands, arches up to a great height.

It was later, that I noticed a change in the constant color of the gardens. The pale, dirty green was growing ever paler and paler, toward white. At last, after a great space, they became greyish-white, and stayed thus for a very long time. Finally, however, the greyness began to fade, even as had the green, into a dead white. And this remained, constant and unchanged. And by this I knew that, at last, snow lay upon all the Northern world.

And so, by millions of years, time winged onward through eternity, to the end —the end, of which, in the old-earth days, I had thought remotely, and in hazily speculative fashion. And now, it was approaching in a manner of which none had ever dreamed.

I recollect that, about this time, I began to have a lively, though morbid, curiosity, as to what would happen when the end came—but I seemed strangely without imaginings.

All this while, the steady process of decay was continuing. The few remaining pieces of glass, had long ago vanished; and, every now and then, a soft thud, and a little cloud of rising dust, would tell of some fragment of fallen mortar or stone.

I looked up again, to the fiery sheet that quaked in the heavens above me and far down into the Southern sky. As I looked, the impression was borne in upon me, that it had lost some of its first brilliancy—that it was duller, deeper hued.

I glanced down, once more, to the blurred white of the worldscape. Sometimes, my look returned to the burning sheet of dulling flame, that was, and yet hid, the sun. At times, I glanced behind me, into the growing dusk of the great, silent room, with its eon-carpet of sleeping dust...

So, I watched through the fleeting ages, lost in soul-wearing thoughts and wonderings, and possessed with a new weariness.

XVII.
The Slowing Rotation

It might have been a million years later, that I perceived, beyond possibility of doubt, that the fiery sheet that lit the world, was indeed darkening.

Another vast space went by, and the whole enormous flame had sunk to a deep, copper color. Gradually, it darkened, from copper to copper-red, and from this, at times, to a deep, heavy, purplish tint, with, in it, a strange loom of blood.

Although the light was decreasing, I could perceive no diminishment in the apparent speed of the sun. It still spread itself in that dazzling veil of speed.

The world, so much of it as I could see, had assumed a dreadful shade of gloom, as though, in very deed, the last day of the worlds approached.

The sun was dying; of that there could be little doubt; and still the earth whirled onward, through space and all the eons. At this time, I remember, an extraordinary sense of bewilderment took me. I found myself, later, wandering, mentally, amid an odd chaos of fragmentary modern theories and the old Biblical story of the world's ending.

Then, for the first time, there flashed across me, the memory that the sun, with its system of planets, was, and had been, traveling through space at an incredible speed. Abruptly, the question rose—*Where?* For a very great time, I pondered this matter; but, finally, with a certain sense of the futility of my puzzlings, I let my thoughts wander to other things. I grew to wondering, how much longer the house would stand. Also, I queried, to myself, whether I should be doomed to stay, bodiless, upon the earth, through the dark-time that I knew was coming. From these thoughts, I fell again to speculations upon the possible direction of the sun's journey through space… And so another great while passed.

Gradually, as time fled, I began to feel the chill of a great winter. Then, I remembered that, with the sun dying, the cold must be, necessarily, extraordinarily intense. Slowly, slowly, as the eons slipped into eternity, the earth sank into a heavier and redder gloom. The dull flame in the firmament took on a deeper tint, very somber and turbid.

Then, at last, it was borne upon me that there was a change. The fiery, gloomy curtain of flame that hung quaking overhead, and down away into the Southern sky, began to thin and contract; and, in it, as one sees the fast vibrations of a jarred harp-string, I saw once more the sun-stream quivering, giddily, North and South.

Slowly, the likeness to a sheet of fire, disappeared, and I saw, plainly, the slowing beat of the sun-stream. Yet, even then, the speed of its swing was inconceivably swift. And all the time, the brightness of the fiery arc grew ever duller. Underneath, the world loomed dimly—an indistinct, ghostly region.

Overhead, the river of flame swayed slower, and even slower; until, at last, it swung to the North and South in great, ponderous beats, that lasted through seconds. A long space went by, and now each sway of the great belt lasted nigh a minute; so that, after a great while, I ceased to distinguish it as a visible movement; and the streaming fire ran in a steady river of dull flame, across the deadly-looking sky.

An indefinite period passed, and it seemed that the arc of fire became less sharply defined. It appeared to me to grow more attenuated, and I thought blackish streaks showed, occasionally. Presently, as I watched, the smooth onward-flow ceased; and I was able to perceive that there came a momentary, but regular, darkening of the world. This grew until, once more, night descended, in short, but periodic, intervals upon the wearying earth.

Longer and longer became the nights, and the days equaled them; so that, at last, the day and the night grew to the duration of seconds in length, and the sun showed, once more, like an almost invisible, coppery-red colored ball, within the glowing mistiness of its flight. Corresponding to the dark lines, showing at times in its trail, there were now distinctly to be seen on the half-visible sun itself, great, dark belts.

Year after year flashed into the past, and the days and nights spread into minutes. The sun had ceased to have the appearance of a tail; and now rose and set—a tremendous globe of a glowing copper-bronze hue; in parts ringed with blood-red bands; in others, with the dusky ones, that I have already mentioned. These circles—both red and black—were of varying thicknesses. For a time, I was at a loss to account for their presence. Then it occurred to me, that it was scarcely likely that the sun would cool evenly all over; and that these markings were due, probably, to differences in temperature of the various areas; the red representing those parts where the heat was still fervent, and the black those portions which were already comparatively cool.

It struck me, as a peculiar thing, that the sun should cool in evenly defined rings; until I remembered that, possibly, they were but isolated patches, to which the enormous rotatory speed of the sun had imparted a beltlike appearance. The sun, itself, was very much greater than the sun I had known in the old-world days; and, from this, I argued that it was considerably nearer.

At nights, the moon still showed; but small and remote;[10] and the light she reflected was so dull and weak that she seemed little more than the small, dim ghost of the olden moon, that I had known.

Gradually, the days and nights lengthened out, until they equaled a space somewhat less than one of the old-earth hours; the sun rising and setting like a great, ruddy bronze disk, crossed with ink-black bars. About this time, I found myself, able once more, to see the gardens, with clearness. For the world had now grown very still, and changeless. Yet, I am not correct in saying, 'gardens;' for there were no gardens—nothing that I knew or recognized. In place thereof, I looked out upon a vast plain, stretching away into distance. A little to my left, there was a low range of hills. Everywhere, there was a uniform, white covering of snow, in places rising into hummocks and ridges.

It was only now, that I recognized how really great had been the snowfall. In places it was vastly deep, as was witnessed by a great, upleaping, wave-shaped hill, away to my right; though it is not impossible, that this was due, in part, to some rise in the surface of the ground. Strangely enough, the range of low hills to my left—already mentioned—was not entirely covered with the universal snow; instead, I could see their bare, dark sides showing in several places. And everywhere and always there reigned an incredible death-silence and desolation. The immutable, awful quiet of a dying world.

All this time, the days and nights were lengthening, perceptibly. Already, each day occupied, maybe, some two hours from dawn to dusk. At night, I had been surprised to find that there were very few stars overhead, and these small, though of an extraordinary brightness; which I attributed to the peculiar, but clear, blackness of the nighttime.

Away to the North, I could discern a nebulous sort of mistiness; not unlike, in appearance, a small portion of the Milky Way. It might have been an extremely remote star-cluster; or—the thought came to me suddenly—perhaps it was the sidereal universe that I had known, and now left far behind, forever—a small, dimly glowing mist of stars, far in the depths of space.

Still, the days and nights lengthened, slowly. Each time, the sun rose duller than it had set. And the dark belts increased in breadth.

About this time, there happened a fresh thing. The sun, earth, and sky were suddenly darkened, and, apparently, blotted out for a brief space. I had a sense, a certain awareness (I could learn little by sight), that the earth was enduring a very great fall of snow. Then, in an instant, the veil that had obscured everything, vanished, and I looked out, once more. A marvelous sight met my gaze. The

[10] No further mention is made of the moon. From what is said here, it is evident that our satellite had greatly increased its distance from the earth. Possibly, at a later age it may even have broken loose from our attraction. I cannot but regret that no light is shed on this point.—Ed.

hollow in which this house, with its gardens, stands, was brimmed with snow.[11] It lipped over the sill of my window. Everywhere, it lay, a great level stretch of white, which caught and reflected, gloomily, the somber coppery glows of the dying sun. The world had become a shadowless plain, from horizon to horizon.

I glanced up at the sun. It shone with an extraordinary, dull clearness. I saw it, now, as one who, until then, had seen it, only through a partially obscuring medium. All about it, the sky had become black, with a clear, deep blackness, frightful in its nearness, and its unmeasured deep, and its utter unfriendliness. For a great time, I looked into it, newly, and shaken and fearful. It was so near. Had I been a child, I might have expressed some of my sensation and distress, by saying that the sky had lost its roof.

Later, I turned, and peered about me, into the room. Everywhere, it was covered with a thin shroud of the all-pervading white. I could see it but dimly, by reason of the somber light that now lit the world. It appeared to cling to the ruined walls; and the thick, soft dust of the years, that covered the floor knee-deep, was nowhere visible. The snow must have blown in through the open framework of the windows. Yet, in no place had it drifted; but lay everywhere about the great, old room, smooth and level. Moreover, there had been no wind these many thousand years. But there was the snow, as I have told.[12]

And all the earth was silent. And there was a cold, such as no living man can ever have known.

The earth was now illuminated, by day, with a most doleful light, beyond my power to describe. It seemed as though I looked at the great plain, through the medium of a bronze-tinted sea.

It was evident that the earth's rotatory movement was departing, steadily.

The end came, all at once. The night had been the longest yet; and when the dying sun showed, at last, above the world's edge, I had grown so wearied of the dark, that I greeted it as a friend. It rose steadily, until about twenty degrees above the horizon. Then, it stopped suddenly, and, after a strange retrograde movement, hung motionless—a great shield in the sky.[13] Only the circular rim of the sun showed bright—only this, and one thin streak of light near the equator.

Gradually, even this thread of light died out; and now, all that was left of our great and glorious sun, was a vast dead disk, rimmed with a thin circle of bronze-red light.

---

[11] Conceivably, frozen air.—Ed.

[12] See previous footnote. This would explain the snow (?) within the room.—Ed.

[13] I am confounded that neither here, nor later on, does the Recluse make any further mention of the continued north and south movement (apparent, of course,) of the sun from solstice to solstice.—Ed.

XVIII.
The Green Star

The world was held in a savage gloom—cold and intolerable. Outside, all was quiet—quiet! From the dark room behind me, came the occasional, soft thud of falling matter—fragments of rotting stone.14 So time passed, and night grasped the world, wrapping it in wrappings of impenetrable blackness.

There was no night-sky, as we know it. Even the few straggling stars had vanished, conclusively. I might have been in a shuttered room, without a light; for all that I could see. Only, in the impalpableness of gloom, opposite, burnt that vast, encircling hair of dull fire. Beyond this, there was no ray in all the vastitude of night that surrounded me; save that, far in the North, that soft, mistlike glow still shone.

Silently, years moved on. What period of time passed, I shall never know. It seemed to me, waiting there, that eternities came and went, stealthily; and still I watched. I could see only the glow of the sun's edge, at times; for now, it had commenced to come and go—lighting up a while, and again becoming extinguished.

All at once, during one of these periods of life, a sudden flame cut across the night—a quick glare that lit up the dead earth, shortly; giving me a glimpse of its flat lonesomeness. The light appeared to come from the sun—shooting out from somewhere near its center, diagonally. A moment, I gazed, startled. Then the leaping flame sank, and the gloom fell again. But now it was not so dark; and the sun was belted by a thin line of vivid, white light. I stared, intently. Had a volcano broken out on the sun? Yet, I negatived the thought, as soon as formed. I felt that the light had been far too intensely white, and large, for such a cause.

Another idea there was, that suggested itself to me. It was, that one of the inner planets had fallen into the sun—becoming incandescent, under that impact. This theory appealed to me, as being more plausible, and accounting more satisfactorily for the extraordinary size and brilliance of the blaze, that had lit up the dead world, so unexpectedly.

---

[14] At this time the sound-carrying atmosphere must have been either incredibly attenuated, or —more probably—nonexistent. In the light of this, it cannot be supposed that these, or any other, noises would have been apparent to living ears—to hearing, as we, in the material body, understand that sense.—Ed.

Full of interest and emotion, I stared, across the darkness, at that line of white fire, cutting the night. One thing it told to me, unmistakably: the sun was yet rotating at an enormous speed.[15] Thus, I knew that the years were still fleeting at an incalculable rate; though so far as the earth was concerned, life, and light, and time, were things belonging to a period lost in the long gone ages.

After that one burst of flame, the light had shown, only as an encircling band of bright fire. Now, however, as I watched, it began slowly to sink into a ruddy tint, and, later, to a dark, copper-red color; much as the sun had done. Presently, it sank to a deeper hue; and, in a still further space of time, it began to fluctuate; having periods of glowing, and anon, dying. Thus, after a great while, it disappeared.

Long before this, the smoldering edge of the sun had deadened into blackness. And so, in that supremely future time, the world, dark and intensely silent, rode on its gloomy orbit around the ponderous mass of the dead sun.

My thoughts, at this period, can be scarcely described. At first, they were chaotic and wanting in coherence. But, later, as the ages came and went, my soul seemed to imbibe the very essence of the oppressive solitude and dreariness, that held the earth.

With this feeling, there came a wonderful clearness of thought, and I realized, despairingly, that the world might wander for ever, through that enormous night. For a while, the unwholesome idea filled me, with a sensation of overbearing desolation; so that I could have cried like a child. In time, however, this feeling grew, almost insensibly, less, and an unreasoning hope possessed me. Patiently, I waited.

From time to time, the noise of dropping particles, behind in the room, came dully to my ears. Once, I heard a loud crash, and turned, instinctively, to look; forgetting, for the moment, the impenetrable night in which every detail was submerged. In a while, my gaze sought the heavens; turning, unconsciously, toward the North. Yes, the nebulous glow still showed. Indeed, I could have almost imagined that it looked somewhat plainer. For a long time, I kept my gaze fixed upon it; feeling, in my lonely soul, that its soft haze was, in some way, a tie with the past. Strange, the trifles from which one can suck comfort! And yet, had I but known—But I shall come to that in its proper time.

For a very long space, I watched, without experiencing any of the desire for sleep, that would so soon have visited me in the old-earth days. How I should have welcomed it; if only to have passed the time, away from my perplexities and thoughts.

Several times, the comfortless sound of some great piece of masonry falling, disturbed my meditations; and, once, it seemed I could hear whispering in the

---

[15] I can only suppose that the time of the earth's yearly journey had ceased to bear its present relative proportion to the period of the sun's rotation.—Ed.

room, behind me. Yet it was utterly useless to try to see anything. Such blackness, as existed, scarcely can be conceived. It was palpable, and hideously brutal to the sense; as though something dead, pressed up against me—something soft, and icily cold.

Under all this, there grew up within my mind, a great and overwhelming distress of uneasiness, that left me, but to drop me into an uncomfortable brooding. I felt that I must fight against it; and, presently, hoping to distract my thoughts, I turned to the window, and looked up toward the North, in search of the nebulous whiteness, which, still, I believed to be the far and misty glowing of the universe we had left. Even as I raised my eyes, I was thrilled with a feeling of wonder; for, now, the hazy light had resolved into a single, great star, of vivid green.

As I stared, astonished, the thought flashed into my mind; that the earth must be traveling toward the star; not away, as I had imagined. Next, that it could not be the universe the earth had left; but, possibly, an outlying star, belonging to some vast star-cluster, hidden in the enormous depths of space. With a sense of commingled awe and curiosity, I watched it, wondering what new thing was to be revealed to me.

For a while, vague thoughts and speculations occupied me, during which my gaze dwelt insatiably upon that one spot of light, in the otherwise pitlike darkness. Hope grew up within me, banishing the oppression of despair, that had seemed to stifle me. Wherever the earth was traveling, it was, at least, going once more toward the realms of light. Light! One must spend an eternity wrapped in soundless night, to understand the full horror of being without it.

Slowly, but surely, the star grew upon my vision, until, in time, it shone as brightly as had the planet Jupiter, in the old-earth days. With increased size, its color became more impressive; reminding me of a huge emerald, scintillating rays of fire across the world.

Years fled away in silence, and the green star grew into a great splash of flame in the sky. A little later, I saw a thing that filled me with amazement. It was the ghostly outline of a vast crescent, in the night; a gigantic new moon, seeming to be growing out of the surrounding gloom. Utterly bemused, I stared at it. It appeared to be quite close—comparatively; and I puzzled to understand how the earth had come so near to it, without my having seen it before.

The light, thrown by the star, grew stronger; and, presently, I was aware that it was possible to see the earthscape again; though indistinctly. Awhile, I stared, trying to make out whether I could distinguish any detail of the world's surface, but I found the light insufficient. In a little, I gave up the attempt, and glanced once more toward the star. Even in the short space, that my attention had been diverted, it had increased considerably, and seemed now, to my bewildered sight, about a quarter of the size of the full moon. The light it threw, was extraordinarily powerful; yet its color was so abominably unfamiliar, that such of the world as I could see, showed unreal; more as though I looked out upon a landscape of shadow, than aught else.

All this time, the great crescent was increasing in brightness, and began, now, to shine with a perceptible shade of green. Steadily, the star increased in size and brilliancy, until it showed, fully as large as half a full moon; and, as it grew greater and brighter, so did the vast crescent throw out more and more light, though of an ever deepening hue of green. Under the combined blaze of their radiances, the wilderness that stretched before me, became steadily more visible. Soon, I seemed able to stare across the whole world, which now appeared, beneath the strange light, terrible in its cold and awful, flat dreariness.

It was a little later, that my attention was drawn to the fact, that the great star of green flame, was slowly sinking out of the North, toward the East. At first, I could scarcely believe that I saw aright; but soon there could be no doubt that it was so. Gradually, it sank, and, as it fell, the vast crescent of glowing green, began to dwindle and dwindle, until it became a mere arc of light, against the livid colored sky. Later it vanished, disappearing in the self-same spot from which I had seen it slowly emerge.

By this time, the star had come to within some thirty degrees of the hidden horizon. In size it could now have rivaled the moon at its full; though, even yet, I could not distinguish its disk. This fact led me to conceive that it was, still, an extraordinary distance away; and, this being so, I knew that its size must be huge, beyond the conception of man to understand or imagine.

Suddenly, as I watched, the lower edge of the star vanished—cut by a straight, dark line. A minute—or a century—passed, and it dipped lower, until the half of it had disappeared from sight. Far away out on the great plain, I saw a monstrous shadow blotting it out, and advancing swiftly. Only a third of the star was visible now. Then, like a flash, the solution of this extraordinary phenomenon revealed itself to me. The star was sinking behind the enormous mass of the dead sun. Or rather, the sun—obedient to its attraction—was rising toward it, with the earth following in its trail.[16] As these thoughts expanded in my mind, the star vanished; being completely hidden by the tremendous bulk of the sun. Over the earth there fell, once more, the brooding night.

With the darkness, came an intolerable feeling of loneliness and dread. For the first time, I thought of the Pit, and its inmates. After that, there rose in my memory the still more terrible Thing, that had haunted the shores of the Sea of Sleep, and lurked in the shadows of this old building. Where were they? I wondered—and shivered with miserable thoughts. For a time, fear held me, and I

---

[16] A careful reading of the MS. suggests that, either the sun is traveling on an orbit of great eccentricity, or else that it was approaching the green star on a lessening orbit. And at this moment, I conceive it to be finally torn directly from its oblique course, by the gravitational pull of the immense star.—Ed.

prayed, wildly and incoherently, for some ray of light with which to dispel the cold blackness that enveloped the world.

How long I waited, it is impossible to say—certainly for a very great period. Then, all at once, I saw a loom of light shine out ahead. Gradually, it became more distinct. Suddenly, a ray of vivid green, flashed across the darkness. At the same moment, I saw a thin line of livid flame, far in the night. An instant, it seemed, and it had grown into a great clot of fire; beneath which, the world lay bathed in a blaze of emerald green light. Steadily it grew, until, presently, the whole of the green star had come into sight again. But now, it could be scarcely called a star; for it had increased to vast proportions, being incomparably greater than the sun had been in the olden time.

"Then, as I stared, I became aware that I could see the edge of the lifeless sun, glowing like a great crescent-moon. Slowly, its lighted surface, broadened out to me, until half of its diameter was visible; and the star began to drop away on my right. Time passed, and the earth moved on, slowly traversing the tremendous face of the dead sun."[17]

Gradually, as the earth traveled forward, the star fell still more to the right; until, at last, it shone on the back of the house, sending a flood of broken rays, in through the skeletonlike walls. Glancing upward, I saw that much of the ceiling had vanished, enabling me to see that the upper storeys were even more decayed. The roof had, evidently, gone entirely; and I could see the green effulgence of the Starlight shining in, slantingly.

---

[17] It will be noticed here that the earth was "slowly traversing the tremendous face of the dead sun." No explanation is given of this, and we must conclude, either that the speed of time had slowed, or else that the earth was actually progressing on its orbit at a rate, slow, when measured by existing standards. A careful study of the MS. however, leads me to conclude that the speed of time had been steadily decreasing for a very considerable period.—Ed.

XIX.
The End of the Solar System

From the abutment, where once had been the windows, through which I had watched that first, fatal dawn, I could see that the sun was hugely greater, than it had been, when first the Star lit the world. So great was it, that its lower edge seemed almost to touch the far horizon. Even as I watched, I imagined that it drew closer. The radiance of green that lit the frozen earth, grew steadily brighter.

Thus, for a long space, things were. Then, on a sudden, I saw that the sun was changing shape, and growing smaller, just as the moon would have done in past time. In a while, only a third of the illuminated part was turned toward the earth. The Star bore away on the left.

Gradually, as the world moved on, the Star shone upon the front of the house, once more; while the sun showed, only as a great bow of green fire. An instant, it seemed, and the sun had vanished. The Star was still fully visible. Then the earth moved into the black shadow of the sun, and all was night—Night, black, starless, and intolerable.

Filled with tumultuous thoughts, I watched across the night—waiting. Years, it may have been, and then, in the dark house behind me, the clotted stillness of the world was broken. I seemed to hear a soft padding of many feet, and a faint, inarticulate whisper of sound, grew on my sense. I looked 'round into the blackness, and saw a multitude of eyes. As I stared, they increased, and appeared to come toward me. For an instant, I stood, unable to move. Then a hideous swine-noise rose up into the night; and, at that, I leapt from the window, out on to the frozen world.[18] I have a confused notion of having run awhile; and, after that, I just waited—waited. Several times, I heard shrieks; but always as though from a distance. Except for these sounds, I had no idea of the whereabouts of the house. Time moved onward. I was conscious of little, save a sensation of cold and hopelessness and fear.

An age, it seemed, and there came a glow, that told of the coming light. It grew, tardily. Then—with a loom of unearthly glory—the first ray from the Green Star, struck over the edge of the dark sun, and lit the world. It fell upon a great, ruined structure, some two hundred yards away. It was the house. Staring, I

---

[18] See first footnote, Chapter 18.

saw a fearsome sight—over its walls crawled a legion of unholy things, almost covering the old building, from tottering towers to base. I could see them, plainly; they were the Swine-creatures.

The world moved out into the light of the Star, and I saw that, now, it seemed to stretch across a quarter of the heavens. The glory of its livid light was so tremendous, that it appeared to fill the sky with quivering flames. Then, I saw the sun. It was so close that half of its diameter lay below the horizon; and, as the world circled across its face, it seemed to tower right up into the sky, a stupendous dome of emerald colored fire. From time to time, I glanced toward the house; but the Swine-things seemed unaware of my proximity.

Years appeared to pass, slowly. The earth had almost reached the center of the sun's disk. The light from the Green *Sun*—as now it must be called—shone through the interstices, that gapped the mouldered walls of the old house, giving them the appearance of being wrapped in green flames. The Swine-creatures still crawled about the walls.

Suddenly, there rose a loud roar of swine-voices, and, up from the center of the roofless house, shot a vast column of blood-red flame. I saw the little, twisted towers and turrets flash into fire; yet still preserving their twisted crookedness. The beams of the Green Sun, beat upon the house, and intermingled with its lurid glows; so that it appeared a blazing furnace of red and green fire.

Fascinated, I watched, until an overwhelming sense of coming danger, drew my attention. I glanced up, and, at once, it was borne upon me, that the sun was closer; so close, in fact, that it seemed to overhang the world. Then—I know not how—I was caught up into strange heights—floating like a bubble in the awful effulgence.

Far below me, I saw the earth, with the burning house leaping into an ever growing mountain of flame, 'round about it, the ground appeared to be glowing; and, in places, heavy wreaths of yellow smoke ascended from the earth. It seemed as though the world were becoming ignited from that one plague-spot of fire. Faintly, I could see the Swine-things. They appeared quite unharmed. Then the ground seemed to cave in, suddenly, and the house, with its load of foul creatures, disappeared into the depths of the earth, sending a strange, blood colored cloud into the heights. I remembered the hell Pit under the house.

In a while, I looked 'round. The huge bulk of the sun, rose high above me. The distance between it and the earth, grew rapidly less. Suddenly, the earth appeared to shoot forward. In a moment, it had traversed the space between it and the sun. I heard no sound; but, out from the sun's face, gushed an ever-growing tongue of dazzling flame. It seemed to leap, almost to the distant Green Sun—shearing through the emerald light, a very cataract of blinding fire. It reached its limit, and sank; and, on the sun, glowed a vast splash of burning white—the grave of the earth.

The sun was very close to me, now. Presently, I found that I was rising higher; until, at last, I rode above it, in the emptiness. The Green Sun was now so huge that its breadth seemed to fill up all the sky, ahead. I looked down, and noted that the sun was passing directly beneath me.

A year may have gone by—or a century—and I was left, suspended, alone. The sun showed far in front—a black, circular mass, against the molten splendor of the great, Green Orb. Near one edge, I observed that a lurid glow had appeared, marking the place where the earth had fallen. By this, I knew that the long-dead sun was still revolving, though with great slowness.

Afar to my right, I seemed to catch, at times, a faint glow of whitish light. For a great time, I was uncertain whether to put this down to fancy or not. Thus, for a while, I stared, with fresh wonderings; until, at last, I knew that it was no imaginary thing; but a reality. It grew brighter; and, presently, there slid out of the green, a pale globe of softest white. It came nearer, and I saw that it was apparently surrounded by a robe of gently glowing clouds. Time passed...

I glanced toward the diminishing sun. It showed, only as a dark blot on the face of the Green Sun. As I watched, I saw it grow smaller, steadily, as though rushing toward the superior orb, at an immense speed. Intently, I stared. What would happen? I was conscious of extraordinary emotions, as I realized that it would strike the Green Sun. It grew no bigger than a pea, and I looked, with my whole soul, to witness the final end of our System—that system which had borne the world through so many eons, with its multitudinous sorrows and joys; and now—

Suddenly, something crossed my vision, cutting from sight all vestige of the spectacle I watched with such soul-interest. What happened to the dead sun, I did not see; but I have no reason—in the light of that which I saw afterward—to disbelieve that it fell into the strange fire of the Green Sun, and so perished.

And then, suddenly, an extraordinary question rose in my mind, whether this stupendous globe of green fire might not be the vast Central Sun—the great sun, 'round which our universe and countless others revolve. I felt confused. I thought of the probable end of the dead sun, and another suggestion came, dumbly—Do the dead stars make the Green Sun their grave? The idea appealed to me with no sense of grotesqueness; but rather as something both possible and probable.

XX.
The Celestial Globes

For a while, many thoughts crowded my mind, so that I was unable to do aught, save stare, blindly, before me. I seemed whelmed in a sea of doubt and wonder and sorrowful remembrance.

It was later, that I came out of my bewilderment. I looked about, dazedly. Thus, I saw so extraordinary a sight that, for a while, I could scarcely believe I was not still wrapped in the visionary tumult of my own thoughts. Out of the reigning green, had grown a boundless river of softly shimmering globes—each one enfolded in a wondrous fleece of pure cloud. They reached, both above and below me, to an unknown distance; and, not only hid the shining of the Green Sun; but supplied, in place thereof, a tender glow of light, that suffused itself around me, like unto nothing I have ever seen, before or since.

In a little, I noticed that there was about these spheres, a sort of transparency, almost as though they were formed of clouded crystal, within which burned a radiance—gentle and subdued. They moved on, past me, continually, floating onward at no great speed; but rather as though they had eternity before them. A great while, I watched, and could perceive no end to them. At times, I seemed to distinguish faces, amid the cloudiness; but strangely indistinct, as though partly real, and partly formed of the mistiness through which they showed.

For a long time, I waited, passively, with a sense of growing content. I had no longer that feeling of unutterable loneliness; but felt, rather, that I was less alone, than I had been for kalpas of years. This feeling of contentment, increased, so that I would have been satisfied to float in company with those celestial globules, forever.

Ages slipped by, and I saw the shadowy faces, with increased frequency, also with greater plainness. Whether this was due to my soul having become more attuned to its surroundings, I cannot tell—probably it was so. But, however this may be, I am assured now, only of the fact that I became steadily more conscious of a new mystery about me, telling me that I had, indeed, penetrated within the borderland of some unthought-of region—some subtle, intangible place, or form, of existence.

The enormous stream of luminous spheres continued to pass me, at an unvarying rate—countless millions; and still they came, showing no signs of ending, nor even diminishing.

Then, as I was borne, silently, upon the unbuoying ether, I felt a sudden, irresistible, forward movement, toward one of the passing globes. An instant, and I was beside it. Then, I slid through, into the interior, without experiencing the least resistance, of any description. For a short while, I could see nothing; and waited, curiously.

All at once, I became aware that a sound broke the inconceivable stillness. It was like the murmur of a great sea at calm—a sea breathing in its sleep. Gradually, the mist that obscured my sight, began to thin away; and so, in time, my vision dwelt once again upon the silent surface of the Sea of Sleep.

For a little, I gazed, and could scarcely believe I saw aright. I glanced 'round. There was the great globe of pale fire, swimming, as I had seen it before, a short distance above the dim horizon. To my left, far across the sea, I discovered, presently, a faint line, as of thin haze, which I guessed to be the shore, where my Love and I had met, during those wonderful periods of soul-wandering, that had been granted to me in the old earth days.

Another, a troubled, memory came to me—of the Formless Thing that had haunted the shores of the Sea of Sleep. The guardian of that silent, echoless place. These, and other, details, I remembered, and knew, without doubt that I was looking out upon that same sea. With the assurance, I was filled with an overwhelming feeling of surprise, and joy, and shaken expectancy, conceiving it possible that I was about to see my Love, again. Intently, I gazed around; but could catch no sight of her. At that, for a little, I felt hopeless. Fervently, I prayed, and ever peered, anxiously... How still was the sea!

Down, far beneath me, I could see the many trails of changeful fire, that had drawn my attention, formerly. Vaguely, I wondered what caused them; also, I remembered that I had intended to ask my dear One about them, as well as many other matters—and I had been forced to leave her, before the half that I had wished to say, was said.

My thoughts came back with a leap. I was conscious that something had touched me. I turned quickly. God, Thou wert indeed gracious—it was She! She looked up into my eyes, with an eager longing, and I looked down to her, with all my soul. I should like to have held her; but the glorious purity of her face, kept me afar. Then, out of the winding mist, she put her dear arms. Her whisper came to me, soft as the rustle of a passing cloud. "Dearest!" she said. That was all; but I had heard, and, in a moment I held her to me—as I prayed—forever.

In a little, she spoke of many things, and I listened. Willingly, would I have done so through all the ages that are to come. At times, I whispered back, and my whispers brought to her spirit face, once more, an indescribably delicate tint—the bloom of love. Later, I spoke more freely, and to each word she listened, and made answer, delightfully; so that, already, I was in Paradise.

She and I; and nothing, save the silent, spacious void to see us; and only the quiet waters of the Sea of Sleep to hear us.

Long before, the floating multitude of cloud-enfolded spheres had vanished into nothingness. Thus, we looked upon the face of the slumberous deeps, and were alone. Alone, God, I would be thus alone in the hereafter, and yet be never lonely! I had her, and, greater than this, she had me. Aye, eon-aged me; and on this thought, and some others, I hope to exist through the few remaining years that may yet lie between us.

XXI.
The Dark Sun

How long our souls lay in the arms of joy, I cannot say; but, all at once, I was waked from my happiness, by a diminution of the pale and gentle light that lit the Sea of Sleep. I turned toward the huge, white orb, with a premonition of coming trouble. One side of it was curving inward, as though a convex, black shadow were sweeping across it. My memory went back. It was thus, that the darkness had come, before our last parting. I turned toward my Love, inquiringly. With a sudden knowledge of woe, I noticed how wan and unreal she had grown, even in that brief space. Her voice seemed to come to me from a distance. The touch of her hands was no more than the gentle pressure of a summer wind, and grew less perceptible.

Already, quite half of the immense globe was shrouded. A feeling of desperation seized me. Was she about to leave me? Would she have to go, as she had gone before? I questioned her, anxiously, frightenedly; and she, nestling closer, explained, in that strange, faraway voice, that it was imperative she should leave me, before the Sun of Darkness—as she termed it—blotted out the light. At this confirmation of my fears, I was overcome with despair; and could only look, voicelessly, across the quiet plains of the silent sea.

How swiftly the darkness spread across the face of the White Orb. Yet, in reality, the time must have been long, beyond human comprehension.

At last, only a crescent of pale fire, lit the, now dim, Sea of Sleep. All this while, she had held me; but, with so soft a caress, that I had been scarcely conscious of it. We waited there, together, she and I; speechless, for very sorrow. In the dimming light, her face showed, shadowy—blending into the dusky mistiness that encircled us.

Then, when a thin, curved line of soft light was all that lit the sea, she released me—pushing me from her, tenderly. Her voice sounded in my ears, "I may not stay longer, Dear One." It ended in a sob.

She seemed to float away from me, and became invisible. Her voice came to me, out of the shadows, faintly; apparently from a great distance:—

"A little while—" It died away, remotely. In a breath, the Sea of Sleep darkened into night. Far to my left, I seemed to see, for a brief instant, a soft glow. It vanished, and, in the same moment, I became aware that I was no longer above the still sea; but once more suspended in infinite space, with the Green Sun—now eclipsed by a vast, dark sphere—before me.

Utterly bewildered, I stared, almost unseeingly, at the ring of green flames, leaping above the dark edge. Even in the chaos of my thoughts, I wondered, dully, at their extraordinary shapes. A multitude of questions assailed me. I thought more of her, I had so lately seen, than of the sight before me. My grief, and thoughts of the future, filled me. Was I doomed to be separated from her, always? Even in the old earth-days, she had been mine, only for a little while; then she had left me, as I thought, forever. Since then, I had seen her but these times, upon the Sea of Sleep.

A feeling of fierce resentment filled me, and miserable questionings. Why could I not have gone with my Love? What reason to keep us apart? Why had I to wait alone, while she slumbered through the years, on the still bosom of the Sea of Sleep? The Sea of Sleep! My thoughts turned, inconsequently, out of their channel of bitterness, to fresh, desperate questionings. Where was it? Where was it? I seemed to have but just parted from my Love, upon its quiet surface, and it had gone, utterly. It could not be far away! And the White Orb which I had seen hidden in the shadow of the Sun of Darkness! My sight dwelt upon the Green Sun—eclipsed. What had eclipsed it? Was there a vast, dead star circling it? Was the *Central* Sun—as I had come to regard it—a double star? The thought had come, almost unbidden; yet why should it not be so?

My thoughts went back to the White Orb. Strange, that it should have been —I stopped. An idea had come, suddenly. The White Orb and the Green Sun! Were they one and the same? My imagination wandered backward, and I remembered the luminous globe to which I had been so unaccountably attracted. It was curious that I should have forgotten it, even momentarily. Where were the others? I reverted again to the globe I had entered. I thought, for a time, and matters became clearer. I conceived that, by entering that impalpable globule, I had passed, at once, into some further, and, until then, invisible dimension; There, the Green Sun was still visible; but as a stupendous sphere of pale, white light—almost as though its ghost showed, and not its material part.

A long time, I mused on the subject. I remembered how, on entering the sphere, I had, immediately, lost all sight of the others. For a still further period, I continued to revolve the different details in my mind.

In a while, my thoughts turned to other things. I came more into the present, and began to look about me, seeingly. For the first time, I perceived that innumerable rays, of a subtle, violet hue, pierced the strange semi-darkness, in all directions. They radiated from the fiery rim of the Green Sun. They seemed to grow upon my vision, so that, in a little, I saw that they were countless. The night was filled with them—spreading outward from the Green Sun, fan-wise. I concluded that I was enabled to see them, by reason of the Sun's glory being cut off by the eclipse. They reached right out into space, and vanished.

Gradually, as I looked, I became aware that fine points of intensely brilliant light, traversed the rays. Many of them seemed to travel from the Green Sun, into distance. Others came out of the void, toward the Sun; but one and all, each kept strictly to the ray in which it traveled. Their speed was inconceivably great; and it was only when they neared the Green Sun, or as they left it, that I could see them as separate specks of light. Further from the sun, they became thin lines of vivid fire within the violet.

The discovery of these rays, and the moving sparks, interested me, extraordinarily. To where did they lead, in such countless profusion? I thought of the worlds in space... And those sparks! Messengers! Possibly, the idea was fantastic; but I was not conscious of its being so. Messengers! Messengers from the Central Sun!

An idea evolved itself, slowly. Was the Green Sun the abode of some vast Intelligence? The thought was bewildering. Visions of the Unnamable rose, vaguely. Had I, indeed, come upon the dwelling-place of the Eternal? For a time, I repelled the thought, dumbly. It was too stupendous. Yet...

Huge, vague thoughts had birth within me. I felt, suddenly, terribly naked. And an awful Nearness, shook me.

And Heaven...! Was that an illusion?

My thoughts came and went, erratically. The Sea of Sleep—and she! Heaven... I came back, with a bound, to the present. Somewhere, out of the void behind me, there rushed an immense, dark body—huge and silent. It was a dead star, hurling onward to the burying place of the stars. It drove between me and the Central Suns—blotting them out from my vision, and plunging me into an impenetrable night.

An age, and I saw again the violet rays. A great while later—aeons it must have been—a circular glow grew in the sky, ahead, and I saw the edge of the receding star, show darkly against it. Thus, I knew that it was nearing the Central Suns. Presently, I saw the bright ring of the Green Sun, show plainly against the night The star had passed into the shadow of the Dead Sun. After that, I just waited. The strange years went slowly, and ever, I watched, intently.

The thing I had expected, came at last—suddenly, awfully. A vast flare of dazzling light. A streaming burst of white flame across the dark void. For an indefinite while, it soared outward—a gigantic mushroom of fire. It ceased to grow. Then, as time went by, it began to sink backward, slowly. I saw, now, that it came from a huge, glowing spot near the center of the Dark Sun. Mighty flames, still soared outward from this. Yet, spite of its size, the grave of the star was no more than the shining of Jupiter upon the face of an ocean, when compared with the inconceivable mass of the Dead Sun.

I may remark here, once more, that no words will ever convey to the imagination, the enormous bulk of the two Central Suns.

XXII. THE DARK NEBULA

Years melted into the past, centuries, eons. The light of the incandescent star, sank to a furious red.

It was later, that I saw the dark nebula—at first, an impalpable cloud, away to my right. It grew, steadily, to a clot of blackness in the night. How long I watched, it is impossible to say; for time, as we count it, was a thing of the past. It came closer, a shapeless monstrosity of darkness—tremendous. It seemed to slip across the night, sleepily—a very hell-fog. Slowly, it slid nearer, and passed into the void, between me and the Central Suns. It was as though a curtain had been drawn before my vision. A strange tremor of fear took me, and a fresh sense of wonder.

The green twilight that had reigned for so many millions of years, had now given place to impenetrable gloom. Motionless, I peered about me. A century fled, and it seemed to me that I detected occasional dull glows of red, passing me at intervals.

Earnestly, I gazed, and, presently, seemed to see circular masses, that showed muddily red, within the clouded blackness. They appeared to be growing out of the nebulous murk. Awhile, and they became plainer to my accustomed vision. I could see them, now, with a fair amount of distinctness—ruddy-tinged spheres, similar, in size, to the luminous globes that I had seen, so long previously.

They floated past me, continually. Gradually, a peculiar uneasiness seized me. I became aware of a growing feeling of repugnance and dread. It was directed against those passing orbs, and seemed born of intuitive knowledge, rather than of any real cause or reason.

Some of the passing globes were brighter than others; and, it was from one of these, that a face looked, suddenly. A face, human in its outline; but so tortured with woe, that I stared, aghast. I had not thought there was such sorrow, as I saw there. I was conscious of an added sense of pain, on perceiving that the eyes, which glared so wildly, were sightless. A while longer, I saw it; then it had passed on, into the surrounding gloom. After this, I saw others—all wearing that look of hopeless sorrow; and blind.

A long time went by, and I became aware that I was nearer to the orbs, than I had been. At this, I grew uneasy; though I was less in fear of those strange globules, than I had been, before seeing their sorrowful inhabitants; for sympathy had tempered my fear.

Later, there was no doubt but that I was being carried closer to the red spheres, and, presently, I floated among them. In awhile, I perceived one bearing down upon me. I was helpless to move from its path. In a minute, it seemed, it was upon me, and I was submerged in a deep red mist. This cleared, and I stared, confusedly, across the immense breadth of the Plain of Silence. It appeared just as I had first seen it. I was moving forward, steadily, across its surface. Away ahead, shone the vast, blood-red ring that lit the place.[19] All around, was spread the extraordinary desolation of stillness, that had so impressed me during my previous wanderings across its starkness.

Presently, I saw, rising up into the ruddy gloom, the distant peaks of the mighty amphitheatre of mountains, where, untold ages before, I had been shown my first glimpse of the terrors that underlie many things; and where, vast and silent, watched by a thousand mute gods, stands the replica of this house of mysteries—this house that I had seen swallowed up in that hell-fire, ere the earth had kissed the sun, and vanished for ever.

Though I could see the crests of the mountain-amphitheatre, yet it was a great while before their lower portions became visible. Possibly, this was due to the strange, ruddy haze, that seemed to cling to the surface of the Plain. However, be this as it may, I saw them at last.

In a still further space of time, I had come so close to the mountains, that they appeared to overhang me. Presently, I saw the great rift, open before me, and I drifted into it; without volition on my part.

Later, I came out upon the breadth of the enormous arena. There, at an apparent distance of some five miles, stood the House, huge, monstrous and silent—lying in the very center of that stupendous amphitheatre. So far as I could see, it had not altered in any way; but looked as though it were only yesterday that I had seen it. Around, the grim, dark mountains frowned down upon me from their lofty silences.

Far to my right, away up among inaccessible peaks, loomed the enormous bulk of the great Beast-god. Higher, I saw the hideous form of the dread goddess, rising up through the red gloom, thousands of fathoms above me. To the left, I made out the monstrous Eyeless-Thing, grey and inscrutable. Further off, reclining on its lofty ledge, the livid Ghoul-Shape showed—a splash of sinister color, among the dark mountains.

Slowly, I moved out across the great arena—floating. As I went, I made out the dim forms of many of the other lurking Horrors that peopled those supreme heights.

[19] Without doubt, the flame-edged mass of the Dead Central Sun, seen from another dimension.—Ed.

Gradually, I neared the House, and my thoughts flashed back across the abyss of years. I remembered the dread Specter of the Place. A short while passed, and I saw that I was being wafted directly toward the enormous mass of that silent building.

About this time, I became aware, in an indifferent sort of way, of a growing sense of numbness, that robbed me of the fear, which I should otherwise have felt, on approaching that awesome Pile. As it was, I viewed it, calmly—much as a man views calamity through the haze of his tobacco smoke.

In a little while, I had come so close to the House, as to be able to distinguish many of the details about it. The longer I looked, the more was I confirmed in my long-ago impressions of its entire similitude to this strange house. Save in its enormous size, I could find nothing unlike.

Suddenly, as I stared, a great feeling of amazement filled me. I had come opposite to that part, where the outer door, leading into the study, is situated. There, lying right across the threshold, lay a great length of coping stone, identical—save in size and color—with the piece I had dislodged in my fight with the Pit-creatures.

I floated nearer, and my astonishment increased, as I noted that the door was broken partly from its hinges, precisely in the manner that my study door had been forced inward, by the assaults of the Swine-things. The sight started a train of thoughts, and I began to trace, dimly, that the attack on this house, might have a far deeper significance than I had, hitherto, imagined. I remembered how, long ago, in the old earth-days, I had half suspected that, in some unexplainable manner, this house, in which I live, was *en rapport*—to use a recognized term—with that other tremendous structure, away in the midst of that incomparable Plain.

Now, however, it began to be borne upon me, that I had but vaguely conceived what the realization of my suspicion meant. I began to understand, with a more than human clearness, that the attack I had repelled, was, in some extraordinary manner, connected with an attack upon that strange edifice.

With a curious inconsequence, my thoughts abruptly left the matter; to dwell, wonderingly, upon the peculiar material, out of which the House was constructed. It was—as I have mentioned, earlier—of a deep, green color. Yet, now that I had come so close to it, I perceived that it fluctuated at times, though slightly—glowing and fading, much as do the fumes of phosphorus, when rubbed upon the hand, in the dark.

Presently, my attention was distracted from this, by coming to the great entrance. Here, for the first time, I was afraid; for, all in a moment, the huge doors swung back, and I drifted in between them, helplessly. Inside, all was blackness, impalpable. In an instant, I had crossed the threshold, and the great doors closed, silently, shutting me in that lightless place.

For a while, I seemed to hang, motionless; suspended amid the darkness. Then, I became conscious that I was moving again; where, I could not tell. Suddenly, far down beneath me, I seemed to hear a murmurous noise of Swine-laughter. It sank away, and the succeeding silence appeared clogged with horror.

Then a door opened somewhere ahead; a white haze of light filtered through, and I floated slowly into a room, that seemed strangely familiar. All at once, there came a bewildering, screaming noise, that deafened me. I saw a blurred vista of visions, flaming before my sight. My senses were dazed, through the space of an eternal moment. Then, my power of seeing, came back to me. The dizzy, hazy feeling passed, and I saw, clearly.

XXIII.
Pepper

I was seated in my chair, back again in this old study. My glance wandered 'round the room. For a minute, it had a strange, quivery appearance—unreal and unsubstantial. This disappeared, and I saw that nothing was altered in any way. I looked toward the end window—the blind was up.

I rose to my feet, shakily. As I did so, a slight noise, in the direction of the door, attracted my attention. I glanced toward it. For a short instant, it appeared to me that it was being closed, gently. I stared, and saw that I must have been mistaken—it seemed closely shut.

With a succession of efforts, I trod my way to the window, and looked out. The sun was just rising, lighting up the tangled wilderness of gardens. For, perhaps, a minute, I stood, and stared. I passed my hand, confusedly, across my forehead.

Presently, amid the chaos of my senses, a sudden thought came to me; I turned, quickly, and called to Pepper. There was no answer, and I stumbled across the room, in a quick access of fear. As I went, I tried to frame his name; but my lips were numb. I reached the table, and stooped down to him, with a catching at my heart. He was lying in the shadow of the table, and I had not been able to see him, distinctly, from the window. Now, as I stooped, I took my breath, shortly. There was no Pepper; instead, I was reaching toward an elongated, little heap of grey, ash-like dust…

I must have remained, in that half-stooped position, for some minutes. I was dazed—stunned. Pepper had really passed into the land of shadows.

XXIV.
The Footsteps in the Garden

Pepper is dead! Even now, at times, I seem scarcely able to realize that this is so. It is many weeks, since I came back from that strange and terrible journey through space and time. Sometimes, in my sleep, I dream about it, and go through, in imagination, the whole of that fearsome happening. When I wake, my thoughts dwell upon it. That Sun—those Suns, were they indeed the great Central Suns, 'round which the whole universe, of the unknown heavens, revolves? Who shall say? And the bright globules, floating forever in the light of the Green Sun! And the Sea of Sleep on which they float! How unbelievable it all is. If it were not for Pepper, I should, even after the many extraordinary things that I have witnessed, be inclined to imagine that it was but a gigantic dream. Then, there is that dreadful, dark nebula (with its multitudes of red spheres) moving always within the shadow of the Dark Sun, sweeping along on its stupendous orbit, wrapped eternally in gloom. And the faces that peered out at me! God, do they, and does such a thing really exist? … There is still that little heap of grey ash, on my study floor. I will not have it touched.

At times, when I am calmer, I have wondered what became of the outer planets of the Solar System. It has occurred to me, that they may have broken loose from the sun's attraction, and whirled away into space. This is, of course, only a surmise. There are so many things, about which I wonder.

Now that I am writing, let me record that I am certain, there is something horrible about to happen. Last night, a thing occurred, which has filled me with an even greater terror, than did the Pit fear. I will write it down now, and, if anything more happens, endeavor to make a note of it, at once. I have a feeling, that there is more in this last affair, than in all those others. I am shaky and nervous, even now, as I write. Somehow, I think death is not very far away. Not that I fear death—as death is understood. Yet, there is that in the air, which bids me fear—an intangible, cold horror. I felt it last night. It was thus:—

Last night, I was sitting here in my study, writing. The door, leading into the garden, was half open. At times, the metallic rattle of a dog's chain, sounded faintly. It belongs to the dog I have bought, since Pepper's death. I will not have him in the house—not after Pepper. Still, I have felt it better to have a dog about the place. They are wonderful creatures.

I was much engrossed in my work, and the time passed, quickly. Suddenly, I heard a soft noise on the path, outside in the garden—pad, pad, pad, it went, with a stealthy, curious sound. I sat upright, with a quick movement, and looked out through the opened door. Again the noise came—pad, pad, pad. It appeared to be approaching. With a slight feeling of nervousness, I stared into the gardens; but the night hid everything.

Then the dog gave a long howl, and I started. For a minute, perhaps, I peered, intently; but could hear nothing. After a little, I picked up the pen, which I had laid down, and recommenced my work. The nervous feeling had gone; for I imagined that the sound I had heard, was nothing more than the dog walking 'round his kennel, at the length of his chain.

A quarter of an hour may have passed; then, all at once, the dog howled again, and with such a plaintively sorrowful note, that I jumped to my feet, dropping my pen, and inking the page on which I was at work.

"Curse that dog!" I muttered, noting what I had done. Then, even as I said the words, there sounded again that queer—pad, pad, pad. It was horribly close—almost by the door, I thought. I knew, now, that it could not be the dog; his chain would not allow him to come so near.

The dog's growl came again, and I noted, subconsciously, the taint of fear in it.

Outside, on the windowsill, I could see Tip, my sister's pet cat. As I looked, it sprang to its feet, its tail swelling, visibly. For an instant it stood thus; seeming to stare, fixedly, at something, in the direction of the door. Then, quickly, it began to back along the sill; until, reaching the wall at the end, it could go no further. There it stood, rigid, as though frozen in an attitude of extraordinary terror.

Frightened, and puzzled, I seized a stick from the corner, and went toward the door, silently; taking one of the candles with me. I had come to within a few paces of it, when, suddenly, a peculiar sense of fear thrilled through me—a fear, palpitant and real; whence, I knew not, nor why. So great was the feeling of terror, that I wasted no time; but retreated straight-way—walking backward, and keeping my gaze, fearfully, on the door. I would have given much, to rush at it, fling it to, and shoot the bolts; for I have had it repaired and strengthened, so that, now, it is far stronger than ever it has been. Like Tip, I continued my, almost unconscious, progress backward, until the wall brought me up. At that, I started, nervously, and glanced 'round, apprehensively. As I did so, my eyes dwelt, momentarily, on the rack of firearms, and I took a step toward them; but stopped, with a curious feeling that they would be needless. Outside, in the gardens, the dog moaned, strangely.

Suddenly, from the cat, there came a fierce, long screech. I glanced, jerkily, in its direction—Something, luminous and ghostly, encircled it, and grew upon my vision. It resolved into a glowing hand, transparent, with a lambent, greenish flame flickering over it. The cat gave a last, awful caterwaul, and I saw it smoke and blaze. My breath came with a gasp, and I leant against the wall. Over that part of the window there spread a smudge, green and fantastic. It hid the thing from me, though the glare of fire shone through, dully. A stench of burning, stole into the room.

Pad, pad, pad—Something passed down the garden path, and a faint, mouldy odor seemed to come in through the open door, and mingle with the burnt smell.

The dog had been silent for a few moments. Now, I heard him yowl, sharply, as though in pain. Then, he was quiet, save for an occasional, subdued whimper of fear.

A minute went by; then the gate on the West side of the gardens, slammed, distantly. After that, nothing; not even the dog's whine.

I must have stood there some minutes. Then a fragment of courage stole into my heart, and I made a frightened rush at the door, dashed it to, and bolted it. After that, for a full half-hour, I sat, helpless—staring before me, rigidly.

Slowly, my life came back into me, and I made my way, shakily, up-stairs to bed.

That is all.

XXV.
The Thing From the Arena

This morning, early, I went through the gardens; but found everything as usual. Near the door, I examined the path, for footprints; yet, here again, there was nothing to tell me whether, or not, I dreamed last night.

It was only when I came to speak to the dog, that I discovered tangible proof, that something did happen. When I went to his kennel, he kept inside, crouching up in one corner, and I had to coax him, to get him out. When, finally, he consented to come, it was in a strangely cowed and subdued manner. As I patted him, my attention was attracted to a greenish patch, on his left flank. On examining it, I found, that the fur and skin had been apparently, burnt off; for the flesh showed, raw and scorched. The shape of the mark was curious, reminding me of the imprint of a large talon or hand.

I stood up, thoughtful. My gaze wandered toward the study window. The rays of the rising sun, shimmered on the smoky patch in the lower corner, causing it to fluctuate from green to red, oddly. Ah! that was undoubtedly another proof; and, suddenly, the horrible Thing I saw last night, rose in my mind. I looked at the dog, again. I knew the cause, now, of that hateful looking wound on his side —I knew, also, that, what I had seen last night, had been a real happening. And a great discomfort filled me. Pepper! Tip! And now this poor animal …! I glanced at the dog again, and noticed that he was licking at his wound.

"Poor brute!" I muttered, and bent to pat his head. At that, he got upon his feet, nosing and licking my hand, wistfully.

Presently, I left him, having other matters to which to attend.

After dinner, I went to see him, again. He seemed quiet, and disinclined to leave his kennel. From my sister, I have learnt that he has refused all food today. She appeared a little puzzled, when she told me; though quite unsuspicious of anything of which to be afraid.

The day has passed, uneventfully enough. After tea, I went, again, to have a look at the dog. He seemed moody, and somewhat restless; yet persisted in remaining in his kennel. Before locking up, for the night, I moved his kennel out, away from the wall, so that I shall be able to watch it from the small window, tonight. The thought came to me, to bring him into the house for the night; but consideration has decided me, to let him remain out. I cannot say that the house is, in any degree, less to be feared than the gardens. Pepper was in the house, and yet...

It is now two o'clock. Since eight, I have watched the kennel, from the small, side window in my study. Yet, nothing has occurred, and I am too tired to watch longer. I will go to bed...

During the night, I was restless. This is unusual for me; but, toward morning, I obtained a few hours' sleep.

I rose early, and, after breakfast, visited the dog. He was quiet; but morose, and refused to leave his kennel. I wish there was some horse doctor near here; I would have the poor brute looked to. All day, he has taken no food; but has shown an evident desire for water—lapping it up, greedily. I was relieved to observe this.

The evening has come, and I am in my study. I intend to follow my plan of last night, and watch the kennel. The door, leading into the garden, is bolted, securely. I am consciously glad there are bars to the windows...

Night:—Midnight has gone. The dog has been silent, up to the present. Through the side window, on my left, I can make out, dimly, the outlines of the kennel. For the first time, the dog moves, and I hear the rattle of his chain. I look out, quickly. As I stare, the dog moves again, restlessly, and I see a small patch of luminous light, shine from the interior of the kennel. It vanishes; then the dog stirs again, and, once more, the gleam comes. I am puzzled. The dog is quiet, and I can see the luminous thing, plainly. It shows distinctly. There is something familiar about the shape of it. For a moment, I wonder; then it comes to me, that it is not unlike the four fingers and thumb of a hand. Like a hand! And I remember the contour of that fearsome wound on the dog's side. It must be the wound I see. It is luminous at night—Why? The minutes pass. My mind is filled with this fresh thing...

Suddenly, I hear a sound, out in the gardens. How it thrills through me. It is approaching. Pad, pad, pad. A prickly sensation traverses my spine, and seems to creep across my scalp. The dog moves in his kennel, and whimpers, frightenedly. He must have turned 'round; for, now, I can no longer see the outline of his shining wound.

Outside, the gardens are silent, once more, and I listen, fearfully. A minute passes, and another; then I hear the padding sound, again. It is quite close, and appears to be coming down the graveled path. The noise is curiously measured and deliberate. It ceases outside the door; and I rise to my feet, and stand motionless. From the door, comes a slight sound—the latch is being slowly raised. A singing noise is in my ears, and I have a sense of pressure about the head—

The latch drops, with a sharp click, into the catch. The noise startles me afresh; jarring, horribly, on my tense nerves. After that, I stand, for a long while, amid an ever-growing quietness. All at once, my knees begin to tremble, and I have to sit, quickly.

An uncertain period of time passes, and, gradually, I begin to shake off the feeling of terror, that has possessed me. Yet, still I sit. I seem to have lost the power of movement. I am strangely tired, and inclined to doze. My eyes open and close, and, presently, I find myself falling asleep, and waking, in fits and starts.

It is some time later, that I am sleepily aware that one of the candles is guttering. When I wake again, it has gone out, and the room is very dim, under the light of the one remaining flame. The semi-darkness troubles me little. I have lost that awful sense of dread, and my only desire seems to be to sleep—sleep.

Suddenly, although there is no noise, I am awake—wide awake. I am acutely conscious of the nearness of some mystery, of some overwhelming Presence. The very air seems pregnant with terror. I sit huddled, and just listen, intently. Still, there is no sound. Nature, herself, seems dead. Then, the oppressive stillness is broken by a little eldritch scream of wind, that sweeps 'round the house, and dies away, remotely.

I let my gaze wander across the half-lighted room. By the great clock in the far corner, is a dark, tall shadow. For a short instant, I stare, frightenedly. Then, I see that it is nothing, and am, momentarily, relieved.

In the time that follows, the thought flashes through my brain, why not leave this house—this house of mystery and terror? Then, as though in answer, there sweeps up, across my sight, a vision of the wondrous Sea of Sleep,—the Sea of Sleep where she and I have been allowed to meet, after the years of separation and sorrow; and I know that I shall stay on here, whatever happens.

Through the side window, I note the somber blackness of the night. My glance wanders away, and 'round the room; resting on one shadowy object and another. Suddenly, I turn, and look at the window on my right; as I do so, I breathe quickly, and bend forward, with a frightened gaze at something outside the window, but close to the bars. I am looking at a vast, misty swine-face, over which fluctuates a flamboyant flame, of a greenish hue. It is the Thing from the arena. The quivering mouth seems to drip with a continual, phosphorescent slaver. The eyes are staring straight into the room, with an inscrutable expression. Thus, I sit rigidly—frozen.

The Thing has begun to move. It is turning, slowly, in my direction. Its face is coming 'round toward me. It sees me. Two huge, inhumanly human, eyes are looking through the dimness at me. I am cold with fear; yet, even now, I am keenly conscious, and note, in an irrelevant way, that the distant stars are blotted out by the mass of the giant face.

A fresh horror has come to me. I am rising from my chair, without the least intention. I am on my feet, and something is impelling me toward the door that leads out into the gardens. I wish to stop; but cannot. Some immutable power is opposed to my will, and I go slowly forward, unwilling and resistant. My glance flies 'round the room, helplessly, and stops at the window. The great swine-face has disappeared, and I hear, again, that stealthy pad, pad, pad. It stops outside the door—the door toward which I am being compelled…

There succeeds a short, intense silence; then there comes a sound. It is the rattle of the latch, being slowly lifted. At that, I am filled with desperation. I will not go forward another step. I make a vast effort to return; but it is, as though I press back, upon an invisible wall. I groan out loud, in the agony of my fear, and the sound of my voice is frightening. Again comes that rattle, and I shiver, clammily. I try—aye, fight and struggle, to hold back, *back*; but it is no use…

I am at the door, and, in a mechanical way, I watch my hand go forward, to undo the topmost bolt. It does so, entirely without my volition. Even as I reach up toward the bolt, the door is violently shaken, and I get a sickly whiff of mouldy air, which seems to drive in through the interstices of the doorway. I draw the bolt back, slowly, fighting, dumbly, the while. It comes out of its socket, with a click, and I begin to shake, aguishly. There are two more; one at the bottom of the door; the other, a massive affair, is placed about the middle.

For, perhaps a minute, I stand, with my arms hanging slackly, by my sides. The influence to meddle with the fastenings of the door, seems to have gone. All at once, there comes the sudden rattle of iron, at my feet. I glance down, quickly, and realize, with an unspeakable terror, that my foot is pushing back the lower bolt. An awful sense of helplessness assails me… The bolt comes out of its hold, with a slight, ringing sound and I stagger on my feet, grasping at the great, central bolt, for support. A minute passes, an eternity; then another—My God, help me! I am being forced to work upon the last fastening. *I will not!* Better to die, than open to the Terror, that is on the other side of the door. Is there no escape …? God help me, I have jerked the bolt half out of its socket! My lips emit a hoarse scream of terror, the bolt is three parts drawn, now, and still my unconscious hands work toward my doom. Only a fraction of steel, between my soul and That. Twice, I scream out in the supreme agony of my fear; then, with a mad effort, I tear my hands away. My eyes seem blinded. A great blackness is falling upon me. Nature has come to my rescue. I feel my knees giving. There is a loud, quick thudding upon the door, and I am falling, falling…

I must have lain there, at least a couple of hours. As I recover, I am aware that the other candle has burnt out, and the room is in an almost total darkness. I cannot rise to my feet, for I am cold, and filled with a terrible cramp. Yet my brain is clear, and there is no longer the strain of that unholy influence.

Cautiously, I get upon my knees, and feel for the central bolt. I find it, and push it securely back into its socket; then the one at the bottom of the door. By this time, I am able to rise to my feet, and so manage to secure the fastening at the top. After that, I go down upon my knees, again, and creep away among the furniture, in the direction of the stairs. By doing this, I am safe from observation from the window.

I reach the opposite door, and, as I leave the study, cast one nervous glance over my shoulder, toward the window. Out in the night, I seem to catch a glimpse of something impalpable; but it may be only a fancy. Then, I am in the passage, and on the stairs.

Reaching my bedroom, I clamber into bed, all clothed as I am, and pull the bedclothes over me. There, after awhile, I begin to regain a little confidence. It is impossible to sleep; but I am grateful for the added warmth of the bedclothes. Presently, I try to think over the happenings of the past night; but, though I cannot sleep, I find that it is useless, to attempt consecutive thought. My brain seems curiously blank.

Toward morning, I begin to toss, uneasily. I cannot rest, and, after awhile, I get out of bed, and pace the floor. The wintry dawn is beginning to creep through the windows, and shows the bare discomfort of the old room. Strange, that, through all these years, it has never occurred to me how dismal the place really is. And so a time passes.

From somewhere down stairs, a sound comes up to me. I go to the bedroom door, and listen. It is Mary, bustling about the great, old kitchen, getting the breakfast ready. I feel little interest. I am not hungry. My thoughts, however; continue to dwell upon her. How little the weird happenings in this house seem to trouble her. Except in the incident of the Pit creatures, she has seemed unconscious of anything unusual occurring. She is old, like myself; yet how little we have to do with one another. Is it because we have nothing in common; or only that, being old, we care less for society, than quietness? These and other matters pass through my mind, as I meditate; and help to distract my attention, for a while, from the oppressive thoughts of the night.

After a time, I go to the window, and, opening it, look out. The sun is now above the horizon, and the air, though cold, is sweet and crisp. Gradually, my brain clears, and a sense of security, for the time being, comes to me. Somewhat happier, I go down stairs, and out into the garden, to have a look at the dog.

As I approach the kennel, I am greeted by the same mouldy stench that assailed me at the door last night. Shaking off a momentary sense of fear, I call to the dog; but he takes no heed, and, after calling once more, I throw a small stone into the kennel. At this, he moves, uneasily, and I shout his name, again; but do not go closer. Presently, my sister comes out, and joins me, in trying to coax him from the kennel.

In a little the poor beast rises, and shambles out lurching queerly. In the daylight he stands swaying from side to side, and blinking stupidly. I look and note that the horrid wound is larger, much larger, and seems to have a whitish, fungoid appearance. My sister moves to fondle him; but I detain her, and explain that I think it will be better not to go too near him for a few days; as it is impossible to tell what may be the matter with him; and it is well to be cautious.

A minute later, she leaves me; coming back with a basin of odd scraps of food. This she places on the ground, near the dog, and I push it into his reach, with the aid of a branch, broken from one of the shrubs. Yet, though the meat should be tempting, he takes no notice of it; but retires to his kennel. There is still water in his drinking vessel, so, after a few moments' talk, we go back to the house. I can see that my sister is much puzzled as to what is the matter with the animal; yet it would be madness, even to hint the truth to her.

The day slips away, uneventfully; and night comes on. I have determined to repeat my experiment of last night. I cannot say that it is wisdom; yet my mind is made up. Still, however, I have taken precautions; for I have driven stout nails in at the back of each of the three bolts, that secure the door, opening from the study into the gardens. This will, at least, prevent a recurrence of the danger I ran last night.

From ten to about two-thirty, I watch; but nothing occurs; and, finally, I stumble off to bed, where I am soon asleep.

XXVI.
The Luminous Speck

I awake suddenly. It is still dark. I turn over, once or twice, in my endeavors to sleep again; but I cannot sleep. My head is aching, slightly; and, by turns I am hot and cold. In a little, I give up the attempt, and stretch out my hand, for the matches. I will light my candle, and read, awhile; perhaps, I shall be able to sleep, after a time. For a few moments, I grope; then my hand touches the box; but, as I open it, I am startled, to see a phosphorescent speck of fire, shining amid the darkness. I put out my other hand, and touch it. It is on my wrist. With a feeling of vague alarm, I strike a light, hurriedly, and look; but can see nothing, save a tiny scratch.

"Fancy!" I mutter, with a half sigh of relief. Then the match burns my finger, and I drop it, quickly. As I fumble for another, the thing shines out again. I know, now, that it is no fancy. This time, I light the candle, and examine the place, more closely. There is a slight, greenish discoloration 'round the scratch. I am puzzled and worried. Then a thought comes to me. I remember the morning after the Thing appeared. I remember that the dog licked my hand. It was this one, with the scratch on it; though I have not been even conscious of the abasement, until now. A horrible fear has come to me. It creeps into my brain—the dog's wound, shines at night. With a dazed feeling, I sit down on the side of the bed, and try to think; but cannot. My brain seems numbed with the sheer horror of this new fear.

Time moves on, unheeded. Once, I rouse up, and try to persuade myself that I am mistaken; but it is no use. In my heart, I have no doubt.

Hour after hour, I sit in the darkness and silence, and shiver, hopelessly…

The day has come and gone, and it is night again.

This morning, early, I shot the dog, and buried it, away among the bushes. My sister is startled and frightened; but I am desperate. Besides, it is better so. The foul growth had almost hidden its left side. And I—the place on my wrist has enlarged, perceptibly. Several times, I have caught myself muttering prayers—little things learnt as a child. God, Almighty God, help me! I shall go mad.

Six days, and I have eaten nothing. It is night. I am sitting in my chair. Ah, God! I wonder have any ever felt the horror of life that I have come to know? I am swathed in terror. I feel ever the burning of this dread growth. It has covered all my right arm and side, and is beginning to creep up my neck. Tomorrow, it will eat into my face. I shall become a terrible mass of living corruption. There is no escape. Yet, a thought has come to me, born of a sight of the gun-rack, on the other side of the room. I have looked again—with the strangest of feelings. The thought grows upon me. God, Thou knowest, Thou must know, that death is better, aye, better a thousand times than This. This! Jesus, forgive me, but I cannot live, cannot, cannot! I dare not! I am beyond all help—there is nothing else left. It will, at least, spare me that final horror...

I think I must have been dozing. I am very weak, and oh! so miserable, so miserable and tired—tired. The rustle of the paper, tries my brain. My hearing seems preternaturally sharp. I will sit awhile and think...

"Hush! I hear something, down—down in the cellars. It is a creaking sound. My God, it is the opening of the great, oak trap. What can be doing that? The scratching of my pen deafens me ... I must listen... There are steps on the stairs; strange padding steps, that come up and nearer... Jesus, be merciful to me, an old man. There is something fumbling at the door handle. O God, help me now! Jesus—The door is opening—slowly. Somethi—"

That is all.[20]

[20] NOTE.—From the unfinished word, it is possible, on the MS., to trace a faint line of ink, which suggests that the pen has trailed away over the paper; possibly, through fright and weakness.—Ed.

XXVII.
Conclusion

I put down the Manuscript, and glanced across at Tonnison: he was sitting, staring out into the dark. I waited a minute; then I spoke.

"Well?" I said.

He turned, slowly, and looked at me. His thoughts seemed to have gone out of him into a great distance.

"Was he mad?" I asked, and indicated the MS., with a half nod.

Tonnison stared at me, unseeingly, a moment; then, his wits came back to him, and, suddenly, he comprehended my question.

"No!" he said.

I opened my lips, to offer a contradictory opinion; for my sense of the saneness of things, would not allow me to take the story literally; then I shut them again, without saying anything. Somehow, the certainty in Tonnison's voice affected my doubts. I felt, all at once, less assured; though I was by no means convinced as yet.

After a few moments' silence, Tonnison rose, stiffly, and began to undress. He seemed disinclined to talk; so I said nothing; but followed his example. I was weary; though still full of the story I had just read.

Somehow, as I rolled into my blankets, there crept into my mind a memory of the old gardens, as we had seen them. I remembered the odd fear that the place had conjured up in our hearts; and it grew upon me, with conviction, that Tonnison was right.

It was very late when we rose—nearly midday; for the greater part of the night had been spent in reading the MS.

Tonnison was grumpy, and I felt out of sorts. It was a somewhat dismal day, and there was a touch of chilliness in the air. There was no mention of going out fishing on either of our parts. We got dinner, and, after that, just sat and smoked in silence.

Presently, Tonnison asked for the Manuscript: I handed it to him, and he spent most of the afternoon in reading it through by himself.

It was while he was thus employed, that a thought came to me:—

"What do you say to having another look at—?" I nodded my head downstream.

Tonnison looked up. "Nothing!" he said, abruptly; and, somehow, I was less annoyed, than relieved, at his answer.

After that, I left him alone.

A little before teatime, he looked up at me, curiously.

"Sorry, old chap, if I was a bit short with you just now;" (just now, indeed! he had not spoken for the last three hours) "but I would not go there again," and he indicated with his head, "for anything that you could offer me. Ugh!" and he put down that history of a man's terror and hope and despair.

The next morning, we rose early, and went for our accustomed swim: we had partly shaken off the depression of the previous day; and so, took our rods when we had finished breakfast, and spent the day at our favorite sport.

After that day, we enjoyed our holiday to the utmost; though both of us looked forward to the time when our driver should come; for we were tremendously anxious to inquire of him, and through him among the people of the tiny hamlet, whether any of them could give us information about that strange garden, lying away by itself in the heart of an almost unknown tract of country.

At last, the day came, on which we expected the driver to come across for us. He arrived early, while we were still abed; and, the first thing we knew, he was at the opening of the tent, inquiring whether we had had good sport. We replied in the affirmative; and then, both together, almost in the same breath, we asked the question that was uppermost in our minds:—Did he know anything about an old garden, and a great pit, and a lake, situated some miles away, down the river; also, had he ever heard of a great house thereabouts?

No, he did not, and had not; yet, stay, he had heard a rumor, once upon a time, of a great, old house standing alone out in the wilderness; but, if he remembered rightly it was a place given over to the fairies; or, if that had not been so, he was certain that there had been something "quare" about it; and, anyway, he had heard nothing of it for a very long while—not since he was quite a gossoon. No, he could not remember anything particular about it; indeed, he did not know he remembered anything "at all, at all" until we questioned him.

"Look here," said Tonnison, finding that this was about all that he could tell us, "just take a walk 'round the village, while we dress, and find out something, if you can."

With a nondescript salute, the man departed on his errand; while we made haste to get into our clothes; after which, we began to prepare breakfast.

We were just sitting down to it, when he returned.

"It's all in bed the lazy divvils is, sor," he said, with a repetition of the salute, and an appreciative eye to the good things spread out on our provision chest, which we utilized as a table.

"Oh, well, sit down," replied my friend, "and have something to eat with us." Which the man did without delay.

After breakfast, Tonnison sent him off again on the same errand, while we sat and smoked. He was away some three-quarters of an hour, and, when he returned, it was evident that he had found out something. It appeared that he had got into conversation with an ancient man of the village, who, probably, knew more—though it was little enough—of the strange house, than any other person living.

The substance of this knowledge was, that, in the "ancient man's" youth—and goodness knows how long back that was—there had stood a great house in the center of the gardens, where now was left only that fragment of ruin. This house had been empty for a great while; years before his—the ancient man's—birth. It was a place shunned by the people of the village, as it had been shunned by their fathers before them. There were many things said about it, and all were of evil. No one ever went near it, either by day or night. In the village it was a synonym of all that is unholy and dreadful.

And then, one day, a man, a stranger, had ridden through the village, and turned off down the river, in the direction of the House, as it was always termed by the villagers. Some hours afterward, he had ridden back, taking the track by which he had come, toward Ardrahan. Then, for three months or so, nothing was heard. At the end of that time, he reappeared; but now, he was accompanied by an elderly woman, and a large number of donkeys, laden with various articles. They had passed through the village without stopping, and gone straight down the bank of the river, in the direction of the House.

Since that time, no one, save the man whom they had chartered to bring over monthly supplies of necessaries from Ardrahan, had ever seen either of them: and him, none had ever induced to talk; evidently, he had been well paid for his trouble.

The years had moved onward, uneventfully enough, in that little hamlet; the man making his monthly journeys, regularly.

One day, he had appeared as usual on his customary errand. He had passed through the village without exchanging more than a surly nod with the inhabitants and gone on toward the House. Usually, it was evening before he made the return journey. On this occasion, however, he had reappeared in the village, a few hours later, in an extraordinary state of excitement, and with the astounding information, that the House had disappeared bodily, and that a stupendous pit now yawned in the place where it had stood.

This news, it appears, so excited the curiosity of the villagers, that they overcame their fears, and marched *en masse* to the place. There, they found everything, just as described by the carrier.

This was all that we could learn. Of the author of the MS., who he was, and whence he came, we shall never know.

His identity is, as he seems to have desired, buried forever.

That same day, we left the lonely village of Kraighten. We have never been there since.

Sometimes, in my dreams, I see that enormous pit, surrounded, as it is, on all sides by wild trees and bushes. And the noise of the water rises upward, and blends—in my sleep—with other and lower noises; while, over all, hangs the eternal shroud of spray.

GRIEF[21]

Fierce hunger reigns within my breast, I had not dreamt that this whole world,
  Crushed in the hand of God, could yield
Such bitter essence of unrest, Such pain as Sorrow now hath hurled
  Out of its dreadful heart, unsealed!
Each sobbing breath is but a cry, My heart-strokes knells of agony,
  And my whole brain has but one thought
That nevermore through life shall I (Save in the ache of memory)
  Touch hands with thee, who now art naught!
Through the whole void of night I search, So dumbly crying out to thee;
  But thou are *not*; and night's vast throne
Becomes an all stupendous church With star-bells knelling unto me
  Who in all space am most alone!
An hungered, to the shore I creep, Perchance some comfort waits on me
  From the old Sea's eternal heart;
But lo! from all the solemn deep, Far voices out of mystery
  Seem questioning why we are apart!
"Where'er I go I am alone Who once, through thee, had all the world.
  My breast is one whole raging pain
For that which *was*, and now is flown Into the Blank where life is hurled
  Where all is not, nor is again!"

/

[21] These stanzas I found, in pencil, upon a piece of foolscap gummed in behind the fly-leaf of the MS. They have all the appearance of having been written at an earlier date than the Manuscript.—Ed.

The Ghost Pirates

1909

"Strange as the glimmer of the ghastly light
That shines from some vast crest of wave at night."

“Olden memories that shine against death’s night—
Quiet stars of sweet enchantments,
That are seen In Life’s lost distances…”

The World of Dreams

AUTHOR'S PREFACE

This book forms the last of three. The first published was *The Boats of the "Glen Carrig,"* the second, *The House on the Borderland*; this, the third, completes what, perhaps, may be termed a trilogy; for, though very different in scope, each of the three books deals with certain conceptions that have an elemental kinship. With this book, the author believes that he closes the door, so far as he is concerned, on a particular phase of constructive thought.

The Hell O! O! Chaunty[22]

Chaunty Man: *Man the capstan, bullies!*
Men: *Ha!-o-o! Ha!-o-o!*
Chaunty Man: *Capstan-bars, you tarry souls!*
Men: *Ha!-o-o! Ha!-o-o!*
Chaunty Man: *Take a turn!*
Men: *Ha!-o-o!*
Chaunty Man: *Stand by to fleet!*
Men: *Ha!-o-o!*
Chaunty Man: *Stand by to surge!*
Men: *Ha!-o-o!*
Chaunty Man: *Ha!—o-o-o-o!*
Men: *TRAMP!*
    And away we go!
Chaunty Man: *Hark to the tramp of the*
    bearded shellbacks!
Men: *Hush!*
    O hear 'em tramp!
Chaunty Man: *Tramping, stamping—*
    treading, vamping,
    While the cable
    comes in ramping.
Men: *Hark!*
    O hear 'em stamp!

[22] a chaunty is a sea shanty, or a work song sung by sailors doing tasks aboard large sailing vessels

Chaunty Man: Surge when it rides!
Surge when it rides!
Round-o-o-o
handsome as it slacks!
Men: Ha!-o-o-o-o!
hear 'em ramp!
Ha!-oo-o-o!
hear 'em stamp!
Ha!-o-o-o-o-oo!
Ha!-o-o-o-o-o-o!
Chorus: They're shouting now; oh! hear 'em
A-bellow as they stamp:—
Ha!-o-o-o! Ha!-o-o-o!
Ha!-o-o-o!
A-shouting as they tramp!
Chaunty Man: O hark to the haunting chorus
of the capstan and the bars!
Chaunty-o-o-o
and rattle crash—
Bash against the stars!
Men: Ha-a!-o-o-o!
Tramp and go!
Ha-a!-o-o-o!
Ha-a!-o-o-o!
Chaunty Man: Hear the pawls a-ranting: with
the bearded men a-chaunting;
While the brazen dome above 'em
Bellows back the "bars."
Men: Hear and hark!
O hear 'em!
Ha-a!-o-o!
Ha-a!-o-o!
Chaunty Man: Hurling songs towards the heavens—!
Men: Ha-a!-o-o!
Ha-a!-o-o!
Chaunty Man: Hush! O hear 'em!
Hark! O hear 'em!
Hurling oaths among their spars!
Men: Hark! O hear 'em!
Hush! O hear 'em!
Chaunty Man: Tramping round between the bars!
Chorus: They're shouting now; oh! hear

A-bellow as they stamp:—
Ha-a!-o-o-o! Ha-a!-o-o-o!
Ha-a!-o-o-o!
A-shouting as they tramp!
Chaunty Man: *O do you hear the*
capstan-chaunty!
Thunder round the pawls!
Men: *Click a-clack,*
a-clatter
Surge!
And scatter bawls!
Chaunty Man: *Click-a-clack, my bonny boys,*
while it comes in handsome!
Men: *Ha-a!-o-o!*
Hear 'em clack!
Chaunty Man: *Ha-a!-o-o! Click-a-clack!*
Men: *Hush! O hear 'em pant!*
Hark! O hear 'em rant!
Chaunty Man: *Click, a-clitter, clicker-clack.*
Men: *Ha-a!-o-o!*
Tramp and go!
Chaunty Man: *Surge! And keep away the slack!*
Men: *Ha-a!-o-o!*
Away the slack:
Ha-a!-o-o!
Click-a-clack
Chaunty Man: *Bustle now each jolly Jack.*
Surging easy! Surging e-a-s-y!!
Men: *Ha-a!-o-o!*
Surging easy
Chaunty Man: *Click-a-clatter—*
Surge; and steady!
Man the stopper there!
All ready?
Men: *Ha-a!-o-o!*
Ha-a!-o-o!
Chaunty Man: *Click-a-clack, my bouncing boys:*
Men: *Ha-a!-o-o!*
Tramp and go!
Chaunty Man: *Lift the pawls, and come back easy.*
Men: *Ha-a!-o-o!*
Steady-o-o-o-o!

Chaunty Man: *Vast the chaunty!*
Vast the capstan!
Drop the pawls! Be-l-a-y!

Men: *Ha-a!-o-o! Unship the bars!*
Ha-a!-o-o! Tramp and go!
Ha-a!-o-o! Shoulder bars!
Ha-a!-o-o! And away we blow!
Ha-a!-o-o-o!
Ha-a!-o-o-o-o!
Ha-a!-o-o-o-o-o!

I.
The Figure Out of the Sea

He began without any circumlocution.

I joined the *Mortzestus* in 'Frisco. I heard before I signed on, that there were some funny yarns floating round about her; but I was pretty nearly on the beach, and too jolly anxious to get away, to worry about trifles. Besides, by all accounts, she was right enough so far as grub and treatment went. When I asked fellows to give it a name, they generally could not. All they could tell me, was that she was unlucky, and made thundering long passages, and had no more than a fair share of dirty weather. Also, that she had twice had the sticks blown out of her, and her cargo shifted. Besides all these, a heap of other things that might happen to any packet, and would not be comfortable to run into. Still, they were the ordinary things, and I was willing enough to risk them, to get home. All the same, if I had been given the chance, I should have shipped in some other vessel as a matter of preference.

When I took my bag down, I found that they had signed on the rest of the crowd. You see, the "home lot" cleared out when they got into 'Frisco, that is, all except one young fellow, a cockney, who had stuck by the ship in port. He told me afterwards, when I got to know him, that he intended to draw a payday out of her, whether anyone else did, or not.

The first night I was in her, I found that it was common talk among the other fellows, that there was something queer about the ship. They spoke of her as if it were an accepted fact that she was haunted; yet they all treated the matter as a joke; all, that is, except the young cockney—Williams—who, instead of laughing at their jests on the subject, seemed to take the whole matter seriously.

This made me rather curious. I began to wonder whether there was, after all, some truth underlying the vague stories I had heard; and I took the first opportunity to ask him whether he had any reasons for believing that there was anything in the yarns about the ship.

At first he was inclined to be a bit offish; but, presently, he came round, and told me that he did not know of any particular incident which could be called unusual in the sense in which I meant. Yet that, at the same time, there were lots of little things which, if you put them together, made you think a bit. For instance, she always made such long passages and had so much dirty weather—nothing but that and calms and headwinds. Then, other things happened; sails that he knew, himself, had been properly stowed, were always blowing adrift *at night*. And then he said a thing that surprised me.

"There's too many bloomin' shadders about this 'ere packet; they gets onter yer nerves like nothin' as ever I seen before in me nat'ral."

He blurted it all out in a heap, and I turned round and looked at him.

"Too many shadows!" I said. "What on earth do you mean?" But he refused to explain himself or tell me anything further—just shook his head, stupidly, when I questioned him. He seemed to have taken a sudden, sulky fit. I felt certain that he was acting dense, purposely. I believe the truth of the matter is that he was, in a way, ashamed of having let himself go like he had, in speaking out his thoughts about "shadders." That type of man may think things at times; but he doesn't often put them into words. Anyhow, I saw it was no use asking any further questions; so I let the matter drop there. Yet, for several days afterwards, I caught myself wondering, at times, what the fellow had meant by "shadders."

We left 'Frisco next day, with a fine, fair wind, that seemed a bit like putting the stopper on the yarns I had heard about the ship's ill luck. And yet—

He hesitated a moment, and then went on again.

For the first couple of weeks out, nothing unusual happened, and the wind still held fair. I began to feel that I had been rather lucky, after all, in the packet into which I had been shunted. Most of the other fellows gave her a good name, and there was a pretty general opinion growing among the crowd, that it was all a silly yarn about her being haunted. And then, just when I was settling down to things, something happened that opened my eyes no end.

It was in the eight to twelve watch, and I was sitting on the steps, on the starboard side, leading up to the fo'cas'le head. The night was fine and there was a splendid moon. Away aft, I heard the timekeeper strike four bells, and the lookout, an old fellow named Jaskett, answered him. As he let go the bell lanyard, he caught sight of me, where I sat quietly, smoking. He leant over the rail, and looked down at me.

"That you, Jessop?" he asked.

"I believe it is," I replied.

"We'd 'ave our gran'mothers an' all the rest of our petticoated relash'ns comin' to sea, if 'twere always like this," he remarked, reflectively—indicating, with a sweep of his pipe and hand, the calmness of the sea and sky.

I saw no reason for denying that, and he continued:

"If this ole packet is 'aunted, as some on 'em seems to think, well all as I can say is, let me 'ave the luck to tumble across another of the same sort. Good grub, an' duff fer Sundays, an' a decent crowd of 'em aft, an' everythin' comfertable like, so as yer can feel yer knows where yer are. As fer 'er bein' 'aunted, that's all 'ellish nonsense. I've comed 'cross lots of 'em before as was said to be 'aunted, an' so some on 'em was; but 'twasn't with ghostesses. One packet I was in, they was that bad yer couldn't sleep a wink in yer watch below, until yer'd 'ad every stitch out yer bunk an' 'ad a reg'lar 'unt. Sometimes—" At that moment, the relief, one of the ordinary seamen, went up the other ladder on to the fo'cas'le head, and the old chap turned to ask him "Why the 'ell" he'd not relieved him a bit smarter. The ordinary made some reply; but what it was, I did not catch; for, abruptly, away aft, my rather sleepy gaze had lighted on something altogether extraordinary and outrageous. It was nothing less than the form of a man stepping inboard over the starboard rail, a little abaft the main rigging. I stood up, and caught at the handrail, and stared.

Behind me, someone spoke. It was the lookout, who had come down off the fo'cas'le head, on his way aft to report the name of his relief to the second mate.

"What is it, mate?" he asked, curiously, seeing my intent attitude.

The thing, whatever it was, had disappeared into the shadows on the lee side of the deck.

"Nothing!" I replied, shortly; for I was too bewildered then, at what my eyes had just shown me, to say anymore. I wanted to think.

The old shellback glanced at me; but only muttered something, and went on his way aft.

For a minute, perhaps, I stood there, watching; but could see nothing. Then I walked slowly aft, as far as the after end of the deck house. From there, I could see most of the main deck; but nothing showed, except, of course, the moving shadows of the ropes and spars and sails, as they swung to and fro in the moonlight.

The old chap who had just come off the lookout had returned forrard again, and I was alone on that part of the deck. And then, all at once, as I stood peering into the shadows to leeward, I remembered what Williams had said about there being too many "shadders." I had been puzzled to understand his real meaning, then. I had no difficulty *now*. There *were* too many shadows. Yet, shadows or no shadows, I realized that for my own peace of mind, I must settle, once and for all, whether the thing I had seemed to see stepping aboard out of the ocean, had been a reality, or simply a phantom, as you might say, of my imagination. My reason said it was nothing more than imagination, a rapid dream—I must have dozed; but something deeper than reason told me that this was not so. I put it to the test, and went straight in amongst the shadows—There was nothing.

I grew bolder. My common sense told me I must have fancied it all. I walked over to the mainmast, and looked behind the pinrail that partly surrounded it, and down into the shadow of the pumps; but here again was nothing. Then I went in under the break of the poop. It was darker under there than out on deck. I looked up both sides of the deck, and saw that they were bare of anything such as I looked for. The assurance was comforting. I glanced at the poop ladders, and remembered that nothing could have gone up there, without the Second Mate or the Time-keeper seeing it. Then I leant my back up against the bulkshead, and thought the whole matter over, rapidly, sucking at my pipe, and keeping my glance about the deck. I concluded my think, and said "No!" out loud. Then something occurred to me, and I said "Unless—" and went over to the starboard bulwarks, and looked over and down into the sea; but there was nothing but sea; and so I turned and made my way forrard. My common sense had triumphed, and I was convinced that my imagination had been playing tricks with me.

I reached the door on the portside, leading into the fo'cas'le, and was about to enter, when something made me look behind. As I did so, I had a shaker. Away aft, a dim, shadowy form stood in the wake of a swaying belt of moonlight, that swept the deck a bit abaft the main-mast.

It was the same figure that I had just been attributing to my fancy. I will admit that I felt more than startled; I was quite a bit frightened. I was convinced now that it was no mere imaginary thing. It was a human figure. And yet, with the flicker of the moonlight and the shadows chasing over it, I was unable to say more than that. Then, as I stood there, irresolute and funky, I got the thought that someone was acting the goat; though for what reason or purpose, I never stopped to consider. I was glad of any suggestion that my common sense assured me was not impossible; and, for the moment, I felt quite relieved. That side to the question had not presented itself to me before. I began to pluck up courage. I accused myself of getting fanciful; otherwise I should have tumbled to it earlier. And then, funnily enough, in spite of all my reasoning, I was still afraid of going aft to discover who that was, standing on the lee side of the maindeck. Yet I felt that if I shirked it, I was only fit to be dumped overboard; and so I went, though not with any great speed, as you can imagine.

I had gone half the distance, and still the figure remained there, motionless and silent—the moonlight and the shadows playing over it with each roll of the ship. I think I tried to be surprised. If it were one of the fellows playing the fool, he must have heard me coming, and why didn't he scoot while he had the chance? And where could he have hidden himself, before? All these things, I asked myself, in a rush, with a queer mixture of doubt and belief; and, you know, in the meantime, I was drawing nearer. I had passed the house, and was not twelve paces distant; when, abruptly, the silent figure made three quick strides to the port rail, and *climbed over it into the sea*.

I rushed to the side, and stared over; but nothing met my gaze, except the shadow of the ship, sweeping over the moonlit sea.

How long I stared down blankly into the water, it would be impossible to say; certainly for a good minute. I felt blank—just horribly blank. It was such a beastly confirmation of the *unnaturalness* of the thing I had concluded to be only a sort of brain fancy. I seemed, for that little time, deprived, you know, of the power of coherent thought. I suppose I was dazed—mentally stunned, in a way.

As I have said, a minute or so must have gone, while I had been staring into the dark of the water under the ship's side. Then, I came suddenly to my ordinary self. The Second Mate was singing out: "Lee fore brace."

I went to the braces, like a chap in a dream.

II.
What Tammy the 'prentices Saw

The next morning, in my watch below, I had a look at the places where that strange thing had come aboard, and left the ship; but I found nothing unusual, and no clue to help me to understand the mystery of the strange man.

For several days after that, all went quietly; though I prowled about the decks at night, trying to discover anything fresh that might tend to throw some light on the matter. I was careful to say nothing to anyone about the thing I had seen. In any case, I felt sure I should only have been laughed at.

Several nights passed away in this manner, and I was no nearer to an understanding of the affair. And then, in the middle watch, something happened.

It was my wheel. Tammy, one of the first voyage 'prenticess, was keeping time —walking up and down the lee side of the poop. The Second Mate was forrard, leaning over the break of the poop, smoking. The weather still continued fine, and the moon, though declining, was sufficiently powerful to make every detail about the poop, stand out distinctly. Three bells had gone, and I'll admit I was feeling sleepy. Indeed, I believe I must have dozed, for the old packet steered very easily, and there was precious little to do, beyond giving her an odd spoke now and again. And then, all at once, it seemed to me that I heard someone calling my name, softly. I could not be certain; and first I glanced forrard to where the Second stood, smoking, and from him, I looked into the binnacle. The ship's head was right on her course, and I felt easier. Then, suddenly, I heard it again. There was no doubt about it this time, and I glanced to leeward. There I saw Tammy reaching over the steering gear, his hand out, in the act of trying to touch my arm. I was about to ask him what the devil he wanted, when he held up his finger for silence, and pointed forrard along the lee side of the poop. In the dim light, his face showed palely, and he seemed much agitated. For a few seconds, I stared in the direction he indicated, but could see nothing.

"What is it?" I asked in an undertone, after a couple of moments' further ineffectual peering. "I can't see anything."

"H'sh!" he muttered, hoarsely, without looking in my direction. Then, all at once, with a quick little gasp, he sprang across the wheel-box, and stood beside me, trembling. His gaze appeared to follow the movements of something I could not see.

I must say that I was startled. His movement had shown such terror; and the way he stared to leeward made me think he saw something uncanny.

"What the deuce is up with you?" I asked, sharply. And then I remembered the Second Mate. I glanced forrard to where he lounged. His back was still towards us, and he had not seen Tammy. Then I turned to the boy.

"For goodness sake, get to looard before the Second sees you!" I said. "If you want to say anything, say it across the wheel-box. You've been dreaming."

Even as I spoke, the little beggar caught at my sleeve with one hand; and, pointing across to the log-reel with the other, screamed: "He's coming! He's coming—" At this instant, the Second Mate came running aft, singing out to know what was the matter. Then, suddenly, crouching under the rail near the log-reel, I saw something that looked like a man; but so hazy and unreal, that I could scarcely say I saw anything. Yet, like a flash, my thoughts ripped back to the silent figure I had seen in the flicker of the moonlight, a week earlier.

The Second Mate reached me, and I pointed, dumbly; and yet, as I did so, it was with the knowledge that *he* would not be able to see what I saw. (Queer, wasn't it?) And then, almost in a breath, I lost sight of the thing, and became aware that Tammy was hugging my knees.

The Second continued to stare at the log-reel for a brief instant; then he turned to me, with a sneer.

"Been asleep, the pair of you, I suppose!" Then, without waiting for my denial, he told Tammy to go to hell out of it and stop his noise, or he'd boot him off the poop.

After that, he walked forward to the break of the poop, and lit his pipe, again —walking forward and aft every few minutes, and eyeing me, at times, I thought, with a strange, half-doubtful, half-puzzled look.

Later, as soon as I was relieved, I hurried down to the 'prentices's berth. I was anxious to speak to Tammy. There were a dozen questions that worried me, and I was in doubt what I ought to do. I found him crouched on a sea-chest, his knees up to his chin, and his gaze fixed on the doorway, with a frightened stare. I put my head into the berth, and he gave a gasp; then he saw who it was, and his face relaxed something of its strained expression.

He said: "Come in," in a low voice, which he tried to steady; and I stepped over the washboard, and sat down on a chest, facing him.

"What was *it?*" he asked; putting his feet down on to the deck, and leaning forward. "For God's sake, tell me what it was!"

His voice had risen, and I put up my hand to warn him.

"H'sh!" I said. "You'll wake the other fellows."

He repeated his question, but in a lower tone. I hesitated, before answering him. I felt, all at once, that it might be better to deny all knowledge—to say I hadn't seen anything unusual. I thought quickly, and made answer on the turn of the moment.

"What was *what?*" I said. "That's just the thing I've come to ask you. A pretty pair of fools you made of the two of us up on the poop just now, with your hysterical tomfoolery."

I concluded my remark in a tone of anger.

"I didn't!" he answered, in a passionate whisper. "You know I didn't. You know *you* saw it yourself. You pointed it out to the Second Mate. I saw you."

The little beggar was nearly crying between fear, and vexation at my assumed unbelief.

"Rot!" I replied. "You know jolly well you were sleeping in your time-keeping. You dreamed something and woke up suddenly. You were off your chump."

I was determined to reassure him, if possible; though, goodness! I wanted assurance myself. If he had known of that other thing, I had seen down on the maindeck, what then?

"I wasn't asleep, any more than you were," he said, bitterly. "And you know it. You're just fooling me. The ship's haunted."

"What!" I said, sharply.

"She's haunted," he said, again. "She's haunted."

"Who says so?" I inquired, in a tone of unbelief.

"I do! And you *know* it. Everybody knows it; but they don't more than half believe it ... I didn't, until tonight."

"Damned rot!" I answered. "That's all a blooming old shellback's yarn.
She's no more haunted than I am."

"It's not damned rot," he replied, totally unconvinced. "And it's not an old shellback's yarn ... Why won't you say you saw it?" he cried, growing almost tearfully excited, and raising his voice again.

I warned him not to wake the sleepers.

"Why won't you say that you saw it?" he repeated.

I got up from the chest, and went towards the door.

"You're a young idiot!" I said. "And I should advise you not to go gassing about like this, round the decks. Take my tip, and turn in and get a sleep. You're talking dotty. Tomorrow you'll perhaps feel what an unholy ass you've made of yourself."

I stepped over the washboard, and left him. I believe he followed me to the door to say something further; but I was halfway forward by then.

For the next couple of days, I avoided him as much as possible, taking care never to let him catch me alone. I was determined, if possible, to convince him that he had been mistaken in supposing that he had seen anything that night. Yet, after all, it was little enough use, as you will soon see. For, on the night of the second day, there was a further extraordinary development, that made denial on my part useless.

III.
The Man up the Main

It occurred in the first watch, just after six bells. I was forward, sitting on the fore-hatch. No one was about the maindeck. The night was exceedingly fine; and the wind had dropped away almost to nothing, so that the ship was very quiet.

Suddenly, I heard the Second Mate's voice—

"In the main-rigging, there! Who's that going aloft?"

I sat up on the hatch, and listened. There succeeded an intense silence.

Then the Second's voice came again. He was evidently getting wild.

"Do you damn well hear me? What the hell are you doing up there? Come down!"

I rose to my feet, and walked up to wind'ard. From there, I could see the break of the poop. The Second Mate was standing by the starboard ladder. He appeared to be looking up at something that was hidden from me by the topsails. As I stared, he broke out again:

"Hell and damnation, you blasted sojer, come down when I tell you!"

He stamped on the poop, and repeated his order, savagely. But there was no answer. I started to walk aft. What had happened? Who had gone aloft? Who would be fool enough to go, without being told? And then, all at once, a thought came to me. The figure Tammy and I had seen. Had the Second Mate seen something—someone? I hurried on, and then stopped, suddenly. In the same moment there came the shrill blast of the Second's whistle; he was whistling for the watch, and I turned and ran to the fo'cas'le to rouse them out. Another minute, and I was hurrying aft with them to see what was wanted.

His voice met us halfway:

"Up the main some of you, smartly now, and find out who that damned fool is up there. See what mischief he's up to."

"i, i, Sir," several of the men sung out, and a couple jumped into the weather rigging. I joined them, and the rest were proceeding to follow; but the Second shouted for some to go up to leeward—in case the fellow tried to get down that side.

As I followed the other two aloft, I heard the Second Mate tell Tammy, whose time-keeping it was, to get down on to the maindeck with the other 'prentices, and keep an eye on the fore and aft stays.

"He may try down one of them if he's cornered," I heard him explain. "If you see anything, just sing out for me, right away."

Tammy hesitated.

"Well?" said the Second Mate, sharply.

"Nothing, Sir," said Tammy, and went down on to the maindeck.

The first man to wind'ard had reached the futtock shrouds; his head was above the top, and he was taking a preliminary look, before venturing higher.

"See anythin', Jock?" asked Plummer, the man next above me.

"Na'!" said Jock, tersely, and climbed over the top, and so disappeared from my sight.

The fellow ahead of me, followed. He reached the futtock rigging, and stopped to expectorate. I was close at his heels, and he looked down to me.

"What's up, anyway?" he said. "What's 'e seen? 'oo're we chasin' after?"

I said I didn't know, and he swung up into the topmast rigging. I followed on. The chaps on the lee side were about level with us. Under the foot of the topsail, I could see Tammy and the other 'prentices down on the maindeck, looking upwards.

The fellows were a bit excited in a sort of subdued way; though I am inclined to think there was far more curiosity and, perhaps, a certain consciousness of the strangeness of it all. I know that, looking to leeward, there was a tendancy to keep well together, in which I sympathized.

"Must be a bloomin' stowaway," one of the men suggested.

I grabbed at the idea, instantly. Perhaps—And then, in a moment, I dismissed it. I remembered how that first thing had stepped over the rail *into the sea. That* matter could not be explained in such a manner. With regard to this, I was curious and anxious. I had seen nothing this time. What could the Second Mate have seen? I wondered. Were we chasing fancies, or was there really someone—something real, among the shadows above us? My thoughts returned to that thing, Tammy and I had seen near the log-reel. I remembered how incapable the Second Mate had been of seeing anything then. I remembered how natural it had seemed that he should not be able to see. I caught the word "stowaway" again. After all, that might explain away *this* affair. It would—

My train of thought was broken suddenly. One of the men was shouting and gesticulating.

"I sees 'im! I sees 'im!" He was pointing upwards over our heads.

"Where?" said the man above me. "Where?"

I was looking up, for all that I was worth. I was conscious of a certain sense of relief. "It is *real* then," I said to myself. I screwed my head round, and looked along the yards above us. Yet, still I could see nothing; nothing except shadows and patches of light.

Down on deck, I caught the Second Mate's voice.

"Have you got him?" he was shouting.

"Not yet, Zur," sung out the lowest man on the lee side.

"We sees 'im, Sir," added Quoin.

"I don't!" I said.

"There 'e is agen," he said.

We had reached the t'gallant rigging, and he was pointing up to the royal yard.

"Ye're a fule, Quoin. That's what ye are."

The voice came from above. It was Jock's, and there was a burst of laughter at Quoin's expense.

I could see Jock now. He was standing in the rigging, just below the yard. He had gone straight away up, while the rest of us were mooning over the top.

"Ye're a fule, Quoin," he said, again, "And I'm thinking the Second's juist as saft."

He began to descend.

"Then there's no one?" I asked.

"Na'," he said, briefly.

As we reached the deck, the Second Mate ran down off the poop. He came towards us, with an expectant air.

"You've got him?" he asked, confidently.

"There wasn't anyone," I said.

"What!" he nearly shouted. "You're hiding something!" he continued, angrily, and glancing from one to another. "Out with it. Who was it?"

"We're hiding nothing," I replied, speaking for the lot. "There's no one up there."

The Second looked round upon us.

"Am I a fool?" he asked, contemptuously.

There was an assenting silence.

"I saw him myself," he continued. "Tammy, here, saw him. He wasn't over the top when I first spotted him. There's no mistake about it. It's all damned rot saying he's not there."

"Well, he's not, Sir," I answered. "Jock went right up to the royal yard."

The Second Mate said nothing, in immediate reply; but went aft a few steps and looked up the main. Then he turned to the two 'prenticess.

"Sure you two boys didn't see anyone coming down from the main?" he inquired, suspiciously.

"Yes, Sir," they answered together.

"Anyway," I heard him mutter to himself, "I'd have spotted him myself, if he had."

"Have you any idea, Sir, who it was you saw?" I asked, at this juncture.

He looked at me, keenly.

"No!" he said.

He thought for a few moments, while we all stood about in silence, waiting for him to let us go.

"By the holy poker!" he exclaimed, suddenly. "But I ought to have thought of that before."

He turned, and eyed us individually.

"You're all here?" he asked.

"Yes, Sir," we said in a chorus. I could see that he was counting us.

Then he spoke again.

"All of you men stay here where you are. Tammy, you go into *your* place and see if the other fellows are in their bunks. Then come and tell me. Smartly now!"

The boy went, and he turned to the other 'prentices.

"You get along forrard to the fo'cas'le," he said. "Count the other watch; then come aft and report to me."

As the youngster disappeared along the deck to the fo'cas'le, Tammy returned from his visit to the Glory Hole, to tell the Second Mate that the other two 'prenticess were sound asleep in their bunks. Whereupon, the Second bundled him off to the Carpenter's and Sailmaker's berth, to see whether they were turned-in.

While he was gone, the other boy came aft, and reported that all the men were in their bunks, and asleep.

"Sure?" the Second asked him.

"Quite, Sir," he answered.

The Second Mate made a quick gesture.

"Go and see if the Steward is in his berth," he said, abruptly. It was plain to me that he was tremendously puzzled.

"You've something to learn yet, Mr. Second Mate," I thought to myself.

Then I fell to wondering to what conclusions he would come.

A few seconds later, Tammy returned to say that the Carpenter, Sailmaker and "Doctor" were all turned-in.

The Second Mate muttered something, and told him to go down into the saloon to see whether the First and Third Mates, by any chance, were not in their berths.

Tammy started off; then halted.

"Shall I have a look into the Old Man's place, Sir, while I'm down there?" he inquired.

"No!" said the Second Mate. "Do what I told you, and then come and tell me. If anyone's to go into the Captain's cabin, it's got to be me."

Tammy said "i, i, Sir," and skipped away, up on to the poop.

While he was gone, the other 'prenticess came up to say that the Steward was in his berth, and that he wanted to know what the hell he was fooling round his part of the ship for.

The Second Mate said nothing, for nearly a minute. Then he turned to us, and told us we might go forrard.

As we moved off in a body, and talking in undertones, Tammy came down from the poop, and went up to the Second Mate. I heard him say that the two Mates were in their berths, asleep. Then he added, as if it were an afterthought—

"So's the Old Man."

"I thought I told you—" the Second Mate began.

"I didn't, Sir," Tammy said. "His cabin door was open."

The Second Mate started to go aft. I caught a fragment of a remark he was making to Tammy.

"—accounted for the whole crew. I'm—"

He went up onto the poop. I did not catch the rest.

I had loitered a moment; now, however, I hurried after the others. As we neared the fo'cas'le, one bell went, and we roused out the other watch, and told them what jinks we had been up to.

"I rec'on 'e must be rocky," one of the men remarked.

"Not 'im," said another, "'e's bin 'avin' forty winks on the break, an' dreemed 'is mother-en-lore 'ad come on 'er visit, friendly like."

There was some laughter at this suggestion, and I caught myself smiling along with the rest; though I had no reason for sharing their belief, that there was nothing in it all.

"Might 'ave been a stowaway, yer know," I heard Quoin, the one who had suggested it before, remark to one of the A.B's named Stubbins—a short, rather surly-looking chap.

"Might have been hell!" returned Stubbins. "Stowaways hain't such fools as all that."

"I dunno," said the first. "I wish I 'ad arsked the Second what 'e thought about it."

"I don't think it was a stowaway, somehow," I said, chipping in. "What would a stowaway want aloft? I guess he'd be trying more for the Steward's pantry."

"You bet he would, hevry time," said Stubbins. He lit his pipe, and sucked at it, slowly.

"I don't hunderstand it, all ther same," he remarked, after a moment's silence.

"Neither do I," I said. And after that I was quiet for a while, listening to the run of conversation on the subject.

Presently, my glance fell upon Williams, the man who had spoken to me about "shadders." He was sitting in his bunk, smoking, and making no effort to join in the talk.

I went across to him.

"What do you think of it, Williams?" I asked. "Do *you* think the Second Mate really saw anything?"

He looked at me, with a sort of gloomy suspicion; but said nothing.

I felt a trifle annoyed by his silence; but took care not to show it.

After a few moments, I went on.

"Do you know, Williams, I'm beginning to understand what you meant that night, when you said there were too many shadows."

"Wot yer mean?" he said, pulling his pipe from out of his mouth, and fairly surprised into answering.

"What I say, of course," I said. "There *are* too many shadows."

He sat up, and leant forward out from his bunk, extending his hand and pipe. His eyes plainly showed his excitement.

"'ave yer seen—" he hesitated, and looked at me, struggling inwardly to express himself.

"Well?" I prompted.

For perhaps a minute he tried to say something. Then his expression altered suddenly from doubt, and something else more indefinite, to a pretty grim look of determination.

He spoke.

"I'm blimed," he said, "ef I don't tike er piy-diy out of 'er, shadders or no shadders."

I looked at him, with astonishment.

"What's it got to do with your getting a payday out of her?" I asked.

He nodded his head, with a sort of stolid resolution.

"Look 'ere," he said.

I waited.

"Ther crowd cleared"; he indicated with his hand and pipe towards the stern.

"You mean in 'Frisco?" I said.

"Yus," he replied; "'an withart er cent of ther piy. I styied."

I comprehended him suddenly.

"You think they saw," I hesitated; then I said "shadows?"

He nodded; but said nothing.

"And so they all bunked?"

He nodded again, and began tapping out his pipe on the edge of his bunk-board.

"And the officers and the Skipper?" I asked.

"Fresh uns," he said, and got out of his bunk; for eight bells was striking.

IV.
The Fooling with the Sail

It was on the Friday night, that the Second Mate had the watch aloft looking for the man up the main; and for the next five days little else was talked about; though, with the exception of Williams, Tammy and myself, no one seemed to think of treating the matter seriously. Perhaps I should not exclude Quoin, who still persisted, on every occasion, that there was a stowaway aboard. As for the Second Mate, I have very little doubt now, but that he was beginning to realize there was something deeper and less understandable than he had at first dreamed of. Yet, all the same, I know he had to keep his guesses and half-formed opinions pretty well to himself; for the Old Man and the First Mate chaffed him unmercifully about his "bogy." This, I got from Tammy, who had heard them both ragging him during the second dog-watch the following day. There was another thing Tammy told me, that showed how the Second Mate bothered about his inability to understand the mysterious appearance and disappearance of the man he had seen go aloft. He had made Tammy give him every detail he could remember about the figure we had seen by the log-reel. What is more, the Second had not even affected to treat the matter lightly, nor as a thing to be sneered at; but had listened seriously, and asked a great many questions. It is very evident to me that he was reaching out towards the only possible conclusion. Though, goodness knows, it was one that was impossible and improbable enough.

It was on the Wednesday night, after the five days of talk I have mentioned, that there came, to me and to those who *knew*, another element of fear. And yet, I can quite understand that, at *that* time, those who had seen nothing, would find little to be afraid of, in all that I am going to tell you. Still, even they were much puzzled and astonished, and perhaps, after all, a little awed. There was so much in the affair that was inexplicable, and yet again such a lot that was natural and commonplace. For, when all is said and done, it was nothing more than the blowing adrift of one of the sails; yet accompanied by what were really significant details—significant, that is, in the light of that which Tammy and I and the Second Mate knew.

Seven bells, and then one, had gone in the first watch, and our side was being roused out to relieve the Mate's. Most of the men were already out of their bunks, and sitting about on their sea-chests, getting into their togs.

Suddenly, one of the 'prenticess in the other watch, put his head in through the doorway on the port side.

"The Mate wants to know," he said, "which of you chaps made fast the fore royal, last watch."

"Wot's 'e want to know that for?" inquired one of the men.

"The lee side's blowing adrift," said the 'prentices. "And he says that the chap who made it fast is to go up and see to it as soon as the watch is relieved."

"Oh! does 'e? Well 'twasn't me, any'ow," replied the man. "You'd better arsk sum of t'others."

"Ask what?" inquired Plummer, getting out of his bunk, sleepily.

The 'prentices repeated his message.

The man yawned and stretched himself.

"Let me see," he muttered, and scratched his head with one hand, while he fumbled for his trousers with the other. "'oo made ther fore r'yal fast?" He got into his trousers, and stood up. "Why, ther Or'nary, er course; 'oo else do yer suppose?"

"That's all I wanted to know!" said the 'prentices, and went away.

"Hi! Tom!" Stubbins sung out to the Ordinary. "Wake up, you lazy young devil. Ther Mate's just sent to hinquire who it was made the fore royal fast. It's all blowin' adrift, and he says you're to get along up as soon as eight bells goes, and make it fast again."

Tom jumped out of his bunk, and began to dress, quickly.

"Blowin' adrift!" he said. "There ain't all that much wind; and I tucked the ends of the gaskets well in under the other turns."

"P'raps one of ther gaskets is rotten, and given way," suggested

Stubbins. "Anyway, you'd better hurry up, it's just on eight bells."

A minute later, eight bells went, and we trooped away aft for roll-call.

As soon as the names were called over, I saw the Mate lean towards the

Second and say something. Then the Second Mate sung out:

"Tom!"

"Sir!" answered Tom.

"Was it you made fast that fore royal, last watch?"

"Yes, Sir."

"How's that it's broken adrift?"

"Carn't say, Sir."

"Well, it has, and you'd better jump aloft and shove the gasket round it again. And mind you make a better job of it this time."

"i, i, Sir," said Tom, and followed the rest of us forrard. Reaching the fore rigging, he climbed into it, and began to make his way leisurely aloft. I could see him with a fair amount of distinctness, as the moon was very clear and bright, though getting old.

I went over to the weather pin-rail, and leaned up against it, watching him, while I filled my pipe. The other men, both the watch on deck and the watch below, had gone into the fo'cas'le, so that I imagined I was the only one about the maindeck. Yet, a minute later, I discovered that I was mistaken; for, as I proceeded to light up, I saw Williams, the young cockney, come out from under the lee of the house, and turn and look up at the Ordinary as he went steadily upwards. I was a little surprised, as I knew he and three of the others had a "poker fight" on, and he'd won over sixty pounds of tobacco. I believe I opened my mouth to sing out to him to know why he wasn't playing; and then, all at once, there came into my mind the memory of my first conversation with him. I remembered that he had said sails were always blowing adrift *at night.* I remembered the, then, unaccountable emphasis he had laid on those two words; and remembering that, I felt suddenly afraid. For, all at once, the absurdity had struck me of a sail—even a badly stowed one—blowing adrift in such fine and calm weather as we were then having. I wondered I had not seen before that there was something queer and unlikely about the affair. Sails don't blow adrift in fine weather, with the sea calm and the ship as steady as a rock. I moved away from the rail and went towards Williams. He knew something, or, at least, he guessed at something that was very much a blankness to me at that time. Up above, the boy was climbing up, to what? That was the thing that made me feel so frightened. Ought I to tell all I knew and guessed? And then, who should I tell? I should only be laughed at—I—

Williams turned towards me, and spoke.

"Gawd!" he said, "it's started agen!"

"What?" I said. Though I knew what he meant.

"Them syles," he answered, and made a gesture towards the fore royal.

I glanced up, briefly. All the lee side of the sail was adrift, from the bunt gasket outwards. Lower, I saw Tom; he was just hoisting himself into the t'gallant rigging.

Williams spoke again.

"We lost two on 'em just sime way, comin' art."

"Two of the men!" I exclaimed.

"Yus!" he said tersely.

"I can't understand," I went on. "I never heard anything about it."

"Who'd yer got ter tell yer abart it?" he asked.

I made no reply to his question; indeed, I had scarcely comprehended it, for the problem of what I ought to do in the matter had risen again in my mind.

"I've a good mind to go aft and tell the Second Mate all I know," I said. "He's seen something himself that he can't explain away, and—and anyway I can't stand this state of things. If the Second Mate knew all—"

"Garn!" he cut in, interrupting me. "An' be told yer're a blastid hidiot. Not yer. Yer sty were yer are."

I stood irresolute. What he had said, was perfectly correct, and I was positively stumped what to do for the best. That there was danger aloft, I was convinced; though if I had been asked my reasons for supposing this, they would have been hard to find. Yet of its existence, I was as certain as though my eyes already saw it. I wondered whether, being so ignorant of the form it would assume, I could stop it by joining Tom on the yard? This thought came as I stared up at the royal. Tom had reached the sail, and was standing on the foot-rope, close in to the bunt. He was bending over the yard, and reaching down for the slack of the sail. And then, as I looked, I saw the belly of the royal tossed up and down abruptly, as though a sudden heavy gust of wind had caught it.

"I'm blimed—!" Williams began, with a sort of excited expectation. And then he stopped as abruptly as he had begun. For, in a moment, the sail had thrashed right over the after side of the yard, apparently knocking Tom clean from off the foot-rope.

"My God!" I shouted out loud. "He's gone!"

For an instant there was a blur over my eyes, and Williams was singing out something that I could not catch. Then, just as quickly, it went, and I could see again, clearly.

Williams was pointing, and I saw something black, swinging below the yard. Williams called out something fresh, and made a run for the forerigging. I caught the last part—

"—ther garskit."

Straightway, I knew that Tom had managed to grab the gasket as he fell, and I bolted after Williams to give him a hand in getting the youngster into safety.

Down on deck, I caught the sound of running feet, and then the Second Mate's voice. He was asking what the devil was up; but I did not trouble to answer him then. I wanted all my breath to help me aloft. I knew very well that some of the gaskets were little better than old shakins; and, unless Tom got hold of something on the t'gallant yard below him, he might come down with a run any moment. I reached the top, and lifted myself over it in quick time. Williams was some distance above me. In less than half a minute, I reached the t'gallant yard. Williams had gone up on to the royal. I slid out on to the t'gallant foot-rope until I was just below Tom; then I sung out to him to let himself down to me, and I would catch him. He made no answer, and I saw that he was hanging in a curiously limp fashion, and by one hand.

Williams's voice came down to me from the royal yard. He was singing out to me to go up and give him a hand to pull Tom up on to the yard. When I reached him, he told me that the gasket had hitched itself round the lad's wrist. I bent beside the yard, and peered down. It was as Williams had said, and I realized how near a thing it had been. Strangely enough, even at that moment, the thought came to me how little wind there was. I remembered the wild way in which the sail had lashed at the boy.

All this time, I was busily working, unreeving the port buntline. I took the end, made a running bowline with it round the gasket, and let the loop slide down over the boy's head and shoulders. Then I took a strain on it and tightened it under his arms. A minute later we had him safely on the yard between us. In the uncertain moonlight, I could just make out the mark of a great lump on his forehead, where the foot of the sail must have caught him when it knocked him over.

As we stood there a moment, taking our breath, I caught the sound of the Second Mate's voice close beneath us. Williams glanced down; then he looked up at me and gave a short, grunting laugh.

"Crikey!" he said.

"What's up?" I asked, quickly.

He jerked his head backwards and downwards. I screwed round a bit, holding the jackstay with one hand, and steadying the insensible Ordinary with the other. In this way I could look below. At first, I could see nothing. Then the Second Mate's voice came up to me again.

"Who the hell are you? What are you doing?"

I saw him now. He was standing at the foot of the weather t'gallant rigging, his face was turned upwards, peering round the after side of the mast. It showed to me only as a blurred, pale-colored oval in the moonlight.

He repeated his question.

"It's Williams and I, Sir," I said. "Tom, here, has had an accident."

I stopped. He began to come up higher towards us. From the rigging to leeward there came suddenly a buzz of men talking.

The Second Mate reached us.

"Well, what's up, anyway?" he inquired, suspiciously. "What's happened?"

He had bent forward, and was peering at Tom. I started to explain; but he cut me short with:

"Is he dead?"

"No, Sir," I said. "I don't think so; but the poor beggar's had a bad fall. He was hanging by the gasket when we got to him. The sail knocked him off the yard."

"What?" he said, sharply.

"The wind caught the sail, and it lashed back over the yard—"

"What wind?" he interrupted. "There's no wind, scarcely." He shifted his weight onto the other foot. "What do you mean?"

"I mean what I say, Sir. The wind brought the foot of the sail over the top of the yard and knocked Tom clean off the foot-rope. Williams and I both saw it happen."

"But there's no wind to do such a thing; you're talking nonsense!"

It seemed to me that there was as much of bewilderment as anything else in his voice; yet I could tell that he was suspicious—though, of what, I doubted whether he himself could have told.

He glanced at Williams, and seemed about to say something. Then, seeming to change his mind, he turned, and sung out to one of the men who had followed him aloft, to go down and pass out a coil of new, three-inch manilla, and a tailblock.

"Smartly now!" he concluded.

"i, i, Sir," said the man, and went down swiftly.

The Second Mate turned to me.

"When you've got Tom below, I shall want a better explanation of all this, than the one you've given me. It won't wash."

"Very well, Sir," I answered. "But you won't get any other."

"What do you mean?" he shouted at me. "I'll let you know I'll have no impertinence from you or any one else."

"I don't mean any impertinence, Sir—I mean that it's the only explanation there is to give."

"I tell you it won't wash!" he repeated. "There's something too damned funny about it all. I shall have to report the matter to the Captain. I can't tell him that yarn—" He broke off abruptly.

"It's not the only damned funny thing that's happened aboard this old hooker," I answered. "You ought to know that, Sir."

"What do you mean?" he asked, quickly.

"Well, Sir," I said, "to be straight, what about that chap you sent us hunting after up the main the other night? That was a funny enough affair, wasn't it? This one isn't half so funny."

"That will do, Jessop!" he said, angrily. "I won't have any back talk." Yet there was something about his tone that told me I had got one in on my own. He seemed all at once less able to appear confident that I was telling him a fairy tale.

After that, for perhaps half a minute, he said nothing. I guessed he was doing some hard thinking. When he spoke again it was on the matter of getting the Ordinary down on deck.

"One of you'll have to go down the lee side and steady him down," he concluded.

He turned and looked downwards.

"Are you bringing that gantline?" he sang out.

"Yes, Sir," I heard one of the men answer.

A moment later, I saw the man's head appear over the top. He had the tail-block slung round his neck, and the end of the gantline over his shoulder.

Very soon we had the gantline rigged, and Tom down on deck. Then we took him into the fo'cas'le and put him in his bunk. The Second Mate had sent for some brandy, and now he started to dose him well with it. At the same time a couple of the men chafed his hands and feet. In a little, he began to show signs of coming round. Presently, after a sudden fit of coughing, he opened his eyes, with a surprised, bewildered stare. Then he caught at the edge of his bunk-board, and sat up, giddily. One of the men steadied him, while the Second Mate stood back, and eyed him, critically. The boy rocked as he sat, and put up his hand to his head.

"Here," said the Second Mate, "take another drink."

Tom caught his breath and choked a little; then he spoke.

"By gum!" he said, "my head does ache."

He put up his hand, again, and felt at the lump on his forehead. Then he bent forward and stared round at the men grouped about his bunk.

"What's up?" he inquired, in a confused sort of way, and seeming as if he could not see us clearly.

"What's up?" he asked again.

"That's just what I want to know!" said the Second Mate, speaking for the first time with some sternness.

"I ain't been snoozin' while there's been a job on?" Tom inquired, anxiously.

He looked round at the men appealingly.

"It's knocked 'im dotty, strikes me," said one of the men, audibly.

"No," I said, answering Tom's question, "you've had—"

"Shut that, Jessop!" said the Second Mate, quickly, interrupting me. "I want to hear what the boy's got to say for himself."

He turned again to Tom.

"You were up at the fore royal," he prompted.

"I carn't say I was, Sir," said Tom, doubtfully. I could see that he had not gripped the Second Mate's meaning.

"But you were!" said the Second, with some impatience. "It was blowing adrift, and I sent you up to shove a gasket round it."

"Blowin' adrift, Sir?" said Tom, dully.

"Yes! blowing adrift. Don't I speak plainly?"

The dullness went from Tom's face, suddenly.

"So it was, Sir," he said, his memory returning. "The bloomin' sail got chock full of wind. It caught me bang in the face."

He paused a moment.

"I believe—" he began, and then stopped once more.

"Go on!" said the Second Mate. "Spit it out!"

"I don't know, Sir," Tom said. "I don't understand—"

He hesitated again.

"That's all I can remember," he muttered, and put his hand up to the bruise on his forehead, as though trying to remember something.

In the momentary silence that succeeded, I caught the voice of Stubbins.

"There hain't hardly no wind," he was saying, in a puzzled tone.

There was a low murmur of assent from the surrounding men.

The Second Mate said nothing, and I glanced at him, curiously. Was he beginning to see, I wondered, how useless it was to try to find any sensible explanation of the affair? Had he begun at last to couple it with that peculiar business of the man up the main? I am inclined *now* to think that this was so; for, after staring a few moments at Tom, in a doubtful sort of way, he went out of the fo'cas'le, saying that he would inquire further into the matter in the morning. Yet, when the morning came, he did no such thing. As for his reporting the affair to the Skipper, I much doubt it. Even did he, it must have been in a very casual way; for we heard nothing more about it; though, of course, we talked it over pretty thoroughly among ourselves.

With regard to the Second Mate, even now I am rather puzzled by his attitude to us aloft. Sometimes I have thought that he must have suspected us of trying to play off some trick on him—perhaps, at the time, he still half suspected one of us of being in some way connected with the other business. Or, again, he may have been trying to fight against the conviction that was being forced upon him, that there was really something impossible and beastly about the old packet. Of course, these are only suppositions.

And then, close upon this, there were further developments.

V.
The End of Williams

As I have said, there was a lot of talk, among the crowd of us forrard, about Tom's strange accident. None of the men knew that Williams and I had seen it *happen*. Stubbins gave it as his opinion that Tom had been sleepy, and missed the foot-rope. Tom, of course, would not have this by any means. Yet, he had no one to appeal to; for, at that time, he was just as ignorant as the rest, that we had seen the sail flap up over the yard.

Stubbins insisted that it stood to reason it couldn't be the wind. There wasn't any, he said; and the rest of the men agreed with him.

"Well," I said, "I don't know about all that. I'm a bit inclined to think Tom's yarn is the truth."

"How do you make that hout?" Stubbins asked, unbelievingly. "There haint nothin' like enough wind."

"What about the place on his forehead?" I inquired, in turn. "How are you going to explain that?"

"I 'spect he knocked himself there when he slipped," he answered.

"Likely 'nuffli," agreed old Jaskett, who was sitting smoking on a chest nearby.

"Well, you're both a damn long way out of it!" Tom chipped in, pretty warm. "I wasn't asleep; an' the sail did bloomin' well hit me."

"Don't you be impertinent, young feller," said Jaskett.

I joined in again.

"There's another thing, Stubbins," I said. "The gasket Tom was hanging by, was on the after side of the yard. That looks as if the sail might have flapped it over? If there were wind enough to do the one, it seems to me that it might have done the other."

"Do you mean that it was hunder ther yard, or hover ther top?" he asked.

"Over the top, of course. What's more, the foot of the sail was hanging over the after part of the yard, in a bight."

Stubbins was plainly surprised at that, and before he was ready with his next objection, Plummer spoke.

"'oo saw it?" he asked.

"I saw it!" I said, a bit sharply. "So did Williams; so—for that matter—did the Second Mate."

Plummer relapsed into silence; and smoked; and Stubbins broke out afresh.

"I reckon Tom must have had a hold of the foot and the gasket, and pulled 'em hover the yard when he tumbled."

"No!" interrupted Tom. "The gasket was under the sail. I couldn't even see it. An' I hadn't time to get hold of the foot of the sail, before it up and caught me smack in the face."

"'ow did yer get 'old er ther gasket, when yer fell, then?" asked Plummer.

"He didn't get hold of it," I answered for Tom. "It had taken a turn round his wrist, and that's how we found him hanging."

"Do you mean to say as 'e 'adn't got 'old of ther garsket?," Quoin inquired, pausing in the lighting of his pipe.

"Of course, I do," I said. "A chap doesn't go hanging on to a rope when he's jolly well been knocked senseless."

"Ye're richt," assented Jock. "Ye're quite richt there, Jessop."

Quoin concluded the lighting of his pipe.

"I dunno," he said.

I went on, without noticing him.

"Anyway, when Williams and I found him, he was hanging by the gasket, and it had a couple of turns round his wrist. And besides that, as I said before, the foot of the sail was hanging over the after side of the yard, and Tom's weight on the gasket was holding it there."

"It's damned queer," said Stubbins, in a puzzled voice. "There don't seem to be no way of gettin' a proper hexplanation to it."

I glanced at Williams, to suggest that I should tell all that we had seen; but he shook his head, and, after a moment's thought, it seemed to me that there was nothing to be gained by so doing. We had no very clear idea of the thing that had happened, and our half facts and guesses would only have tended to make the matter appear more grotesque and unlikely. The only thing to be done was to wait and watch. If we could only get hold of something tangible, then we might hope to tell all that we knew, without being made into laughing-stocks.

I came out from my think, abruptly.

Stubbins was speaking again. He was arguing the matter with one of the other men.

"You see, with there bein' no wind, scarcely, ther thing's himpossible, an' yet—"

The other man interrupted with some remark I did not catch.

"No," I heard Stubbins say. "I'm hout of my reckonin'. I don't savvy it one bit. It's too much like a damned fairy tale."

"Look at his wrist!" I said.

Tom held out his right hand and arm for inspection. It was considerably swollen where the rope had been round it.

"Yes," admitted Stubbins. "That's right enough; but it don't tell you nothin'."

I made no reply. As Stubbins said, it told you "nothin'." And there I let it drop. Yet, I have told you this, as showing how the matter was regarded in the fo'cas'le.

Still, it did not occupy our minds very long; for, as I have said, there were further developments.

The three following nights passed quietly; and then, on the fourth, all those curious signs and hints culminated suddenly in something extraordinarily grim. Yet, everything had been so subtle and intangible, and, indeed, so was the affair itself, that only those who had actually come in touch with the invading fear, seemed really capable of comprehending the terror of the thing. The men, for the most part, began to say the ship was unlucky, and, of course, as usual! there was some talk of there being a Jonah in the ship. Still, I cannot say that none of the men realized there was anything horrible and frightening in it all; for I am sure that some did, a little; and I think Stubbins was certainly one of them; though I feel certain that he did not, at that time, you know, grasp a quarter of the real significance that underlay the several queer matters that had disturbed our nights. He seemed to fail, somehow, to grasp the element of personal danger that, to me, was already plain. He lacked sufficient imagination, I suppose, to piece the things together—to trace the natural sequence of the events, and their development. Yet I must not forget, of course, that he had no knowledge of those two first incidents. If he had, perhaps he might have stood where I did. As it was, he had not seemed to reach out at all, you know, not even in the matter of Tom and the fore royal. Now, however, after the thing I am about to tell you, he seemed to see a little way into the darkness, and realize possibilities.

I remember the fourth night, well. It was a clear, starlit, moonless sort of night: at least, I think there was no moon; or, at any rate, the moon could have been little more than a thin crescent, for it was near the dark time.

The wind had breezed up a bit; but still remained steady. We were slipping along at about six or seven knots an hour. It was our middle watch on deck, and the ship was full of the blow and hum of the wind aloft. Williams and I were the only ones about the maindeck. He was leaning over the weather pin-rail, smoking; while I was pacing up and down, between him and the fore hatch. Stubbins was on the lookout.

Two bells had gone some minutes, and I was wishing to goodness that it was eight, and time to turn in. Suddenly, overhead, there sounded a sharp crack, like the report of a rifle shot. It was followed instantly by the rattle and crash of sailcloth thrashing in the wind.

Williams jumped away from the rail, and ran aft a few steps. I followed him, and, together, we stared upwards to see what had gone. Indistinctly, I made out that the weather sheet of the fore t'gallant had carried away, and the clew of the sail was whirling and banging about in the air, and, every few moments, hitting the steel yard a blow, like the thump of a great sledge hammer.

"It's the shackle, or one of the links that's gone, I think," I shouted to Williams, above the noise of the sail. "That's the spectacle that's hitting the yard."

"Yus!" he shouted back, and went to get hold of the clewline. I ran to give him a hand. At the same moment, I caught the Second Mate's voice away aft, shouting. Then came the noise of running feet, and the rest of the watch, and the Second Mate, were with us almost at the same moment. In a few minutes we had the yard lowered and the sail clewed up. Then Williams and I went aloft to see where the sheet had gone. It was much as I had supposed; the spectacle was all right, but the pin had gone out of the shackle, and the shackle itself was jammed into the sheavehole in the yard arm.

Williams sent me down for another pin, while he unbent the clewline, and overhauled it down to the sheet. When I returned with the fresh pin, I screwed it into the shackle, clipped on the clewline, and sung out to the men to take a pull on the rope. This they did, and at the second heave the shackle came away. When it was high enough, I went up on to the t'gallant yard, and held the chain, while Williams shackled it into the spectacle. Then he bent on the clewline afresh, and sung out to the Second Mate that we were ready to hoist away.

"Yer'd better go down an' give 'em a 'aul," he said. "I'll sty an' light up ther syle."

"Right ho, Williams," I said, getting into the rigging. "Don't let the ship's bogy run away with you."

This remark I made in a moment of light-heartedness, such as will come to anyone aloft, at times. I was exhilarated for the time being, and quite free from the sense of fear that had been with me so much of late. I suppose this was due to the freshness of the wind.

"There's more'n one!" he said, in that curiously short way of his.

"What?" I asked.

He repeated his remark.

I was suddenly serious. The *reality* of all the impossible details of the past weeks came back to me, vivid, and beastly.

"What do you mean, Williams?" I asked him.

But he had shut up, and would say nothing.

"What do you know—how much do you know?" I went on, quickly. "Why did you never tell me that you—"

The Second Mate's voice interrupted me, abruptly:

"Now then, up there! Are you going to keep us waiting all night? One of you come down and give us a pull with the ha'lyards. The other stay up and light up the gear."

"i, i, Sir," I shouted back.

Then I turned to Williams, hurriedly.

"Look here, Williams," I said. "If you think there is *really* a danger in your being alone up here—" I hesitated for words to express what I meant. Then I went on. "Well, I'll jolly well stay up with you."

The Second Mate's voice came again.

"Come on now, one of you! Make a move! What the hell are you doing?"

"Coming, Sir!" I sung out.

"Shall I stay?" I asked definitely.

"Garn!" he said. "Don't yer fret yerself. I'll tike er bloomin' piy-diy out of 'er. Blarst 'em. I ain't funky of 'em."

I went. That was the last word Williams spoke to anyone living.

I reached the decks, and tailed on to the haulyards.

We had nearly mast-headed the yard, and the Second Mate was looking up at the dark outline of the sail, ready to sing out "Belay"; when, all at once, there came a queer sort of muffled shout from Williams.

"Vast hauling, you men," shouted the Second Mate.

We stood silent, and listened.

"What's that, Williams?" he sung out. "Are you all clear?"

For nearly half a minute we stood, listening; but there came no reply. Some of the men said afterwards that they had noticed a curious rattling and vibrating noise aloft that sounded faintly above the hum and swirl of the wind. Like the sound of loose ropes being shaken and slatted together, you know. Whether this noise was really heard, or whether it was something that had no existence outside of their imaginations, I cannot say. I heard nothing of it; but then I was at the tail end of the rope, and furthest from the fore rigging; while those who heard it were on the fore part of the haulyards, and close up to the shrouds.

The Second Mate put his hands to his mouth.

"Are you all clear there?" he shouted again.

The answer came, unintelligible and unexpected. It ran like this:

"Blarst yer … I've styed … Did yer think … drive … bloody piy-diy." And then there was a sudden silence.

I stared up at the dim sail, astonished.

"He's dotty!" said Stubbins, who had been told to come off the lookout and give us a pull.

"'e's as mad as a bloomin' 'atter," said Quoin, who was standing foreside of me. "'e's been queer all along."

"Silence there!" shouted the Second Mate. Then:

"Williams!"

No answer.

"Williams!" more loudly.

Still no answer.

Then:

"Damn you, you jumped-up cockney crocodile! Can't you hear? Are you blooming-well deaf?"

There was no answer, and the Second Mate turned to me.

"Jump aloft, smartly now, Jessop, and see what's wrong!"

"i, i, Sir," I said and made a run for the rigging. I felt a bit queer. Had Williams gone mad? He certainly always had been a bit funny. Or—and the thought came with a jump—had he seen—I did not finish. Suddenly, up aloft, there sounded a frightful scream. I stopped, with my hand on the sheerpole. The next instant, something fell out of the darkness—a heavy body, that struck the deck near the waiting men, with a tremendous crash and a loud, ringing, wheezy sound that sickened me. Several of the men shouted out loud in their fright, and let go of the haulyards; but luckily the stopper held it, and the yard did not come down. Then, for the space of several seconds, there was a dead silence among the crowd; and it seemed to me that the wind had in it a strange moaning note.

The Second Mate was the first to speak. His voice came so abruptly that it startled me.

"Get a light, one of you, quick now!"

There was a moment's hesitation.

"Fetch one of the binnacle lamps, you, Tammy."

"i, i, Sir," the youngster said, in a quavering voice, and ran aft.

In less than a minute I saw the light coming towards us along the deck.

The boy was running. He reached us, and handed the lamp to the Second Mate, who took it and went towards the dark, huddled heap on the deck.

He held the light out before him, and peered at the thing.

"My God!" he said. "It's Williams!"

He stooped lower with the light, and I saw details. It was Williams right enough. The Second Mate told a couple of the men to lift him and straighten him out on the hatch. Then he went aft to call the Skipper. He returned in a couple of minutes with an old ensign which he spread over the poor beggar. Almost directly, the Captain came hurrying forward along the decks. He pulled back one end of the ensign, and looked; then he put it back quietly, and the Second Mate explained all that we knew, in a few words.

"Would you leave him where he is, Sir?" he asked, after he had told everything.

"The night's fine," said the Captain. "You may as well leave the poor devil there."

He turned, and went aft, slowly. The man who was holding the light, swept it round so that it showed the place where Williams had struck the deck.

The Second Mate spoke abruptly.

"Get a broom and a couple of buckets, some of you."

He turned sharply, and ordered Tammy on to the poop.

As soon as he had seen the yard mast-headed, and the ropes cleared up, he followed Tammy. He knew well enough that it would not do for the youngster to let his mind dwell too much on the poor chap on the hatch, and I found out, a little later, that he gave the boy something to occupy his thoughts.

After they had gone aft, we went into the fo'cas'le. Every one was moody and frightened. For a little while, we sat about in our bunks and on the chests, and no one said a word. The watch below were all asleep, and not one of them knew what had happened.

All at once, Plummer, whose wheel it was, stepped over the starboard washboard, into the fo'cas'le.

"What's up, anyway?" he asked. "Is Williams much 'urt?"

"Sh!" I said. "You'll wake the others. Who's taken your wheel?"

"Tammy—ther Second sent 'im. 'e said I could go forrard an' 'ave er smoke. 'e said Williams 'ad 'ad er fall."

He broke off, and looked across the fo'cas'le.

"Where is 'e?" he inquired, in a puzzled voice.

I glanced at the others; but no one seemed inclined to start yarning about it.

"He fell from the t'gallant rigging!" I said.

"Where is 'e?" he repeated.

"Smashed up," I said. "He's lying on the hatch."

"Dead?" he asked.

I nodded.

"I guessed 'twere somethin' pretty bad, when I saw the Old Man come forrard. 'ow did it 'appen?"

He looked round at the lot of us sitting there silent and smoking.

"No one knows," I said, and glanced at Stubbins. I caught him eyeing me, doubtfully.

After a moment's silence, Plummer spoke again.

"I 'eard 'im screech, when I was at ther wheel. 'e must 'ave got 'urt up aloft."

Stubbins struck a match and proceeded to relight his pipe.

"How d'yer mean?" he asked, speaking for the first time.

"'ow do I mean? Well, I can't say. Maybe 'e jammed 'is fingers between ther parrel an' ther mast."

"What about 'is swearin' at ther Second Mate? Was that 'cause 'e'd jammed 'is fingers?" put in Quoin.

"I never 'eard about that," said Plummer. "'oo 'eard 'im?

"I should think heverybody in ther bloomin' ship heard him," Stubbins answered. "All ther same, I hain't sure he *was* swearin' at ther Second Mate. I thought at first he'd gone dotty an' was cussin' him; but somehow it don't seem likely, now I come to think. It don't stand to reason he should go to cuss ther man. There was nothin' to go cussin' about. What's more, he didn't seem ter be talkin' down to us on deck—what I could make hout. 'sides, what would he want ter go talkin' to ther Second about his payday?"

He looked across to where I was sitting. Jock, who was smoking, quietly, on the chest next to me, took his pipe slowly out from between his teeth.

"Ye're no far oot, Stubbins, I'm thinkin'. Ye're no far oot," he said, nodding his head.

Stubbins still continued to gaze at me.

"What's your idee?" he said, abruptly.

It may have been my fancy, but it seemed to me that there was something deeper than the mere sense the question conveyed.

I glanced at him. I couldn't have said, myself, just what my idea was.

"I don't know!" I answered, a little adrift. "He didn't strike me as cursing at the Second Mate. That is, I should say, after the first minute."

"Just what I say," he replied. "Another thing—don't it strike you as bein' bloomin' queer about Tom nearly comin' down by ther run, an' then *this?*"

I nodded.

"It would have been all hup with Tom, if it hadn't been for ther gasket."

He paused. After a moment, he went on again.

"That was honly three or four nights ago!"

"Well," said Plummer. "What are yer drivin' at?"

"Nothin'," answered Stubbins. "Honly it's damned queer. Looks as though ther ship might be unlucky, after all."

"Well," agreed Plummer. "Things 'as been a bit funny lately; and then there's what's 'appened ter-night. I shall 'ang on pretty tight ther next time I go aloft."

Old Jaskett took his pipe from his mouth, and sighed.

"Things is going wrong 'most every night," he said, almost pathetically. "It's as diff'rent as chalk 'n' cheese ter what it were w'en we started this 'ere trip. I thought it were all 'ellish rot about 'er bein' 'aunted; but it's not, seem'ly."

He stopped and expectorated.

"She hain't haunted," said Stubbins. "Leastways, not like you mean—"

He paused, as though trying to grasp some elusive thought.

"Eh?" said Jaskett, in the interval.

Stubbins continued, without noticing the query. He appeared to be answering some half-formed thought in his own brain, rather than Jaskett:

"Things is queer—an' it's been a bad job tonight. I don't savvy one bit what Williams was sayin' of hup aloft. I've thought sometimes he'd somethin' on 'is mind—"

Then, after a pause of about half a minute, he said this:

"*Who* was he sayin' that to?"

"Eh?" said Jaskett, again, with a puzzled expression.

"I was thinkin'," said Stubbins, knocking out his pipe on the edge of the chest. "P'raps you're right, hafter all."

VI.
Another Man to the Wheel

The conversation had slacked off. We were all moody and shaken, and I know I, for one, was thinking some rather troublesome thoughts.

Suddenly, I heard the sound of the Second's whistle. Then his voice came along the deck:

"Another man to the wheel!"

"'e's singin' out for some one to go aft an' relieve ther wheel," said Quoin, who had gone to the door to listen. "Yer'd better 'urry up, Plummer."

"What's ther time?" asked Plummer, standing up and knocking out his pipe. "Must be close on ter four bells, 'oo's next wheel is it?"

"It's all right, Plummer," I said, getting up from the chest on which I had been sitting. "I'll go along. It's my wheel, and it only wants a couple of minutes to four bells."

Plummer sat down again, and I went out of the fo'cas'le. Reaching the poop, I met Tammy on the lee side, pacing up and down.

"Who's at the wheel?" I asked him, in astonishment.

"The Second Mate," he said, in a shaky sort of voice. "He's waiting to be relieved. I'll tell you all about it as soon as I get a chance."

I went on aft to the wheel.

"Who's that?" the Second inquired.

"It's Jessop, Sir," I answered.

He gave me the course, and then, without another word, went forrard along the poop. On the break, I heard him call Tammy's name, and then for some minutes he was talking to him; though what he was saying, I could not possibly hear. For my part, I was tremendously curious to know why the Second Mate had taken the wheel. I knew that if it were just a matter of bad steering on Tammy's part, he would not have dreamt of doing such a thing. There had been something queer happening, about which I had yet to learn; of this, I felt sure.

Presently, the Second Mate left Tammy, and commenced to walk the weather side of the deck. Once he came right aft, and, stooping down, peered under the wheel-box; but never addressed a word to me. Sometime later, he went down the weather ladder on to the main-deck. Directly afterwards, Tammy came running up to the lee side of the wheel-box.

"I've seen it again!" he said, gasping with sheer nervousness.

"What?" I said.

"That *thing*," he answered. Then he leant across the wheel-box, and lowered his voice.

"It came over the lee rail—*up out of the sea*," he added, with an air of telling something unbelievable.

I turned more towards him; but it was too dark to see his face with any distinctness. I felt suddenly husky. "My God!" I thought. And then I made a silly effort to protest; but he cut me short with a certain impatient hopelessness.

"For God's sake, Jessop," he said, "do stow all that! It's no good. I must have someone to talk to, or I shall go dotty."

I saw how useless it was to pretend any sort of ignorance. Indeed, really, I had known it all along, and avoided the youngster on that very account, as you know.

"Go on," I said. "I'll listen; but you'd better keep an eye for the

Second Mate; he may pop up any minute."

For a moment, he said nothing, and I saw him peering stealthily about the poop.

"Go on," I said. "You'd better make haste, or he'll be up before you're halfway through. What was he doing at the wheel when I came up to relieve it? Why did he send you away from it?"

"He didn't," Tammy replied, turning his face towards me. "I bunked away from it."

"What for?" I asked.

"Wait a minute," he answered, "and I'll tell you the whole business. You know the Second Mate sent me to the wheel, after *that*—" He nodded his head forrard.

"Yes," I said.

"Well, I'd been here about ten minutes, or a quarter of an hour, and I was feeling rotten about Williams, and trying to forget it all and keep the ship on her course, and all that; when, all at once, I happened to glance to loo'ard, and there I saw it climbing over the rail. My God! I didn't know what to do. The Second Mate was standing forrard on the break of the poop, and I was here all by myself. I felt as if I were frozen stiff. When it came towards me, I let go of the wheel, and yelled and bunked forrard to the Second Mate. He caught hold of me and shook me; but I was so jolly frightened, I couldn't say a word. I could only keep on pointing. The Second kept asking me 'Where?' And then, all at once, I found I couldn't see the thing. I don't know whether he saw it. I'm not at all certain he did. He just told me to damn well get back to the wheel, and stop making a damned fool of myself. I said out straight I wouldn't go. So he blew his whistle, and sung out for someone to come aft and take it. Then he ran and got hold of the wheel himself. You know the rest."

"You're quite sure it wasn't thinking about Williams made you imagine you saw something?" I said, more to gain a moment to think, than because I believed that it was the case.

"I thought you were going to listen to me, seriously!" he said, bitterly. "If you won't believe me; what about the chap the Second Mate saw? What about Tom? What about Williams? For goodness sake! don't try to put me off like you did last time. I nearly went cracked with wanting to tell someone who would listen to me, and wouldn't laugh. I could stand anything, but this being alone. There's a good chap, don't pretend you don't understand. Tell me what it all means. What is this horrible man that I've twice seen? You know you know something, and I believe you're afraid to tell anyone, for fear of being laughed at. Why don't you tell me? You needn't be afraid of my laughing."

He stopped, suddenly. For the moment, I said nothing in reply.

"Don't treat me like a kid, Jessop!" he exclaimed, quite passionately.

"I won't," I said, with a sudden resolve to tell him everything. "I need someone to talk to, just as badly as you do."

"What does it all mean, then?" he burst out. "Are they real? I always used to think it was all a yarn about such things."

"I'm sure I don't know what it all means, Tammy," I answered. "I'm just as much in the dark, there, as you are. And I don't know whether they're real—that is, not as we consider things real. You don't know that I saw a queer figure down on the maindeck, several nights before you saw that thing up here."

"Didn't you see this one?" he cut in, quickly.

"Yes," I answered.

"Then, why did you pretend not to have?" he said, in a reproachful voice. "You don't know what a state you put me into, what with my being certain that I had seen it and then you being so jolly positive that there had been nothing. At one time I thought I was going clean off my dot—until the Second Mate saw that man go up the main. Then, I knew that there must be something in the thing I was certain I'd seen."

"I thought, perhaps, that if I told you I hadn't seen it, you would think you'd been mistaken," I said. "I wanted you to think it was imagination, or a dream, or something of that sort."

"And all the time, you knew about that other thing you'd seen?" he asked.

"Yes," I replied.

"It was thundering decent of you," he said. "But it wasn't any good."

He paused a moment. Then he went on:

"It's terrible about Williams. Do you think he saw something, up aloft?"

"I don't know, Tammy," I said. "It's impossible to say. It *may* have been only an accident." I hesitated to tell him what I really thought.

"What was he saying about his payday? Who was he saying it to?"

"I don't know," I said, again. "He was always cracked about taking a payday out of her. You know, he stayed in her, on purpose, when all the others left. He told me that he wasn't going to be done out of it, for anyone."

"What did the other lot leave for?" he asked. Then, as the idea seemed to strike him—"Jove! do you think they saw something, and got scared? It's quite possible. You know, we only joined her in 'Frisco. She had no 'prenticess on the passage out. Our ship was sold; so they sent us aboard here to come home."

"They may have," I said. "Indeed, from things I've heard Williams say, I'm pretty certain, he for one, guessed or knew a jolly sight more than we've any idea of."

"And now he's dead!" said Tammy, solemnly. "We'll never be able to find out from him now."

For a few moments, he was silent. Then he went off on another track.

"Doesn't anything ever happen in the Mate's watch?"

"Yes," I answered. "There's several things happened lately, that seem pretty queer. Some of his side have been talking about them. But he's too jolly pig-headed to see anything. He just curses his chaps, and puts it all down to them."

"Still," he persisted, "things seem to happen more in our watch than in his—I mean, bigger things. Look at tonight."

"We've no proof, you know," I said.

He shook his head, doubtfully.

"I shall always funk going aloft, now."

"Nonsense!" I told him. "It may only have been an accident."

"Don't!" he said. "You know you don't think so, really."

I answered nothing, just then; for I knew very well that he was right.

We were silent for a couple of moments. Then he spoke again:

"Is the ship haunted?"

For an instant I hesitated.

"No," I said, at length. "I don't think she is. I mean, not in that way."

"What way, then?"

"Well, I've formed a bit of a theory, that seems wise one minute, and cracked the next. Of course, it's as likely to be all wrong; but it's the only thing that seems to me to fit in with all the beastly things we've had lately."

"Go on!" he said, with an impatient, nervous movement.

"Well, I've an idea that it's nothing *in* the ship that's likely to hurt us. I scarcely know how to put it; but, if I'm right in what I think, it's the ship herself that's the cause of everything."

"What do you mean?" he asked, in a puzzled voice. "Do you mean that the ship *is* haunted, after all?"

"No!" I answered. "I've just told you I didn't. Wait until I've finished what I was going to say."

"All right!" he said.

"About that thing you saw tonight," I went on. "You say it came over the lee rail, up on to the poop?"

"Yes," he answered.

"Well, the thing I saw, came up out of the sea, and went back into the sea."

"Jove!" he said; and then: "Yes, go on!"

"My idea is, that this ship is open to be boarded by those things," I explained. "What they are, of course I don't know. They look like men—in lots of ways. But —well, the Lord knows what's in the sea. Though we don't want to go imagining silly things, of course. And then, again, you know, it seems fat-headed, calling anything silly. That's how I keep going, in a sort of blessed circle. I don't know a bit whether they're flesh and blood, or whether they're what we should call ghosts or spirits."

"They can't be flesh and blood," Tammy interrupted. "Where would they live? Besides, that first one I saw, I thought I could see through it. And this last one— the Second Mate would have seen it. And they would drown—"

"Not necessarily," I said.

"Oh, but I'm sure they're not," he insisted. "It's impossible—"

"So are ghosts—when you're feeling sensible," I answered. "But I'm not saying they *are* flesh and blood; though, at the same time, I'm not going to say straight out they're ghosts—not yet, at any rate."

"Where do they come from?" he asked, stupidly enough.

"Out of the sea," I told him. "You saw for yourself!"

"Then why don't other vessels have them coming aboard?" he said. "How do you account for that?"

"In a way—though sometimes it seems cracky—I think I can, according to my idea," I answered.

"How?" he inquired again.

"Why, I believe that this ship is open, as I've told you—exposed, unprotected, or whatever you like to call it. I should say it's reasonable to think that all the things of the material world are barred, as it were, from the immaterial; but that in some cases the barrier may be broken down. That's what may have happened to this ship. And if it has, she may be naked to the attacks of beings belonging to some other state of existence."

"What's made her like that?" he asked, in a really awed sort of tone.

"The Lord knows!" I answered. "Perhaps something to do with magnetic stresses; but you'd not understand, and I don't, really. And, I suppose, inside of me, I don't believe it's anything of the kind, for a minute. I'm not built that way. And yet I don't know! Perhaps, there may have been some rotten thing done aboard of her. Or, again, it's a heap more likely to be something quite outside of anything I know."

"If they're immaterial then, they're spirits?" he questioned.

"I don't know," I said. "It's so hard to say what I really think, you know. I've got a queer idea, that my head-piece likes to think good; but I don't believe my tummy believes it."

"Go on!" he said.

"Well," I said. "Suppose the earth were inhabited by two kinds of life. We're one, and *they're* the other."

"Go on!" he said.

"Well," I said. "Don't you see, in a normal state we may not be capable of appreciating the *realness* of the other? But they may be just as *real* and material to *them*, as *we* are to *us*. Do you see?"

"Yes," he said. "Go on!"

"Well," I said. "The earth may be just as *real* to them, as to us. I mean that it may have qualities as material to them, as it has to us; but neither of us could appreciate the other's realness, or the quality of realness in the earth, which was real to the other. It's so difficult to explain. Don't you understand?"

"Yes," he said. "Go on!"

"Well, if we were in what I might call a healthy atmosphere, they would be quite beyond our power to see or feel, or anything. And the same with them; but the more we're like *this*, the more *real* and actual they could grow *to us*. See? That is, the more we should become able to appreciate their form of materialness. That's all. I can't make it any clearer."

"Then, after all, you *really* think they're ghosts, or something of that sort?" Tammy said.

"I suppose it does come to that," I answered. "I mean that, anyway, I don't think they're our ideas of flesh and blood. But, of course, it's silly to say much; and, after all, you must remember that I may be all wrong."

"I think you ought to tell the Second Mate all this," he said. "If it's really as you say, the ship ought to be put into the nearest port, and jolly well burnt."

"The Second Mate couldn't do anything," I replied. "Even if he believed it all; which we're not certain he would."

"Perhaps not," Tammy answered. "But if you could get him to believe it, he might explain the whole business to the Skipper, and then something might be done. It's not safe as it is."

"He'd only get jeered at again," I said, rather hopelessly.

"No," said Tammy. "Not after what's happened tonight."

"Perhaps not," I replied, doubtfully. And just then the Second Mate came back on to the poop, and Tammy cleared away from the wheel-box, leaving me with a worrying feeling that I ought to do something.

VII.
The Coming of the Mist and That Which It Ushered

We buried Williams at midday. Poor beggar! It had been so sudden. All day the men were awed and gloomy, and there was a lot of talk about there being a Jonah aboard. If they'd only known what Tammy and I, and perhaps the Second Mate, knew!

And then the next thing came—the mist. I cannot remember now, whether it was on the day we buried Williams that we first saw it, or the day after.

When first I noticed it, like everybody else aboard, I took it to be some form of haze, due to the heat of the sun; for it was broad daylight when the thing came.

The wind had died away to a light breeze, and I was working at the main rigging, along with Plummer, putting on seizings.

"Looks as if 'twere middlin' 'ot," he remarked.

"Yes," I said; and, for the time, took no further notice.

Presently he spoke again:

"It's gettin' quite 'azy!" and his tone showed he was surprised.

I glanced up, quickly. At first, I could see nothing. Then, I saw what he meant. The air had a wavy, strange, unnatural appearance; something like the heated air over the top of an engine's funnel, that you can often see when no smoke is coming out.

"Must be the heat," I said. "Though I don't remember ever seeing anything just like it before."

"Nor me," Plummer agreed.

It could not have been a minute later when I looked up again, and was astonished to find that the whole ship was surrounded by a thinnish haze that quite hid the horizon.

"By Jove! Plummer," I said. "How queer!"

"Yes," he said, looking round. "I never seen anythin' like it before—not in these parts."

"Heat wouldn't do that!" I said.

"N—no," he said, doubtfully.

We went on with our work again—occasionally exchanging an odd word or two. Presently, after a little time of silence, I bent forward and asked him to pass me up the spike. He stooped and picked it up from the deck, where it had tumbled. As he held it out to me, I saw the stolid expression on his face, change suddenly to a look of complete surprise. He opened his mouth.

"By gum!" he said. "It's gone."

I turned quickly, and looked. And so it had—the whole sea showing clear and bright, right away to the horizon.

I stared at Plummer, and he stared at me.

"Well, I'm blowed!" he exclaimed.

I do not think I made any reply; for I had a sudden, queer feeling that the thing was not right. And then, in a minute, I called myself an ass; but I could not really shake off the feeling. I had another good look at the sea. I had a vague idea that something was different. The sea looked brighter, somehow, and the air clearer, I thought, and I missed something; but not much, you know. And it was not until a couple of days later, that I knew that it was several vessels on the horizon, which had been quite in sight before the mist, and now were gone.

During the rest of the watch, and indeed all day, there was no further sign of anything unusual. Only, when the evening came (in the second dog-watch it was) I saw the mist rise faintly—the setting sun shining through it, dim and unreal.

I knew then, as a certainty, that it was not caused by heat.

And that was the beginning of it.

The next day, I kept a pretty close watch, during all my time on deck; but the atmosphere remained clear. Yet, I heard from one of the chaps in the Mate's watch, that it had been hazy during part of the time he was at the wheel.

"Comin' an' goin', like," he described it to me, when I questioned him about it. He thought it might be heat.

But though I knew otherwise, I did not contradict him. At that time, no one, not even Plummer, seemed to think very much of the matter. And when I mentioned it to Tammy, and asked him whether he'd noticed it, he only remarked that it must have been heat, or else the sun drawing up water. I let it stay at that; for there was nothing to be gained by suggesting that the thing had more to it.

Then, on the following day, something happened that set me wondering more than ever, and showed me how right I had been in feeling the mist to be something unnatural. It was in this way.

Five bells, in the eight to twelve morning watch, had gone. I was at the wheel. The sky was perfectly clear—not a cloud to be seen, even on the horizon. It was hot, standing at the wheel; for there was scarcely any wind, and I was feeling drowsy. The Second Mate was down on the maindeck with the men, seeing about some job he wanted done; so that I was on the poop alone.

Presently, with the heat, and the sun beating right down on to me, I grew thirsty; and, for want of something better, I pulled out a bit of plug I had on me, and bit off a chew; though, as a rule, it is not a habit of mine. After a little, naturally enough, I glanced round for the spittoon; but discovered that it was not there. Probably it had been taken forrard when the decks were washed, to give it a scrub. So, as there was no one on the poop, I left the wheel, and stepped aft to the taffrail. It was thus that I came to see something altogether unthought of—a full-rigged ship, close-hauled on the port tack, a few hundred yards on our starboard quarter. Her sails were scarcely filled by the light breeze, and flapped as she lifted to the swell of the sea. She appeared to have very little way through the water, certainly not more than a knot an hour. Away aft, hanging from the gaff-end, was a string of flags. Evidently, she was signalling to us. All this, I saw in a flash, and I just stood and stared, astonished. I was astonished because I had not seen her earlier. In that light breeze, I knew that she must have been in sight for at least a couple of hours. Yet I could think of nothing rational to satisfy my wonder. There she was—of that much, I was certain. And yet, how had she come there without my seeing her, before?

All at once, as I stood, staring, I heard the wheel behind me, spin rapidly. Instinctively, I jumped to get hold of the spokes; for I did not want the steering gear jammed. Then I turned again to have another look at the other ship; but, to my utter bewilderment, *there was no sign of her*—nothing but the calm ocean, spreading away to the distant horizon. I blinked my eyelids a bit, and pushed the hair off my forehead. Then, I stared again; but there was no vestige of her—nothing, you know; and absolutely nothing unusual, except a faint, tremulous quiver in the air. And the blank surface of the sea reaching everywhere to the empty horizon.

Had she foundered? I asked myself, naturally enough; and, for the moment, I really wondered. I searched round the sea for wreckage; but there was nothing, not even an odd hen-coop, or a piece of deck furniture; and so I threw away that idea, as impossible.

Then, as I stood, I got another thought, or, perhaps, an intuition and I asked myself seriously whether this disappearing ship might not be in some way connected with the other queer things. It occurred to me then, that the vessel I had seen was nothing real, and, perhaps, did not exist outside of my own brain. I considered the idea, gravely. It helped to explain the thing, and I could think of nothing else that would. Had she been real, I felt sure that others aboard us would have been bound to have seen her long before I had—I got a bit muddled there, with trying to think it out; and then, abruptly, the reality of the other ship, came back to me—every rope and sail and spar, you know. And I remembered how she had lifted to the heave of the sea, and how the sails had flapped in the light breeze. And the string of flags! She had been signalling. At that last, I found it just as impossible to believe that she had not been real.

I had reached to this point of irresolution, and was standing with my back, partly turned to the wheel. I was holding it steady with my left hand, while I looked over the sea, to try to find something to help me to understand.

All at once, as I stared, I seemed to see the ship again.

She was more on the beam now, than on the quarter; but I thought little of that, in the astonishment of seeing her once more. It was only a glimpse, I caught of her—dim and wavering, as though I looked at her through the convolutions of heated air. Then she grew indistinct, and vanished again; but I was convinced now that she was real, and had been in sight all the time, if I could have seen her. That curious, dim, wavering appearance had suggested something to me. I remembered the strange, wavy look of the air, a few days previously, just before the mist had surrounded the ship. And in my mind, I connected the two. It was nothing about the other packet that was strange. The strangeness was with us. It was something that was about (or invested) our ship that prevented me—or indeed, any one else aboard from seeing that other. It was evident that she had been able to see us, as was proved by her signalling. In an irrelevant sort of way, I wondered what the people aboard of her thought of our apparently intentional disregard of their signals.

After that, I thought of the strangeness of it all. Even at that minute, they could see us, plainly; and yet, so far as we were concerned, the whole ocean seemed empty. It appeared to me, at that time, to be the weirdest thing that could happen to us.

And then a fresh thought came to me. How long had we been like that? I puzzled for a few moments. It was now that I recollected that we had sighted several vessels on the morning of the day when the mist appeared; and since then, we had seen nothing. This, to say the least, should have struck me as queer; for some of the other packets were homeward bound along with us, and steering the same course. Consequently, with the weather being fine, and the wind next to nothing, they should have been in sight all the time. This reasoning seemed to me to show, unmistakably, some connection between the coming of the mist, and our inability to *see*. So that it is possible we had been in that extraordinary state of blindness for nearly three days.

In my mind, the last glimpse of that ship on the quarter, came back to me. And, I remember, a curious thought got me, that I had looked at her from out of some other dimension. For a while, you know, I really believed the mystery of the idea, and that it might be the actual truth, took me; instead of my realising just all that it might mean. It seemed so exactly to express all the half-defined thoughts that had come, since seeing that other packet on the quarter.

Suddenly, behind me, there came a rustle and rattle of the sails; and, in the same instant, I heard the Skipper saying:

"Where the devil have you got her to, Jessop?"

I whirled round to the wheel.

"I don't know—Sir," I faltered.

I had forgotten even that I was at the wheel.

"Don't know!" he shouted. "I should damned well think you don't. Starboard your helm, you fool. You'll have us all aback!"

"i, i, Sir," I answered, and hove the wheel over. I did it almost mechanically; for I was still dazed, and had not yet had time to collect my senses.

During the following half-minute, I was only conscious, in a confused sort of way, that the Old Man was ranting at me. This feeling of bewilderment passed off, and I found that I was peering blankly into the binnacle, at the compass-card; yet, until then, entirely without being aware of the fact. Now, however, I saw that the ship was coming back on to her course. Goodness knows how much she had been off!

With the realisation that I had let the ship get almost aback, there came a sudden memory of the alteration in the position of the other vessel. She had appeared last on the beam, instead of on the quarter. Now, however, as my brain began to work, I saw the cause of this apparent and, until then, inexplicable change. It was due, of course, to our having come up, until we had brought the other packet on to the beam.

It is curious how all this flashed through my mind, and held my attention—although only momentarily—in the face of the Skipper's storming. I think I had hardly realized he was still singing out at me. Anyhow, the next thing I remember, he was shaking my arm.

"What's the matter with you, man?" he was shouting. And I just stared into his face, like an ass, without saying a word. I seemed still incapable, you know, of actual, reasoning speech.

"Are you damned well off your head?" he went on shouting. "Are you a lunatic? Have you had sunstroke? Speak, you gaping idiot!"

I tried to say something; but the words would not come clearly.

"I—I—I—" I said, and stopped, stupidly. I was all right, really; but I was so bewildered with the thing I had found out; and, in a way, I seemed almost to have come back out of a distance, you know.

"You're a lunatic!" he said, again. He repeated the statement several times, as if it were the only thing that sufficiently expressed his opinion of me. Then he let go of my arm, and stepped back a couple of paces.

"I'm not a lunatic!" I said, with a sudden gasp. "I'm not a lunatic, Sir, any more than you are."

"Why the devil don't you answer my questions then?" he shouted, angrily.

"What's the matter with you? What have you been doing with the ship? Answer me now!"

"I was looking at that ship away on the starboard quarter, Sir," I blurted out. "She's been signalling—"

"What!" he cut me short with disbelief. "What ship?"

He turned, quickly, and looked over the quarter. Then he wheeled round to me again.

"There's no ship! What do you mean by trying to spin up a cuffer like that?"

"There is, Sir," I answered. "It's out there—" I pointed.

"Hold your tongue!" he said. "Don't talk rubbish to me. Do you think I'm blind?"

"I saw it, Sir," I persisted.

"Don't you talk back to me!" he snapped, with a quick burst of temper. "I won't have it!"

Then, just as suddenly, he was silent. He came a step towards me, and stared into my face. I believe the old ass thought I was a bit mad; anyway, without another word, he went to the break of the poop.

"Mr. Tulipson," he sung out.

"Yes, Sir," I heard the Second Mate reply.

"Send another man to the wheel."

"Very good, Sir," the Second answered.

A couple of minutes later, old Jaskett came up to relieve me. I gave him the course, and he repeated it.

"What's up, mate?" he asked me, as I stepped off the grating.

"Nothing much," I said, and went forrard to where the Skipper was standing on the break of the poop. I gave him the course; but the crabby old devil took no notice of me, whatever. When I got down on to the maindeck, I went up to the Second, and gave it to him. He answered me civilly enough, and then asked me what I had been doing to put the Old Man's back up.

"I told him there's a ship on the starboard quarter, signalling us," I said.

"There's no ship out there, Jessop," the Second Mate replied, looking at me with a queer, inscrutable expression.

"There is, Sir," I began. "I—"

"That will do, Jessop!" he said. "Go forrard and have a smoke. I shall want you then to give a hand with these foot-ropes. You'd better bring a serving-mallet aft with you, when you come."

I hesitated a moment, partly in anger; but more, I think, in doubt.

"i, i, Sir," I muttered at length, and went forrard.

VIII.
After the Coming of the Mist

After the coming of the mist, things seemed to develop pretty quickly. In the following two or three days a good deal happened.

On the night of the day on which the Skipper had sent me away from the wheel, it was our watch on deck from eight o' clock to twelve, and my lookout from ten to twelve.

As I paced slowly to and fro across the fo'cas'le head, I was thinking about the affair of the morning. At first, my thoughts were about the Old Man. I cursed him thoroughly to myself, for being a pig-headed old fool, until it occurred to me that if I had been in his place, and come on deck to find the ship almost aback, and the fellow at the wheel staring out across the sea, instead of attending to his business, I should most certainly have kicked up a thundering row. And then, I had been an ass to tell him about the ship. I should never have done such a thing, if I had not been a bit adrift. Most likely the old chap thought I was cracked.

I ceased to bother my head about him, and fell to wondering why the Second Mate had looked at me so queerly in the morning. Did he guess more of the truth than I supposed? And if that were the case, why had he refused to listen to me?

After that, I went to puzzling about the mist. I had thought a great deal about it, during the day. One idea appealed to me, very strongly. It was that the actual, visible mist was a materialized expression of an extraordinarily subtle atmosphere, in which we were moving.

Abruptly, as I walked backwards and forwards, taking occasional glances over the sea (which was almost calm), my eye caught the glow of a light out in the darkness. I stood still, and stared. I wondered whether it was the light of a vessel. In that case we were no longer enveloped in that extraordinary atmosphere. I bent forward, and gave the thing my more immediate attention. I saw then that it was undoubtedly the green light of a vessel on our port bow. It was plain that she was bent on crossing our bows. What was more, she was dangerously near—the size and brightness of her light showed that. She would be close-hauled, while we were going free, so that, of course, it was our place to get out of her way. Instantly, I turned and, putting my hands up to my mouth, hailed the Second Mate:

"Light on the port bow, Sir."

The next moment his hail came back:

"Whereabouts?"

"He must be blind," I said to myself.

"About two points on the bow, Sir," I sung out.

Then I turned to see whether she had shifted her position at all. Yet, when I came to look, there was no light visible. I ran forrard to the bows, and leant over the rail, and stared; but there was nothing—absolutely nothing except the darkness all about us. For perhaps a few seconds I stood thus, and a suspicion swept across me, that the whole business was practically a repetition of the affair of the morning. Evidently, the impalpable something that invested the ship, had thinned for an instant, thus allowing me to see the light ahead. Now, it had closed again. Yet, whether I could see, or not, I did not doubt the fact that, there was a vessel ahead, and very close ahead, too. We might run on top of her any minute. My only hope was that, seeing we were not getting out of her way, she had put her helm up, so as to let us pass, with the intention of then crossing under our stern. I waited, pretty anxiously, watching and listening. Then, all at once, I heard steps coming along the deck, forrard, and the 'prentices, whose time-keeping it was, came up onto the fo'cas'le head.

"The Second Mate says he can't see any light Jessop," he said, coming over to where I stood. "Whereabouts is it?"

"I don't know," I answered. "I've lost sight of it myself. It was a green light, about a couple of points on the port bow. It seemed fairly close."

"Perhaps their lamp's gone out," he suggested, after peering out pretty hard into the night for a minute or so.

"Perhaps," I said.

I did not tell him that the light had been so close that, even in the darkness, we should *now* have been able to see the ship herself.

"You're quite sure it was a light, and not a star?" he asked, doubtfully, after another long stare.

"Oh! no," I said. "It may have been the moon, now I come to think about it."

"Don't rot," he replied. "It's easy enough to make a mistake. What shall I say to the Second Mate?"

"Tell him it's disappeared, of course!"

"Where to?" he asked.

"How the devil should I know?" I told him. "Don't ask silly questions!"

"All right, keep your rag in," he said, and went aft to report to the Second Mate.

Five minutes later, it might have been, I saw the light again. It was broad on the bow, and told me plainly enough that she had up with her helm to escape being run down. I did not wait a moment; but sung out to the Second Mate that there was a green light about four points on the port bow. By Jove! it must have been a close shave. The light did not *seem* to be more than about a hundred yards away. It was fortunate that we had not much way through the water.

"Now," I thought to myself, "the Second will see the thing. And perhaps Mr. Blooming 'prentices will be able to give the star its proper name."

Even as the thought came into my head, the light faded and vanished; and I caught the Second Mate's voice.

"Whereaway?" he was singing out.

"It's gone again, Sir," I answered.

A minute later, I heard him coming along the deck.

He reached the foot of the starboard ladder.

"Where are you, Jessop?" he inquired.

"Here, Sir," I said, and went to the top of the weather ladder.

He came up slowly on to the fo'cas'le head.

"What's this you've been singing out about a light?" he asked. "Just point out exactly where it was you last saw it."

This I did, and he went over to the port rail, and stared away into the night; but without seeing anything.

"It's gone, Sir," I ventured to remind him. "Though I've seen it twice now—once, about a couple of points on the bow, and this last time, broad away on the bow; but it disappeared both times, almost at once."

"I don't understand it at all, Jessop," he said, in a puzzled voice. "Are you sure it was a ship's light?"

"Yes, Sir. A green light. It was quite close."

"I don't understand," he said again. "Run aft and ask the 'prentices to pass you down my night glasses. Be as smart as you can."

"i, i, Sir," I replied, and ran aft.

In less than a minute, I was back with his binoculars; and, with them, he stared for some time at the sea to leeward.

All at once he dropped them to his side, and faced round on me with a sudden question:

"Where's she gone to? If she's shifted her bearing as quickly as all that, she must be precious close. We should be able to see her spars and sails, or her cabin light, or her binnacle light, or something!"

"It's queer, Sir," I assented.

"Damned queer," he said. "So damned queer that I'm inclined to think you've made a mistake."

"No, Sir. I'm certain it was a light."

"Where's the ship then?" he asked.

"I can't say, Sir. That's just what's been puzzling me."

The Second said nothing in reply; but took a couple of quick turns across the fo'cas'le head—stopping at the port rail, and taking another look to leeward through his night glasses. Perhaps a minute he stood there. Then, without a word, he went down the lee ladder, and away aft along the main deck to the poop.

"He's jolly well puzzled," I thought to myself. "Or else he thinks I've been imagining things." Either way, I guessed he'd think that.

In a little, I began to wonder whether, after all, he had any idea of what might be the truth. One minute, I would feel certain he had; and the next, I was just as sure that he guessed nothing. I got one of my fits of asking myself whether it would not have been better to have told him everything. It seemed to me that he must have seen sufficient to make him inclined to listen to me. And yet, I could not by any means be certain. I might only have been making an ass of myself, in his eyes. Or set him thinking I was dotty.

I was walking about the fo'cas'le head, feeling like this, when I saw the light for the third time. It was very bright and big, and I could see it move, as I watched. This again showed me that it must be very close.

"Surely," I thought, "the Second Mate must see it now, for himself."

I did not sing out this time, right away. I thought I would let the Second see for himself that I had not been mistaken. Besides, I was not going to risk its vanishing again, the instant I had spoken. For quite half a minute, I watched it, and there was no sign of its disappearing. Every moment, I expected to hear the Second Mate's hail, showing that he had spotted it at last; but none came.

I could stand it no longer, and I ran to the rail, on the after part of the fo'cas'le head.

"Green light a little abaft the beam, Sir!" I sung out, at the top of my voice.

But I had waited too long. Even as I shouted, the light blurred and vanished.

I stamped my foot and swore. The thing was making a fool of me. Yet, I had a faint hope that those aft had seen it just before it disappeared; but this I knew was vain, directly I heard the Second's voice.

"Light be damned!" he shouted.

Then he blew his whistle, and one of the men ran aft, out of the fo'cas'le, to see what it was he wanted.

"Whose next lookout is it?" I heard him ask.

"Jaskett's, Sir."

"Then tell Jaskett to relieve Jessop at once. Do you hear?"

"Yes, Sir," said the man, and came forrard.

In a minute, Jaskett stumbled up onto the fo'cas'le head.

"What's up, mate?" he asked sleepily.

"It's that fool of a Second Mate!" I said, savagely. "I've reported a light to him three times, and, because the blind fool can't see it, he's sent you up to relieve me!"

"Where is it, mate?" he inquired.

He looked round at the dark sea.

"I don't see no light," he remarked, after a few moments.

"No," I said. "It's gone."

"Eh?" he inquired.

"It's gone!" I repeated, irritably.

He turned and regarded me silently, through the dark.

"I'd go an' 'ave a sleep, mate," he said, at length. "I've been that way meself. Ther's nothin' like a snooze w'en yer gets like that."

"What!" I said. "Like what?"

"It's all right, mate. Yer'll be all right in ther mornin'. Don't yer worry 'bout me." His tone was sympathetic.

"Hell!" was all I said, and walked down off the fo'cas'le head. I wondered whether the old fellow thought I was going silly.

"Have a sleep, by Jove!" I muttered to myself. "I wonder who'd feel like having a sleep after what I've seen and stood today!"

I felt rotten, with no one understanding what was really the matter. I seemed to be all alone, through the things I had learnt. Then the thought came to me to go aft and talk the matter over with Tammy. I knew he would be able to understand, of course; and it would be such a relief.

On the impulse, I turned and went aft, along the deck to the 'prenticess' berth. As I neared the break of the poop, I looked up and saw the dark shape of the Second Mate, leaning over the rail above me.

"Who's that?" he asked.

"It's Jessop, Sir," I said.

"What do you want in this part of the ship?" he inquired.

"I'd come aft to speak to Tammy, Sir," I replied.

"You go along forrard and turn in," he said, not altogether unkindly. "A sleep will do you more good than yarning about. You know, you're getting to fancy things too much!"

"I'm sure I'm not, Sir! I'm perfectly well. I—"

"That will do!" he interrupted, sharply. "You go and have a sleep."

I gave a short curse, under my breath, and went slowly forrard. I was getting maddened with being treated as if I were not quite sane.

"By God!" I said to myself. "Wait till the fools know what I know—just wait!"

I entered the fo'cas'le, through the port doorway, and went across to my chest, and sat down. I felt angry and tired, and miserable.

Quoin and Plummer were sitting close by, playing cards, and smoking. Stubbins lay in his bunk, watching them, and also smoking. As I sat down, he put his head forward over the bunk-board, and regarded me in a curious, meditative way.

"What's hup with ther Second hofficer?" he asked, after a short stare.

I looked at him, and the other two men looked up at me. I felt I should go off with a bang, if I did not say something, and I let out pretty stiffly, telling them the whole business. Yet, I had seen enough to know that it was no good trying to explain things; so I just told them the plain, bold facts, and left explanations as much alone as possible.

"Three times, you say?" said Stubbins when I had finished.

"Yes," I assented.

"An' ther Old Man sent yer from ther wheel this mornin', 'cause yer 'appened ter see a ship 'e couldn't," Plummer added in a reflective tone.

"Yes," I said, again.

I thought I saw him look at Quoin, significantly; but Stubbins, I noticed, looked only at me.

"I reckon ther Second thinks you're a bit hoff color," he remarked, after a short pause.

"The Second Mate's a fool!" I said, with some bitterness. "A confounded fool!"

"I hain't so sure about that," he replied. "It's bound ter seem queer ter him. I don't understand it myself—"

He lapsed into silence, and smoked.

"I carn't understand 'ow it is ther Second Mate didn't 'appen to spot it," Quoin said, in a puzzled voice.

It seemed to me that Plummer nudged him to be quiet. It looked as if Plummer shared the Second Mate's opinion, and the idea made me savage. But Stubbins's next remark drew my attention.

"I don't hunderstand it," he said, again; speaking with deliberation. "All ther same, ther Second should have savvied enough not to have slung you hoff ther look-hout."

He nodded his head, slowly, keeping his gaze fixed on my face.

"How do you mean?" I asked, puzzled; yet with a vague sense that the man understood more, perhaps, than I had hitherto thought.

"I mean what's ther Second so blessed cocksure about?"

He took a draw at his pipe, removed it, and leant forward somewhat, over his bunk-board.

"Didn't he say nothin' ter you, after you came hoff ther look-hout?" he asked.

"Yes," I replied; "he spotted me going aft. He told me I was getting to imagining things too much. He said I'd better come forrard and get a sleep."

"An' what did you say?"

"Nothing. I came forrard."

"Why didn't you bloomin' well harsk him if he weren't doin' ther imaginin' trick when he sent us chasin' hup ther main, hafter that bogyman of his?"

"I never thought of it," I told him.

"Well, yer ought ter have."

He paused, and sat up in his bunk, and asked for a match.

As I passed him my box, Quoin looked up from his game.

"It might 'ave been a stowaway, yer know. Yer carn't say as it's ever been proved as it wasn't."

Stubbins passed the box back to me, and went on without noticing Quoin's remark:

"Told you to go an' have a snooze, did he? I don't hunderstand what he's bluffin' at."

"How do you mean, bluffing?" I asked.

He nodded his head, sagely.

"It's my hidea he knows you saw that light, just as bloomin' well as I do."

Plummer looked up from his game, at this speech; but said nothing.

"Then *you* don't doubt that I really saw it?" I asked, with a certain surprise.

"Not me," he remarked, with assurance. "You hain't likely ter make that kind of mistake three times runnin'."

"No," I said. "I *know* I saw the light, right enough; but"—I hesitated a moment—"it's blessed queer."

"It *is* blessed queer!" he agreed. "It's damned queer! An' there's a lot of other damn queer things happenin' aboard this packet lately."

He was silent for a few seconds. Then he spoke suddenly:

"It's not nat'ral, I'm damned sure of that much."

He took a couple of draws at his pipe, and in the momentary silence, I caught Jaskett's voice, above us. He was hailing the poop.

"Red light on the starboard quarter, Sir," I heard him sing out.

"There you are," I said with a jerk of my head. "That's about where that packet I spotted, ought to be by now. She couldn't cross our bows, so she up helm, and let us pass, and now she's hauled up again and gone under our stern."

I got up from the chest, and went to the door, the other three following. As we stepped out on deck, I heard the Second Mate shouting out, away aft, to know the whereabouts of the light.

"By Jove! Stubbins," I said. "I believe the blessed thing's gone again."

We ran to the starboard side, in a body, and looked over; but there was no sign of a light in the darkness astern.

"I carn't say as *I* see any light," said Quoin.

Plummer said nothing.

I looked up at the fo'cas'le head. There, I could faintly distinguish the outlines of Jaskett. He was standing by the starboard rail, with his hands up, shading his eyes, evidently staring towards the place where he had last seen the light.

"Where's she got to, Jaskett?" I called out.

"I can't say, mate," he answered. "It's the most 'ellishly funny thing I've ever comed across. She were there as plain as me 'att one minnit, an' ther next she were gone—clean gone."

I turned to Plummer.

"What do you think about it, *now*?" I asked him.

"Well," he said. "I'll admit I thought at first 'twere somethin' an' nothin'. I thought yer was mistaken; but it seems yer did see somethin'."

Away aft, we heard the sound of steps, along the deck.

"Ther Second's comin' forrard for a hexplanation, Jaskett," Stubbins sung out. "You'd better go down an' change yer breeks."

The Second Mate passed us, and went up the starboard ladder.

"What's up now, Jaskett?" he said quickly. "Where is this light? Neither the 'prentices nor I can see it!"

"Ther damn thing's clean gone, Sir," Jaskett replied.

"Gone!" the Second Mate said. "Gone! What do you mean?"

"She were there one minnit, Sir, as plain as me 'att, an' ther next, she'd gone."

"That's a damn silly yarn to tell me!" the Second replied. "You don't expect me to believe it, do you?"

"It's Gospel trewth any'ow, Sir," Jaskett answered. "An' Jessop seen it just ther same."

He seemed to have added that last part as an afterthought. Evidently, the old beggar had changed his opinion as to my need for sleep.

"You're an old fool, Jaskett," the Second said, sharply. "And that idiot Jessop has been putting things into your silly old head."

He paused, an instant. Then he continued:

"What the devil's the matter with you all, that you've taken to this sort of game? You know very well that you saw no light! I sent Jessop off the lookout, and then you must go and start the same game."

"We 'aven't—" Jaskett started to say; but the Second silenced him.

"Stow it!" he said, and turned and went down the ladder, passing us quickly, without a word.

"Doesn't look to *me*, Stubbins," I said, "as though the Second did believe we've seen the light."

"I hain't so sure," he answered. "He's a puzzler."

The rest of the watch passed away quietly; and at eight bells I made haste to turn in, for I was tremendously tired.

When we were called again for the four to eight watch on deck, I learnt that one of the men in the Mate's watch had seen a light, soon after we had gone below, and had reported it, only for it to disappear immediately. This, I found, had happened twice, and the Mate had got so wild (being under the impression that the man was playing the fool) that he had nearly came to blows with him—finally ordering him off the lookout, and sending another man up in his place. If this last man saw the light, he took good care not to let the Mate know; so that the matter had ended there.

And then, on the following night, before we had ceased to talk about the matter of the vanishing lights, something else occurred that temporarily drove from my mind all memory of the mist, and the extraordinary, blind atmosphere it had seemed to usher.

IX.
The Man Who Cried for Help

It was, as I have said, on the following night that something further happened. And it brought home pretty vividly to me, if not to any of the others, the sense of a personal danger aboard.

We had gone below for the eight to twelve watch, and my last impression of the weather at eight o'clock, was that the wind was freshening. There had been a great bank of cloud rising astern, which had looked as if it were going to breeze up still more.

At a quarter to twelve, when we were called for our twelve to four watch on deck, I could tell at once, by the sound, that there was a fresh breeze blowing; at the same time, I heard the voices of the men on the other watch, singing out as they hauled on the ropes. I caught the rattle of canvas in the wind, and guessed that they were taking the royals off her. I looked at my watch, which I always kept hanging in my bunk. It showed the time to be just after the quarter; so that, with luck, we should escape having to go up to the sails.

I dressed quickly, and then went to the door to look at the weather. I found that the wind had shifted from the starboard quarter, to right aft; and, by the look of the sky, there seemed to be a promise of more, before long.

Up aloft, I could make out faintly the fore and mizzen royals flapping in the wind. The main had been left for a while longer. In the fore riggings, Jacobs, the Ordinary Seaman in the Mate's watch, was following another of the men aloft to the sail. The Mate's two 'prenticess were already up at the mizzen. Down on deck, the rest of the men were busy clearing up the ropes.

I went back to my bunk, and looked at my watch—the time was only a few minutes off eight bells; so I got my oilskins ready, for it looked like rain outside. As I was doing this, Jock went to the door for a look.

"What's it doin', Jock?" Tom asked, getting out of his bunk, hurriedly.

"I'm thinkin' maybe it's goin' to blow a wee, and ye'll be needin' yer' oilskins," Jock answered.

When eight bells went, and we mustered aft for roll-call, there was a considerable delay, owing to the Mate refusing to call the roll until Tom (who as usual, had only turned out of his bunk at the last minute) came aft to answer his name. When, at last, he did come, the Second and the Mate joined in giving him a good dressing down for a lazy sojer; so that several minutes passed before we were on our way forrard again. This was a small enough matter in itself, and yet really terrible in its consequence to one of our number; for, just as we reached the fore rigging, there was a shout aloft, loud above the noise of the wind, and the next moment, something crashed down into our midst, with a great, slogging thud—something bulky and weighty, that struck full upon Jock, so that he went down with a loud, horrible, ringing "ugg," and never said a word. From the whole crowd of us there went up a yell of fear, and then, with one accord, there was a run for the lighted fo'cas'le. I am not ashamed to say that I ran with the rest. A blind, unreasoning fright had seized me, and I did not stop to think.

Once in the fo'cas'le and the light, there was a reaction. We all stood and looked blankly at one another for a few moments. Then someone asked a question, and there was a general murmur of denial. We all felt ashamed, and someone reached up and unhooked the lantern on the port side. I did the same with the starboard one; and there was a quick movement towards the doors. As we streamed out on deck, I caught the sound of the Mates' voices. They had evidently come down from off the poop to find out what had happened; but it was too dark to see their whereabouts.

"Where the hell have you all got to?" I heard the Mate shout.

The next instant, they must have seen the light from our lanterns; for I heard their footsteps, coming along the deck at a run. They came the starboard side, and just abaft the fore rigging, one of them stumbled and fell over something. It was the First Mate who had tripped. I knew this by the cursing that came directly afterwards. He picked himself up, and, apparently without stopping to see what manner of thing it was that he had fallen over, made a rush to the pin-rail. The Second Mate ran into the circle of light thrown by our lanterns, and stopped, dead—eyeing us doubtfully. I am not surprised at this, *now*, nor at the behaviour of the Mate, the following instant; but at that time, I must say I could not conceive what had come to them, particularly the First Mate. He came out at us from the darkness with a rush and a roar like a bull and brandishing a belaying-pin. I had failed to take into account the scene which his eyes must have shown him:—the whole crowd of men in the fo'cas'le—both watches—pouring out on to the deck in utter confusion, and greatly excited, with a couple of fellows at their head, carrying lanterns. And before this, there had been the cry aloft and the crash down on deck, followed by the shouts of the frightened crew, and the sounds of many feet running. He may well have taken the cry for a signal, and our actions for something not far short of mutiny. Indeed, his words told us that this was his very thought.

"I'll knock the face off the first man that comes a step further aft!" he shouted, shaking the pin in my face. "I'll show yer who's master here! What the hell do yer mean by this? Get forrard into yer kennel!"

There was a low growl from the men at the last remark, and the old bully stepped back a couple of paces.

"Hold on, you fellows!" I sung out. "Shut up a minute."

"Mr. Tulipson!" I called out to the Second, who had not been able to get a word in edgeways, "I don't know what the devil's the matter with the First Mate; but he'll not find it pay to talk to a crowd like ours, in that sort of fashion, or there'll be ructions aboard."

"Come! Come! Jessop! This won't do! I can't have you talking like that about the Mate!" he said, sharply. "Let me know what's to-do, and then go forrard again, the lot of you."

"We'd have told you at first, Sir," I said, "only the Mate wouldn't give any of us a chance to speak. There's been an awful accident, Sir. Something's fallen from aloft, right onto Jock—"

I stopped suddenly; for there was a loud crying aloft.

"Help! help! help!" someone was shouting, and then it rose from a shout into a scream.

"My God! Sir!" I shouted. "That's one of the men up at the fore royal!"

"Listen!" ordered the Second Mate. "Listen!" Even as he spoke, it came again —broken and, as it were, in gasps.

"Help!... Oh!... God!... Oh!... Help! H-e-l-p!"

Abruptly, Stubbins's voice struck in.

"Hup with us, lads! By God! hup with us!" and he made a spring into the fore rigging. I shoved the handle of the lantern between my teeth, and followed. Plummer was coming; but the Second Mate pulled him back.

"That's sufficient," he said. "I'm going," and he came up after me.

We went over the foretop, racing like fiends. The light from the lantern prevented me from seeing to any distance in the darkness; but, at the crosstrees, Stubbins, who was some ratlines ahead, shouted out all at once, and in gasps:

"They're fightin' ... like ... hell!"

"What?" called the Second Mate, breathlessly.

Apparently, Stubbins did not hear him; for he made no reply. We cleared the crosstrees, and climbed into the t'gallant rigging. The wind was fairly fresh up there, and overhead, there sounded the flap, flap of sailcloth flying in the wind; but since we had left the deck, there had been no other sound from above.

Now, abruptly, there came again a wild crying from the darkness over us. A strange, wild medley it was of screams for help, mixed up with violent, breathless curses.

Beneath the royal yard, Stubbins halted, and looked down to me.

"Hurry hup ... with ther ... lantern ... Jessop!" he shouted, catching his breath between the words. "There'll be ... murder done ... hin a minute!"

I reached him, and held the light up for him to catch. He stooped, and took it from me. Then, holding it above his head, he went a few ratlines higher. In this manner, he reached to a level with the royal yard. From my position, a little below him, the lantern seemed but to throw a few straggling, flickering rays along the spar; yet they showed me something. My first glance had been to wind'ard, and I had seen at once, that there was nothing on the weather yard arm. From there my gaze went to leeward. Indistinctly, I saw something upon the yard, that clung, struggling. Stubbins bent towards it with the light; thus I saw it more clearly. It was Jacobs, the Ordinary Seaman. He had his right arm tightly round the yard; with the other, he appeared to be fending himself from something on the other side of him, and further out upon the yard. At times, moans and gasps came from him, and sometimes curses. Once, as he appeared to be dragged partly from his hold, he screamed like a woman. His whole attitude suggested stubborn despair. I can scarcely tell you how this extraordinary sight affected me. I seemed to stare at it without realising that the affair was a real happening.

During the few seconds which I had spent staring and breathless, Stubbins had climbed round the after side of the mast, and now I began again to follow him.

From his position below me, the Second had not been able to see the thing that was occurring on the yard, and he sung out to me to know what was happening.

"It's Jacobs, Sir," I called back. "He seems to be fighting with someone to looard of him. I can't see very plainly yet."

Stubbins had got round on to the lee foot-rope, and now he held the lantern up, peering, and I made my way quickly alongside of him. The Second Mate followed; but instead of getting down on to the foot-rope, he got on the yard, and stood there holding on to the tie. He sung out for one of us to pass him up the lantern, which I did, Stubbins handing it to me. The Second held it out at arm's length, so that it lit up the lee part of the yard. The light showed through the darkness, as far as to where Jacobs struggled so weirdly. Beyond him, nothing was distinct.

There had been a moment's delay while we were passing the lantern up to the Second Mate. Now, however, Stubbins and I moved out slowly along the foot-rope. We went slowly; but we did well to go at all, with any show of boldness; for the whole business was so abominably uncanny. It seems impossible to convey truly to you, the strange scene on the royal yard. You may be able to picture it yourselves. The Second Mate standing upon the spar, holding the lantern; his body swaying with each roll of the ship, and his head craned forward as he peered along the yard. On our left, Jacobs, mad, fighting, cursing, praying, gasping; and outside of him, shadows and the night.

The Second Mate spoke, abruptly.

"Hold on a moment!" he said. Then:

"Jacobs!" he shouted. "Jacobs, do you hear me?"

There was no reply, only the continual gasping and cursing.

"Go on," the Second Mate said to us. "But be careful. Keep a tight hold!"

He held the lantern higher and we went out cautiously.

Stubbins reached the Ordinary, and put his hand on his shoulder, with a soothing gesture.

"Steady hon now, Jacobs," he said. "Steady hon."

At his touch, as though by magic, the young fellow calmed down, and Stubbins—reaching round him—grasped the jackstay on the other side.

"Get a hold of him your side, Jessop," he sung out. "I'll get this side."

This, I did, and Stubbins climbed round him.

"There hain't no one here," Stubbins called to me; but his voice expressed no surprise.

"What!" sung out the Second Mate. "No one there! Where's Svensen, then?"

I did not catch Stubbins's reply; for suddenly, it seemed to me that I saw something shadowy at the extreme end of the yard, out by the lift. I stared. It rose up, on the yard, and I saw that it was the figure of a man. It grasped at the lift, and commenced to swarm up, quickly. It passed diagonally above Stubbins's head, and reached down a vague hand and arm.

"Look out! Stubbins!" I shouted. "Look out!"

"What's up now?" he called, in a startled voice. At the same instant, his cap went whirling away to leeward.

"Damn the wind!" he burst out.

Then all at once, Jacobs, who had only been giving an occasional moan, commenced to shriek and struggle.

"Hold fast onto him!" Stubbins yelled. "He'll be throwin' himself off the yard."

I put my left arm round the Ordinary's body—getting hold of the jackstay on the other side. Then I looked up. Above us, I seemed to see something dark and indistinct, that moved rapidly up the lift.

"Keep tight hold of him, while I get a gasket," I heard the Second Mate sing out.

A moment later there was a crash, and the light disappeared.

"Damn and set fire to the sail!" shouted the Second Mate.

I twisted round, somewhat, and looked in his direction. I could dimly make him out on the yard. He had evidently been in the act of getting down on to the foot-rope, when the lantern was smashed. From him, my gaze jumped to the lee rigging. It seemed that I made out some shadowy thing stealing down through the darkness; but I could not be sure; and then, in a breath, it had gone.

"Anything wrong, Sir?" I called out.

"Yes," he answered. "I've dropped the lantern. The blessed sail knocked it out of my hand!"

"We'll be all right, Sir," I replied. "I think we can manage without it. Jacobs seems to be quieter now."

"Well, be careful as you come in," he warned us.

"Come on, Jacobs," I said. "Come on; we'll go down on deck."

"Go along, young feller," Stubbins put in. "You're right now. We'll take care of you." And we started to guide him along the yard.

He went willingly enough, though without saying a word. He seemed like a child. Once or twice he shivered; but said nothing.

We got him in to the lee rigging. Then, one going beside him, and the other keeping below, we made our way slowly down on deck. We went very slowly—so slowly, in fact, that the Second Mate—who had stayed a minute to shove the gasket round the lee side of the sail—was almost as soon down.

"Take Jacobs forrard to his bunk," he said, and went away aft to where a crowd of the men, one with a lantern, stood round the door of an empty berth under the break of the poop on the starboard side.

We hurried forrard to the fo'cas'le. There we found all in darkness.

"They're haft with Jock, and Svenson!" Stubbins had hesitated an instant before saying the name.

"Yes," I replied. "That's what it must have been, right enough."

"I kind of knew it all ther time," he said.

I stepped in through the doorway, and struck a match. Stubbins followed, guiding Jacobs before him, and, together, we got him into his bunk. We covered him up with his blankets, for he was pretty shivery. Then we came out. During the whole time, he had not spoken a word.

As we went aft, Stubbins remarked that he thought the business must have made him a bit dotty.

"It's driven him clean barmy," he went on. "He don't hunderstand a word that's said ter him."

"He may be different in the morning," I answered.

As we neared the poop, and the crowd of waiting men, he spoke again:

"They've put 'em hinter ther Second's hempty berth."

"Yes," I said. "Poor beggars."

We reached the other men, and they opened out, and allowed us to get near the door. Several of them asked in low tones, whether Jacobs was all right, and I told them, "Yes;" not saying anything then about his condition.

I got close up to the doorway, and looked into the berth. The lamp was lit, and I could see, plainly. There were two bunks in the place, and a man had been laid in each. The Skipper was there, leaning up against a bulkshead. He looked worried; but was silent—seeming to be mooding in his own thoughts. The Second Mate was busy with a couple of flags, which he was spreading over the bodies. The First Mate was talking, evidently telling him something; but his tone was so low that I caught his words only with difficulty. It struck me that he seemed pretty subdued. I got parts of his sentences in patches, as it were.

"…broken," I heard him say. "And the Dutchman…"

"I've seen him," the Second Mate said, shortly.

"Two, straight off the reel," said the Mate "…three in…"

The Second made no reply.

"Of course, yer know … accident." The First Mate went on.

"Is it!" the Second said, in a queer voice.

I saw the Mate glance at him, in a doubtful sort of way; but the Second was covering poor old Jock's dead face, and did not appear to notice his look.

"It—it—" the mate said, and stopped.

After a moment's hesitation, he said something further, that I could not catch; but there seemed a lot of funk in his voice.

The Second Mate appeared not to have heard him; at any rate, he made no reply; but bent, and straightened out a corner of the flag over the rigid figure in the lower bunk. There was a certain niceness in his action which made me warm towards him.

"He's white!" I thought to myself.

Out loud, I said:

"We've put Jacobs into his bunk, Sir."

The Mate jumped; then whizzed round, and stared at me as though I had been a ghost. The Second Mate turned also; but before he could speak, the Skipper took a step towards me.

"Is he all right?" he asked.

"Well, Sir," I said. "He's a bit queer; but I think it's possible he may be better, after a sleep."

"I hope so, too," he replied, and stepped out on deck. He went towards the starboard poop ladder, walking slowly. The Second went and stood by the lamp, and the Mate, after a quick glance at him, came out and followed the Skipper up on to the poop. It occurred to me then, like a flash, that the man had stumbled upon a portion of the *truth*. This accident coming so soon after that other! It was evident that, in his mind, he had connected them. I recollected the fragments of his remarks to the Second Mate. Then, those many minor happenings that had cropped up at different times, and at which he had sneered. I wondered whether he would begin to comprehend their significance—their beastly, sinister significance.

"Ah! Mr. Bully-Mate," I thought to myself. "You're in for a bad time if you've begun to understand."

Abruptly, my thoughts jumped to the vague future before us.

"God help us!" I muttered.

The Second Mate, after a look round, turned down the wick of the lamp, and came out, closing the door after him.

"Now, you men," he said to the Mate's watch, "get forrard; we can't do anything more. You'd better go and get some sleep."

"i, i, Sir," they said, in a chorus.

Then, as we all turned to go forrard, he asked if anyone had relieved the lookout.

"No, sir," answered Quoin.

"Is it yours?" the Second asked.

"Yes, Sir," he replied.

"Hurry up and relieve him then," the Second said.

"i, i, Sir," the man answered, and went forrard with the rest of us.

As we went, I asked Plummer who was at the wheel.

"Tom," he said.

As he spoke, several spots of rain fell, and I glanced up at the sky. It had become thickly clouded.

"Looks as if it were going to breeze up," I said.

"Yes," he replied. "We'll be shortenin' 'er down 'fore long."

"May be an all-hands job," I remarked.

"Yes," he answered again. "'Twon't be no use their turnin' in, if it is."

The man who was carrying the lantern, went into the fo'cas'le, and we followed.

"Where's ther one, belongin' to our side?" Plummer asked.

"Got smashed hupstairs," answered Stubbins.

"'ow were that?" Plummer inquired.

Stubbins hesitated.

"The Second Mate dropped it," I replied. "The sail hit it, or something."

The men in the other watch seemed to have no immediate intention of turning-in; but sat in their bunks, and around on the chests. There was a general lighting of pipes, in the midst of which there came a sudden moan from one of the bunks in the forepart of the fo'cas'le—a part that was always a bit gloomy, and was more so now, on account of our having only one lamp.

"Wot's that?" asked one of the men belonging to the other side.

"S—sh!" said Stubbins. "It's him."

"'oo?" inquired Plummer. "Jacobs?"

"Yes," I replied. "Poor devil!"

"Wot were 'appenin' w'en yer got hup *ther*?" asked the man on the other side, indicating with a jerk of his head, the fore royal.

Before I could reply, Stubbins jumped up from his sea-chest.

"Ther Second Mate's whistlin'!" he said. "Come hon," and he ran out on deck.

Plummer, Jaskett and I followed quickly. Outside, it had started to rain pretty heavily. As we went, the Second Mate's voice came to us through the darkness.

"Stand by the main royal clewlines and buntlines," I heard him shout, and the next instant came the hollow thutter of the sail as he started to lower away.

In a few minutes we had it hauled up.

"Up and furl it, a couple of you," he sung out.

I went towards the starboard rigging; then I hesitated. No one else had moved.

The Second Mate came among us.

"Come on now, lads," he said. "Make a move. It's got to be done."

"I'll go," I said. "If someone else will come."

Still, no one stirred, and no one answered.

Tammy came across to me.

"I'll come," he volunteered, in a nervous voice.

"No, by God, no!" said the Second Mate, abruptly.

He jumped into the main rigging himself. "Come along, Jessop!" he shouted.

I followed him; but I was astonished. I had fully expected him to get on to the other fellows' tracks like a ton of bricks. It had not occurred to me that he was making allowances. I was simply puzzled then; but afterwards it dawned upon me.

No sooner had I followed the Second Mate, than, straightway, Stubbins,

Plummer, and Jaskett came up after us at a run.

About halfway to the maintop, the Second Mate stopped, and looked down.

"Who's that coming up below you, Jessop?" he asked.

Before I could, speak, Stubbins answered:

"It's me, Sir, an' Plummer an' Jaskett."

"Who the devil told you to come *now*? Go straight down, the lot of you!"

"We're comin' hup ter keep you company, Sir," was his reply.

At that, I was confident of a burst of temper from the Second; and yet, for the second time within a couple of minutes I was wrong. Instead of cursing Stubbins, he, after a moment's pause, went on up the rigging, without another word, and the rest of us followed. We reached the royal, and made short work of it; indeed, there were sufficient of us to have eaten it. When we had finished, I noticed that the Second Mate remained on the yard until we were all in the rigging. Evidently, he had determined to take a full share of any risk there might be; but I took care to keep pretty close to him; so as to be on hand if anything happened; yet we reached the deck again, without anything having occurred. I have said, without anything having occurred; but I am not really correct in this; for, as the Second Mate came down over the crosstrees, he gave a short, abrupt cry.

"Anything wrong, Sir?" I asked.

"No—o!" he said. "Nothing! I banged my knee."

And yet *now*, I believe he was lying. For, that same watch, I was to hear men giving just such cries; but, God knows, they had reason enough.

X.
Hands That Plucked

Directly we reached the deck, the Second Mate gave the order: "Mizzen t'gallant clewlines and buntlines," and led the way up onto the poop. He went and stood by the haulyards, ready to lower away. As I walked across to the starboard clewline, I saw that the Old Man was on deck, and as I took hold of the rope, I heard him sing out to the Second Mate.

"Call all hands to shorten sail, Mr. Tulipson."

"Very good, Sir," the Second Mate replied. Then he raised his voice:

"Go forrard, you, Jessop, and call all hands to shorten sail. You'd better give them a call in the bosun's place, as you go."

"i, i, Sir," I sung out, and hurried off.

As I went, I heard him tell Tammy to go down and call the Mate.

Reaching the fo'cas'le, I put my head in through the starboard doorway, and found some of the men beginning to turn in.

"It's all hands on deck, shorten sail," I sung out.

I stepped inside.

"Just wot I said," grumbled one of the men.

"They don't damn well think we're goin' aloft tonight, after what's happened?" asked another.

"We've been up to the main royal," I answered. "The Second Mate went with us."

"Wot?" said the first man. "Ther Second Mate hisself?"

"Yes," I replied. "The whole blooming watch went up."

"An' wot 'appened?" he asked.

"Nothing," I said. "Nothing at all. We just made a mouthful apiece of it, and came down again."

"All the same," remarked the second man, "I don't fancy goin' upstairs, after what's happened."

"Well," I replied. "It's not a matter of fancy. We've got to get the sail off her, or there'll be a mess. One of the 'prenticess told me the glass is falling."

"Come erlong, boys. We've got ter du it," said one of the older men, rising from a chest, at this point. "What's it duin' outside, mate?"

"Raining," I said. "You'll want your oilskins."

I hesitated a moment before going on deck again. From the bunk forrard among the shadows, I had seemed to hear a faint moan.

"Poor beggar!" I thought to myself.

Then the old chap who had last spoken, broke in upon my attention.

"It's awl right, mate!" he said, rather testily. "Yer needn't wait. We'll be out in er minit."

"That's all right. I wasn't thinking about you lot," I replied, and walked forrard to Jacobs's bunk. Sometime before, he had rigged up a pair of curtains, cut out of an old sack, to keep off the draft. These, someone had drawn, so that I had to pull them aside to see him. He was lying on his back, breathing in a queer, jerky fashion. I could not see his face, plainly; but it seemed rather pale, in the half-light.

"Jacobs," I said. "Jacobs, how do you feel now?" but he made no sign to show that he had heard me. And so, after a few moments, I drew the curtains to again, and left him.

"What like does 'e seem?" asked one of the fellows, as I went towards the door.

"Bad," I said. "Damn bad! I think the Steward ought to be told to come and have a look at him. I'll mention it to the Second when I get a chance."

I stepped out on deck, and ran aft again to give them a hand with the sail. We got it hauled up, and then went forrard to the fore t'gallant. And, a minute later, the other watch were out, and, with the Mate, were busy at the main.

By the time the main was ready for making fast, we had the fore hauled up, so that now all three t'gallants were in the ropes, and ready for stowing. Then came the order:

"Up aloft and furl!"

"Up with you, lads," the Second Mate said. "Don't let's have any hanging back this time."

Away aft by the main, the men in the Mate's watch seemed to be standing in a clump by the mast; but it was too dark to see clearly. I heard the Mate start to curse; then there came a growl, and he shut up.

"Be handy, men! Be handy!" the Second Mate sung out.

At that, Stubbins jumped into the rigging.

"Come hon!" he shouted. "We'll have ther bloomin' sail fast, an' down hon deck again before they're started."

Plummer followed; then Jaskett, I, and Quoin who had been called down off the lookout to give a hand.

"That's the style, lads!" the Second sung out, encouragingly. Then he ran aft to the Mate's crowd. I heard him and the Mate talking to the men, and presently, when we were going over the foretop, I made out that they were beginning to get into the rigging.

I found out, afterwards, that as soon as the Second Mate had seen them off the deck, he went up to the mizzen t'gallant, along with the four 'prenticess.

On our part, we made our way slowly aloft, keeping one hand for ourselves and the other for the ship, as you can fancy. In this manner we had gone as far as the crosstrees, at least, Stubbins, who was first, had; when, all at once, he gave out just another such cry as had the Second Mate a little earlier, only that in his case he followed it by turning round and blasting Plummer.

"You might have blarsted well sent me flyin' down hon deck," he shouted. "If you bloody well think it's a joke, try it hon someone else—"

"It wasn't me!" interrupted Plummer. "I 'aven't touched yer. 'oo the 'ell are yer swearin' at?"

"At you—!" I heard him reply; but what more he may have said, was lost in a loud shout from Plummer.

"What's up, Plummer?" I sung out. "For God's sake, you two, don't get fighting, up aloft!"

But a loud, frightened curse was all the answer he gave. Then straightway, he began to shout at the top of his voice, and in the lulls of his noise, I caught the voice of Stubbins, cursing savagely.

"They'll come down with a run!" I shouted, helplessly. "They'll come down as sure as nuts."

I caught Jaskett by the boot.

"What are they doing? What are they doing?" I sung out. "Can't you see?" I shook his leg as I spoke. But at my touch, the old idiot—as I thought him at the moment—began to shout in a frightened voice:

"Oh! Oh! Help! Hel—!"

"Shut up!" I bellowed. "Shut up, you old fool. If you won't do anything, let me get past you."

Yet he only cried out the more. And then, abruptly, I caught the sound of a frightened clamor of men's voices, away down somewhere about the maintop—curses, cries of fear, even shrieks, and above it all, someone shouting to go down on deck:

"Get down! get down! down! down! Blarst—" The rest was drowned in a fresh outburst of hoarse crying in the night.

I tried to get past old Jaskett; but he was clinging to the rigging, sprawled on to it, is the best way to describe his attitude, so much of it as I could see in the darkness. Up above him, Stubbins and Plummer still shouted and cursed, and the shrouds quivered and shook, as though the two were fighting desperately.

Stubbins seemed to be shouting something definite; but whatever it was, I could not catch.

At my helplessness, I grew angry, and shook and prodded Jaskett, to make him move.

"Damn you, Jaskett!" I roared. "Damn you for a funky old fool! Let me get past! Let me get past, will you!"

But, instead of letting me pass, I found that he was beginning to make his way down. At that, I caught him by the slack of his trousers, near the stern, with my right hand, and with the other, I got hold of the after shroud somewhere above his left hip; by these means, I fairly hoisted myself up on to the old fellow's back. Then, with my right, I could reach to the forrard shroud, over his right shoulder, and having got a grip, I shifted my left to a level with it; at the same moment, I was able to get my foot onto the splice of a ratline and so give myself a further lift. Then I paused an instant, and glanced up.

"Stubbins! Stubbins!" I shouted. "Plummer! Plummer!"

And even as I called, Plummer's foot—reaching down through the gloom—alighted full on my upturned face. I let go from the rigging with my right hand, and struck furiously at his leg, cursing him for his clumsiness. He lifted his foot, and in the same instant a sentence from Stubbins floated down to me, with a strange distinctness:

"For God's sake tell 'em to get down hon deck!" he was shouting.

Even as the words came to me, something in the darkness gripped my waist. I made a desperate clutch at the rigging with my disengaged right hand, and it was well for me that I secured the hold so quickly, for the same instant, I was wrenched at with a brutal ferocity that appalled me. I said nothing, but lashed out into the night with my left foot. It is queer, but I cannot say with certainty that I struck anything; I was too downright desperate with funk, to be sure; and yet it seemed to me that my foot encountered something soft, that gave under the blow. It may have been nothing more than an imagined sensation; yet I am inclined to think otherwise; for, instantly, the hold about my waist was released; and I commenced to scramble down, clutching the shrouds pretty desperately.

I have only a very uncertain remembrance of that which followed. Whether I slid over Jaskett, or whether he gave way to me, I cannot tell. I know only that I reached the deck, in a blind whirl of fear and excitement, and the next thing I remember, I was among a crowd of shouting, half-mad sailor-men.

XI.
The Search for Stubbins

In a confused way, I was conscious that the Skipper and the Mates were down among us, trying to get us into some state of calmness. Eventually they succeeded, and we were told to go aft to the Saloon door, which we did in a body. Here, the Skipper himself served out a large tot of rum to each of us. Then, at his orders, the Second Mate called the roll.

He called over the Mate's watch first, and everyone answered. Then he came to ours, and he must have been much agitated; for the first name he sung out was Jock's.

Among us there came a moment of dead silence, and I noticed the wail and moan of the wind aloft, and the flap, flap of the three unfurled t'gallan's'ls.

The Second Mate called the next name, hurriedly:

"Jaskett," he sung out.

"Sir," Jaskett answered.

"Quoin."

"Yes, Sir."

"Jessop."

"Sir," I replied.

"Stubbins."

There was no answer.

"Stubbins," again called the Second Mate.

Again there was no reply.

"Is Stubbins here?—anyone!" The Second's voice sounded sharp and anxious.

There was a moment's pause. Then one of the men spoke:

"He's not here, Sir."

"Who saw him last?" the Second asked.

Plummer stepped forward into the light that streamed through the Saloon doorway. He had on neither coat nor cap, and his shirt seemed to be hanging about him in tatters.

"It were me, Sir," he said.

The Old Man, who was standing next to the Second Mate, took a pace towards him, and stopped and stared; but it was the Second who spoke.

"Where?" he asked.

"'e were just above me, in ther crosstrees, when, when—" the man broke off short.

"Yes! Yes!" the Second Mate replied. Then he turned to the Skipper.

"Someone will have to go up, Sir, and see—" He hesitated.

"But—" said the Old Man, and stopped.

The Second Mate cut in.

"I shall go up, for one, Sir," he said, quietly.

Then he turned back to the crowd of us.

"Tammy," he sung out. "Get a couple of lamps out of the lamp-locker."

"i, i, Sir," Tammy replied, and ran off.

"Now," said the Second Mate, addressing us. "I want a couple of men to jump aloft along with me and take a look for Stubbins."

Not a man replied. I would have liked to step out and offer; but the memory of that horrible clutch was with me, and for the life of me, I could not summon up the courage.

"Come! Come, men!" he said. "We can't leave him up there. We shall take lanterns. Who'll come now?"

I walked out to the front. I was in a horrible funk; but, for very shame, I could not stand back any longer.

"I'll come with you, Sir," I said, not very loud, and feeling fairly twisted up with nervousness.

"That's more the tune, Jessop!" he replied, in a tone that made me glad I had stood out.

At this point, Tammy came up, with the lights. He brought them to the Second, who took one, and told him to give the other to me. The Second Mate held his light above his head, and looked round at the hesitating men.

"Now, men!" he sung out. "You're not going to let Jessop and me go up alone. Come along, another one or two of you! Don't act like a damned lot of cowards!"

Quoin stood out, and spoke for the crowd.

"I dunno as we're actin' like cowyards, Sir; but just look at 'im," and he pointed at Plummer, who still stood full in the light from the Saloon doorway.

"What sort of a Thing is it 'as done that, Sir?" he went on. "An' then yer arsks us ter go up agen! It aren't likely as we're in a 'urry."

The Second Mate looked at Plummer, and surely, as I have before mentioned, the poor beggar was in a state; his ripped-up shirt was fairly flapping in the breeze that came through the doorway.

The Second looked; yet he said nothing. It was as though the realization of Plummer's condition had left him without a word more to say. It was Plummer himself who finally broke the silence.

"I'll come with yer, Sir," he said. "Only yer ought ter 'ave more light than them two lanterns. 'Twon't be no use, unless we 'as plenty er light."

The man had grit; and I was astonished at his offering to go, after what he must have gone through. Yet, I was to have even a greater astonishment; for, abruptly, The Skipper—who all this time had scarcely spoken—stepped forward a pace, and put his hand on the Second Mate's shoulder.

"I'll come with you, Mr. Tulipson," he said.

The Second Mate twisted his head round, and stared at him a moment, in astonishment. Then he opened his mouth.

"No, Sir; I don't think—" he began.

"That's sufficient, Mr. Tulipson," the Old Man interrupted. "I've made up my mind."

He turned to the First Mate, who had stood by without a word.

"Mr. Grainge," he said. "Take a couple of the 'prenticess down with you, and pass out a box of blue-lights and some flare-ups."

The Mate answered something, and hurried away into the Saloon, with the two 'prenticess in his watch. Then the Old Man spoke to the men.

"Now, men!" he began. "This is no time for dilly-dallying. The Second Mate and I will go aloft, and I want about half a dozen of you to come along with us, and carry lights. Plummer and Jessop here, have volunteered. I want four or five more of you. Step out now, some of you!"

There was no hesitation whatever, now; and the first man to come forward was Quoin. After him followed three of the Mate's crowd, and then old Jaskett.

"That will do; that will do," said the Old Man.

He turned to the Second Mate.

"Has Mr. Grainge come with those lights yet?" he asked, with a certain irritability.

"Here, Sir," said the First Mate's voice, behind him in the Saloon doorway. He had the box of blue-lights in his hands, and behind him, came the two boys carrying the flares.

The Skipper took the box from him, with a quick gesture, and opened it.

"Now, one of you men, come here," he ordered.

One of the men in the Mate's watch ran to him.

He took several of the lights from the box, and handed them to the man.

"See here," he said. "When we go aloft, you get into the foretop, and keep one of these going all the time, do you hear?"

"Yes, Sir," replied the man.

"You know how to strike them?" the Skipper asked, abruptly.

"Yes, Sir," he answered.

The Skipper sung out to the Second Mate:

"Where's that boy of yours—Tammy, Mr. Tulipson?"

"Here, Sir," said Tammy, answering for himself.

The Old Man took another light from the box.

"Listen to me, boy!" he said. "Take this, and stand-by on the forrard deck house. When we go aloft, you must give us a light until the man gets his going in the top. You understand?"

"Yes, Sir," answered Tammy, and took the light.

"One minute!" said the Old Man, and stooped and took a second light from the box. "Your first light may go out before we're ready. You'd better have another, in case it does."

Tammy took the second light, and moved away.

"Those flares all ready for lighting there, Mr. Grainge?" the Captain asked.

"All ready, Sir," replied the Mate.

The Old Man pushed one of the blue-lights into his coat pocket, and stood upright.

"Very well," he said. "Give each of the men one apiece. And just see that they all have matches."

He spoke to the men particularly:

"As soon as we are ready, the other two men in the Mate's watch will get up into the cranelines, and keep their flares going there. Take your paraffin tins with you. When we reach the upper topsail, Quoin and Jaskett will get out on the yard-arms, and show their flares there. Be careful to keep your lights away from the sails. Plummer and Jessop will come up with the Second Mate and myself. Does every man clearly understand?"

"Yes, Sir," said the men in a chorus.

A sudden idea seemed to occur to the Skipper, and he turned, and went through the doorway into the Saloon. In about a minute, he came back, and handed something to the Second Mate, that shone in the light from the lanterns. I saw that it was a revolver, and he held another in his other hand, and this I saw him put into his side pocket.

The Second Mate held the pistol a moment, looking a bit doubtful.

"I don't think, Sir—" he began. But the Skipper cut him short.

"You don't know!" he said. "Put it in your pocket."

Then he turned to the First Mate.

"You will take charge of the deck, Mr. Grainge, while we're aloft," he said.

"i, i, Sir," the Mate answered and sung out to one of his 'prenticess to take the blue-light box back into the cabin.

The Old Man turned and led the way forrard. As we went, the light from the two lanterns shone upon the decks, showing the litter of the t'gallant gear. The ropes were foul of one another in a regular "bunch o' buffers." This had been caused, I suppose, by the crowd trampling over them in their excitement, when they reached the deck. And then, suddenly, as though the sight had waked me up to a more vivid comprehension, you know, it came to me new and fresh, how damned strange was the whole business… I got a little touch of despair, and asked myself what was going to be the end of all these beastly happenings. You can understand?

Abruptly, I heard the Skipper shouting, away forward. He was singing out to Tammy to get up on to the house with his blue-light. We reached the fore rigging, and, the same instant, the strange, ghastly flare of Tammy's blue-light burst out into the night causing every rope, sail, and spar to jump out weirdly.

I saw now that the Second Mate was already in the starboard rigging, with his lantern. He was shouting to Tammy to keep the drip from his light clear of the staysail, which was stowed upon the house. Then, from somewhere on the port side, I heard the Skipper shout to us to hurry.

"Smartly now, you men," he was saying. "Smartly now."

The man who had been told to take up a station in the fore-top, was just behind the Second Mate. Plummer was a couple of ratlines lower.

I caught the Old Man's voice again.

"Where's Jessop with that other lantern?" I heard him shout.

"Here, Sir," I sung out.

"Bring it over this side," he ordered. "You don't want the two lanterns on one side."

I ran round the fore side of the house. Then I saw him. He was in the rigging, and making his way smartly aloft. One of the Mate's watch and Quoin were with him. This, I saw as I came round the house. Then I made a jump, gripped the sheerpole, and swung myself up on to the rail. And then, all at once, Tammy's blue-light went out, and there came, what seemed by contrast, pitchy darkness. I stood where I was—one foot on the rail and my knee upon the sheerpole. The light from my lantern seemed no more than a sickly yellow glow against the gloom, and higher, some forty or fifty feet, and a few ratlines below the futtock rigging on the starboard side, there was another glow of yellowness in the night. Apart from these, all was blackness. And then from above—high above—there wailed down through the darkness a weird, sobbing cry. What it was, I do not know; but it sounded horrible.

The Skipper's voice came down, jerkily.

"Smartly with that light, boy!" he shouted. And the blue glare blazed out again, almost before he had finished speaking.

I stared up at the Skipper. He was standing where I had seen him before the light went out, and so were the two men. As I looked, he commenced to climb again. I glanced across to starboard. Jaskett, and the other man in the Mate's watch, were about midway between the deck of the house and the foretop. Their faces showed extraordinary pale in the dead glare of the blue-light. Higher, I saw the Second Mate in the futtock rigging, holding his light up over the edge of the top. Then he went further, and disappeared. The man with the blue-lights followed, and also vanished from view. On the port side, and more directly above me, the Skipper's feet were just stepping out of the futtock shrouds. At that I made haste to follow.

Then, suddenly, when I was close under the top, there came from above me the sharp flare of a blue-light, and almost in the same instant, Tammy's went out.

I glanced down at the decks. They were filled with flickering, grotesque shadows cast by the dripping light above. A group of the men stood by the port galley door—their faces upturned and pale and unreal under the gleam of the light.

Then I was in the futtock rigging, and a moment afterwards, standing in the top, beside the Old Man. He was shouting to the men who had gone out on the craneline. It seemed that the man on the port side was bungling; but at last—nearly a minute after the other man had lit his flare—he got going. In that time, the man in the top had lit his second blue-light, and we were ready to get into the topmast rigging. First, however, the Skipper leant over the afterside of the top, and sung out to the First Mate to send a man up on to the fo'cas'le head with a flare. The Mate replied, and then we started again, the Old Man leading.

Fortunately, the rain had ceased, and there seemed to be no increase in the wind; indeed, if anything, there appeared to be rather less; yet what there was drove the flames of the flare-ups out into occasional, twisting serpents of fire at least a yard long.

About halfway up the topmast rigging, the Second Mate sung out to the Skipper, to know whether Plummer should light his flare; but the Old Man said he had better wait until we reached the crosstrees, as then he could get out away from the gear to where there would be less danger of setting fire to anything.

We neared the crosstrees, and the Old Man stopped and sung out to me to pass him the lantern by Quoin. A few ratlines more, and both he and the Second Mate stopped almost simultaneously, holding their lanterns as high as possible, and peered up into the darkness.

"See any signs of him, Mr. Tulipson?" the Old Man asked.

"No, Sir," replied the Second. "Not a sign."

He raised his voice.

"Stubbins," he sung out. "Stubbins, are you there?"

We listened; but nothing came to us beyond the blowing moan of the wind, and the flap, flap of the bellying t'gallant above.

The Second Mate climbed over the crosstrees, and Plummer followed. The man got out by the royal backstay, and lit his flare. By its light we could see, plainly; but there was no vestige of Stubbins, so far as the light went.

"Get out on to the yard-arms with those flares, you two men," shouted the Skipper. "Be smart now! Keep them away from the sail!"

The men got on to the foot-ropes—Quoin on the port, and Jaskett on the starboard side. By the light from Plummer's flare, I could see them clearly, as they lay out upon the yard. It occurred to me that they went gingerly—which is no surprising thing. And then, as they drew near to the yard-arms, they passed beyond the brilliance of the light; so that I could not see them clearly. A few seconds passed, and then the light from Quoin's flare streamed out upon the wind; yet nearly a minute went by, and there was no sign of Jaskett's.

Then out from the semi-darkness at the starboard yard-arm, there came a curse from Jaskett, followed almost immediately by a noise of something vibrating.

"What's up?" shouted the Second Mate. "What's up, Jaskett?"

"It's ther foot-rope, Sir-r-r!" he drew out the last word into a sort of gasp.

The Second Mate bent quickly, with the lantern. I craned round the after side of the top-mast, and looked.

"What is the matter, Mr. Tulipson?" I heard the Old Man singing out.

Out on the yard-arm, Jaskett began to shout for help, and then, all at once, in the light from the Second Mate's lantern, I saw that the starboard foot-rope on the upper topsail yard was being violently shaken—savagely shaken, is perhaps a better word. And then, almost in the same instant, the Second Mate shifted the lantern from his right to his left hand. He put the right into his pocket and brought out his gun with a jerk. He extended his hand and arm, as though pointing at something a little below the yard. Then a quick flash spat out across the shadows, followed immediately by a sharp, ringing crack. In the same moment, I saw that the foot-rope ceased to shake.

"Light your flare! Light your flare, Jaskett!" the Second shouted. "Be smart now!"

Out at the yard-arm there came a splutter of a match, and then, straightaway, a great spurt of fire as the flare took light.

"That's better, Jaskett. You're all right now!" the Second Mate called out to him.

"What was it, Mr. Tulipson?" I heard the Skipper ask.

I looked up, and saw that he had sprung across to where the Second Mate was standing. The Second Mate explained to him; but he did not speak loud enough for me to catch what he said.

I had been struck by Jaskett's attitude, when the light of his flare had first revealed him. He had been crouched with his right knee cocked over the yard, and his left leg down between it and the foot-rope, while his elbows had been crooked over the yard for support, as he was lighting the flare. Now, however, he had slid both feet back on to the foot-rope, and was lying on his belly, over the yard, with the flare held a little below the head of the sail. It was thus, with the light being on the foreside of the sail, that I saw a small hole a little below the foot-rope, through which a ray of the light shone. It was undoubtedly the hole which the bullet from the Second Mate's revolver had made in the sail.

Then I heard the Old Man shouting to Jaskett.

"Be careful with that flare there!" he sung out. "You'll be having that sail scorched!"

He left the Second Mate, and came back on to the port side of the mast.

To my right, Plummer's flares seemed to be dwindling. I glanced up at his face through the smoke. He was paying no attention to it; instead, he was staring up above his head.

"Shove some paraffin on to it, Plummer," I called to him. "It'll be out in a minute."

He looked down quickly to the light, and did as I suggested. Then he held it out at arm's length, and peered up again into the darkness.

"See anything?" asked the Old Man, suddenly observing his attitude.

Plummer glanced at him, with a start.

"It's ther r'yal, Sir," he explained. "It's all adrift."

"What!" said the Old Man.

He was standing a few ratlines up the t'gallant rigging, and he bent his body outwards to get a better look.

"Mr. Tulipson!" he shouted. "Do you know that the royal's all adrift?"

"No, Sir," answered the Second Mate. "If it is, it's more of this devilish work!"

"It's adrift right enough," said the Skipper, and he and the Second went a few ratlines higher, keeping level with one another.

I had now got above the crosstrees, and was just at the Old Man's heels.

Suddenly, he shouted out:

"There he is!—Stubbins! Stubbins!"

"Where, Sir?" asked the Second, eagerly. "I can't see him!"

"There! There!" replied the Skipper, pointing.

I leant out from the rigging, and looked up along his back, in the direction his finger indicated. At first, I could see nothing; then, slowly, you know, there grew upon my sight a dim figure crouching upon the bunt of the royal, and partly hidden by the mast. I stared, and gradually it came to me that there was a couple of them, and further out upon the yard, a hump that might have been anything, and was only visible indistinctly amid the flutter of the canvas.

"Stubbins!" the Skipper sung out. "Stubbins, come down out of that! Do you hear me?"

But no one came, and there was no answer.

"There's two—" I began; but he was shouting again:

"Come down out of that! Do you damned well hear me?"

Still there was no reply.

"I'm hanged if I can see him at all, Sir!" the Second Mate called out from his side of the mast.

"Can't see him!" said the Old Man, now thoroughly angry. "I'll soon let you see him!"

He bent down to me with the lantern.

"Catch hold, Jessop," he said, which I did.

Then he pulled the blue light from his pocket, and as he was doing so, I saw the Second peek round the back side of the mast at him. Evidently, in the uncertain light, he must have mistaken the Skipper's action; for, all at once, he shouted out in a frightened voice:

"Don't shoot, Sir! For God's sake, don't shoot!"

"Shoot be damned!" exclaimed the Old Man. "Watch!"

He pulled off the cap of the light.

"There's two of them, Sir," I called again to him.

"What!" he said in a loud voice, and at the same instant he rubbed the end of the light across the cap, and it burst into fire.

He held it up so that it lit the royal yard like day, and straightway, a couple of shapes dropped silently from the royal on to the t'gallant yard. At the same moment, the humped Something, midway out upon the yard, rose up. It ran in to the mast, and I lost sight of it.

"God!" I heard the Skipper gasp, and he fumbled in his side pocket.

I saw the two figures which had dropped on to the t'gallant, run swiftly along the yard—one to the starboard and the other to the port yard-arms.

On the other side of the mast, the Second Mate's pistol cracked out twice, sharply. Then, from over my head the Skipper fired twice, and then again; but with what effect, I could not tell. Abruptly, as he fired his last shot, I was aware of an indistinct Something, gliding down the starboard royal backstay. It was descending full upon Plummer, who, all unconscious of the thing, was staring towards the t'gallant yard.

"Look out above you, Plummer!" I almost shrieked.

"What? Where?" he called, and grabbed at the stay, and waved his flare, excitedly.

Down on the upper topsail yard, Quoin's and Jaskett's voices rose simultaneously, and in the identical instant, their flares went out. Then Plummer shouted, and his light went utterly. There were left only the two lanterns, and the blue-light held by the Skipper, and that, a few seconds afterwards, finished and died out.

The Skipper and the Second Mate were shouting to the men upon the yard, and I heard them answer, in shaky voices. Out on the crosstrees, I could see, by the light from my lantern, that Plummer was holding in a dazed fashion to the backstay.

"Are you all right, Plummer?" I called.

"Yes," he said, after a little pause; and then he swore.

"Come in off that yard, you men!" the Skipper was singing out. "Come in! Come in!"

Down on deck, I heard someone calling; but could not distinguish the words. Above me, pistol in hand, the Skipper was glancing about, uneasily.

"Hold up that light, Jessop," he said. "I can't see!"

Below us, the men got off the yard, into the rigging.

"Down on deck with you!" ordered the Old Man.

"As smartly as you can!"

"Come in off there, Plummer!" sung out the Second Mate. "Get down with the others!"

"Down with you, Jessop!" said the Skipper, speaking rapidly. "Down with you!"

I got over the crosstrees, and he followed. On the other side, the Second Mate was level with us. He had passed his lantern to Plummer, and I caught the glint of his revolver in his right hand. In this fashion, we reached the top. The man who had been stationed there with the blue-lights, had gone. Afterwards, I found that he went down on deck as soon as they were finished. There was no sign of the man with the flare on the starboard craneline. He also, I learnt later, had slid down one of the backstays on to the deck, only a very short while before we reached the top. He swore that a great black shadow of a man had come suddenly upon him from aloft. When I heard that, I remembered the thing I had seen descending upon Plummer. Yet the man who had gone out upon the port craneline—the one who had bungled with the lighting of his flare—was still where we had left him; though his light was burning now but dimly.

"Come in out of that, *you!*" the Old Man sung out "Smartly now, and get down on deck!"

"i, i, Sir," the man replied, and started to make his way in.

The Skipper waited until he had got into the main rigging, and then he told me to get down out of the top. He was in the act of following, when, all at once, there rose a loud outcry on deck, and then came the sound of a man screaming.

"Get out of my way, Jessop!" the Skipper roared, and swung himself down alongside of me.

I heard the Second Mate shout something from the starboard rigging. Then we were all racing down as hard as we could go. I had caught a momentary glimpse of a man running from the doorway on the port side of the fo'cas'le. In less than half a minute we were upon the deck, and among a crowd of the men who were grouped round something. Yet, strangely enough, they were not looking at the thing among them; but away aft at something in the darkness.

"It's on the rail!" cried several voices.

"Overboard!" called somebody, in an excited voice. "It's jumped over the side!"

"Ther' wer'n't nothin'!" said a man in the crowd.

"Silence!" shouted the Old Man. "Where's the Mate? What's happened?"

"Here, Sir," called the First Mate, shakily, from near the centre of the group. "It's Jacobs, Sir. He—he—"

"What!" said the Skipper. "What!"

"He—he's—he's—dead I think!" said the First Mate, in jerks.

"Let me see," said the Old Man, in a quieter tone.

The men had stood to one side to give him room, and he knelt beside the man upon the deck.

"Pass the lantern here, Jessop," he said.

I stood by him, and held the light. The man was lying face downwards on the deck. Under the light from the lantern, the Skipper turned him over and looked at him.

"Yes," he said, after a short examination. "He's dead."

He stood up and regarded the body a moment, in silence. Then he turned to the Second Mate, who had been standing by, during the last couple of minutes.

"Three!" he said, in a grim undertone.

The Second Mate nodded, and cleared his voice.

He seemed on the point of saying something; then he turned and looked at Jacobs, and said nothing.

"Three," repeated the Old Man. "Since eight bells!"

He stooped and looked again at Jacobs.

"Poor devil! poor devil!" he muttered.

The Second Mate grunted some of the huskiness out of his throat, and spoke.

"Where must we take him?" he asked, quietly. "The two bunks are full."

"You'll have to put him down on the deck by the lower bunk," replied the Skipper.

As they carried him away, I heard the Old Man make a sound that was almost a groan. The rest of the men had gone forrard, and I do not think he realized that I was standing by him

"My God! O, my God!" he muttered, and began to walk slowly aft.

He had cause enough for groaning. There were three dead, and Stubbins had gone utterly and completely. We never saw him again.

XII.
The Council

A few minutes later, the Second Mate came forrard again. I was still standing near the rigging, holding the lantern, in an aimless sort of way.

"That you, Plummer?" he asked.

"No, Sir," I said. "It's Jessop."

"Where's Plummer, then?" he inquired.

"I don't know, Sir," I answered. "I expect he's gone forrard. Shall I go and tell him you want him?"

"No, there's no need," he said. "Tie your lamp up in the rigging—on the sheerpole there. Then go and get his, and shove it up on the starboard side. After that you'd better go aft and give the two 'prenticess a hand in the lamp locker."

"i, i, Sir," I replied, and proceeded to do as he directed. After I had got the light from Plummer, and lashed it up to the starboard sherpole, I hurried aft. I found Tammy and the other 'prentices in our watch, busy in the locker, lighting lamps.

"What are we doing?" I asked.

"The Old Man's given orders to lash all the spare lamps we can find, in the rigging, so as to have the decks light," said Tammy. "And a damned good job too!"

He handed me a couple of the lamps, and took two himself.

"Come on," he said, and stepped out on deck. "We'll fix these in the main rigging, and then I want to talk to you."

"What about the mizzen?" I inquired.

"Oh," he replied. "He" (meaning the other 'prentices) "will see to that. Anyway, it'll be daylight directly."

We shoved the lamps up on the sherpoles—two on each side. Then he came across to me.

"Look here, Jessop!" he said, without any hesitation. "You'll have to jolly well tell the Skipper and the Second Mate all you know about all this."

"How do you mean?" I asked.

"Why, that it's something about the ship herself that's the cause of what's happened," he replied. "If you'd only explained to the Second Mate when I told you to, this might never have been!"

"But I don't *know*," I said. "I may be all wrong. It's only an idea of mine. I've no proofs—"

"Proofs!" he cut in with. "Proofs! what about tonight? We've had all the proofs ever I want!"

I hesitated before answering him.

"So have I, for that matter," I said, at length. "What I mean is, I've nothing that the Skipper and the Second Mate would consider as proofs. They'd never listen seriously to me."

"They'd listen fast enough," he replied. "After what's happened this watch, they'd listen to anything. Anyway, it's jolly well your duty to tell them!"

"What could they do, anyway?" I said, despondently. "As things are going, we'll all be dead before another week is over, at this rate."

"You tell them," he answered. "That's what you've got to do. If you can only get them to realize that you're right, they'll be glad to put into the nearest port, and send us all ashore."

I shook my head.

"Well, anyway, they'll have to do something," he replied, in answer to my gesture. "We can't go round the Horn, with the number of men we've lost. We haven't enough to handle her, if it comes on to blow."

"You've forgotten, Tammy," I said. "Even if I could get the Old Man to believe I'd got at the truth of the matter, he couldn't do anything. Don't you see, if I'm right, we couldn't even see the land, if we made it. We're like blind men…"

"What on earth do you mean?" he interrupted. "How do you make out we're like blind men? Of course we could see the land—"

"Wait a minute! wait a minute!" I said. "You don't understand. Didn't I tell you?"

"Tell what?" he asked.

"About the ship I spotted," I said. "I thought you knew!"

"No," he said. "When?"

"Why," I replied. "You know when the Old Man sent me away from the wheel?"

"Yes," he answered. "You mean in the morning watch, day before yesterday?"

"Yes," I said. "Well, don't you know what was the matter?"

"No," he replied. "That is, I heard you were snoozing at the wheel, and the Old Man came up and caught you."

"That's all a darned silly yarn!" I said. And then I told him the whole truth of the affair. After I had done that, I explained my idea about it, to him.

"Now you see what I mean?" I asked.

"You mean that this strange atmosphere—or whatever it is—we're in, would not allow us to see another ship?" he asked, a bit awestruck.

"Yes," I said. "But the point I wanted you to see, is that if we can't see another vessel, even when she's quite close, then, in the same way, we shouldn't be able to see land. To all intents and purposes we're blind. Just you think of it! We're out in the middle of the briny, doing a sort of eternal blind man's hop. The Old Man couldn't put into port, even if he wanted to. He'd run us bang on shore, without our ever seeing it."

"What are we going to do, then?" he asked, in a despairing sort of way. "Do you mean to say we can't do anything? Surely something can be done! It's terrible!"

For perhaps a minute, we walked up and down, in the light from the different lanterns. Then he spoke again.

"We might be run down, then," he said, "and never even see the other vessel?"

"It's possible," I replied. "Though, from what I saw, it's evident that *we're* quite visible; so that it would be easy for them to see us, and steer clear of us, even though we couldn't see them."

"And we might run into something, and never see it?" he asked me, following up the train of thought.

"Yes," I said. "Only there's nothing to stop the other ship from getting out of our way."

"But if it wasn't a vessel?" he persisted. "It might be an iceberg, or a rock, or even a derelict."

"In that case," I said, putting it a bit flippantly, naturally, "we'd probably damage it."

He made no answer to this and for a few moments, we were quiet.

Then he spoke abruptly, as though the idea had come suddenly to him.

"Those lights the other night!" he said. "Were they a ship's lights?"

"Yes," I replied. "Why?"

"Why," he answered. "Don't you see, if they were really lights, we *could* see them?"

"Well, I should think I ought to know that," I replied. "You seem to forget that the Second Mate slung me off the lookout for daring to do that very thing."

"I don't mean that," he said. "Don't you see that if we could see them at all, it showed that the atmosphere-thing wasn't round us then?"

"Not necessarily," I answered. "It may have been nothing more than a rift in it; though, of course, I may be all wrong. But, anyway, the fact that the lights disappeared almost as soon as they were seen, shows that it was very much round the ship."

That made him feel a bit the way I did, and when next he spoke, his tone had lost its hopefulness.

"Then you think it'll be no use telling the Second Mate and the Skipper anything?" he asked.

"I don't know," I replied. "I've been thinking about it, and it can't do any harm. I've a very good mind to."

"I should," he said. "You needn't be afraid of anybody laughing at you, now. It might do some good. You've seen more than anyone else."

He stopped in his walk, and looked round.

"Wait a minute," he said, and ran aft a few steps. I saw him look up at the break of the poop; then he came back.

"Come along now," he said. "The Old Man's up on the poop, talking to the Second Mate. You'll never get a better chance."

Still I hesitated; but he caught me by the sleeve, and almost dragged me to the lee ladder.

"All right," I said, when I got there. "All right, I'll come. Only I'm hanged if I know what to say when I get there."

"Just tell them you want to speak to them," he said. "They'll ask what you want, and then you spit out all you know. They'll find it interesting enough."

"You'd better come too," I suggested. "You'll be able to back me up in lots of things."

"I'll come, fast enough," he replied. "You go up."

I went up the ladder, and walked across to where the Skipper and the Second Mate stood talking earnestly, by the rail. Tammy kept behind. As I came near to them, I caught two or three words; though I attached no meaning then to them. They were: "...send for him." Then the two of them turned and looked at me, and the Second Mate asked what I wanted.

"I want to speak to you and the Old M—Captain, Sir," I answered.

"What is it, Jessop?" the Skipper inquired.

"I scarcely know how to put it, Sir," I said. "It's—it's about these—these things."

"What things? Speak out, man," he said.

"Well, Sir," I blurted out. "There's some dreadful thing or things come aboard this ship, since we left port."

I saw him give one quick glance at the Second Mate, and the Second looked back.

Then the Skipper replied.

"How do you mean, come aboard?" he asked.

"Out of the sea, Sir," I said. "I've seen them. So's Tammy, here."

"Ah!" he exclaimed, and it seemed to me, from his face, that he was understanding something better. "Out of the Sea!"

Again he looked at the Second Mate; but the Second was staring at me.

"Yes Sir," I said. "It's the *ship*. She's not safe! I've watched. I think I understand a bit; but there's a lot I don't."

I stopped. The Skipper had turned to the Second Mate. The Second nodded, gravely. Then I heard him mutter, in a low voice, and the Old Man replied; after which he turned to me again.

"Look here, Jessop," he said. "I'm going to talk straight to you. You strike me as being a cut above the ordinary shellback, and I think you've sense enough to hold your tongue."

"I've got my mate's ticket, Sir," I said, simply.

Behind me, I heard Tammy give a little start. He had not known about it until then.

The Skipper nodded.

"So much the better," he answered. "I may have to speak to you about that, later on."

He paused, and the Second Mate said something to him, in an undertone.

"Yes," he said, as though in reply to what the Second had been saying.

Then he spoke to me again.

"You've seen things come out of the sea, you say?" he questioned. "Now just tell me all you can remember, from the very beginning."

I set to, and told him everything in detail, commencing with the strange figure that had stepped aboard out of the sea, and continuing my yarn, up to the things that had happened in that very watch.

I stuck well to solid facts; and now and then he and the Second Mate would look at one another, and nod. At the end, he turned to me with an abrupt gesture.

"You still hold, then, that you saw a ship the other morning, when I sent you from the wheel?" he asked.

"Yes, Sir," I said. "I most certainly do."

"But you knew there wasn't any!" he said.

"Yes, Sir," I replied, in an apologetic tone. "There was; and, if you will let me, I believe that I can explain it a bit."

"Well," he said. "Go on."

Now that I knew he was willing to listen to me in a serious manner all my funk of telling him had gone, and I went ahead and told him my ideas about the mist, and the thing it seemed to have ushered, you know. I finished up, by telling him how Tammy had worried me to come and tell what I knew.

"He thought then, Sir," I went on, "that you might wish to put into the nearest port; but I told him that I didn't think you could, even if you wanted to."

"How's that?" he asked, profoundly interested.

"Well, Sir," I replied. "If we're unable to see other vessels, we shouldn't be able to see the land. You'd be piling the ship up, without ever seeing where you were putting her."

This view of the matter, affected the Old Man in an extraordinary manner; as it did, I believe, the Second Mate. And neither spoke for a moment. Then the Skipper burst out.

"By Gad! Jessop," he said. "If you're right, the Lord have mercy on us."

He thought for a couple of seconds. Then he spoke again, and I could see that he was pretty well twisted up:

"My God!… if you're right!"

The Second Mate spoke.

"The men mustn't know, Sir," he warned him. "It'd be a mess if they did!"

"Yes," said the Old Man.

He spoke to me.

"Remember that, Jessop," he said. "Whatever you do, don't go yarning about this, forrard."

"No, Sir," I replied.

"And you too, boy," said the Skipper. "Keep your tongue between your teeth. We're in a bad enough mess, without your making it worse. Do you hear?"

"Yes, Sir," answered Tammy.

The Old Man turned to me again.

"These things, or creatures that you say come out of the sea," he said.

"You've never seen them, except after nightfall?" he asked.

"No, Sir," I replied. "Never."

He turned to the Second Mate.

"So far as I can make out, Mr. Tulipson," he remarked, "the danger seems to be only at night."

"It's always been at night, Sir," the Second answered.

The Old Man nodded.

"Have you anything to propose, Mr. Tulipson?" he asked.

"Well, Sir," replied the Second Mate. "I think you ought to have her snugged down every night, before dark!"

He spoke with considerable emphasis. Then he glanced aloft, and jerked his head in the direction of the unfurled t'gallants.

"It's a damned good thing, Sir," he said, "that it didn't come on to blow any harder."

The Old Man nodded again.

"Yes," he remarked. "We shall have to do it; but God knows when we'll get home!"

"Better late than not at all," I heard the Second mutter, under his breath.

Out loud, he said:

"And the lights, Sir?"

"Yes," said the Old Man. "I will have lamps in the rigging every night, after dark."

"Very good, Sir," assented the Second. Then he turned to us.

"It's getting daylight, Jessop," he remarked, with a glance at the sky. "You'd better take Tammy with you, and shove those lamps back again into the locker."

"i, i, Sir," I said, and went down off the poop with Tammy.

XIII.
The Shadow in the Sea

When eight bells went, at four o'clock, and the other watch came on deck to relieve us, it had been broad daylight for some time. Before we went below, the Second Mate had the three t'gallants set; and now that it was light, we were pretty curious to have a look aloft, especially up the fore; and Tom, who had been up to overhaul the gear, was questioned a lot, when he came down, as to whether there were any signs of anything queer up there. But he told us there was nothing unusual to be seen.

At eight o'clock, when we came on deck for the eight to twelve watch, I saw the Sailmaker coming forrard along the deck, from the Second Mate's old berth. He had his rule in his hand, and I knew he had been measuring the poor beggars in there, for their burial outfit. From breakfast time until near noon, he worked, shaping out three canvas wrappers from some old sailcloth. Then, with the aid of the Second Mate and one of the hands, he brought out the three dead chaps on to the after hatch, and there sewed them up, with a few lumps of holy stone at their feet. He was just finishing when eight bells went, and I heard the Old Man tell the Second Mate to call all hands aft for the burial. This was done, and one of the gangways unshipped.

We had no decent grating big enough, so they had to get off one of the hatches, and use it instead. The wind had died away during the morning, and the sea was almost a calm—the ship lifting ever so slightly to an occasional glassy heave. The only sounds that struck on the ear were the soft, slow rustle and occasional shiver of the sails, and the continuous and monotonous creak, creak of the spars and gear at the gentle movements of the vessel. And it was in this solemn half-quietness that the Skipper read the burial service.

They had put the Dutchman first upon the hatch (I could tell him by his stumpiness), and when at last the Old Man gave the signal, the Second Mate tilted his end, and he slid off, and down into the dark.

"Poor old Dutchie," I heard one of the men say, and I fancy we all felt a bit like that.

Then they lifted Jacobs on to the hatch, and when he had gone, Jock. When Jock was lifted, a sort of sudden shiver ran through the crowd. He had been a favourite in a quiet way, and I know I felt, all at once, just a bit queer. I was standing by the rail, upon the after bollard, and Tammy was next to me; while

Plummer stood a little behind. As the Second Mate tilted the hatch for the last time, a little, hoarse chorus broke from the men:

"S'long, Jock! So long, Jock!"

And then, at the sudden plunge, they rushed to the side to see the last of him as he went downwards. Even the Second Mate was not able to resist this universal feeling, and he, too, peered over. From where I had been standing, I had been able to see the body take the water, and now, for a brief couple of seconds, I saw the white of the canvas, blurred by the blue of the water, dwindle and dwindle in the extreme depth. Abruptly, as I stared, it disappeared—too abruptly, it seemed to me.

"Gone!" I heard several voices say, and then our watch began to go slowly forrard, while one or two of the other, started to replace the hatch.

Tammy pointed, and nudged me.

"See, Jessop," he said. "What is it?"

"What?" I asked.

"That queer shadow," he replied. "Look!"

And then I saw what he meant. It was something big and shadowy, that appeared to be growing clearer. It occupied the exact place—so it seemed to me —in which Jock had disappeared.

"Look at it!" said Tammy, again. "It's getting bigger!"

He was pretty excited, and so was I.

I was peering down. The thing seemed to be rising out of the depths. It was taking shape. As I realized what the shape was, a queer, cold funk took me.

"See," said Tammy. "It's just like the shadow of a ship!"

And it was. The shadow of a ship rising out of the unexplored immensity beneath our keel. Plummer, who had not yet gone forrard, caught Tammy's last remark, and glanced over.

"What's 'e mean?" he asked.

"That!" replied Tammy, and pointed.

I jabbed my elbow into his ribs; but it was too late. Plummer had seen. Curiously enough, though, he seemed to think nothing of it.

"That ain't nothin', 'cept ther shadder er ther ship," he said.

Tammy, after my hint, let it go at that. But when Plummer had gone forrard with the others, I told him not to go telling everything round the decks, like that.

"We've got to be thundering careful!" I remarked. "You know what the Old Man said, last watch!"

"Yes," said Tammy. "I wasn't thinking; I'll be careful next time."

A little way from me the Second Mate was still staring down into the water. I turned, and spoke to him.

"What do you make it out to be, Sir?" I asked.

"God knows!" he said, with a quick glance round to see whether any of the men were about.

He got down from the rail, and turned to go up on to the poop. At the top of the ladder, he leant over the break.

"You may as well ship that gangway, you two," he told us. "And mind, Jessop, keep your mouth shut about this."

"i, i, Sir," I answered.

"And you too, youngster!" he added and went aft along the poop.

Tammy and I were busy with the gangway when the Second came back. He had brought the Skipper.

"Right under the gangway, Sir" I heard the Second say, and he pointed down into the water.

For a little while, the Old Man stared. Then I heard him speak.

"I don't see anything," he said.

At that, the Second Mate bent more forward and peered down. So did I; but the thing, whatever it was, had gone completely.

"It's gone, Sir," said the Second. "It was there right enough when I came for you."

About a minute later, having finished shipping the gangway, I was going forrard, when the Second's voice called me back

"Tell the Captain what it was you saw just now," he said, in a low voice.

"I can't say exactly, Sir," I replied. "But it seemed to me like the shadow of a ship, rising up through the water."

"There, Sir," remarked the Second Mate to the Old Man. "Just what I told you."

The Skipper stared at me.

"You're quite sure?" he asked.

"Yes, Sir," I answered. "Tammy saw it, too."

I waited a minute. Then they turned to go aft. The Second was saying something.

"Can I go, Sir?" I asked.

"Yes, that will do, Jessop," he said, over his shoulder. But the Old Man came back to the break, and spoke to me.

"Remember, not a word of this forrard!" he said.

"No Sir," I replied, and he went back to the Second Mate; while I walked forrard to the fo'cas'le to get something to eat.

"Your whack's in the kettle, Jessop," said Tom, as I stepped in over the washboard. "An' I got your lime-juice in a pannikin."

"Thanks," I said, and sat down.

As I stowed away my grub, I took no notice of the chatter of the others. I was too stuffed with my own thoughts. That shadow of a vessel rising, you know, out of the profound deeps, had impressed me tremendously. It had not been imagination. Three of us had seen it—really four; for Plummer distinctly saw it; though he failed to recognise it as anything extraordinary.

As you can understand, I thought a lot about this shadow of a vessel. But, I am sure, for a time, my ideas must just have gone in an everlasting, blind circle. And then I got another thought; for I got thinking of the figures I had seen aloft in the early morning; and I began to imagine fresh things. You see, that first thing that had come up over the side, had come *out of the sea.* And it had gone back. And now there was this shadow vessel-thing—ghost-ship I called it. It was a damned good name, too. And the dark, noiseless men ... I thought a lot on these lines. Unconsciously, I put a question to myself, aloud:

"Were they the crew?"

"Eh?" said Jaskett, who was on the next chest.

I took hold of myself, as it were, and glanced at him, in an apparently careless manner.

"Did I speak?" I asked.

"Yes, mate," he replied, eyeing me, curiously. "Yer said sumthin' about a crew."

"I must have been dreaming," I said; and rose up to put away my plate.

XIV.
THE GHOST SHIPS

At four o'clock, when again we went on deck, the Second Mate told me to go on with a paunch mat I was making; while Tammy, he sent to get out his sinnet. I had the mat slug on the fore side of the mainmast, between it and the after end of the house; and, in a few minutes, Tammy brought his sinnet and yarns to the mast, and made fast to one of the pins.

"What do you think it was, Jessop?" he asked, abruptly, after a short silence.

I looked at him.

"What do you think?" I replied.

"I don't know what to think," he said. "But I've a feeling that it's something to do with all the rest," and he indicated aloft, with his head.

"I've been thinking, too," I remarked.

"That it is?" he inquired.

"Yes," I answered, and told him how the idea had come to me at my dinner, that the strange men-shadows which came aboard, might come from that indistinct vessel we had seen down in the sea.

"Good Lord!" he exclaimed, as he got my meaning. And then for a little, he stood and thought.

"That's where they live, you mean?" he said, at last, and paused again.

"Well," I replied. "It can't be the sort of existence *we* should call life."

He nodded, doubtfully.

"No," he said, and was silent again.

Presently, he put out an idea that had come to him.

"You *think*, then, that that—vessel has been with us for some time, if we'd only known?" he asked.

"All along," I replied. "I mean ever since these things started."

"Supposing there are others," he said, suddenly.

I looked at him.

"If there are," I said. "You can pray to God that they won't stumble across us. It strikes me that whether they're ghosts, or not ghosts, they're blood-gutted pirates.

"It seems horrible," he said solemnly, "to be talking seriously like this, about—you know, about such things."

"I've tried to stop thinking that way," I told him. "I've felt I should go cracked, if I didn't. There's damned queer things happen at sea, I know; but this isn't one of them."

"It seems so strange and unreal, one moment, doesn't it?" he said. "And the next, you *know* it's really true, and you can't understand why you didn't always know. And yet they'd never believe, if you told them ashore about it."

"They'd believe, if they'd been in this packet in the middle watch this morning," I said.

"Besides," I went on. "They don't understand. We didn't ... I shall always feel different now, when I read that some packet hasn't been heard of."

Tammy stared at me.

"I've heard some of the old shellbacks talking about things," he said.

"But I never took them really seriously."

"Well," I said. "I guess we'll have to take this seriously. I wish to God we were home!"

"My God! so do I," he said.

For a good while after that, we both worked on in silence; but, presently, he went off on another tack.

"Do you think we'll really shorten her down every night before it gets dark?" he asked.

"Certainly," I replied. "They'll never get the men to go aloft at night, after what's happened."

"But, but—supposing they *ordered* us aloft—" he began.

"Would you go?" I interrupted.

"No!" he said, emphatically. "I'd jolly well be put in irons first!"

"That settles it, then," I replied. "You wouldn't go, nor would anyone else."

At this moment the Second Mate came along.

"Shove that mat and that sinnet away, you two," he said. "Then get your brooms and clear up."

"i, i, Sir," we said, and he went on forrard.

"Jump on the house, Tammy," I said. "And let go the other end of this rope, will you?"

"Right" he said, and did as I had asked him. When he came back, I got him to give me a hand to roll up the mat, which was a very large one.

"I'll finish stopping it," I said. "You go and put your sinnet away."

"Wait a minute," he replied, and gathered up a double handful of shakins from the deck, under where I had been working. Then he ran to the side.

"Here!" I said. "Don't go dumping those. They'll only float, and the Second Mate or the Skipper will be sure to spot them."

"Come here, Jessop!" he interrupted, in a low voice, and taking no notice of what I had been saying.

I got up off the hatch, where I was kneeling. He was staring over the side.

"What's up?" I asked.

"For God's sake, hurry!" he said, and I ran, and jumped on to the spar, alongside of him.

"Look!" he said, and pointed with a handful of shakins, right down, directly beneath us.

Some of the shakins dropped from his hand, and blurred the water, momentarily, so that I could not see. Then, as the ripples cleared away, I saw what he meant.

"Two of them!" he said, in a voice that was scarcely above a whisper. "And there's another out there," and he pointed again with the handful of shakins.

"There's another a little further aft," I muttered.

"Where?—where?" he asked.

"There," I said, and pointed.

"That's four," he whispered. "Four of them!"

I said nothing; but continued to stare. They appeared to me to be a great way down in the sea, and quite motionless. Yet, though their outlines were somewhat blurred and indistinct, there was no mistaking that they were very like exact, though shadowy, representations of vessels. For some minutes we watched them, without speaking. At last Tammy spoke.

"They're real, right enough," he said, in a low voice.

"I don't know," I answered.

"I mean we weren't mistaken this morning," he said.

"No," I replied. "I never thought we were."

Away forrard, I heard the Second Mate, returning aft. He came nearer, and saw us.

"What's up now, you two?" he called, sharply. "This isn't clearing up!"

I put out my hand to warn him not to shout, and draw the attention of the rest of the men.

He took several steps towards me.

"What is it? what is it?" he said, with a certain irritability; but in a lower voice.

"You'd better take a look over the side, Sir," I replied.

My tone must have given him an inkling that we had discovered something fresh; for, at my words, he made one spring, and stood on the spar, alongside of me.

"Look, Sir," said Tammy. "There's four of them."

The Second Mate glanced down, saw something and bent sharply forward.

"My God!" I heard him mutter, under his breath.

After that, for some half-minute, he stared, without a word.

"There are two more out there, Sir," I told him, and indicated the place with my finger.

It was a little time before he managed to locate these and when he did, he gave them only a short glance. Then he got down off the spar, and spoke to us.

"Come down off there," he said, quickly. "Get your brooms and clear up. Don't say a word!—It may be nothing."

He appeared to add that last bit, as an afterthought, and we both knew it meant nothing. Then he turned and went swiftly aft.

"I expect he's gone to tell the Old Man," Tammy remarked, as we went forrard, carrying the mat and his sinnet.

"H'm," I said, scarcely noticing what he was saying; for I was full of the thought of those four shadowy craft, waiting quietly down there.

We got our brooms, and went aft. On the way, the Second Mate and the Skipper passed us. They went forrard too by the fore brace, and got up on the spar. I saw the Second point up at the brace and he appeared to be saying something about the gear. I guessed that this was done purposely, to act as a blind, should any of the other men be looking. Then the Old Man glanced down over the side, in a casual sort of manner; so did the Second Mate. A minute or two later, they came aft, and went back, up on to the poop. I caught a glimpse of the Skipper's face as he passed me, on his return. He struck me as looking worried—bewildered, perhaps, would be a better word.

Both Tammy and I were tremendously keen to have another look; but when at last we got a chance, the sky reflected so much on the water, we could see nothing below.

We had just finished sweeping up when four bells went, and we cleared below for tea. Some of the men got chatting while they were grubbing.

"I 'ave 'eard," remarked Quoin, "as we're goin' ter shorten 'er down afore dark."

"Eh?" said old Jaskett, over his pannikin of tea.

Quoin repeated his remark.

"'oo says so?" inquired Plummer.

"I 'eard it from ther Doc," answered Quoin, "'e got it from ther Stooard."

"'ow would 'ee know?" asked Plummer.

"I dunno," said Quoin. "I 'spect 'e's 'eard 'em talkin' 'bout it arft."

Plummer turned to me.

"'ave you 'eard anythin', Jessop?" he inquired.

"What, about shortening down?" I replied.

"Yes," he said. "Weren't ther Old Man talkin' ter yer, up on ther poop this mornin'?"

"Yes," I answered. "He said something to the Second Mate about shortening down; but it wasn't to me."

"They are!" said Quoin, "'aven't I just said so?"

At that instant, one of the chaps in the other watch, poked his head in through the starboard doorway.

"All hands shorten sail!" he sung out; at the same moment the Mate's whistle came sharp along the decks.

Plummer stood up, and reached for his cap.

"Well," he said. "It's evydent they ain't goin' ter lose no more of us!"

Then we went out on deck.

It was a dead calm; but all the same, we furled the three royals, and then the three t'gallants. After that, we hauled up the main and foresail, and stowed them. The crossjack, of course, had been furled some time, with the wind being plumb aft.

It was while we were up at the foresail, that the sun went over the edge of the horizon. We had finished stowing the sail, out upon the yard, and I was waiting for the others to clear in, and let me get off the foot-rope. Thus it happened that having nothing to do for nearly a minute, I stood watching the sun set, and so saw something that otherwise I should, most probably, have missed. The sun had dipped nearly halfway below the horizon, and was showing like a great, red dome of dull fire. Abruptly, far away on the starboard bow, a faint mist drove up out of the sea. It spread across the face of the sun, so that its light shone now as though it came through a dim haze of smoke. Quickly, this mist or haze grew thicker; but, at the same time, separating and taking strange shapes, so that the red of the sun struck through ruddily between them. Then, as I watched, the weird mistiness collected and shaped and rose into three towers. These became more definite, and there was something elongated beneath them. The shaping and forming continued, and almost suddenly I saw that the thing had taken on the shape of a great ship. Directly afterwards, I saw that it was moving. It had been broadside on to the sun. Now it was swinging. The bows came round with a stately movement, until the three masts bore in a line. It was heading directly towards us. It grew larger; but yet less distinct. Astern of it, I saw now that the sun had sunk to a mere line of light. Then, in the gathering dusk it seemed to me that the ship was sinking back into the ocean. The sun went beneath the sea, and the thing I had seen became merged, as it were, into the monotonous grayness of the coming night.

A voice came to me from the rigging. It was the Second Mate's. He had been up to give us a hand.

"Now then, Jessop," he was saying. "Come along! come along!"

I turned quickly, and realized that the fellows were nearly all off the yard.

"i, i, Sir," I muttered, and slid in along the foot-rope, and went down on deck. I felt fresh dazed and frightened.

A little later, eight bells went, and, after roll call, I cleared up, on to the poop, to relieve the wheel. For a while as I stood at the wheel my mind seemed blank, and incapable of receiving impressions. This sensation went, after a time, and I realized that there was a great stillness over the sea. There was absolutely no wind, and even the everlasting creak, creak of the gear seemed to ease off at times.

At the wheel there was nothing whatever to do. I might just as well have been forrard, smoking in the fo'cas'le. Down on the main-deck, I could see the loom of the lanterns that had been lashed up to the sherpoles in the fore and main rigging. Yet they showed less than they might, owing to the fact that they had been shaded on their after sides, so as not to blind the officer of the watch more than need be.

The night had come down strangely dark, and yet of the dark and the stillness and the lanterns, I was only conscious in occasional flashes of comprehension. For, now that my mind was working, I was thinking chiefly of that queer, vast phantom of mist, I had seen rise from the sea, and take shape.

I kept staring into the night, towards the West, and then all round me; for, naturally, the memory predominated that she had been coming towards us when the darkness came, and it was a pretty disquieting sort of thing to think about. I had such a horrible feeling that something beastly was going to happen any minute.

Yet, two bells came and went, and still all was quiet—strangely quiet, it seemed to me. And, of course, besides the queer, misty vessel I had seen in the West I was all the time remembering the four shadowy craft lying down in the sea, under our port side. Every time I remembered them, I felt thankful for the lanterns round the maindeck, and I wondered why none had been put in the mizzen rigging. I wished to goodness that they had, and made up my mind I would speak to the Second Mate about it, next time he came aft. At the time, he was leaning over the rail across the break of the poop. He was not smoking, as I could tell; for had he been, I should have seen the glow of his pipe, now and then. It was plain to me that he was uneasy. Three times already he had been down on to the maindeck, prowling about. I guessed that he had been to look down into the sea, for any signs of those four grim craft. I wondered whether they would be visible at night.

Suddenly, the time-keeper struck three bells, and the deeper notes of the bell forrard, answered them. I gave a start. It seemed to me that they had been struck close to my elbow. There was something unaccountably strange in the air that night. Then, even as the Second Mate answered the lookout's "All's well," there came the sharp whir and rattle of running gear, on the port side of the mainmast. Simultaneously, there was the shrieking of a parrel, up the main; and I knew that someone, or something, had let go the main-topsail haul-yards. From aloft there came the sound of something parting; then the crash of the yard as it ceased falling.

The Second Mate shouted out something unintelligible, and jumped for the ladder. From the maindeck there came the sound of running feet, and the voices of the watch, shouting. Then I caught the Skipper's voice; he must have run out on deck, through the Saloon doorway.

"Get some more lamps! Get some more lamps!" he was singing out. Then he swore.

He sung out something further. I caught the last two words.

"...carried away," they sounded like.

"No, Sir," shouted the Second Mate. "I don't think so."

A minute of some confusion followed; and then came the click of pawls. I could tell that they had taken the haulyards to the after capstan. Odd words floated up to me.

"...all this water?" I heard in the Old Man's voice. He appeared to be asking a question.

"Can't say, Sir," came the Second Mate's.

There was a period of time, filled only by the clicking of the pawls and the sounds of the creaking parrel and the running gear. Then the Second Mate's voice came again.

"Seems all right, Sir," I heard him say.

I never heard the Old Man's reply; for in the same moment, there came to me a chill of cold breath at my back. I turned sharply, and saw something peering over the taffrail. It had eyes that reflected the binnacle light, weirdly, with a frightful, tigerish gleam; but beyond that, I could see nothing with any distinctness. For the moment, I just stared. I seemed frozen. It was so close. Then movement came to me, and I jumped to the binnacle and snatched out the lamp. I twitched round, and shone the light towards it. The thing, whatever it was, had come more forward over the rail; but now, before the light, it recoiled with a queer, horrible litheness. It slid back, and down, and so out of sight. I have only a confused notion of a wet glistening Something, and two vile eyes. Then I was running, crazy, towards the break of the poop. I sprang down the ladder, and missed my footing, and landed on my stern, at the bottom. In my left hand I held the still burning binnacle lamp. The men were putting away the capstan-bars; but at my abrupt appearance, and the yell I gave out at falling, one or two of them fairly ran backwards a short distance, in sheer funk, before they realized what it was.

From somewhere further forrard, the Old Man and the Second Mate came running aft.

"What the devil's up now?" sung out the Second, stopping and bending to stare at me. "What's to do, that you're away from the wheel?"

I stood up and tried to answer him; but I was so shaken that I could only stammer.

"I—I—there—" I stuttered.

"Damnation!" shouted the Second Mate, angrily. "Get back to the wheel!"

I hesitated, and tried to explain.

"Do you damned well hear me?" he sung out.

"Yes, Sir; but—" I began.

"Get up on to the poop, Jessop!" he said.

I went. I meant to explain, when he came up. At the top of the ladder, I stopped. I was not going back alone to that wheel. Down below, I heard the Old Man speaking.

"What on earth is it now, Mr. Tulipson?" he was saying.

The Second Mate made no immediate reply; but turned to the men, who were evidently crowding near.

"That will do, men!" he said, somewhat sharply.

I heard the watch start to go forrard. There came a mutter of talk from them. Then the Second Mate answered the Old Man. He could not have known that I was near enough to overhear him.

"It's Jessop, Sir. He must have seen something; but we mustn't frighten the crowd more than need be."

"No," said the Skipper's voice.

They turned and came up the ladder, and I ran back a few steps, as far as the skylight. I heard the Old Man speak as they came up.

"How is it there are no lamps, Mr. Tulipson?" he said, in a surprised tone.

"I thought there would be no need up here, Sir," the Second Mate replied. Then he added something about saving oil.

"Better have them, I think," I heard the Skipper say.

"Very good, Sir," answered the Second, and sung out to the timekeeper to bring up a couple of lamps.

Then the two of them walked aft, to where I stood by the skylight.

"What are you doing, away from the wheel?" asked the Old Man, in a stern voice.

I had collected my wits somewhat by now.

"I won't go, Sir, till there's a light," I said.

The Skipper stamped his foot, angrily; but the Second Mate stepped forward.

"Come! Come, Jessop!" he exclaimed. "This won't do, you know! You'd better get back to the wheel without further bother."

"Wait a minute," said the Skipper, at this juncture. "What objection have you to going back to the wheel?" he asked.

"I saw something," I said. "It was climbing over the taffrail, Sir—"

"Ah!" he said, interrupting me with a quick gesture. Then, abruptly:

"Sit down! sit down; you're all in a shake, man."

I flopped down on to the skylight seat. I was, as he had said, all in a shake, and the binnacle lamp was wobbling in my hand, so that the light from it went dancing here and there across the deck.

"Now," he went on. "Just tell us what you saw."

I told them, at length, and while I was doing so, the time-keeper brought up the lights and lashed one up on the sheerpole in each rigging.

"Shove one under the spanker boom," the Old Man sung out, as the boy finished lashing up the other two. "Be smart now."

"i, i, Sir," said the 'prentices, and hurried off.

"Now then," remarked the Skipper when this had been done "You needn't be afraid to go back to the wheel. There's a light over the stern, and the Second Mate or myself will be up here all the time."

I stood up.

"Thank you, Sir," I said, and went aft. I replaced my lamp in the binnacle, and took hold of the wheel; yet, time and again, I glanced behind and I was very thankful when, a few minutes later, four bells went, and I was relieved.

Though the rest of the chaps were forrard in the fo'cas'le, I did not go there. I shirked being questioned about my sudden appearance at the foot of the poop ladder; and so I lit my pipe and wandered about the maindeck. I did not feel particularly nervous, as there were now two lanterns in each rigging, and a couple standing upon each of the spare top-masts under the bulwarks.

Yet, a little after five bells, it seemed to me that I saw a shadowy face peer over the rail, a little abaft the fore lanyards. I snatched up one of the lanterns from off the spar, and flashed the light towards it, whereupon there was nothing. Only, on my mind, more than my sight, I fancy, a queer knowledge remained of wet, peery eyes. Afterwards, when I thought about them, I felt extra beastly. I knew then how brutal they had been … Inscrutable, you know. Once more in that same watch I had a somewhat similar experience, only in this instance it had vanished even before I had time to reach a light. And then came eight bells, and our watch below.

XV.
The Great Ghost Ship

When we were called again, at a quarter to four, the man who roused us out, had some queer information.

"Toppin's gone—clean vanished!" he told us, as we began to turn out. "I never was in such a damned, hair-raisin' hooker as this here. It ain't safe to go about the bloomin' decks."

"'oo's gone?" asked Plummer, sitting up suddenly and throwing his legs over his bunk-board.

"Toppin, one of the 'prenticess," replied the man. "We've been huntin' all over the bloomin' show. We're still at it—but we'll never find him," he ended, with a sort of gloomy assurance.

"Oh, I dunno," said Quoin. "P'raps 'e's snoozin' somewheres 'bout."

"Not him," replied the man. "I tell you we've turned everythin' upside down. He's not aboard the bloomin' ship.

"Where was he when they last saw him?" I asked.

"Someone must know something, you know!"

"Keepin' time up on the poop," he replied. "The Old Man's nearly shook the life out of the Mate and the chap at the wheel. And they say they don't know nothin'."

"How do you mean?" I inquired. "How do you mean, nothing?"

"Well," he answered. "The youngster was there one minute, and then the next thing they knew, he'd gone. They've both sworn black an' blue that there wasn't a whisper. He's just disappeared off of the face of the bloomin' earth."

I got down on to my chest, and reached for my boots.

Before I could speak again, the man was saying something fresh.

"See here, mates," he went on. "If things is goin' on like this, I'd like to know where you an' me'll be befor' long!"

"We'll be in 'ell," said Plummer.

"I dunno as I like to think 'bout it," said Quoin.

"We'll have to think about it!" replied the man. "We've got to think a bloomin' lot about it. I've talked to our side, an' they're game."

"Game for what?" I asked.

"To go an' talk straight to the bloomin' Capting," he said, wagging his finger at me. "It's make tracks for the nearest bloomin' port, an' don't you make no bloomin' mistake."

I opened my mouth to tell him that the probability was we should not be able to make it, even if he could get the Old Man to see the matter from his point of view. Then I remembered that the chap had no idea of the things I had seen, and *thought out*; so, instead, I said:

"Supposing he won't?"

"Then we'll have to bloomin' well make him," he replied.

"And when you got there," I said. "What then? You'd be jolly well locked up for mutiny."

"I'd sooner be locked up," he said. "It don't kill you!"

There was a murmur of agreement from the others, and then a moment of silence, in which, I know, the men were thinking.

Jaskett's voice broke into it.

"I never thought at first as she was 'aunted—" he commenced; but Plummer cut in across his speech.

"We mustn't 'urt any one, yer know," he said. "That'd mean 'angin', an' they ain't been er bad crowd."

"No," assented everyone, including the chap who had come to call us.

"All the same," he added. "It's got to be up hellum, an' shove her into the nearest bloomin' port."

"Yes," said everyone, and then eight bells went, and we cleared out on deck.

Presently, after roll-call—in which there had come a queer, awkward little pause at Toppin's name—Tammy came over to me. The rest of the men had gone forrard, and I guessed they were talking over mad plans for forcing the Skipper's hand, and making him put into port—poor beggars!

I was leaning over the port rail, by the fore brace-lock, staring down into the sea, when Tammy came to me. For perhaps a minute he said nothing. When at last he spoke, it was to say that the shadow vessels had not been there since daylight.

"What?" I said, in some surprise. "How do you know?"

"I woke up when they were searching for Toppin," he replied. "I've not been asleep since. I came here, right away." He began to say something further; but stopped short.

"Yes," I said encouragingly.

"I didn't know—" he began, and broke off. He caught my arm. "Oh, Jessop!" he exclaimed. "What's going to be the end of it all? Surely something can be done?"

I said nothing. I had a desperate feeling that there was very little we could do to help ourselves.

"Can't we do something?" he asked, and shook my arm. "Anything's better than *this*! We're being *murdered!*"

Still, I said nothing; but stared moodily down into the water. I could plan nothing; though I would get mad, feverish fits of thinking.

"Do you hear?" he said. He was almost crying.

"Yes, Tammy," I replied. "But I don't know! I *don't* know!"

"You don't know!" he exclaimed. "You don't know! Do you mean we're just to give in, and be murdered, one after another?"

"We've done all we can," I replied. "I don't know what else we can do, unless we go below and lock ourselves in, every night."

"That would be better than this," he said. "There'll be no one to go below, or anything else, soon!"

"But what if it came on to blow?" I asked. "We'd be having the sticks blown out of her."

"What if it came on to blow *now*?" he returned. "No one would go aloft, if it were dark, you said, yourself! Besides, we could shorten her *right* down, first. I tell you, in a few days there won't be a chap alive aboard this packet unless they jolly well do something!"

"Don't shout," I warned him. "You'll have the Old Man hearing you." But the young beggar was wound up, and would take no notice.

"I will shout," he replied. "I want the Old Man to hear. I've a good mind to go up and tell him."

He started on a fresh tack.

"Why don't the men do something?" he began. "They ought to damn well make the Old Man put us into port! They ought—"

"For goodness sake, shut up, you little fool!" I said. "What's the good of talking a lot of damned rot like that? You'll be getting yourself into trouble."

"I don't care," he replied. "I'm not going to be murdered!"

"Look here," I said. "I told you before, that we shouldn't be able to see the land, even if we made it."

"You've no proof," he answered. "It's only your idea."

"Well," I replied. "Proof, or no proof, the Skipper would only pile her up, if he tried to make the land, with things as they are now."

"Let him pile her up," he answered. "Let him jolly well pile her up! That would be better than staying out here to be pulled overboard, or chucked down from aloft!"

"Look here, Tammy—" I began; but just then the Second Mate sung out for him, and he had to go. When he came back, I had started to walk to and from, across the fore side of the mainmast. He joined me, and after a minute, he started his wild talk again.

"Look here, Tammy," I said, once more. "It's no use your talking like you've been doing. Things are as they are, and it's no one's fault, and nobody can help it. If you want to talk sensibly, I'll listen; if not, then go and gas to someone else."

With that, I returned to the port side, and got up on the spar, again, intending to sit on the pinrail and have a bit of a talk with him. Before sitting down I glanced over, into the sea. The action had been almost mechanical; yet, after a few instants, I was in a state of the most intense excitement, and without withdrawing my gaze, I reached out and caught Tammy's arm to attract his attention.

"My God!" I muttered. "Look!"

"What is it?" he asked, and bent over the rail, beside me. And this is what we saw: a little distance below the surface there lay a pale-colored, slightly-domed disc. It seemed only a few feet down. Below it, we saw quite clearly, after a few moment's staring, the shadow of a royal-yard, and, deeper, the gear and standing-rigging of a great mast. Far down among the shadows I thought, presently, that I could make out the immense, indefinite stretch of vast decks.

"My God!" whispered Tammy, and shut up. But presently, he gave out a short exclamation, as though an idea had come to him; and got down off the spar, and ran forrard on to the fo'cas'le head. He came running back, after a short look into the sea, to tell me that there was the truck of another great mast coming up there, a bit off the bow, to within a few feet of the surface of the sea.

In the meantime, you know, I had been staring like mad down through the water at the huge, shadowy mast just below me. I had traced out bit by bit, until now I could clearly see the jackstay, running along the top of the royal mast; and, you know, the royal itself was *set*.

But, you know, what was getting at me more than anything, was a feeling that there was movement down in the water there, among the rigging. I *thought* I could actually see, at times, things moving and glinting faintly and rapidly to and fro in the gear. And once, I was practically certain that something was on the royal-yard, moving in to the mast; as though, you know, it might have come up the leech of the sail. And this way, I got a beastly feeling that there were things swarming down there.

Unconsciously, I must have leant further and further out over the side, staring; and suddenly—good Lord! how I yelled—I overbalanced. I made a sweeping grab, and caught the fore brace, and with that, I was back in a moment upon the spar. In the same second, almost, it seemed to me that the surface of the water above the submerged truck was broken, and I am sure *now, I* saw something a moment in the air against the ship's side—a sort of shadow in the air; though I did not realize it at the time. Anyway, the next instant, Tammy gave out an awful scream, and was head downwards over the rail, in a second. I had an idea *then* that he was jumping overboard. I collared him by the waist of his britchers, and one knee, and then I had him down on the deck, and sat plump on him; for he was struggling and shouting all the time, and I was so breathless and shaken and gone to mush, I could not have trusted my hands to hold him. You see, I never thought *then* it was anything but some influence at work on him; and that he was trying to get loose to go over the side. But I know *now* that I saw the shadow-man that had him. Only, at the time, I was so mixed up, and with the one idea in my head, I was not really able to notice anything, properly. But, afterwards, I comprehended a bit (you can understand, can't you?) what I had seen at the time without taking in.

And even now looking back, I know that the shadow was only like a faint-seen grayness in the daylight, against the whiteness of the decks, clinging against Tammy.

And there was I, all breathless and sweating, and quivery with my own tumble, sitting on the little screeching beggar, and he fighting like a mad thing; so that I thought I should never hold him.

And then I heard the Second Mate shouting and there came running feet along the deck. Then many hands were pulling and hauling, to get me off him.

"Bloody cowyard!" sung out someone.

"Hold him! Hold him!" I shouted. "He'll be overboard!"

At that, they seemed to understand that I was not ill-treating the youngster; for they stopped manhandling me, and allowed me to rise; while two of them took hold of Tammy, and kept him safe.

"What's the matter with him?" the Second Mate was singing out. "What's happened?"

"He's gone off his head, I think," I said.

"What?" asked the Second Mate. But before I could answer him, Tammy ceased suddenly to struggle, and flopped down upon the deck.

"'e's fainted," said Plummer, with some sympathy. He looked at me, with a puzzled, suspicious air. "What's 'appened? What's 'e been doin'?"

"Take him aft into the berth!" ordered the Second Mate, a bit abruptly. It struck me that he wished to prevent questions. He must have tumbled to the fact that we had seen something, about which it would be better not to tell the crowd.

Plummer stooped to lift the boy.

"No," said the Second Mate. "Not you, Plummer. Jessop, you take him." He turned to the rest of the men. "That will do," he told them and they went forrard, muttering a little.

I lifted the boy, and carried him aft.

"No need to take him into the berth," said the Second Mate. "Put him down on the after hatch. I've sent the other lad for some brandy."

Then the brandy came, we dosed Tammy and soon brought him round. He sat up, with a somewhat dazed air. Otherwise, he seemed quiet and sane enough.

"What's up?" he asked. He caught sight of the Second Mate. "Have I been ill, Sir?" he exclaimed.

"You're right enough now, youngster," said the Second Mate. "You've been a bit off. You'd better go and lie down for a bit."

"I'm all right now, Sir," replied Tammy. "I don't think—"

"You do as you're told!" interrupted the Second. "Don't always have to be told twice! If I want you, I'll send for you."

Tammy stood up, and made his way, in rather an unsteady fashion, into the berth. I fancy he was glad enough to lie down.

"Now then, Jessop," exclaimed the Second Mate, turning to me. "What's been the cause of all this? Out with it now, smart!"

I commenced to tell him; but, almost directly, he put up his hand.

"Hold on a minute," he said. "There's the breeze!"

He jumped up the port ladder, and sung out to the chap at the wheel. Then down again.

"Starboard fore brace," he sung out. He turned to me. "You'll have to finish telling me afterwards," he said.

"i, i, Sir," I replied, and went to join the other chaps at the braces.

As soon as we were braced sharp up on the port tack, he sent some of the watch up to loose the sails. Then he sung out for me.

"Go on with your yarn now, Jessop," he said.

I told him about the great shadow vessel, and I said something about Tammy—I mean about my not being sure *now* whether he *had* tried to jump overboard. Because, you see, I began to realize that I had seen the shadow; and I remembered the stirring of the water above the submerged truck. But the Second did not wait, of course, for any theories, but was away, like a shot, to see for himself. He ran to the side, and looked down. I followed, and stood beside him; yet, now that the surface of the water was blurred by the wind, we could see nothing.

"It's no good," he remarked, after a minute. "You'd better get away from the rail before any of the others see you. Just be taking those halyards aft to the capstan."

From then, until eight bells, we were hard at work getting the sail upon her, and when at last eight bells went, I made haste to swallow my breakfast, and get a sleep.

At midday, when we went on deck for the afternoon watch, I ran to the side; but there was no sign of the great shadow ship. All that watch, the Second Mate kept me working at my paunch mat, and Tammy he put on to his sinnet, telling me to keep an eye on the youngster. But the boy was right enough; as I scarcely doubted now, you know; though—a most unusual thing—he hardly opened his lips the whole afternoon. Then at four o'clock, we went below for tea.

At four bells, when we came on deck again, I found that the light breeze, which had kept us going during the day, had dropped, and we were only just moving. The sun was low down, and the sky clear. Once or twice, as I glanced across to the horizon, it seemed to me that I caught again that odd quiver in the air that had preceded the coming of the mist; and, indeed on two separate occasions, I saw a thin whisp of haze drive up, apparently out of the sea. This was at some little distance on our port beam; otherwise, all was quiet and peaceful; and though I stared into the water, I could make out no vestige of that great shadow ship, down in the sea.

It was some little time after six bells that the order came for all hands to shorten sail for the night. We took in the royals and t'gallants, and then the three courses. It was shortly after this, that a rumour went round the ship that there was to be no lookout that night after eight o'clock. This naturally created a good deal of talk among the men; especially as the yarn went that the fo'cas'le doors were to be shut and fastened as soon as it was dark, and that no one was to be allowed on deck.

"'oo's goin' ter take ther wheel?" I heard Plummer ask.

"I s'pose they'll 'ave us take 'em as usual," replied one of the men. "One of ther officers is bound ter be on ther poop; so we'll 'ave company."

Apart from these remarks, there was a general opinion that—if it were true—it was a sensible act on the part of the Skipper. As one of the men said:

"It ain't likely that there'll be any of us missin' in ther mornin', if we stays in our bunks all ther blessed night."

And soon after this, eight bells went.

XVI.
The Ghost Pirates

At the moment when eight bells actually went, I was in the fo'cas'le, talking to four of the other watch. Suddenly, away aft, I heard shouting, and then on the deck overhead, came the loud thudding of someone pomping with a capstan-bar. Straightway, I turned and made a run for the port doorway, along with the four other men. We rushed out through the doorway on to the deck. It was getting dusk; but that did not hide from me a terrible and extraordinary sight. All along the port rail there was a queer, undulating grayness, that moved downwards inboard, and spread over the decks. As I looked, I found that I saw more clearly, in a most extraordinary way. And, suddenly, all the moving grayness resolved into hundreds of strange men. In the half-light, they looked unreal and impossible, as though there had come upon us the inhabitants of some fantastic dream-world. My God! I thought I was mad. They swarmed in upon us in a great wave of murderous, living shadows. From some of the men who must have been going aft for roll-call, there rose into the evening air a loud, awful shouting.

"Aloft!" yelled someone; but, as I looked aloft, I saw that the horrible things were swarming there in scores and scores.

"Jesus Christ—!" shrieked a man's voice, cut short, and my glance dropped from aloft, to find two of the men who had come out from the fo'cas'le with me, rolling upon the deck. They were two indistinguishable masses that writhed here and there across the planks. The brutes fairly covered them. From them, came muffled little shrieks and gasps; and there I stood, and with me were the other two men. A man darted past us into the fo'cas'le, with two gray men on his back, and I heard them kill him. The two men by me, ran suddenly across the fore hatch, and up the starboard ladder on to the fo'cas'le head. Yet, almost in the same instant, I saw several of the gray men disappear up the other ladder. From the fo'cas'le head above, I heard the two men commence to shout, and this died away into a loud scuffling. At that, I turned to see whether I could get away. I stared round, hopelessly; and then with two jumps, I was on the pigsty, and from there upon the top of the deckhouse. I threw myself flat, and waited, breathlessly.

All at once, it seemed to me that it was darker than it had been the previous moment, and I raised my head, very cautiously. I saw that the ship was enveloped in great billows of mist, and then, not six feet from me, I made out someone lying, face downwards. It was Tammy. I felt safer now that we were hidden by the mist, and I crawled to him. He gave a quick gasp of terror when I touched him; but when he saw who it was, he started to sob like a little kid.

"Hush!" I said. "For God's sake be quiet!" But I need not have troubled; for the shrieks of the men being killed, down on the decks all around us, drowned every other sound.

I knelt up, and glanced round and then aloft. Overhead, I could make out dimly the spars and sails, and now as I looked, I saw that the t'gallants and royals had been unloosed and were hanging in the buntlines. Almost in the same moment, the terrible crying of the poor beggars about the decks, ceased; and there succeeded an awful silence, in which I could distinctly hear Tammy sobbing. I reached out, and shook him.

"Be quiet! Be quiet!" I whispered, intensely. "THEY'LL hear us!"

At my touch and whisper, he struggled to become silent; and then, overhead, I saw the six yards being swiftly mast-headed. Scarcely were the sails set, when I heard the swish and flick of gaskets being cast adrift on the lower yards, and realized that ghostly things were at work there.

For a moment or so there was silence, and I made my way cautiously to the after end of the house, and peered over. Yet, because of the mist, I could see nothing. Then, abruptly, from behind me, came a single wail of sudden pain and terror from Tammy. It ended instantly in a sort of choke. I stood up in the mist and ran back to where I had left the kid; but he had gone. I stood dazed. I felt like shrieking out loud. Above me I heard the flaps of the course being tumbled off the yards. Down upon the decks, there were the noises of a multitude working in a weird, inhuman silence. Then came the squeal and rattle of blocks and braces aloft. They were squaring the yards.

I remained standing. I watched the yards squared, and then I saw the sails fill suddenly. An instant later, the deck of the house upon which I stood, became canted forrard. The slope increased, so that I could scarcely stand, and I grabbed at one of the wire-winches. I wondered, in a stunned sort of way, what was happening. Almost directly afterwards, from the deck on the port side of the house, there came a sudden, loud, human scream; and immediately, from different parts of the decks, there rose, afresh, some most horrible shouts of agony from odd men. This grew into an intense screaming that shook my heart up; and there came again a noise of desperate, brief fighting. Then a breath of cold wind seemed to play in the mist, and I could see down the slope of the deck. I looked below me, towards the bows. The jibboom was plunged right into the water, and, as I stared, the bows disappeared into the sea. The deck of the house became a wall to me, and I was swinging from the winch, which was now above my head. I watched the ocean lap over the edge of the fo'cas'le head, and rush down on to the maindeck, roaring into the empty fo'cas'le. And still all around me came crying of the lost sailor-men. I heard something strike the corner of the house above me, with a dull thud, and then I saw Plummer plunge down into the flood beneath. I remembered that he had been at the wheel. The next instant, the water had leapt to my feet; there came a drear chorus of bubbling screams, a roar of waters, and I was going swiftly down into the darkness. I let go of the winch, and struck out madly, trying to hold my breath. There was a loud singing in my ears. It grew louder. I opened my mouth. I felt I was dying. And then, thank God! I was at the surface, breathing. For the moment, I was blinded with the water, and my agony of breathlessness. Then, growing easier, I brushed the water from my eyes and so, not three hundred yards away, I made out a large ship, floating almost motionless. At first, I could scarcely believe I saw aright. Then, as I realized that indeed there was yet a chance of living, I started to swim towards you.

You know the rest—

"And you think—?" said the Captain, interrogatively, and stopped short.

"No," replied Jessop. "I don't think. I _know. None of us *think*. It's a gospel fact. People *talk* about queer things happening at sea; but this isn't one of them. This is one of the *real* things. You've all seen queer things; perhaps more than I have. It depends. But they don't go down in the log. These kinds of things never do. This one won't; at least, not as it's really happened."

He nodded his head, slowly, and went on, addressing the Captain more particularly.

"I'll bet," he said, deliberately, "that you'll enter it in the log-book, something like this:

"'May 18th. Lat.—S. Long.—W. 2 p.m. Light winds from the South and East. Sighted a full-rigged ship on the starboard bow. Overhauled her in the first dog-watch. Signalled her; but received no response. During the second dog-watch she steadily refused to communicate. About eight bells, it was observed that she seemed to be settling by the head, and a minute later she foundered suddenly, bows foremost, with all her crew. Put out a boat and picked up one of the men, an A.B. by the name of Jessop. He was quite unable to give any explanation of the catastrophe.'

"And you two," he made a gesture at the First and Second Mates, "will probably sign your names to it, and so will I, and perhaps one of your A.B.s. Then when we get home they'll print a report of it in the newspapers, and people will talk about the unseaworthy ships. Maybe some of the experts will talk rot about rivets and defective plates and so forth."

He laughed, cynically. Then he went on.

"And you know, when you come to think of it, there's no one except our own selves will ever know how it happened—really. The shellbacks don't count. They're only 'beastly, drunken brutes of *common sailors*'—poor devils! No one would think of taking anything they said, as anything more than a damned cuffer. Besides, the beggars only tell these things when they're half-boozed. They wouldn't then (for fear of being laughed at), only they're not responsible—"

He broke off, and looked round at us.

The Skipper and the two Mates nodded their heads, in silent assent.

APPENDIX: THE SILENT SHIP

I'm the Third Mate of the *Sangier*, the vessel that picked up Jessop, you know; and he's asked us to write a short note of what we saw from our side, and sign it. The Old Man's set me on the job, as he says I can put it better than he can.

Well, it was in the first dog-watch that we came up with her, the *Mortzestus* I mean; but it was in the second dog-watch that it happened. The Mate and I were on the poop watching her. You see, we'd signaled her, and she'd not taken any notice, and that seemed queer, as we couldn't have been more than three or four hundred yards off her port beam, and it was a fine evening; so that we could almost have had a tea-fight, if they'd seemed a pleasant crowd. As it was, we called them a set of sulky swine, and left it at that, though we still kept our hoist up.

All the same, you know, we watched her a lot; and I remember even then I thought it queer how quiet she was. We couldn't even hear her bell go and I spoke to the Mate about it, and he said he'd been noticing the same thing.

Then, about six bells they shortened her right down to top-sails; and I can tell you that made us stare more than ever, as anyone can imagine. And I remember we noticed then especially that we couldn't hear a single sound from her even when the haul yards were let go; and, you know, without the glass, I saw their Old Man singing out something; but we didn't get a sound of it and we *should* have been able to hear every word.

Then, just before eight bells, the thing Jessop's told us about happened. Both the Mate and the Old Man said they could see men going up her side a bit indistinct, you know, because it was getting dusk; but the Second Mate and I half thought we did and half thought we didn't; but there was something queer; we all knew that; and it looked like a sort of moving mist along her side. I know I felt pretty funny; but it wasn't the sort of thing, of course, to be too sure and serious about until you *were* sure.

After the Mate and the Captain had said they saw the men boarding her, we began to hear sounds from her; very queer at first and rather like a phonograph makes when it's getting up speed. Then the sounds came properly from her, and we heard them shouting and yelling; and, you know, I don't know even now just what I really thought. I was all so queer and mixed.

The next thing I remember there was a thick mist round the ship; and then all the noise was shut off, as if it were all the other side of a door. But we could still see her masts and spars and sails above the misty stuff; and both the Captain and the Mate said they could see men aloft; and I thought I could; but the Second Mate wasn't sure. All the same though, the sails were all loosed in about a minute, it seemed, and the yards mastheaded. We couldn't see the courses above the mist; but Jessop says they were loosed too and sheeted home along with the upper sails. Then we saw the yards squared and I saw the sails fill bang up with wind; and yet, you know, ours were slatting.

The next thing was the one that hit me more than anything. Her masts took a cant forrard, and then I saw her stem come up out of the mist that was round her. Then, all in an instant, we could hear sounds from the vessel again. And I tell you, the men didn't seem to be shouting, but screaming. Her stern went higher. It was most extraordinary to look at; and then she went plunk down, head foremost, right bang into the mist-stuff.

It's all right what Jessop says, and when we saw him swimming (I was the one who spotted him) we got out a boat quicker than a wind-jammer ever got out a boat before, I should think.

The Captain and the Mate and the Second and I are all going to sign this.

(SIGNED)
WILLIAM NAWSTON
MASTER.
J.E.G. ADAMS
FIRST MATE.
ED. BROWN
SECOND MATE.
JACK T. EVAN
THIRD MATE.

/

About the Author

William Hope Hodgson (1877-1918) was an English author and sailor, best known for his works of horror and supernatural fiction. He was born in Blackmore End, Essex, England, to a family of clergymen. At the age of 13, Hodgson ran away from home and joined the Merchant Navy. He published his first collection of stories after leaving the military and went on to write several other works of horror and supernatural fiction, including *The Night Land* and the *Carnacki, the Ghost Finder* collection. Hodgson's life was cut short when he was killed in action during World War I in 1918, at the age of 40. Despite his relatively short career, his work has had a lasting impact on the horror and supernatural fiction genres.

/

www.ingramcontent.com/pod-product-compliance
Lightning Source LLC
Chambersburg PA
CBHW010403310726
48979CB00005B/1051
* 9 7 8 1 9 5 5 3 8 2 2 6 7 *

HORROR HISTORIA presents your favorite frightening classics:

Dracula
Bram Stoker

The Elemental Trilogy:
The Boats of the "Glen Carrig," The House on the Borderland, & The Ghost Pirates
William Hope Hodgson

Frankenstein
Mary Shelley

Innominato: The Wizard of the Mountain
William Gilbert

The Lancashire Witches
William Harrison Ainsworth

The Phantom of the Opera
Gaston Leroux

The Picture of Dorian Gray
Oscar Wilde

Satan's Signature: Jekyll and Hyde, the Invisible Man, and Other Mad Scientists
Robert Louis Stevenson, H. G. Wells, and others

She
H. Rider Haggard

Wolf/Man: A Tandem of Werewolf Classics
The Door of the Unreal & The Undying Monster
Gerald Biss & Jessie Douglas Kerruish

and more…

About the Editor

C.S.R. CALLOWAY is a prolific writer across a multitude of mediums and genres. His horror novels include *Desiderio*, *The Ungodly Hours*, and *The Veil and the Shade*. He created, curated, and edited the entire HORROR HISTORIA anthology. Best known as creator and showrunner of the award-winning series *Pretty Dudes*, Calloway currently lives in Los Angeles with his Venus flytraps Betsy, Bootsie and Itsy Bitsy.

CHANCECALLOWAY.COM

/